A Man of Honor

or HORATIO'S CONFESSIONS

J.A. NELSON

Quill Point Press

This is a work of fiction. Although some characters, dates, and settings are based on the historical record, the work as a whole is a product of the author's imagination.

A MAN OF HONOR, or HORATIO'S CONFESSIONS.
Copyright © 2019 by Jennifer A. Nelson.
All rights reserved.

Published in the United States of America by
Quill Point Press
8116 Arlington Blvd, #323
Falls Church, VA 22042
www.quillpointpress.com.

Maps "Denmark and Environs of Northern Christendom, 1520"
and "Kingdom of Denmark, 1512-1520"
Designed by Nat Case / INCase LLC.
Copyright © 2019 by Jennifer A. Nelson.

Translation of text within the *Gesta Danorum*'s frontispiece
by Absolute Translations, Ltd.
© 2019 by Jennifer A. Nelson.

Cover Design by Patrick Knowles / patrickknowlesdesign.com.
Interior Design by Mark Thomas / coverness.com.
Paperback set in Minion Pro.
Headings set in IM Fell English Pro.

No part of this book may be used, reproduced, or transmitted in any form or by any means whatsoever without written prior permission of the publisher except in the case of brief quotations embodied in critical articles and reviews, or where permitted by law.

ISBN 978-1-7333475-0-1 (paperback)
ISBN 978-1-7333475-1-8 (eBook)

*To Ed and Mom,
and
in loving memory of
Pete Loomer*

DENMARK AND ENVIRONS OF NORTHERN CHRISTENDOM, 1520

Whether discommended or commended thou do thy duty.
(or, *Act the part which is worthy of you.*)

Marcus Aurelius Antoninus, Roman Emperor
The Meditations, Sixth Book, II

Remember withal through how many things
Thou hast already passed, and how many
Thou hast been able to endure;
So that now the legend of thy life is full,
And thy charge is accomplished.

Marcus Aurelius Antoninus, Roman Emperor
The Meditations, Fifth Book, XXV

I.

I cradled Hamlet, my dear friend, so like a brother. He lay, sweat-damp and quaking, across my lap where I sat upon the floor of Krogen Castle's dim Freyja Hall. The blood-speckled shells that were his eyes peered at me. Despite his creeping death tremors, Hamlet was strangely calm. He was resigned—an unnatural demeanor for Hamlet, for madness had lately gripped him—but I, panicking, whisked crimson droplets from his temples.

The sour incense of death, that cruel invader, exuded from the dead surrounding us. Our king, stabbed and poisoned by Hamlet, his nephew. Our queen, Hamlet's mother, poisoned accidentally by a tainted goblet. Hamlet's dueling opponent, Laertes, poisoned by his own sword, which also mortally wounded Hamlet. Two dozen nobles attending to them wailed over the deceased and prayed. The souls of these dead surely burned like kindling for their parts in Hamlet's demise.

I alone tended to Hamlet. I kissed his bristly cheek. "What will come of our plans? Our university for peasant boys... They would have forged a better world. Our good works would have..." My words snagged on a sob. Hamlet and I, as older students at the age of thirty years, had finally heard our calling, perceived our legacy. How could it all be lost now? I told him, "Now our hope is destroyed, and I can't save you."

Hamlet's gaze wavered. "Help me, Horatio. My soul will be damned if my honor is ruined. Tell all who care to know the full truth about my purpose. Then, perhaps heaven will receive me. But if not, and hell is full, Goddess Freyja—"

"Hamlet, blaspheme will surely damn you."

"She will bring me to Valhalla."

"Though we harbor our beloved old beliefs, Hamlet, we must not speak of them. If someone hears you, what priest will absolve your soul? How will I defend you against the Church's doctrines?"

His gaze fixed upon me. "I will feast with Freyja and Odin's slain warriors... awaiting the final battle. Horatio, dare to tell the truth. Promise: endure every burden to report my story."

"You once made me swear not to tell of your schemes. You would make me break that oath to God?"

"I am sorry for that." Hamlet coughed. I raised his head to help him breathe.

"Enemies of the House of Hamlet will not tolerate your glorification. It would be treason. Cristiern condemned your parents as wicked pretenders. He will hang me for extolling the virtues of your family."

"I-I know the difficulty I ask... of you. Dare to stand in the open and tell the truth, Horatio."

I bore Hamlet's heavy, challenging stare and the too familiar stab of guilt. God's blood, my every attempt to help him had only tempted calamity and worsened his fate. For my failure, I deserved the horrors of eternal punishment starkly depicted in the religious manuals. Devils would feed me my disemboweled gut. I looked upward and begged, "Oh, blessed Christ, savior of souls, redeem me. Give me strength." I hoped for a comforting sign. Above, I saw, past the tapestries and the limp banners of crests with hearts, dogs, and flowering trees, the hall's timbers. They bowed from the ceiling down to the floor and seemed not like rungs toward heaven or Valhalla, but rather like the overturned hull of a sunken Viking ship.

Not far from my grasp, upon the floor, sat the dark, poisonous cup. Some liquid remained therein. For Hamlet and me, I would do what was best.

"Hamlet, I cannot wage a war against obscurity. I'm not like Wiglaf the Dane, who built, for all to see, the legendary funeral pyre in memory of his friend Beowulf. Rather, I'm like an antique Roman, one of the Horatii, who honored their brotherhood by vowing to die together in battle."

"No, Horatio," Hamlet warned. "You must be a Dane, bent on honor through memorial."

I grasped the tankard.

Hamlet hissed, "Horatio, give me the cup. Now is not the time for sacrifice."

The world seemed out of balance. My hands shook as I looked into the goblet I held. A tiny pool of glossy, black liquid spun at the bottom. "We learn to love the idea of death. It's an arranged marriage." I tilted the rim to my lips.

Hamlet lurched and gripped my hand. "God forbids self-slaughter. If you kill yourself, your damnation is absolute."

Again, I sensed the nearness of Hades. Boiling. Skinning. Mind-splitting torments.

"And you are no longer my brother."

That excommunication, I truly could not bear. Heartsick, I surrendered the cup to Hamlet.

The poison raging through Hamlet's body was claiming him. To speed his death, he swallowed the final ruinous drops.

He lay back, into my lap. Bubbling spittle collected on his lips. "You are the right man to tell my story. Although you are a commoner, you became like a brother to a prince." A corner of Hamlet's mouth twitched, a weak grin. Then his breast heaved upward.

Almighty God, do not take him. I held Hamlet's cold, perspiring hands and prayed. "*Pater noster, qui es in caelis—*"

"Hallowed be thy name." Hamlet, choking, finished the Lord's Prayer. He said to me, "One day we will consider the grandest philosophies, you and I. Together we will speak..." His voice faltered. Hamlet's body rattled as if pinned under a great weight.

My tongue lay dumb, entombed in the trench of my jaw. I felt that, all at once, I was fire at the heart and frost in the flesh.

He whispered, "The rest is silence."

I saw Hamlet's lips close on those words that, once spoken, seemed to roll away his body's burden.

Dazed, I held my friend to my aching breast. "Good night, sweet prince. May flights of angels sing thee to thy rest." I touched my forehead to his. *First Papa, now Hamlet.* Loneliness, heavy and hollow, sat with me.

How strange it is that a man's heart can break with such force, yet others do not hear the calamity.

If the old beliefs held true, the Furious Host, that thundering sleigh of death, should have swooped among us to gather the honorable dead, to collect them so that Freyja and Odin could choose among them for Valhalla. But it did not come.

Hamlet's death was a bad death, so unlike the promise of Pentecost. He should have been properly reposed as he died, clad in robes befitting his high station. One hundred prostrate monks should have prayed the Office of the Dead to herald his good passing. Instead, Hamlet received no extreme unction. His soul was in peril, and I had to be his champion.

Moans and sobs rose in the hall. I looked to my left and saw four young noblemen praying over Laertes. His bulging eyes were like marble. By the platform steps to my right, leading to the thrones, two robed elders pulled a longsword from Claudius's slumped body that still wore Helsingør's crown. Hamlet, never one to make a point lightly, had pinned Claudius to the wooden feet of Old Hamlet's statue. The arms of that memorialized chest-bare warrior, as burly as the guildsmen who carved them, reached upward in praise.

At the hall's opposite side, by the massive arch of the open portal, was the statue of the Virgin. Her stoic demeanor and outstretched arms loomed above the crumpled body of Queen Gertrude. In death her chalk face was vein-streaked and her parted lips gray. The queen's principal lady, Margrete, ministered to the corpse. She tried to press Gertrude's gold-ringed hands into a prayerful posture. To retain that dignified pose, Margrete removed her own cap, allowing her amber hair to fall to her shoulders, to wrap Gertrude's hands together. Margrete cried but her gaze never wavered from her task. Her eyes soft. Jaw firm. Her age not greater than my own, probably. Her elegant silk, her lace-trimmed bodice—she was lovely and noble. Her grace deserved adoration, not judgment for her reputation. Only the most fiendish swine could have forced upon her the ruin that, as gossip told it, had soiled her virtue. Margrete's fallen status surely offended the Almighty, however it seemed not to have mattered to the queen, who had retained Margrete in her service. Neither, then, would I condemn such a woman. Margrete's care for her dead mistress evidenced, in my estimation, unblemished honor.

The single crack of a cannon startled me. It was the signal of an approaching dignitary. The others, tending to the bodies, moaned. Margrete cried out, "Who now will protect Helsingør from its enemies?"

Were the Hamlets' rivals breaching our gate? Was it Cristiern of Denmark's ruling House of Oldenburg? Old Hamlet's sword and warrior's might had asserted the House of Hamlet's lordship over Helsingør and its northern provinces for four decades. But when Old Hamlet died and his brother, Claudius, who had no reputation as a soldier, took the crown, Cristiern had directed an embargo, less costly to him than battle, to wrest the throne from the Hamlets. From his throne in Copenhagen, Cristiern had starved Helsingør's fortress, Krogen, and its village. He declared he would slay all people loyal to the House of Hamlet. With our royal family now dead, he could overtake and murder us all.

Or was the invader Fortinbras, Prince of Norway? Did Fortinbras come to defy Cristiern, to take Helsingør's throne before Cristiern could claim it? Perhaps also to avenge his father, who Hamlet's father had killed in battle?

A cannon blasted again. I bent over Hamlet to shield his corpse. A woman shrieked, "Cristiern attacks."

The hum and foot beats of a multitude, approaching from the corridor, filled the hall.

"Hide the bodies," Margrete cried out. She rose and gripped Gertrude's body under the arms. "They must not be burned by our foes in retribution. Tear down those tapestries. Let us roll the dead within so that we may bury them tonight."

Another woman and a man joined Margrete to drag Gertrude toward a drapery hanging between the wall's timbered ribs. Six men yanked the tapestry from its hooks. It thudded upon the floor. Margrete pulled Gertrude onto the tapestry and, from her own earlobe, unclipped a gilt-stud earring. She fastened it to Gertrude's shiny black collar. Margrete kissed Gertrude's wrapped hands a final time, then stepped back to allow three men to roll Gertrude within the tapestry. So, too, they encased Claudius and Laertes each within a tapestry, and then laid the three cylinders beside a wall and piled a few benches there. To all appearances, it was the debris of a past festivity.

Beyond the corridor, perhaps in the courtyard garden, a trumpet blared. Drums pounded. The nobles clustered by the open arch, and a few stepped into the corridor to scout the cause of the alert. I, however, remained upon the floor and held Hamlet. Some men with Margrete came to take Hamlet from me, but I gripped him tighter. In my sight they melted.

I wiped my eyes and saw the entirety of Krogen's noblemen and women, more than one hundred souls, enter the hall. They moved stiffly, as if prodded by pikes. They avoided the blood smears upon the floor. I supposed that an army herded them. But only two men, the last to pass through the portal's round arch, appeared.

One man—perhaps twenty-five years, of average height and girth— wore a breastplate smeared with blackened blood. A sword dangled from a loop that belted leather pantaloons. Upon each ankle rested a bunched sleeve of tarnished mail that jangled with each step. Scars marked his brows and cheeks. His sandy pallor seemed crisped from heat and toil, and his fists were large and rough, dyed by grime. The briny reek of animal sweat reached me where I sat, clutching Hamlet's corpse, trembling for fear that this was Cristiern. Would he imprison or kill us?

The nobles knelt, heads bowed.

I leaned over Hamlet's corpse and dared to regard the other man. He was not a general, for he sauntered, rather than stomped, into the room. His garb was entirely black except for his white shirt and brown mud marring his strapped boots. From his wide-brimmed hat a dark mane flowed upon his shoulders. His cape, elegant and sleek, shrouded his torso like a raven's folded wings. He stood, broad shoulders rolled back, and calmly regarded us. He noticed the bloody marks upon the floor, where no one stood, and then said to the armored man beside him, "*Mon Dieu*, a riot has occurred."

I recognized by his French accent that did not gutturalize the Rs that he was a Burgundian. Likely older than me by only a few years, his bearing, Roman aquiline nose and face, as if molded by a fine chisel and branded by a slender moustache, was noble. Most compelling about this man was his confidence, which seemed genuine to him, not dependent upon a weapon, for he held none.

The man in armor glared at the prostrate crowd. Clusters of people gripped hands. A few whimpered.

In the corridor outside the hall, one of Krogen's guards, the old Italian, Marcellus, raised a horn and blasted a clarion note. He called out, announcing the armored man who stood before us. "All hail, Fortinbras of Norway."

Not Cristiern. Relief washed over us. Men rose from their knees but remained stooped, bowing. Ladies curtsied low.

Rather than signal that all may rise, Fortinbras opened his arms, then dropped them to his sides as he beheld the empty thrones upon the platform. "Where is Claudius? Lanier, this is no diplomatic arrangement."

Lanier, the Frenchman, sniffed the air and grimaced. He walked among the people toward a bloody patch but paused and stooped to retrieve a scarf dropped by a crying woman. After Lanier placed it into her hand, he proceeded to the grim smear. He bent to touch the sticky blood. Brow rumpled, he glanced across the hall and spied the three rolled tapestries lying against the wall. Lanier's boots knocked the floor in deliberate stride toward the hidden bodies. He pulled away the benches and unrolled one tube. Gertrude slid out and lay upon her side. Her hands rested askew, no longer wrapped as if in supplication.

Margrete bent, clutching her middle as though ill.

Next, Lanier strode to the second roll and yanked upon it. The tube unfurled to expel Laertes facedown, arms and legs outspread.

"No king yet," Lanier said in French-accented Danish, adding some syllables.

Then, Lanier hunched over the third tube and pulled hard upon it. The tapestry unrolled, sending Claudius's body and crown tumbling across the floor in the direction of Fortinbras. Nobles cried out and scattered. Sorrow and the dung stench of fresh death made my belly clench.

Lanier pointed at the pinch-faced corpse. With a dry, sardonic tone, he said, "*Mon seigneur*, I present Claudius, Denmark's king of Helsingør's provinces. He cannot receive you. However, you may receive him." If not for the dire moment, I would have laughed; I liked Lanier's demeanor.

Fortinbras went to the body and stared down at his pale, stiffening rival. A grin of satisfaction spread across his lips. "What bedlam is this?"

Lanier looked to me and Hamlet's cold corpse, which I held close. He approached, and when he crouched beside me the scent of cloves lingered. His dark, vulpine eyes regarded me. "*Mon ami*, was it this man or the younger dead one?" A full baritone, hardly nasal. His black, leather-gloved hands opened. "*Rendre le corps*."

I could not release Hamlet to him.

"I will bear him gently." Lanier's thumb wiped each wing of his dark mustache. "The body is nothing but a vessel."

Hamlet must be buried, I thought. Relenting, I lowered Hamlet like an armful of splintered glass to the floor beside me. His face was as white as Helsingør's sand. As was true of all men of his house, his fair skin was as smooth as a calf's except near the eyes, which bore the print of age, and his eyes were as blue as Øresund Bay. I touched Hamlet's cooling forehead and slowly made the sign of the cross upon his brow.

Lanier lifted Hamlet as if taking his own child into his arms and hoisted his limp body across his shoulders. He stood and, turning away from me, staggered slightly beneath the weight.

I reached for Hamlet's trailing arm, for the debris of my chosen family and future, but my friend was beyond my grasp. He never heard my assurances, because I never answered his request while he lived. Determined, I stood. "I swear, I will not allow the world to forget or malign you."

Shuffling under his burden, Lanier slowed, then halted. He pivoted slowly to regard me. His brows, beneath the brim of his hat, arched and he nodded slightly to me as if in respect.

I had accepted the deadly charge. The act would be treason against Cristiern, and I would be killed for it if discovered. Worse, a failed promise would dishonor me and bring the same consequence, death, with the additional grant of eternal torture. My oath would forever bind me.

Three noblemen pushed a rattling cart from the corridor into the hall. They and Lanier lifted the bodies onto the cart and laid them across one another. I shuddered at the sight.

Margrete approached me, her hands clasped at her middle in formality. Her voice was moderate in pitch and tempo. "Your pledge does Hamlet immense honor." She took my hand. Her fingers were soft and lithe, yet firm. Margrete's empathy stirred me. Despite her grief, she had reached to comfort others, to assure them. To earn her touch again… and for my promise, I would find a way to affirm Hamlet's reputation. Perhaps I could be a storyteller. A hero needn't always be a warrior.

Fortinbras opened his arms and roared to the crowd, "Was this a coup? Did these nobles attack their king? Who will tell me what happened in this place?"

An idea sparked. I saw how I could fulfill my promise and survive it, could save my brother whose death I had unwittingly hastened. I would begin by telling Fortinbras Hamlet's story, then present it to the nobles when I gave Hamlet's funeral eulogy. If next I could gain Fortinbras's patronage, I could safely journey south to other lands to tell Hamlet's story. Then, I could return north and finish my task if Fortinbras battled Cristiern and became monarch of the Kalmar Union—ruler of Denmark, Norway, Sweden, and other lands to the west. Or perhaps, through Fortinbras, I could appeal to those rulers. Their royal and noble families already opposed Cristiern by daring to crown their own kings.

Fortinbras was my only hope for necessary assistance. I had no direct access to any other king, royal, or pocket-gilded noble to sponsor the telling of Hamlet's story beyond Helsingør. Further, I had no purse to afford journeys across the globe.

My breast pounded. I planted myself before Fortinbras, bowed deeply at the waist, then straightened. "Highness, I was Hamlet's closest friend, although I am a commoner. I can tell you why these people are worth saving. I can tell you of schemes and folly, of how this carnage came to be, and how Prince Hamlet, a man of heart who prized loyalty, strove to honor his murdered father."

Margrete leaned closer. Her warm, full bodice lit my senses. She whispered, "Ask that he defend us. Appeal to his vanity."

Indeed, I would help these people. I could convince Fortinbras of their value and influence his commitment to them. After all, my prowess in debate had earned my peers' esteem as Hamlet and I had paired to spar against the best minds at Wittenberg's Leucorea University. Persuasion could be my best weapon against the arrogance of power.

"Your Majesty," I continued, "we praise the hosts of heaven that the Almighty has brought you to us. Cristiern is our enemy and yours as well. He's starved the people of Krogen and the village of Helsingør. Your defense of Krogen would be your first stroke in taking hold of the Kalmar Union from Cristiern. Under your protection, we would no longer suffer."

"What defense do these people deserve?" Fortinbras's face bunched in anger. He bore down upon me. With each step, the links in his mail clicked. "They cheered my father's death when Old Hamlet killed him." Fortinbras pointed at the cart full of bodies. "The Hamlets were murderers, and they had no rights, whether by birth or grant, to this land. Old Hamlet was born a commoner. His wife, Gertrude, a high noble and a thief. They seized the castle Krogen for its sound toll monies, crowned themselves rulers of Helsingør and Zealand's northwest region. Why should I trust their nobles and minions?"

"Well done," Margrete muttered to me.

Under other circumstances I would have enjoyed her sardonic quip, an art I adore.

Margrete opened her quaking hands to Fortinbras. "I beg Your Highness's mercy. We are a loyal people."

Fortinbras's brow scrunched. "Woman, I did not bid you to address me."

Margrete bowed her head and clutched her hands at her middle. "After the death of Polonius, the king's counselor, as the queen's principal lady I was the most trusted personage of this court. My purpose is to serve. Please forgive it, Your Majesty."

Another piercing blast issued from Marcellus's horn. He declared, "His Excellency, the Ambassador of England."

A man bedecked in a gold livery collar and black damask robe stepped into the hall. He pushed through the crowd of nobles to stand before the platform. He spoke to Fortinbras in an authoritative lilt. "England fulfilled the order for execution of the criminals Rosenkrantz and Gyldenstierne. Who will deliver to King Henry the respect due His Majesty?"

Steady and reserved, Margrete said to the ambassador, "Dear sir, if the queen were alive, she would tell you that is a lie. I humbly assure you that the Hamlets did not issue that order." Apparently, Fortinbras's rebuke had not wilted Margrete's courage to engage other officials.

The ambassador reached into his overcoat pocket. He withdrew a small packet, unfolded it, and waved it at her. "Signed by Claudius of Denmark, Sovereign of Helsingør."

The letter he held was one that Hamlet had forged in Claudius's name, requiring that England execute his devious escorts, Niels Rosenkrantz and Knud Gyldenstierne. Hamlet had told me of it and given me the real order Claudius had written, asking England to kill Hamlet. When I felt for the folded death writ in my pocket, its seams crackled, but that evidence of deceit remained safe.

"Who else would have issued the order?" The ambassador waggled the false letter at us.

"A good question," said Fortinbras. He leveled his stare like a ready crossbow at me. "You said that you can tell me what occurred here. Do you know something of this matter as well?"

I had to build Hamlet's stature in Fortinbras's esteem, to deserve his patronage and reinforce Hamlet's reputation and honor. A fib trickled from my tongue. "Hamlet had nothing to do with it."

A shaft of sunlight, from the high windows of Freyja Hall, landed upon the ambassador. He winced and, covering his brow with his hand, stepped closer to Fortinbras. "We care *not* whether the squanderer king, Claudius, or mad Prince Hamlet, or their stable boy ordered the executions. England's diligence deserves compensation."

I cringed at the rumor of Hamlet's madness. "I assure you, Hamlet had no hand in their demise."

Fortinbras's eyes narrowed in assessment of me.

I felt Margrete's pointed stare. I did not look to her. When she leaned close, her citrus scent beguiled me. But then she whispered, "Why are you lying to Fortinbras?"

"It'll come to good," I said but did not explain more. She would never understand my reasons. She had always been a noble, protected since her birth, not a commoner shielded only by her wits.

The ambassador rubbed his hands as if to warm them. He may have intended his slow steps, returning to the channel of bright light, to give Fortinbras time to reconsider. The ambassador asked, "Should I report to His Majesty, the king of England, that you refuse to pay your predecessor's debt for the favor performed?"

Fortinbras, arms folded, scoffed. "Their agreements do not bind me because they never had the right to rule Helsingør in the first place."

The ambassador's cheek twitched. "England's understanding is that Gertrude was a cousin to Cristiern's father who never battled the House of Hamlet for sovereignty over Helsingør. Further, Gertrude and Old Hamlet created their tribe, residency, and rights to the provincial Danish throne of Helsingør by moving the region's nobility from their lands to live in this castle." The ambassador raised a hand as if saluting the pennants of Krogen's noble families.

Fortinbras clenched the hilt of the sword hanging from his belt. "Norway has rights to Helsingør. Cristiern is not the only Norse royal injured by the Hamlets' usurpation of land and throne. Old Hamlet murdered my father. Today, due to Fortune's blessing, I was passing through this region, returning from battle against the Poles and bound for my home"—Fortinbras slowly walked to the cart of corpses—"when I stopped here to pay Norway's required tribute to the Hamlets. However, instead I found this naked prospect."

The ambassador returned Fortinbras's stare across a gulf of disdain. "You choose to rule Helsingør but ignore its obligations." With a disgusted grunt, the ambassador strode through the crowd toward the hall's arched entryway. Nearly at the threshold, he stopped and turned on his heel. "Prince Fortinbras, although you take Helsingør's throne, it will not strengthen your defenses against Cristiern. Indeed, it will cost you more than you will be able to defend from Norway. *That* crown, your primary inheritance, will never be absolutely yours as long as Denmark rules the Kalmar Union. You will need your friends to defend you, but you have offended King Henry. Do not bother to request England's service again." The ambassador left the hall.

Fortinbras smirked. He reached into the mass of bodies and, from it, plucked Claudius's crown. He placed the jeweled band well-centered upon his own head. "Let it be recorded that today, the tenth day of June, in the year of our Lord 1513, I claimed reign over Helsingør and its fortress, Krogen Castle. With sad regret, I accept my destiny."

With regret, indeed. For centuries Krogen Castle, sitting upon Helsingør's knob of land jutting into Øresund Bay, collected sound tolls from the sun-blistered hands of passing ship captains. Helsingør would yield Fortinbras a fat treasury.

"My king." A tattered, bruised, and bloody man stumbled into the hall. He carried a crossbow but no quiver of arrows.

"Geirbjorn." Fortinbras hurried to greet the man. "Where are your fellows? What happened?"

"Our men, returning from Poland, landed upon southern Denmark, at the tip near Falster. Our army is destroyed, sire. Cristiern was waiting for us. His bombards were a storm of devils."

Fortinbras blanched. Agape and wide-eyed, he bent and braced his hands against his knees. "My entire force. Lost?"

The scout continued, "Cristiern is marching northbound. He will reach Copenhagen in one week."

"To Helsingør?"

"I don't know, sire." The scout knelt, covered his face, and began to shake.

The nobles moaned. The crowd churned. A buxom woman cried out, "Once they reach Copenhagen, they could be here within one day."

Fortinbras straightened and folded his arms. His clenched jaw pulsed. "Not one day. Three, perhaps four days, to transport battle carts from Copenhagen." Then he barked at the nobles, "You have only decrepit Italians and Spaniards as guards. I have not seen one soldier. Why?" Fortinbras flung his hand in the direction of Marcellus, who was leaning against the portal's stone doorjamb, and jeered at him.

"My good liege," said a wavering voice. An elder noble wearing a brocade tunic and a stiff square hat warily approached Fortinbras. The noble removed his hat and bowed. "Claudius did not maintain his army as did his brother, Old Hamlet. But Claudius used his treasury for our good, for entertainments to bear up our spirits when the blockade began."

Turning to the old man, Fortinbras said, "Claudius wagered that Sweden, Denmark, and Norway would clash like giants and destroy one another before they would attack his tiny province. He was a fool."

Fortinbras passed the nobleman and stormed to Lanier. "You must get me soldiers. These old relics"—he jerked his thumb at Marcellus—"were probably rejected by the Holy Roman Emperor. Not even fit for his Papal Wars. Christ's bones, Lanier, you are my aide-de-camp. You must get me a horde of mercenaries, or I will terminate your services and return you to France."

Lanier frowned. He looked to the floor and, fists clenched, said, "Tonight, I will search."

The elder noble entreated Fortinbras, "Do not abandon us."

A young woman of tender years, tears dropping down her cheeks, said, "Protect us."

The people pressed themselves lower to the ground. They groveled and pled.

Margrete slowly approached. Before Fortinbras, she curtsied and remained stooped. Her persistence amazed me. "Your Excellency, behold your people. We depend wholly upon your care and wisdom. Cristiern's embargo...months have passed since we last saw the flags of the Hanseatic trade ships. Our guildsmen need the markets and fairs. You can save us." Her voice's register was a bit lower now. "We will help to defend our home. We beg you, instruct us, men and women, in how to do battle."

Fortinbras sucked his teeth.

I could not allow Margrete to suffer Fortinbras's judgment alone. I knelt beside her, before Fortinbras's glare, and said, "The lady speaks the truth. While I have resided at Krogen I have seen their resilience and care despite growing hunger because of empty docks."

A young man called out, "We will fight to keep this place if you will protect us."

I looked to the tall youth. If his exuberant edge could be filed down, he would be a fine warrior.

Fortinbras's face, a frown-cleft stone, softened. But then he spat on the ground. "Courtiers do not understand war. They are leeches with stingers, otherwise unreliable."

Lanier pulled off his gloves and tucked them into his belt. "*Mon seigneur*, we can teach these Helsingør noblemen to fight. I count one hundred fifty in all, but for children. Enough men and women to defend the battlements until reinforcements come...from Sweden...perhaps."

"What could these nobles learn within a few days?" Fortinbras asked.

Lanier stroked his chin. "Fundamental skills: bow, sword, munitions, murder hole, and bucket defenses."

"I should trust people loyal to the man who murdered my father?" Fortinbras's eyes glistened with sadness. "Perhaps they themselves killed Claudius and the others. The castle and fortress are worth saving and probably the village. But train this soft, weak herd?"

Fortinbras paced the length of the crowd. Grit crackled beneath his boots. He wiped his face with one hand. Then, he turned and regarded us suspiciously. "I will decide after this one"—he pointed at me—"who is not a noble, reports the facts about how the Hamlets were killed." He scowled at me as if I were a worm swimming in his gruel.

"King Fortinbras—" Old Marcellus, hobbling toward us, pointed the narrow end of his horn at me, where I remained kneeling beside Margrete. "Horatio can tell you much, even about how your father died. He saw your father and Old Hamlet on that icy battlefield. Did you not, Horatio?"

I regarded Marcellus and, with a slight swipe of my hand, gestured for silence. True, I had once told him and the Spanish guard, Barnardo, that I had seen that deadly fight. I had said so only to gain their trust. To me, that glorious victory seemed like a memory because Hamlet had related the story to me many times. In fact, however, I had never witnessed Old Hamlet in battle.

A prickly sensation warned me to locate its source. To my immediate left, I saw that Margrete's grim frown and strained eyes were due to more than sorrow's mark or pain from maintaining her curtsy. Her stare was that of a tired magistrate. She whispered, "Horatio, I pray you. Do not lie to Fortinbras. If he discovers any falsehoods, we will be punished."

"Lady, you have little faith in the art of scholars. Ours is neither a black nor white craft, and we deal in a variety of truths."

Margrete's brow bunched. Disapproval seeped from her pressed lips. "How many truths are there from which to choose?"

I felt Marcellus's shaking hand upon my shoulder. "Horatio, tell him." Marcellus then turned to Fortinbras. "Horatio also saw Old Hamlet's ghost—remember, Horatio? You were with us on the ramparts before you told Hamlet of its visitation."

Fortinbras's stare was as cold and sharp as a winter warrior's blade. "Rise, commoner. You saw Old Hamlet's ghost?"

I stood and replied, "I did, Your Highness."

"How did Hamlet manage to conjure his father's spirit?"

"The ghost willed the encounters."

"For years I dreamt of besting Old Hamlet. Instead, circumstance was the victor."

I regarded Fortinbras. *The cherubs of Mars must have wept for you,* I thought.

"Commoner, who besides the dead committed these crimes? Tell me the truth."

"No one, majesty," I said.

"I will execute any who helped Old Hamlet murder my father."

"At Krogen, treachery was aimed inward. It's unlikely that Helsingør's nobles conspired against your father."

Fortinbras's chin raised, and his sharp stare pinioned me. "We will go to the royal suite, immediately, where you will tell me everything. Take me there." He turned toward the hall's pocked archway. Over his shoulder he called out, "Lanier, get me an army of mercenaries." The click of his heels striking the stone-paved corridor bid that I follow.

I hastily bid Margrete good day, then pushed through the crowd and ran out of the hall after Fortinbras. His armor and leather-clad figure strode toward the corner stairway. My feet pounded in exact cadence with my thundering fear. Would my testimony secure Fortinbras's patronage and his defense of Krogen's people? Or would failure of my promise and honor force me to find more poison and relinquish my soul?

II.

Claudius and Gertrude's wood-paneled bedchamber smelled of rust and the stillness of life stopped. Prickly fear crept down my neck. I stood near the broad window, away from the imposing tapestry and wardrobe and the dead hearth interring clumps of ash, and awaited a signal from Fortinbras that I should begin telling Hamlet's story.

I watched Fortinbras open the wardrobe's wide doors and peer within at the colorful multitude of folded tunics and shirts and hanging robes and frocks. He seemed to prefer to search the royal possessions more than hear my deposition. But then he asked, as he stared at the garments, "Why did the Hamlets lay dead upon my arrival at this castle? Did Cristiern expect that the fall of the Hamlets would trap me?"

"I can't pledge that there are no evil daemons at work, majesty, but I'm certain that the deaths weren't a trap set to capture you."

"How long ago did Old Hamlet die?"

"Two months."

Surely, Fortinbras knew that fact. I felt as though he tested me. My gut squirmed. Defense of Helsingør's nobles relied upon my ability to convince Fortinbras of their goodness, that they were no threat to him.

Fortinbras grunted acknowledgement of my answer. He banged the wardrobe doors shut, turned to face the canopied bed, and swept his hands down its curtains' gathered red and purple folds as if feeling for something hidden. Next, he went to a dim corner, beyond the bed, where stood a triangular metal frame as tall as a man. It racked eight large unlit candles. He lifted one to inspect its bottom surface. "You said that you saw Old Hamlet's ghost."

"Yes, sire."

"I want to see my father's spirit." Fortinbras set down the candle and regarded me. "Can you summon my father's ghost?"

"Highness, I didn't beckon him." To escape, if needed, I looked to the doors. One opened directly into the corridor, and another, beside the hearth, led, probably, to a sitting room.

"You can try to call him. I have tried." Fortinbras bent over a plush black robe draped across the corner of the bed. He prodded the robe's pockets. "Tell me about the appearance of Old Hamlet's ghost."

"I stood high upon the battlements with the guards. They had seen the phantom and asked me to watch with them. Past midnight but before dawn, clouds crossed the moon's half face, shading the ramparts. The wind tore at us. Pebbles and debris rose from the battlements, becoming a whirling cloud of rock. It spun fast and threw sparks like striking flint. Then it compressed into the form of a man. He wore armor, visor up. I saw his pallid brow, and his black and silver beard. I bid the phantom speak to me, but it didn't reply. It wanted only to address Hamlet, I thought. The following night I brought Hamlet with me. The specter was mute in my presence, but it lured Hamlet away and spoke to him."

Fortinbras regarded me. His brow crumpled. "Why did the guards first tell you and not Hamlet?"

"They feared judgment. They expected I would know how to tell Hamlet."

I paused. Did I dare tell Fortinbras the truth? Did I dare unmask myself, tell him how I had contributed to Hamlet's death? Perhaps he would respect my will to honor my friend. He might take pity and agree to be my patron.

I continued, "I told Hamlet about his father's ghost because I believed it would help Hamlet grieve his father's passing. But I was wrong and ignorant. By introducing Old Hamlet's ghost to his son, I put Hamlet on a path to destruction."

"I do not believe it. Each man invites his own damnation." Fortinbras crossed the tawny floorboards. In his path lay the queen's heeled, red silk shoes, one upside down. As he passed them, his foot swatted both away. "Did Hamlet's encounter with his father's ghost cause his madness?"

By the saints, I thought with relief. *Now I'll start to fulfill my promise.*

I began by telling Fortinbras of Hamlet's downfall. I did not expect that Hamlet's story, or mine, would become my confessions made in ink.

※

One month previous, Hamlet and I stood gasping for breath near Krogen's East Gate upon the moonlit killing field, once a curving moat and now a grassy expanse between the fortress's glowing inner and outer walls. Suddenly, Hamlet, scowling, drew his sword against me. The blade's point wavered at my face like a night wasp. A cruel, heartbreaking threat. Through a choking sob, he said, "If you try to stop me again, I will make a ghost of *you*."

Christ's bones. Hamlet turned against me. His father's ghost had just spoken to him and overpowered his reason. I had only wanted the spirit to settle and my friend's grief to quell. What wicked seed had I sowed by bringing Hamlet to the phantom?

My heart pounded in my throat, from fear and my pursuit of my friend down the rampart's stairs. "Hamlet, of course I would intervene. I journeyed from Wittenberg to Helsingør to help you grieve your father's death. Not to stand idle while you chase a sprit and endanger your soul."

The glinting tip shook at me, too close. I clenched my eyes against it.

"You lied, Horatio. You said that when you saw my father's ghost walk upon the battlements last night, he appeared sad, not enraged. He suffers..."

I opened my eyes and saw Hamlet gawking, weeping. His weapon had dipped, now was level with my heart. Helpless, I opened my hands. "I wanted to soften news of the visitation, to spare you. Hamlet, you must be wary of a phantom, not confront it. It could be evil. Trap you. Take another shape and force you to kill yourself."

The blade dropped. I gulped a breath, relieved at first. Hamlet laid it on the ground.

The sky flickered as if in a signal to retreat.

Hamlet, trembling, turned to the gate's bars and reached high, grasping as if to scale the high-mounted crest of the House of Hamlet—a spire and three lions. A sudden wind tore through the killing field. Above the gate, a small lantern rattled. Past the gate and dock, the dark skin of Øresund Bay rippled as if pricked by fear.

"The ghost spoke to you?" I asked.

"I must not divulge...it is a secret."

"I won't tell anyone."

Hamlet released the gate and turned to me. "The spirit confirmed my worst suspicions. In Denmark, every man or woman who seems to be a malefactor is, indeed, a scoundrel no matter his ambition or her birthright."

I snorted. "That isn't even a rumor. Why would a ghost rise to tell us an obvious fact?"

Hamlet laid his sword upon the ground. "Before I can risk telling you more, you must swear upon this sword."

Objecting, I put up my hands.

From the ground, a voice drummed, "Swear. Swear. Swear."

The gate's lantern, swinging above our heads, shattered. Glass and metal showered upon us. I flung my arms over my head. But Hamlet opened his arms wide in supplication, or perhaps in triumph. "Hear the old man, commanding us from the grave."

I cried, "What chaos was this?"

Before us, the gate's bars formed a glowering brow and snarling mouth.

I knelt before the sword. It pivoted on the ground then aimed at me. My heart hammered within my ribs. I made the sign of the cross. "I swear," I said.

Hamlet sank upon his knees beside me. He sobbed to the sky. Spittle dripped from his lips. "I am cursed with a duty. My father commanded me to avenge his murder. Poisoned by my uncle for his crown and bride. He died without last rites."

My stomach lurched. Sour bile burned my throat. I wanted to retch for fear. "Your father has burdened you with a horrible charge."

Hamlet flattened his hand upon the blade. "Father, I will avenge your death, even if to do so I must seem to be crazed." Hamlet looked to me.

"You must pledge never to disavow that I am mad."

"But you are *not* mad, Hamlet." Although I had seen his temperament vacillate between extremes—reserve and wild leaps, charging enthusiasm and retreating wistfulness—he did not appear to be mad.

"You lied about my father's condition, yet you will not fib about mine? Say to others that I am mad. This will divert them from discovering my true purpose."

"Swear," roared the metal mouth and jumble of teeth.

"I do swear it," I cried. "Almighty God, forgive me."

The rumbling ceased. The clouds rolled off the moon's face, shedding its light. Bright moonlight swept the fortress. The last cloud thinned. The heavens unfolded as a dusky expanse, clear and deep.

The gate's bars loomed straight and thick again.

"Peace, troubled ghost," Hamlet said. He wiped his flushed face. Then, watching the bars, he hesitantly crouched to retrieve his sword and, standing, slid it through his belt loop.

I cinched my courage and stood. "What matter crafts these supernatural marvels?"

"Something more than our dreams and philosophy, Horatio, cradles all of earth and heaven's possibilities."

What of Hades's fortune, I would have sardonically asked, had not an idea struck. In lieu of my failing influence, perhaps philosophy could lure Hamlet's reason.

I said, "Not every dream renders blessing. Some bring a curse, Hamlet, not Aristotle's Golden Mean. Let's seek that ideal balance. Let's quit these environs, return to Wittenberg and find life's normalcy again. Resume our studies and our plans for the school we will build."

"Horatio, you are the greatest of friends. I love you as a brother, if you would still have me. I am wretched. Let us simply bid good night."

To protect Hamlet, I had to break the ghost's powerful influence over him, because I had caused the spark that lit a destructive blaze.

Thus, I swallowed to force a vicious knot in my throat to sink, and then leaned close to Hamlet. "I'll obey my promise to you, brother, but now you must make a promise to me."

Hamlet regarded me warily.

I continued, "Before taking any action of vengeance you must validate this ghost's intent."

"Horatio, have you ever known me to commit upon impulse?"

"Your father's soul, in purgatory, may wander in terror. Its sense may not be calibrated. It may be a devil."

Hamlet rubbed his forehead. "I should not believe my father?"

"Swear to me, Hamlet."

"I promise."

I rested my hand upon his shoulder and steered him toward the tunnel through Krogen's inner wall. "Do nothing but rest. At breakfast we'll decide how we'll test the ghost's veracity."

❦

Fortinbras stared upward at the faded grand tapestry. It filled the bedchamber wall between the broad window and the canopy bed. The woven depiction was a primitive Danish treasure. The sticklike bodies, blockish heads, and skirts of red, green, and gold were the first known images of the queen of Denmark, previously queen of Norway, Margaret Fredkulla and her court, who lived four hundred years ago. If she, a Swedish princess, could become queen of Norway and Denmark through marriage, Fortinbras, an ambitious Norwegian prince, could become monarch over the Kalmar Union by defeating Cristiern in battle.

Was that the thought that occupied him? I stood beside Fortinbras, wondering if he had heard anything I had said.

"I have more to tell, majesty."

"When did the court believe that Hamlet was mad? Which nobles knew of it and loyally protected him?" Fortinbras crossed his arms and continued to stare at the tapestry.

"Hamlet first pretended madness in the private company of his betrothed, Ophelia. After that—in public. Gossip spread, and Ophelia's father, Polonius, who was also Claudius's counselor, reported to Claudius and Gertrude that Hamlet was mad. When Ophelia rejected Hamlet's courtship, Hamlet was enraged."

Fortinbras scoffed. "That rift must have saddened her father."

"I believe he encouraged it. Others sought to obstruct and cage Hamlet. When our onetime school friends, Rosenkrantz and Gyldenstierne, arrived, Hamlet suspected that they were Claudius's spies. He was not wrong."

Fortinbras looked to me. His eyes narrowed. "Did Hamlet suspect everyone of treachery? Did he seek proof of his accusations?"

"Indeed, he did. Hamlet created a plan that I wish I had never agreed to assist." I covered my face with my hands.

☙❧

The morning after Old Hamlet appeared to Hamlet and me, I attended Lauds devotions, but I did not pray. Instead, I devised a way to resolve our troubles. My scheme spilled from my tongue the instant Hamlet and I sat at breakfast in crowded Freyja Hall, as we drank our first cup of thin beer.

I leaned forward for some privacy, despite the filled benches at tables surrounding us. I whispered across the table to Hamlet, "This is how we'll verify the spirit's nature. We'll watch for its visitation, but this time we'll bring the priest from Saint Olai Church. He'll question the ghost. If it's a daemon, he'll exorcise it and we'll be safe. If it's a good spirit, the priest will give it absolution, easing the soul through purgatory. No vengeance needed. This plan resolves the matter."

I drank from my tankard, then set it upon the table and regarded Hamlet. His garb was not solemn black as usual. Rather, he wore a white shirt and an embroidered purple tunic and leggings. Lively. A sign of his lighter disposition, I hoped.

Hamlet said nothing. He calmly regarded me and pulled from his tunic pocket a square-folded sheet. He dropped it on the table before me as if it was his winning card.

I did not take the packet. "What's this?"

"Additional lines I wrote for insertion into a Roman play. It will be performed tonight in this hall."

He had already acted upon his decision. That was why Hamlet ignored my plan. Worried, I quaffed my cup.

Hamlet pushed aside his empty tankard and scooted over the sticky tabletop to sit on the bench beside me. He curled his shoulder for privacy, shielding us from a guzzling neighbor. "You and I will spy on Claudius during the performance."

"We will?"

"We will watch Claudius's response throughout but especially during those new lines. Should he even flinch I will deem him guilty and the ghost trustworthy."

"That's treason, Hamlet."

He grinned triumphantly.

I folded my arms. "Perhaps you *are* mad. When John the Baptist confronted King Herod and condemned his marriage to his dead brother's wife, what happened to him? Like John, we may be executed."

Hamlet said, tapping the tabletop to punctuate his argument, "We will have our answer tonight, long before any visitation or time taken for Saint Olai's priest to drag his ancient hide to our gate."

"Claudius's guilty appearance won't mean that the ghost is virtuous. Why do you choose to scrutinize a man but not a phantom?"

"I need your help." Hamlet steadily regarded me. "I cannot trust anyone but you, Horatio. You are ruled by reason, by balance. You are the most reserved, rational man I have ever known. Indeed, you are my brother."

Overwhelmed by this cherished bond, I looked to the floor. I lost my words.

"You will not assist me?" he asked.

I glanced up at Hamlet. His eyes sharpened. I realized that the ghost still wielded tremendous influence over him. There was no other option for me but friendship in proving the ghost's malicious purpose. Thus, I clasped Hamlet's shoulder to assure him, and I took the page.

He pointed to it. "At these prompts, observe any sign of guilt."

Hamlet left, and I remained with text in hand. I read the lines, once, twice, thrice, and each time concluded that not only were they, in sum, a trap and therefore sedition, some individual sentences surely were treasonous. I could not explain how I perceived such duplicity and yet agreed to help in this crime. Perhaps, compared to everyone at Krogen, I was the maddest of all. That consideration, however, did not deter me. Because of my oath to support Hamlet's pretense of lost wits and my love of his brotherhood, I proceeded.

That evening I joined one hundred fifty nobles scurrying within

Freyja Hall, crawling among its benches like bees across the combs of a royal hive, searching for perfect seats. Men wearing tight-waisted doublets, generous codpieces, and sleek capes guided ladies packed into stiff gowns. Once gingerly seated, all buzzed louder.

To claim a place upon the aisle and near the stage, I pressed between two thick-throated, prattling women leaning together, nearly joined at their ample, jeweled bosoms. I separated those great boulders.

Upon my chosen bench I observed two kinds of performances, the players upon their stage and the royal family seated on that same platform but to one side where they could be admired by all. As the scenes progressed, revealing a scheming pretender's plans to steal his brother's crown and bride through murder, I observed Claudius's fist dig ever deeper into his cheek. His brow grew ever more knotted. When the wicked brother poured poison in the ear of the sleeping king, Claudius jolted up straight. "Oh," he cried.

Scores of elegantly coiffed heads turned in unison to assess the alert, like a herd of elk sensing danger. Seemingly confused, they issued a patter of applause.

I saw Claudius flush. He leapt to his feet. "I have seen enough."

Claudius's descending boot struck the stage's platform steps, and Gertrude followed him, shaking her head.

Like a wave's upward thrust, the audience rose. I lunged into the aisle, ahead of the crowd, and ran to the doors. When I reached the corridor, I turned around to observe Claudius's expression. His was the shocked, enraged face of a man trapped by his own sin—the very stamp of a murderer.

The ghost was correct. At this realization, my strength fled from me. I staggered backward to avoid being trampled by Claudius and the raging current of nobles as they passed by. However, Hamlet captured me and kissed me on both cheeks. Then he shook a celebratory fist at the stage.

"The ghost spoke truth. Did you see how the text I added lured the king's conscience?"

That paper—where was it? I thrust my hands into my pockets. Empty. My stomach dropped. Had I lost the evidence of our treason? Shaking, I dashed back to my bench and searched, to no avail. Then I looked throughout the hall but did not find the sheet of lines.

Quivering, I thought, *Someone will discover those lines and recognize Hamlet's scrawl.* To avoid execution, I decided that Hamlet and I had to depart Helsingør for Wittenberg immediately, despite the moonless night.

But where was Hamlet? He had left the room.

I dashed from Freyja Hall into the passageway and up the spiraling stairs. Exiting onto Wiglaf Corridor I ran to the west corridor, where the royal suites were situated. Wall-mounted torches lit my path to my left, and I was chilled by night-blackened windows to my right. Midway ahead stood the Spanish guard, Barnardo, leaning against his pike. A short distance beyond were Hamlet's chambers.

I was about to pass Barnardo when suddenly a door swung into my path. Claudius, clad in a thick gray robe, stepped into the hallway. The instant he saw me, his face flashed crimson. To avoid careening into him, I crouched. Although his broad-shouldered mantle gave him ballast, I lost my balance and fell but quickly recovered. Then I bowed deeply, daring not to look directly at this ruler whom I had so closely scrutinized only an hour earlier. I looked down at my scuffed boots and could see something fluttering in his shaking hand. I recognized the creased, crisp folds and Hamlet's elegant ink script. It was the page of lines.

Treason discovered. For a moment I could not breathe.

"How fortunate, Horatio, that you have come in search of this material. I was about to send for you. Step into my chambers."

Claudius pointed at his door, embellished by iron-wrought curls, and Barnardo opened it. I entered directly into a candlelit bedchamber overlooking the western fortress wall and passed the fire lapping in the hearth to stand before the broad window. I might have jumped out of it but for the small panes' metal frames that seemed keen to impale a fool.

Behind me, the door slammed. I turned into the brunt of Claudius's charge. "You and Hamlet played a dangerous trick upon us tonight. Incited the court to believe that fratricide gave me the crown and my queen. An abomination." Claudius thrust the crumpled page at me. "Hamlet wrote these lines. You held them. Why?"

I took the sheet, glanced down at it. "The play was good drama but not excellent, sire. The additional text was only meant to improve the story, to raise the dramatic effect for your enjoyment."

"Enjoyment?" Claudius's face swelled red with rage. With one outstretched hand he gripped a post of the birch canopy bed as if to choke it. From its capping rails carved angels peered down upon the mattress, and snarling dragons warned off approaching thieves.

"It is a fiction, highness." To feign calm, I slowly laid the page upon the plush bed.

Claudius plucked up the page and shook it at me. "You are protecting Hamlet. Report to me everything about his plans, his madness."

Quaking, wishing for a place to hide, I looked down at the tawny, polished floorboards, so unlike the cold, pine floor of my beloved cell at Leucorea. "I beg your mercy, sire. To help both you and Hamlet, may I leave with him for Wittenberg?"

"You refuse my command?" Claudius scoffed. His arms swept wide. "Why do you think you are here? Who, do you suppose, summoned you from Leucorea University to attend to your grieving friend? It was not Hamlet."

"The letter was signed in his name," I muttered. However, then I recalled that Hamlet's greeting, after I had arrived, was one of surprise. Hamlet had not expected me. Why had the king and queen tricked me into making that journey?

Claudius turned his back to me and, carrying the page of lines, walked toward the door. "You are not Hamlet's only school friend here. I sent to Vallo Castle for Rosenkrantz. To Kalundborg for Gyldenstierne. They have recently arrived. I grant your request to leave Helsingør, but you will be in a shroud." Claudius pushed open the door. "Barnardo, take Horatio—"

Gertrude strode through the open threshold, pulling the shimmering train of her low-collared gown, a shade darker than her long, snowy-blond locks. Her heeled slippers hammered the floorboards, jiggling her bosom. Chin high, she faced Claudius and glared at him.

Claudius watched her warily. He rubbed his blunt chin.

Gertrude flipped her tresses off her shoulder and then, reaching, snatched the page from Claudius's hand. She turned and strode to the hearth. Her fists twisted the sheet into a stick, and she thrust the small rod into the fire. "Let us look to true matters, not supposition."

The page buckled upon its creases and curled, glowing orange and gray.

Claudius passed his hand across his gawking face as if to wipe away anger or disbelief. He tersely said, "That was evidence, my dear."

Gertrude leaned toward Claudius. "Of what? And what more rumors would fly about the court should you act only upon your suspicions?" She smoothed his velvet mantle to correct its sheen. "Dearest, you should want to salve Hamlet's grief, not rage against him. Not accuse innocents. Be patient and just in your judgments."

Claudius scowled at Gertrude. She patted his breast and smiled. "All is better."

I glanced at the smoking remnant. *Yes, much better but for the king's wrath.*

Gertrude swept toward me, arms open, waggling and swaying. "Horatio, we trust you. Tell me: Is my son mad? My husband thinks so."

Remembering my oath, I replied, "It appears so, madame."

She regarded me for a long moment, her face flushed. Worry's burden slipped from her brow to fill her eyes. Then she blinked away tears.

I added, "He loved his father."

Gertrude said with pinched mouth, "Your friendship with Hamlet is his treasure." She hooked her arm inside my elbow and guided me toward the door. "Thank you for remaining at Krogen. You must stay. Hamlet needs you."

Before I could reply, Claudius gripped my other arm and yanked me forward. He pushed open the door and shoved me into the corridor. "You," he whispered hoarsely, "will stay but do as I order. Await my command. I will watch you and Hamlet. If you tell anyone of this, I will take you to the killing field and cut your throat myself."

Claudius retreated into the room and slammed the door.

Straightening my tunic, I silently replied: *Unless your wife dispatches your weapon.*

My arse was fixed in a crevice between the marital cannons of two monarchs. I was not the only one so situated, I realized, when I saw the corridor's other occupant, Barnardo, the guard. Nearby, he stood as straight as a plank, gripping his pike and staring ahead, ignoring me.

So, too, I disregarded Barnardo. To locate Hamlet, I ran to his chambers. As I pounded upon the door, I cursed myself for my negligence. *Stupid wretch. How could I lose that blasted page? Because of me, my brother is in worse danger now—Claudius thinks Hamlet's his enemy. I threw oil on their smoldering hate. Well done. This would not have happened if I never conspired.*

Hamlet did not open his door. He could not likely sleep through such racket. Rattled with fright, I searched for him in Freyja Hall where perhaps he sought more drink to celebrate his success. He was neither there nor in the chapel praying for his father's soul—I could not find him anywhere. I crept to my chambers and, for the second consecutive night, lay awake until sleep's agent, exhaustion, took pity and clubbed me senseless.

※※※

I looked again to the bedchamber's hearth and ashes. Recollection of Claudius's threats issued in that place made my knees quake like shaking dice.

Beside me, Fortinbras bent to examine a stone block within the hearth's frame. He picked at its loose mortar and asked, "Was Hamlet apprehended?" Then, he tugged a corner of the stone, seemingly testing whether it concealed a compartment.

"Not immediately. First, he killed Ophelia's father."

Fortinbras straightened, brows arching over his hard stare. "Hamlet killed the king's counselor?"

"It was an accident."

Fortinbras's head jerked back. "You are certain Hamlet had no hand in killing those noblemen—what were their names? Rosengyld and Krantzenstierne?"

I clasped my hands behind my back. The truth would not please Fortinbras... but I told it as Hamlet had divulged it to me. "Hamlet was in private conversation with his mother. He heard a noise and believed it was Claudius, spying on him."

Fortinbras opened his arms wide and glared at me. "Hamlet wanted to stab the king. Instead he killed the royal counselor, Polonius. Yet you think Hamlet deserves honor?" He reached for the door to the left of the hearth. Fortinbras pushed upon the latch, opened the door, and entered the sitting room.

Was I dismissed already? My breast pounded. I had not finished explaining Hamlet's cause, and I needed Fortinbras as my benefactor. I had no money that could sustain me as a storyteller, traveling thief-infested roads throughout Europe to proselytize about Hamlet. Alone, I could not influence the tribes across the globe to learn Hamlet's story. The heat of pending failure lapped at me. I could sense the Devil's knives ready to slice across my ribs.

Saint Niels, give me courage, I thought of my patron saint, as I followed Fortinbras into the sitting room.

III.

The two dozen chairs that lined the walls of Claudius's sitting room were for men awaiting audience with the king. The seat I needed was a prayer bench to beg the Almighty: *Let Fortinbras hear the remainder of Hamlet's story. Let him hear my request for patronage.* My flailing heart was whipping itself into pieces.

Fortinbras reached up toward two crossed swords mounted upon the wall. "Were any nobles involved in Polonius's death?" Fortinbras yanked the weapon from its anchor. He extended the sword, then with bent elbow shook it to test its weight.

I mopped my beading forehead with my cuff. "None assisted Hamlet. But one noble especially suffered as a result of the judgments, schemes, and slaughter. Although I tried to help her, I failed … in all my efforts."

☙❦❧

On the morning that followed Claudius's threats and my futile search for Hamlet, the housemaster, Tomas, an older, thin fellow, rapped upon my chamber door. When I opened it to him, I beheld his full head of white hair, coifed with a touch of wax, to sweep back at the temples.

"I'm sorry, Tomas, that I neglected Mass this morning. I am feeling a bit tired."

"It is not that, Horatio. Overnight, the king and queen appointed you as nursemaid to Ophelia."

Hamlet's lady needs my assistance? I rubbed my face to wipe away amazement and sleep. "What happened?"

"Her father is dead. Killed by Hamlet. As I took the prince to the dungeon, he asked if it was the king he had stabbed. Madness. Within an hour Claudius ordered Hamlet sent to England. I put him on a ship before dawn this morning."

My mind froze. Claudius had spared Hamlet...through exile. "When will he return?"

Tomas grunted uncertainly. "Report to myself or Claudius anything that Ophelia says concerning Hamlet." He wiped his nose with his long finger. "The lady is grieving. Her brother is away and there is no mother to help. Claudius wanted you, as Hamlet's closest friend, to attend to her. Remember: report anything of concern to us. Well...good fortune to you."

He turned on his heel and strode away.

"But I don't know how to care for a sad woman," I called after him. Tomas shrugged, continuing toward the stairwell.

During a fortnight, Ophelia and I often sat on her sparse chamber's cool floor among thick shadows, tufts of blond hair, and shredded bandages. With each sliver that fell from the moon, Ophelia lost a piece of her wits. Ophelia's flaxen frock, its ties barely secured at the waist, hid little of her pillowy flesh. Long scratches trailed from her neck into the crease of her bosom. Bloody scabs marred her scalp. Only two weeks prior, her weepy, red-rimmed eyes had been blue sapphires, but now her entire face was the gray of anguish.

Ophelia sometimes imagined a harvest of flowers. She sat beside her straw-stuffed mattress, which lay flat upon the floor, and pulled dry stalks out of its shredded corner. One day she told me, "These fertile fields could never be my father's graveyard. He left me, cannot bless my nuptials." Then, wide-eyed and clutching her pretend tokens, she asked, "Where is my beloved? What has happened to him? I beg you, Horatio, tell me."

"He will return to you, pretty dear," I said, hoping to quell the elements that were baking lunacy in her brain. I added, "How, Ophelia, can I restore your good nature?"

"Bring me Hamlet."

I shook my head. "The date of his return is not within my influence, but…" I reached for her fists to receive a share of her invented mementos, "I can take these petals for the priest's blessing and place them into your mattress for good fortune in marriage."

Ophelia, glaring, pulled back from me. "Counterfeit consecration by worthless men. You can do nothing."

She might have included the court physician in her judgment, for neither could he work healing magic. Administering at Gertrude's request, he forced vinegar pastes into Ophelia's mouth and nose and applied leeches for bloodletting. When she flailed, double-fisted, at him he declared her obstinate. I learned from the physician that his more determined purging treatments, such as potions rubbed into her mouth, vagina, and anus, produced nothing from her but screams, vomit, and filth. Even exorcism performed by Saint Olai's priest, and which I was commanded to attend as witness, yielded no benefit. The threads of Ophelia's mind unwound faster than I could gather them.

Never, I privately vowed, would my failure to assist Ophelia cause Hamlet to suffer a pitiful marriage, should they wed after his return. I had long been skeptical of his intent to marry, for his distrust of women seemed only to intensify his allure to the many ambitious ladies who perceived his broken sensibilities and wished to fix him. Nevertheless, if it was Ophelia he desired to marry, I had to repair her so that, upon his return, Hamlet, Ophelia, and I would immediately depart for Wittenberg, never again to return to Helsingør.

Each day, to ease Ophelia's spirits I recited stories and lectures and anything that might ease her upturned mind. When my tongue tired of wagging, I sat quietly with her. Held her hand gingerly, avoiding her torn fingernails. Fed her and withstood the half-chewed wads she spat at me. Prayed for her every evening before I departed her company. Usually, Ophelia rocked, murmuring, "Hamlet." Increasingly, she stood between me and her chamber door, raising her hem and wiggling her bare self at me. When Ophelia greedily rubbed her hands inside her thighs, she smoldered. To avoid more abusive cures, I did not report these behaviors to the housemaster or Claudius.

One morning Marcellus, the old, droop-jowled guard, came to my door. "Ophelia is dead," he rasped.

Hollow-eyed, he told me that in the middle of the night she had tricked him and escaped her room. The other two guards assisted his search. At dawn, too late, they found Ophelia's submerged body within the evil water known as the Pond of Hearts. She, as many souls determined to die, had pinned herself under its submerged rock. Not all who died there likely wished to perish. Many decades earlier, Old Hamlet's youngest brother, Jons, mysteriously drowned while playing with his older brother, Claudius. Ophelia, however, probably intended to die. Her death glare, as Marcellus described it, was a frozen grin of hysterical determination.

Marcellus, standing before me, melted into tears. For fear and shame, I wept with him for Ophelia's bad death, condemning her eternal soul to torture, and the additional grief that I anticipated would wrack Hamlet. Some bitterly blamed Hamlet for causing the grief for her father that killed Ophelia. Gertrude, I was told, cried for Ophelia's loss and wailed that her own familial line might be lost. All was my failure, I confess it. I sensed Hell's licking flames rising and searing the tender arches of my own feet.

How soon might I suffer the chop of Claudius's death blade? It had been suspended only by Gertrude's whim, which could vanish due to anger at my negligence, and the guard's. I wanted to remain in Helsingør, however, to intercept Hamlet upon his return and make our way to Wittenberg, to Leucorea. Thus, I avoided the king and queen by leaving my chambers during the hard, dark hours for morning devotions in the chapel, taking bits of bread and fish offered at the cook's door behind Freyja Hall, and sitting upon the dock until sunset, scouting the bay's horizon for the sail of Hamlet's returning ship.

On the seventh morning, the tenth day of June, as I exited the East Gate for the dock, the guard, Francisco, mentioned that Ophelia would be buried that afternoon in a corner of Helsingør's graveyard. That morning, I glumly watched the bay's gray horizon. At noon a ship's rotund sail appeared. Surprised, I stood and eagerly watched its approach. Its anchor dropped, and a tiny boat slid down the starboard side. A lone man pulled upon its oars, thumping through the current toward me. He waved. It was Hamlet.

He climbed upon the dock and we embraced. I stepped back to

behold my brother. He wore a torn black doublet with leggings and a white shirt. His swirling bristles gave him a Viking appearance, not the smooth-cheeked Germanic fashion we usually preferred. Most different was his lack of steadiness. I wondered what was wrong with him.

I took Hamlet by his elbow. "Claudius suspects us of treason. We must leave Helsingør. We can take your ship—"

Hamlet waved dismissively. "Those pirates brought me here for payment. But where is my uncle? My father is not yet avenged. I will fix that fault in nature."

The scuff of Francisco's boots, nearby, was my reminder. I moved up the dock toward the trail that met the East Gate. "There's much I must tell you, Hamlet. Come with me. We'll discuss privately."

Hamlet, looking up at clouds bunched like matted gray fleece, winced. "Then we will find Claudius."

Thinking of the probable funeral entourage, I replied, "He likely will come to us."

I led Hamlet down the hill and past the village, past Saint Olai Church to Helsingør's unconsecrated graveyard. There, we walked upon the field pockmarked by sunken tombs and swollen with memorial mounds.

As fat raindrops began to strike, I attempted a most thorny conversation. "Something terrible has happened, Hamlet. Today there will be a funeral…"

The heavens cracked. Rain fell faster. Although I shielded my eyes against the onslaught, Hamlet stood at the edge of an open pit and looked down into it—the only grave prepared for a burial. I guessed it would be Ophelia's.

I tried to continue. "Hamlet, when Polonius died—"

"Men of busy tongues and rotting hearts walk among us." Hamlet stooped to pluck a chipped skull from the ground. "Why do we often smell but not see their ruin until it is too late."

"Ophelia went mad."

Hamlet wiped the skull's congealed remains on his sleeve. His abhorrence seemed to turn to fascination as he caressed the bumps and cracks in the bone.

I wondered if he had heard me. Moving nearer, I said, "I need to tell you that—"

"Death comes to all of us at the appointed time," Hamlet said to the craggy relic in his hand. He bent and set the skull atop the edge of the pit.

He seemed too resigned to the moment of mortal release. Had Hamlet somehow already heard of Ophelia's death?

In the chilly rain, a creaking wagon pulled by four peasants rounded a nearby mound. Behind the cart bearing a shroud-wrapped corpse walked a dozen black-robed mourners wearing their hoods up. Among them were Claudius, Gertrude, Ophelia's brother, Laertes, and Margrete, the queen's principal lady.

I pulled Hamlet behind a tall bush and hastened to explain. "Hamlet, I grieve with you. I know that you loved her. I did my best to protect Ophelia."

He blinked. "What?"

Beyond our hiding place, beside the grave, we heard a man beg, "She deserves more rights. Ophelia was a good woman. She feared God."

"That is Ophelia's brother, Laertes." Hamlet, pale, turned to me. Drops fell from his rain-dotted brow but not from his eyes. "Horatio, is Ophelia dead?"

Would grief enrage Hamlet? With dread, I replied, "Yes."

Hamlet dove through the scratchy bushes. I followed to stand beside him before the open tomb and the entourage. He declared, "It is I, Hamlet the Dane. My sorrow honors Ophelia best."

Our sudden appearance beside Ophelia's grave jolted Gertrude and startled Margrete whose emerald gaze regarded Hamlet, then me. Hers was the loveliest scowl ever to beset me.

Not attractive was Claudius's rage. His hood, deflecting the plummeting rain, did nothing to mask a vein storming down his crimson forehead. "We recognize you, nephew. No need for fanfare."

Laertes pulled the corpse from its wagon and jumped with it into the grave. Hamlet leapt also into that long hole. They scrambled in the mud, arms flailing. Ophelia's gray arm trailed through an opening in the shroud. Never before had I witnessed two men claw one another for a deceased girl. It was the most macabre expression of pride I had ever seen. While Hamlet chose his actions and, I have come to see, must bear his own cross for his sins, I confess my part in his ruin. Had I, in proper time and fashion, disclosed to Hamlet the facts of Ophelia's death, he might have met his grief with honor. Instead, a trap, built by the distress of men, awaited us.

When Hamlet, covered in brown filth, pulled himself from the grave, he said nothing and ran away. I chased, slipping in muck as rain pelted me, among the graves, past the church and village to the uphill trail. When Hamlet, far ahead of me on the rising path, reached the East Gate, I lost view of him. However, I guessed his destination because I feared his harmful intent. I would shepherd him to safety, far from Helsingør.

I remained on the road that passed the East Gate and curled along the fortress's northeast wall. Then, upon a slim path of white sand, I arrived at a ring of birch trees that encircled the Pond of Hearts. Beside the spring, Hamlet sat on a rock. He was clean and dripping from submersion in his clothes.

The rain had stopped, and Hamlet looked across the misty pond. His gaze, blue and steady, seemed at ease, calm and quiet. Nothing like the storm of temperament in the grave only minutes earlier. This oddness in him stirred discomfort in me.

I climbed upon a boulder's round haunches to sit beside Hamlet. "Don't do it. We must finish our master's of arts degrees. You will be the royal patron and I soon a doctor of divinity, the chancellor, and we will charter our school."

"My father's ghost tells me I have proven my mettle to dispatch a man."

His abrupt topic was like a cold splash. I stammered, "But you didn't mean to kill Polonius."

"Not him. Rosenkrantz and Gyldenstierne, however…" Hamlet pulled from his pocket a folded missive and pressed it into my open hand.

Hamlet had killed his longtime friends. Was it by sword, as he had once threatened me on the killing field? The beetle of fear that had been creeping up my neck burrowed under my skin.

"I found this in Gyldenstierne's possession," he said. "My uncle did not send me away for recovery or exile. He sent me to be murdered. Here was his demand of England."

> *The twenty-fourth day of May in the year of our Lord 1513*
> *To His Majesty, Henry VIII of England:*
> *Traitors often rise from within one's own family.*
> *I call upon you to consider the crimes of my nephew,*

Hamlet, who killed my counselor and, I believe, intends to murder my person.

If you will lend your assistance, do not delay. Execute Hamlet, who came to you by ship in the company of the men who bore this letter to you. Your ambassador will be rewarded at the court of Helsingør once the favor is done.

As for the style of execution, I recommend beheading. I hear it is not your practice in England. Likely, however, it will become so once you observe the method, which is effective and painless compared to hanging or the fiery stake.

With Greatest Regard,
Claudius, Sovereign of Helsingør, Denmark

I stuffed the letter into my tunic pocket. Then I picked up a stone and cast it hard at the water.

"They chose to act against me." Hamlet turned to me and held my gaze. He seemed strangely tranquil. "I know how I will kill my uncle. Do not squint at me, friend. He deserves drowning in the Pond of Hearts."

Before I could object to Hamlet's plan, a curly-headed young man approached. He told Hamlet of a challenge proposed by Claudius—a longsword duel against Laertes in Freyja Hall, immediately, to settle their differences. Hamlet accepted the terms. The man nodded and left.

"You must decline," I told Hamlet. "I will go to Claudius, tell him you're ill—ate a bad herring. Or I could substitute for you. And the blades must be thoroughly tested for strength, else neither you nor I will play. Should Laertes's weapon break while attacking...it could be deadly."

Hamlet, rubbing his forehead, refused. "Every man has an appointed time to win or to lose, to choose between his honor and his life."

I spread my arms. "Why not leave this matter to God? Why must you be the agent of revenge?" I knew when I said this that I, too, wished to fashion the outcome I desired.

Hamlet shifted upon our bolder. He ground a pebble beneath his heel. "We cannot change what must be. If I die in the act of honoring my oath to my father, it is well. Since I will die sometime, let it be now if that is fate's dictate."

I saw that Hamlet, decided and calm, was at peace with his plan. But I did not recognize him. Hamlet was now free from mercurial escalations and melancholy depths. Absent gripping doubts. Showed no fear of his father's disapproval. While of concern, those factors were the oars Hamlet had pulled upon and fought against throughout life. Balance was not his normal instrument. Thus, I realized that now, indeed, Hamlet was mad.

Christ's blood, I thought. This terrain was uncharted. Hamlet still rejected my reasoning, and he remained set upon committing regicide. No absolution for that. I had to help Hamlet navigate and survive.

"I'll get you out of this fight." I slid down from the rock and began to run up the sandy path toward the fortress.

Hamlet pursued me. I heard his crunching boot gain upon me. When he leapt on me, we toppled. I lay on my belly, squirming for breath. Hamlet shifted away, allowing me to roll onto my back.

Wheezing, I said, "Come with me to Saint Olai Church. Or the castle's chapel. Pray and receive God's forgiveness. Heal your soul before the duel."

Hamlet shook his head. "I accepted the terms. We must go now."

Lying upon my back, I looked up at Hamlet. He stood at his ease, arms still at his sides. I asked once more, "Let us go to Wittenberg now and—"

"After this duel, when I bring an end to my uncle, then we will return to Leucorea."

Hamlet reached down, gripped my hand, and pulled me to my feet.

Within the hour Freyja Hall became a battlefield.

☙❦❧

Did Fortinbras accept Hamlet's story of sacrifice? Would not his own heart beat with Hamlet's desire to justly avenge a father? In silent agony I followed Fortinbras from the sitting room into the bedchamber. With each stride his mail leg sleeves, bunched at his ankles, clicked.

Fortinbras stood at the toilet table, before the sun-glazed window. He held the pilfered sword point down, in one rough hand, and, with the other, picked through items. A square mirror. Bristly, flat brushes. A razor in its bone handle. A solitary gold ring—slender and beautiful. I leaned closer and saw that it bore four delicate ridges and an embedded ruby. When Fortinbras set it down, I took it and read its external inscription of love and carnal seduction. *Venus bless us.* It was probably Gertrude's wedding band. She had left it when she went to applaud her son as he fought the killer sponsored by her husband.

Fortinbras held out his hand. "Not yours to ogle, commoner." I dropped the ring into his palm. He inspected it again. "Did Gertrude know she was married to a murderer?"

I looked again to the ring. "I didn't believe so. But now...I'm not certain."

Fortinbras slid the ring into his belt pouch. He glared at me. "The noble who proposed the duel—he must have known of the intent to kill Hamlet."

I would tell the truth. "No, sire. He was a judge during the duel and ruled several hits in Hamlet's favor. Laertes was the treacherous noble. After he and Hamlet dueled, Laertes used his poisoned sword to cut Hamlet; Hamlet used the same to stab Laertes, who admitted, as he lay dying, that he and Claudius had conspired to poison Hamlet first with the cup. If that didn't work, the poisoned blade would kill him. But they didn't expect that Gertrude would drink from the cup to toast Hamlet. When she cried out that she had been poisoned and then died, Hamlet realized that the duel was a trap... as I had feared but couldn't protect him from. Hamlet's revenge was thorough. He attacked Claudius, poured much of the cup's poison into his mouth, and speared him with the baited sword."

The dropping sun angled a shaft at us. I sensed the flame of Fortinbras's irritation. The sword in his hand glinted. He turned the point downward, but the blade's edge aimed at my leg. "Have you told me everything?"

My hands shook. I clasped them behind my back. "I have told you all that I know and all that I did as a loyal friend and a true subject..."

"Your name is Horatio? Hor-a-ti-o. That is an odd name. Why do you not sound like a Dane? Your crunching Germanic tongue must make your mouth bleed."

"My native town is Tønderensis, in the Schleswig region, not far from the Germanic territories. Sire, I request your patronage so that I may fulfill my promise to my friend, for his honor and mine. I would tell his story."

"Not only are you a Germanic-yammering Dane. You are a beggar, too." He regarded me and rubbed his chin. "Why would I pay for your wandering storytelling? I must buy soldiers."

My hope for patronage drooped as low as the setting sun, which flashed its dying golden salvo upon the window. I made a closed smile to hide my gritted teeth. "Sire, your patronage would ensure Hamlet's remembrance and will rain blessings upon you for your generosity."

"Hamlet deserves punishment, not celebration." Fortinbras slid the sword into his belt loop. He began to pace. "You told me nothing useful."

"Majesty," I moved into the path of his march.

Fortinbras advanced on me. "Step aside, peasant."

I retreated and stood by the bed. "Sire, gifted with your patronage I would journey across all of Europe, telling of your kindness to the beleaguered people of Helsingør. If you defended them against Cristiern, you could gain sainthood, as one who protects those who suffer."

"It is Hamlet's story you wish to tell."

"Without that context, who could understand the peril from which you saved us?"

Fortinbras glared, slowly chewing the prideful notions I fed him. I thought, *Perhaps I persuaded him.* But then, he pointed at me. "You are no better than your prince. By your own account, you committed treason against your king. And you have proven nothing to me about how these nobles supported their monarch." He hammered his fist into his palm. "Did no one see what was developing? Intercede for the king in any way, especially after his counselor was killed?"

I looked to the floor. "Perhaps, majesty, some nobles attempted to assist Claudius, and I do not know of it." My legs tingled as if I wobbled on a precipice.

"Why should I trust that these nobles will not betray me and surrender to Cristiern?"

I walked to Fortinbras, knelt, and touched my forehead to the cold floor before his boots. "Forgive me, sire, that my story did not please you. I beg Your Highness..."

"I deny your request. No patronage."

I looked up at him. Fortinbras's hand raised and flicked away my hope.

That sow-loving, Devil-ordained wallop. I had bared myself to him, but he gave me not even a speck of consideration.

My fury boiled. It bubbled upward and flooded my tongue. To still the tempest that would ruin me if I spoke, I closed my eyes, clenched my jaw.

"Go," he said.

I opened my eyes and stood. The itch of revenge dared me. I surrendered to it and tossed my effort of truth-telling upon the hearth's ash heap. "Earlier today, sire, you asked whether Hamlet conjured his father's spirit. He did not. But you may be interested...I've heard of a spell that will beckon any ghost."

Fortinbras's brows arched. "What is it? In three ceremonies I have summoned my father's spirit, but he did not appear."

"It is said that for a phantom to emerge your humors must balance with the ghost's. This can happen if you drain your strength."

"Tell me."

"You must erect a small tent in a field. At midnight you must enter that tent, light candles within, and then speak certain incantations while pleasuring yourself until spent. Your act invokes regulating balance. The phantom will appear to you that night."

Fortinbras nodded at me, frowning. "I will try your spell. Give it to me."

He went into the sitting room and returned with a stick of charcoal and a small square of parchment. I scribbled in Latin a fantastical incantation I concocted, which I believed Fortinbras was learned enough to read yet not translate.

> *Entwined in ecstasy with The Fates,*
> *Eat of Eve and the fruit that woke her,*
> *Pray that your penis survives.*

I extended the tiny fragment and its hex to Fortinbras and relished the thought of his humiliation—an audience secreted in a dark field watching his enlarged shadow cast within his tent.

"Go," Fortinbras said. I left the chambers.

That trick wasn't wise, I thought woefully, as I quickly turned away. Although I told the story, it had not inspired Fortinbras's respect or honor for Hamlet. My grief stung anew. I thought, *I failed again*. Perhaps more poison could be found in Laertes's chambers?

Mulling, I walked east to my chambers in Wiglaf Corridor. Before I could take any other action, I would give Hamlet's eulogy at his funeral the next day. That was another way to tell his story...or begin to tell it, I realized. If it appealed to my audience and they lauded it, perhaps Fortinbras would see that they were loyal and deserved protection, and that his patronage of them would serve good purpose. The eulogy was my final opportunity to fulfill my life's obligation to Hamlet and to God.

Sleep beckoned, promising the rejuvenation I needed to write a sublime eulogy. But sleep is a witch, a master deceiver. I fell to fitful slumber and suffered two dreams.

One was a nightmare. I stood at a ship's rail in the night. Without warning, something pushed me overboard. I fell into a black ocean. My soaked clothing made my arms and legs heavy, easy prey for the creatures and daemons swimming there. As I sank, my breath squeezed from my chest. I saw, floating above my head, wavering streaks of moonlight. I reached toward them, kicking and thrashing. At last, I broke through the glimmering surface. "Pray, help me," I cried.

The surrounding water bubbled. The moon's silvery threads shot like lightning through the water, prickling my body. Something broke the surface beside me. It rolled like a log caught in a tumultuous current. I believed I would be pulled under and mauled by a monster, and I struggled to flee.

I saw that the tumbling figure was a man.

Suddenly all motion ceased. The body slowly turned to face upward. Its skin was blanched and streaked. The blond hair matted. His decay horrified me. But it was Hamlet. I grasped him and held him close.

He rasped in my ear, "Tell my story."

His arms wrapped about me like tentacles. I did not struggle. Together, we sank.

The other dream was less frightening but a strange vision, nonetheless. I stood with Hamlet in Helsingør's village graveyard. As when we had visited, he held a skull and examined how that brain vault also contained the soul, as clerics maintain. But then he handed the skull to me. Suddenly, Hamlet disappeared. I stood in his place, in the graveyard, holding the skull—which I knew was Hamlet's. Instantly, Lanier, the Burgundian who was Fortinbras's aide, appeared with a little girl unknown to me. Lanier held her by her hand. I offered Hamlet's skull to Lanier. He took it, bent to the girl, and gave it to her. Curiosity and intelligence shone in her face as she turned that cradle of bone over and over in her tiny hands.

I woke in the morning exhausted. I shaved my whiskers while pondering the meaning of my dreams. While I believed the first one was a torment wielded by the Devil, the second vision was a strange comfort to me. The skull did not seem wicked or cursed. I felt I was not alone because I shared it with others. I thought, *Perhaps the skull represents my promise.*

My friend's story. I would tell it next as Hamlet's eulogy. Unwritten, it mustered in my imagination. Finally, I sat at my table and wrote my notes. That afternoon I went to the crypt for Hamlet's burial.

We mourners congregated in the low-ceiled cave that lay beneath the castle. Leaning, peaked tomb markers and long sarcophagi lids filled the crypt. Dozens of shelves, dug into the walls, bore corpses hardened into tan, brittle sinews. Skeletons lay upon their backs, their arms splayed and jaws gaping in unholy appeal. Some lay on their sides. Their contracted limbs, pulled to hollow breasts, had returned to their fetal origins. Through their re-internment at Krogen, all had helped Gertrude and her husband stake claim to Helsingør.

I stood, unshaven and feeling as though I had been turned inside out. The priest placed me, standing at the head of Hamlet's bier. I looked down upon my dear friend's body. His head was squared by a warrior's shiny helmet that Hamlet never would have donned in life. He wore a gray feather cape, perhaps to fly his soul across the mythical River Styx. If his cloak's wings failed, the coins that, in our stubborn tradition, shielded his flat eyes would pay the river's ferryman. Hamlet's ringed hands, once dramatic instruments of gesticulation, lay still and flat upon his breast. His length, abruptly capped at the feet by pointed boots, seemed shortened by death.

A MAN OF HONOR

A wave of grief swept over me. My heart was like a fisherman's line weight, suspended by thin twine, hanging still in a cold ocean. I felt separate from the living. Black-cowled mourners whispered to one another. Their gold neck chains and brocade belts caught and held the torchlight. Sculpted effigies on the tombs seemed to blink at me. They appeared to await Hamlet's eulogy—the most important speech of my life.

I glanced down at the pages of notes I held. Were they sufficient? Strength drained through my heels. I bent my knees to bear the moment's burden.

The ceremony began. The priest stood beside me. He was as tall as a birch tree and hunched to avoid scraping his head on the ceiling. He droned the incantation. After the prayer, the people slid back their hoods. Among them stood Margrete, her hair braided behind her head. Her strained eyes and face bore the bruise of grief. Beside her, Fortinbras stood cloaked in a large robe, arms crossed.

I could not give ground to doubt, that creeping, gray fiend. I coughed to clear my throat, then read aloud:

> Hamlet was our prince. He was born on the twenty-fourth day of November in the year of our Lord 1482 to Gertrude and Old Hamlet, Sovereigns of Helsingør. He was your brother in blood. He was mine in spirit.
>
> I knew him as a true student of humanitas, of the divine role and will of man in God's creation. He sought, in exquisite delight and frustrated wonder, to understand man's complex state. But because of the principles of humanitas he found optimism to exist in man, and man's ability to locate truth.

I shared his certainty in that discipline. We learned it at Leucorea University in Wittenberg, a magnificent citadel of new thinking. Hamlet and I matriculated in 1502 among its original inductees. We met and paired as debate partners. Hamlet sometimes struggled to close the debate, but he excelled at crafting the argument. We won nearly every challenge. Together, we would have graduated. Hamlet would have returned to you, ruled Helsingør. I would have earned my doctoral degree in theology and the faculty seat that went to that bitter thorn, Martin Luther—

"Pardon me." I paused to wipe my eyes. "Never mind Luther."

Greater than shared blood is commonality of mind. Hamlet and I expected to found a new school at Helsingør. Its bright spires would have cast away scholastic darkness in the northern lands. Hamlet, as royal patron, and I, as chancellor administering the school and its holdings, would have sponsored poor students—never requiring their status to be as low as servitor.

I looked down upon Hamlet's gaunt face. Ours would have been good deaths.

One hundred and fifty pairs of frowning eyes filling the squat room pulled my attention to them. In Margrete's open, listening face, I saw tolerance. Fortinbras, however, glared impatience.

> *But death is a cruel editor. And we are allowed only so much ink at our quill's point to craft our life's plot.*

The people nodded.

> *Let us remember Hamlet. His adoration of books. And of plays and performance.*

Smiles. A few murmurs of agreement.

> *His care for people.*

Consent melted. Feet shuffled against the dirt, and a grumble rolled at the back of the crypt. Fortinbras grinned. Margrete looked down to the ground. Hot panic swept through me.

> *Hamlet's adoration of his father. Hamlet's grief for his deceased father consumed him. I had never seen him struggle so mightily. His grief was compounded by a charge. He was ordered to avenge Old Hamlet's murder.*

Stares of disbelief bore upon me. Some stood with mouths agape like netted fish, others groused with furrowed brows. The strain of silence was like an iron string pulled to its limit.

> *The command came from Old Hamlet's ghost. I witnessed it twice and saw it beckon to Hamlet. The*

ghost burdened him terribly, told him that Claudius had poisoned Old Hamlet to steal his crown and his queen.

Shrieks broke out across the crypt. Mouths and eyes, wide in horror, objected. The truth held no appeal for them.

I looked down at the quivering papers I held and read aloud the next paragraph. Fear stretched my voice above its usual register.

Hamlet sought vengeance to honor his father and to aid his suffering soul. In his fervor he mistook Polonius for Claudius and accidentally killed him. Claudius blamed Hamlet, but Hamlet was the faction that was wronged.

The crowd began to grumble. "These accusations," a middling-aged, red-bearded man called out to me, "are treason against the souls of the Hamlet monarchs."

I wanted nothing more than to finish. I ignored several pages and found the last lines. At that time, I dared neither break my oath by telling of Hamlet's pretend madness, nor risk his dishonor by admitting his true madness.

Many thought that Hamlet was mad. It has been said that madness was poor Hamlet's enemy. Let it be known throughout Denmark and the world that the rumor of Hamlet's madness is false. His harsh actions were those of a loving son and a proud prince who desired to ease his father's soul and to deliver just punishment. Let us remember Hamlet for his better self.

"Amen," said some.

I looked to Margrete. She gave a pitying smile.

The tide of mourners receded down the aisles of the dead to exit into the tunnels. Before I could escape, Fortinbras moved close and rasped into my ear, "You said nothing that convinced me that the House of Hamlet deserved victory over my father. Nothing that proved I should trust these people, waste even one goldgulden in their defense."

I bowed, not daring to look at him. "I beg your pardon, sire."

Fortinbras turned on his heel. I straightened and watched him push through the crowd as it hastily parted for him.

Failure's cursed tendrils squeezed my heart. My legs were as weak as sea froth. Grief burrowed deeper, doubling its possession of me. I looked to the surrounding tombs for solace. Lonely for my chosen family, I wondered what graveyard held Papa, my adopted, beloved guiding star. Where was his comforting hand that would never again rest upon my shoulder?

I trudged to my chambers, sat at my toilet table. After removing my tunic, I rolled up my undershirt's cuff, baring my arm. I held my shaving razor open and stared at the glint of its edge.

Hamlet's funeral eulogy would be added to the royal documents within Krogen's muniment room, the royal treasury. There, it would be safekept for posterity, albeit locked away and accessible to only a few. Perhaps an angel would discover it and give it wings.

How can I carry forth Hamlet's legacy when I can't conceive of my own? How can I save him?

I felt as I had when, as a small child, upon my little knees, I had begged God's mercy. I did not mean to cause my mother's death. Surely my father knew that. However, when he took me to the orphanage gate, released my hand, and told me that my hurried birth had killed my mother—my five-year-old heart had no voice to object. Whether my father surrendered me for my punishment, our grief, or both, I will never know. Even today my father's concussive voice overpowers my adult logic, muffling my denial of blame to a mere whimper.

Once my father abandoned me, I never again felt safe. Lies became my haven. But now, for my failure, I warranted no harbor. I deserved the Devil's impaling spears.

I thought, because Hamlet had killed a king and died without extreme unction, and my honor was dead, we would accompany one another in death, after all.

I thumbed the razor's edge. It was sharp enough. I pressed the blade to my wrist and felt its bite.

IV.

The razor sliced my skin, making a thin flap. Aiming again, I pressed the blade against my left wrist's blue trail of veins.

I ignored the clanging midday bells of Helsingør's priories and Krogen's Chapel, calling all to Sext prayer. My *Book of Hours* lay closed upon my toilet table where I sat.

A knock landed upon my bedchamber door.

Let me be, I thought. I wanted to tumble into Lethe, the mythical waters of forgetfulness.

My door's ragged latch rattled as someone grasped it.

Guilty and alone no more. I will be with Hamlet. I pressed again, harder this time. The blade's edge bit farther into my skin. Blood trickled from my wrist, dropped to the floor.

My opening door cackled. I had forgotten to lock it.

Footsteps. I did not turn around.

A thick hand rested upon my shoulder. *Papa*, I thought—but that touch was not his ghost's.

A barely familiar voice said, "I heard the eulogy."

I looked up to see Lanier, the Burgundian, aide to Fortinbras, black-clad in wide-brimmed hat, cape, and pantaloons. His long mane, too, was black. Only his shirt was white.

"That was not an easy thing you tried, *mon ami*. I have seen less bravery in executioners and curfew watchmen." His hand slid from my shoulder to smooth the corners of his moustache.

I said, "You keep low company."

Lanier calmly took a shaving cloth that lay before me upon my toilet table. He pressed it to my wrist. "Hold it like this. Raise your arm above your head."

I set my knife upon the table and did as I was told.

"I know desperation; I recognize it." He nodded at the knife. "Also, I know the distracting balm of work." Lanier removed his hat and laid it upon my writing table in the corner. He grasped a nearby chair and sat. Elbows upon his knees, he leaned toward me. "But you are not a man of the workbench. A scholar, are you not? What is your experience of court politics?"

"As an observer, mostly, during two months here, at Krogen Castle," I said.

"Ah. How long did you keep yourself in your scholar's cell at university?"

"Ten and four years. But I was in town often, wasn't bound by the university's walls. I didn't live in a monastery."

"Half of your lifetime in school."

"Nearly so."

"Pah. You know nothing about the games between a court and a new king taking his enemy's throne. You have never seen cats claw the dogs, dogs chew the rats."

"I've seen much of that. *You* know nothing of academia."

"Well, you will miss your cloister, but—" he slapped my shoulder in encouragement, which I thought meant I should lower my arm. "No. Up," he said. "You have a bad cut."

I raised my arm again. It tingled, but I bore the discomfort.

"*Mon ami*, you need work." Lanier twisted his crest-stamped ring.

"Thank you, but I don't need help."

"You do not?" He regarded me, one eye slightly closed as if inspecting. "As a Hanseatic agent, I have positioned men with guilds, with trade ships to fight against pirates." He absently reached within his shirt for the chain of his small, silver crucifix. Embroidered on his cuff was a small shield identical to the crest in his ring. He noticed my interest and informed me, "The House of Valois."

"The noble line that fractured? You're related to the French king, Louis?"

Lanier looked away. "*Oui*. Bloodshed divided the Burgundian and Orleans lines."

"Why don't you serve Louis rather than a Norwegian monarch?"

He coughed into his fist. "Even work-starved men do not ask so many questions." Lanier again looked quizzically at me. "What if I found for you—"

Another knock. "Horatio?" It was a woman's voice. Kind—but authoritative.

The door pushed open. Margrete stood alone at my threshold. She held a wooden bowl and a wide roll of parchment. I forgot the sting in my wrist as I beheld her fair skin. Lovely auburn tresses, the rustic copper of autumn, cascaded from her lace cap. They trailed down her tall collar and rested on the full green bodice of her gown. From her belt sash hung a loop of wooden paternoster beads. Her shining elegance in tapered sleeves made my breath catch. I realized that I was exceedingly hungry.

Eyes wide, she beheld me as well. "You are hurt." She entered the room and noticed the knife on my table. "Did you men fight?"

I shook my head, then lowered my arm and held the cloth in place.

Lanier stood slowly. He pulled his black leather gloves from his belt and tugged them onto his hands. "I fished for mercenaries yesterday at the village, but my net remains empty. I must consult the village tavern keeper." When he passed Margrete, he doffed his hat to her. Lanier exited the room, but while closing the door he peered at me through the gap. He beckoned me with a wave and, fingers pinched, raised them to his lips as if drinking. Then, he shut the door.

Margrete came to me. She set down the rolled document and the sloshing bowl on my writing table, among my quills, inkpots, ink packets, and celestial globe.

"Horatio, what did you intend with that blade?"

"I don't know. All is lost."

"Why? Your audience with Fortinbras, did you…" Margrete paused, then looked to the cloth upon my wrist. She removed it. One drop fell from my stinging slice. She said, "First we will attend to your health—and then I will ask you a question."

Margrete lifted her cap and pulled, from the auburn waves piled atop her head, two ribbons. Her hair fell to her shoulders, and she replaced her cap upon her head of cascaded hair. She reached for my wound. "Hold the dressing on your cut," she said. Margrete tied one ribbon to secure the cloth, bandaging my wrist. The grip of her fingers was like the clamp of a smith's tongs, despite her delicate appearance. "I saw your dispute with Hamlet over the poisoned cup. Like him, are you habitually interested in death?"

By what right did she question me? "Before today, I never thought of it. Have you?"

Margrete blanched. "No, I have not." She looked down at my wrapped wrist, avoided my stare. "I can see that you do not really want to die. No man would choose to spend his last moments arguing with a woman."

She tied the second ribbon to secure the other end of my bandage and said, in steady cadence, "Apparently, you have heard of my disgrace. I am not surprised. Rumors fly like bats from Krogen's spires. It is true that a brute robbed me of my dignity. For his cruelty, he was expelled from Krogen. Horatio, another fact is this: neither my father nor Gertrude relegated me to a convent because they rightly perceived that, although I was... I am a fallen woman, I was useful to the court. I thank the gods for the queen's kindness. She kept me as her principal lady. That restored part of my honor. And so you see that you need not concern yourself about my virtue."

Behind Margrete's firm smile I sensed a flare of indignation. Her poise, however, was remarkable. The lone gold and pearl earring she wore—the other having been sacrificed to Gertrude's corpse—caught the sunny gleam of my chamber window. I beheld her visage of precious metal and skin of pink pearl. Delicate strength and exquisite. I noticed that Margrete wore no wedding ring. Such an attractive woman could not go unclaimed. The thought of her in fleshy, tumbling liaison made my member rise. The difference between our stations should have dampened my aspirations, however—*Why not a commoner?* I thought. Noblemen, demanding a marriage of good repute, probably would not dismiss her past. Indeed, why not elect me? Women have said I appeared more bred than motley, with high cheekbones, a mild brow, and medium height. My hair, albeit dull brown, at least was straight and easily cut at my square jaw, not unkempt like a boar's tuft atop the head as is true with some of us men, no matter our efforts.

I sat up, spine straight, and said, "My apologies. Just as I needn't be concerned about your status, you needn't fret about my wound. And I am no brute." I had meant to reassure her, but she glanced warily at me.

To ease the moment, I rolled back my shoulders, a bit exaggerated for humor, to show that I could muster some force, but not that of a ruffian. Margrete's countenance softened. She rewarded my jest with a laugh, light and rich.

After a moment, I said, "I offended you. I apologize. I'm not myself."

Margrete moved to the table and began to open the rolled document. "When you ended the eulogy you looked wan, unwell. You must regain your balance of humors."

She set the bowl before me. Within it I glimpsed several pale, thin leeches lying in a pool of water. Years before, I had once used those creatures to restore my health from a bilious sickness. Their application was no worry to me, if I handled them.

"Give me your arm," Margrete said.

I jolted in horror. "A female barber-surgeon? You won't practice upon me."

"I may practice upon you if I wish, as a noble upon a commoner."

Lacking any protections, I squirmed. "Women must not perform the physician's trade. It is forbidden by the *Malleus Maleficarum*. Have you heard of it?"

"You think I am a witch?" Margrete unrolled the parchment and anchored each corner under a candle. It was a chart of the human body.

Each quarter section was labeled with the months of a season accompanied by its drawn zodiac signs. Her materials were proper for the work at hand. I knew this from my lessons about the bodily humors in university.

"Your father permits your study?"

Margrete nodded. "He encouraged me to read charts of the body's zodiac regions and interpret celestial influences." Margrete's finger rested upon a line on her chart. She studied the drawing. "What is your zodiac month?" she asked me.

Her question was correct. It was the first step of inquiry when assessing fitness for bleeding. I was impressed by her knowledge, I admit. Thus, I answered, "Leo. Why would a woman of position, of native noble birth such as yourself, want to practice medicine? For a woman it is base—"

"We ladies do what we must, especially if men's sins obligate us to it."

"—unnatural and manly—"

"You accuse me of manliness?" She smiled slightly and thumbed my razor's blade. She looked again to the chart. Then she regarded me in wonder, as though I had grown faerie ears. "Your month is Leo? Can that be correct?"

I admitted, "I'm not certain."

Margrete's mouth opened, aghast, and then clamped shut, but she could not contain her opinion. "How can you not know your month? Your parents were cruel by not telling you. How could they expect accurate calculations for treatments?"

"My mother didn't survive my delivery. My father excused himself from raising me. I only know the year of my birth. Fourteen hundred eighty-three."

The lives of commoners must have been distant from Margrete's region. She gazed at me, woefully. "You estimated your sign. That is dangerous."

I felt naked. "I know the zodiac. Studied it at—"

"Ah, yes. Leucorea University; you and Hamlet." She nodded, seemingly satisfied that either I was learned enough or that I was a horse's posterior. Or both.

I said, "My humors, I believe, are between black bile and phlegm."

Margrete's finger traced a circle connecting melancholy's easterly earth element with phlegm's southerly water element. She nodded. "Your birth month could be between autumn and winter."

I thought of my mother, and in memory I heard my father's accusation that my birth had killed her. Guilt is a hungry predator. I said, "I'll be dishonored and condemned to Hades if I do not achieve my promise to Hamlet."

She regarded me for a long moment, then sat in the chair beside me that Lanier had so recently occupied. "Such loyalty makes for a noble friend, and for heartbreak when deciding."

"Deciding what?"

"Which part of your heart to honor while denying the other deserving parts." Margrete looked away from me. She touched the corners of her eyes.

"I'm to blame for Hamlet's death."

"Horatio, you could not control Hamlet's destiny or actions. He was impulsive and brilliant. Even the most steadfast, loyal friend could never make Hamlet walk a straight, logical line. No one could have saved him from himself, or from fate."

"I failed Hamlet many times."

"That cannot be so. All depends upon the value we assign, good or bad, to our actions."

I shook my head. "Never again will I neglect to rescue a friend."

Margrete dabbed her eyes but could not swab away the hollow cast of grief. "By your logic, I am to blame, as principal lady, for Gertrude's death. I did not test or guard the cup that poisoned her." Margrete stroked her arm as if to warm herself. "Why did you want to drink from Hamlet's poisoned cup?"

A chill rolled through me. "My legacy was joined with Hamlet's, but now it's gone. I don't know how to build another."

Margrete folded her hands in her lap and looked down at them. "I know only how to serve as a principal lady. I hear that Fortinbras has no queen."

"Surely there are many who depend upon you, given our state of uncertainty," I said.

"I will do all I can to help the people of Helsingør Village and the nobles of Krogen Castle." Margrete stood and touched her paternoster beads looped from her belt sash. Then, she returned to my corner table. She turned the celestial globe on its axis, found the moon's position, and calculated its pull upon my blood. While Margrete worked, I watched her graceful sway from hip to hip. She stroked an auburn tress against the curve of her nape.

"It is good," she said. "The moon is not aligned with Leo. Bleeding you will not worsen your malady. Now, I beg you, give me your arm."

I opened my hand, demanding the leech. "I will apply it."

Margrete sighed. She dipped her hand into the water, took an emaciated leech by its triangular head, and dropped the twisting creature onto my palm.

I placed it upon my arm, inside the elbow. Margrete, sitting beside me, stroked its undulating body with her slender fingers unadorned by rings. The worm's mouth affixed. I felt its suction as it began to gorge itself.

Margrete sat beside me. She sighed and regarded me as if scrutinizing a mason's level. "Horatio, please tell me that everything you reported to Fortinbras was true."

I nodded, "I truly reported Hamlet's story."

Her steady stare was prickly, but I did not wince. "You told him no lies?"

I thought of the lewd spell I had devised to summon ghosts. "Perhaps one artful embellishment." I shrugged.

Margrete's head dropped, chin to her bosom. When she looked up at me, her open mouth pronounced nothing...initially. Then she said, "Horatio, yesterday, in Freyja Hall, I asked you not to lie to Fortinbras. But today, in Hamlet's eulogy, you said that Hamlet was not mad."

"He wasn't...not as people usually think of it." I glanced at the window and beheld the sky, an indigo sheet streaked with chalk and charcoal. "They're strategic lies, told for good purpose. They don't hurt anyone. I can't allow Hamlet's honor to suffer...or my own." I regarded Margrete for her reaction.

Her nose wrinkled as if she smelled burning rot. "Lying is a grave sin."

I gave a dismissive wave. "There can be little offense from a lie that advances a greater truth."

"Do you realize that you are endangering our lives by lying to our new king?"

My neck suddenly ached. I turned my head, looking away, to stretch.

"Yesterday, you told Fortinbras that Hamlet had nothing to do with the deaths of Rosenkrantz and Gyldenstierne. Hamlet must have been the one who ordered their deaths. The facts are: Claudius and Gertrude expected their return from England, and Hamlet was the only man sailing with them to England who possessed a royal signet ring required to seal their death writ."

Grief ate of me. I ached for her understanding, and for food. I had not eaten in more than a day. "I'm hungry."

Margrete went to the door and, calling into the corridor, instructed a servant who, I assume, was standing idle at the nearby stairwell. Then she returned and sat again, hands folded in her lap, back straight and poised. Her gaze did not waver from me. She awaited my response to her observations about my truth telling, I guessed. I did not, however, feel obligated to explain my methods.

"I don't mind that you study me," I said.

She laughed. "You believe that you fascinate me?"

I shrugged at her, grinned a little.

Margrete smiled slightly. "Perhaps you do." She reached for the bowl and swirled the water to moisten the leeches. "You have no children, no wife?"

I shook my head.

"Brothers or sisters?"

Her question brought a sudden wave of grief. "Hamlet was my brother. I also have lost Papa."

"We all will mourn Hamlet. And I am sorry that your father is dead."

"Whether my father is alive, I don't know. I chose another man, a teacher I adored, to be my papa. God's grace brought him to me."

"Did he raise you?"

"No. As a boy, in Tønderensis, from the age of five I was a ward in our foundling hospital. I despised my chores and wanted to learn to read. The nuns and nurses told me of a legendary teacher, Walthur Willadsen, in our town known for his success in helping boys enter university. I wanted education, but I had no patron. To get money, I left the hospital in my early youth, and I indentured myself to the town cooper, lived in a hut with his other servant. Cask-making is bone-bending, hard work. At the age of ten and six years, when I had a small sum, one day after supper I went to introduce myself to Schoolmaster Willadsen. I found him alone in his classroom. His door was open."

"Reading to children?"

"They had finished their class and gone. Willadsen stood alone, arms braced against his table, whistling, soft and melodious, studying the positions of chess pieces on the board before him."

Margrete grinned. "Was he the giant you expected?"

"In time, he became so. But his height was only moderate. A round face. Waves of copper hair, burnished but not yet silver, swept behind his head. I interrupted his deliberations to ask, 'Do they talk to you?' He looked at me seriously, with a dramatic arc in his brow, and told me, 'Sometimes they do.' His voice was a rich baritone. Then he asked me, 'Do you play?'"

I imitated for Margrete Papa's typical gesture: an open hand rotating, palm upward, with a flourish, as if counterbalancing the stone ring he wore. He seemed to hold a question for delicate examination.

"Soon I began lessons with Willadsen in Latin and rhetoric after dusk. The fee I could pay was only a fraction of his usual price. At times he did not charge me. And his lessons... he was marvelous. His teaching was a performance: recitation and lecture, comic mimicry of man and animal, storytelling, and song—all with wondrous command of voice.

He was a consummate weaver—his family were loomers—of lessons and entertainment. I gloried in his mind. I took him to my heart as my papa."

Margrete regarded me, tapped her chin with her fingertips. "You are happy when you remember him."

"Papa saved me. He supported my admission to university by submitting documents proving my mastery of subjects. I matriculated at Leucorea at the age of ten and nine years, older than some novices. And he gave me my name. By rechristening me 'Horatio' he gifted me with a new line of ancestors, legendary Romans: Horatio Cocles and the Horatii brothers. Papa saw that I was a frightened whelp, that I needed heroes. He was a miracle to me—a modest man with forceful opinions, and he knew his paternal power. As Papa helped me, I want to help others."

Margrete stood and walked to the window. She turned a latch and pushed open the pane to vent my stuffy chambers. Margrete peered down at the courtyard garden. "My father and I sit sometimes, among the herbs of the garden. He tells me stories of our family, as though I am still a little girl. He teaches me every day."

"When Papa and I walked together in the town, he taught me songs. Told me of reputed wonders, inventions, and music emerging in Europe. He would marvel and say, 'Exquisite. Do you see?'"

"And did you?"

"Not always. He was so proud of his students' achievements that I never wanted to admit when I felt adrift or confused. Yet, Papa always assured me, 'Oh, yes, you see it. You understand it all.'"

I glanced at the pulsing leech on my arm. I tapped its darkening purple rump. "When he died, I lost the person who understood me best."

Margrete regarded me. She bit her lip, seemed to puzzle. "Your papa would not advise you to surrender to grief, would he?"

I shook my head. "He often told me, 'Act the part which is worthy of you.' Those words, of the Roman emperor Marcus Aurelius, helped Papa when he was young, a soldier, before he became a teacher."

I looked again to Margrete at the window. The afternoon's light kissed her cheeks and forehead. She said, "An honorable man may be born worthy of his duty and act it well, while others reach for honor and by acting well become worthy of it. Some, however, choose a dishonorable part, damning their souls."

"Papa taught me to strive for honor."

Margrete left the window and sat in the chair beside me. Her hands lay still in her lap. "How was lying to Fortinbras acting well your part?"

Margrete's accusation was a sharp barb. Never would I admit to her that Papa likely would have agreed with her assessment—when listening to my troubles he often detected my lies.

I did not know how to answer Margrete. I lifted my bandage to examine the cuts on my wrist. My wounds were dry and dark scarlet. Instead, I said, "I may have to leave soon and return to Leucorea. I must keep my promise to Hamlet, although I don't know how I'll do it. I may need my friends at the school to help me."

I pulled off the leech and dropped it in the bowl.

A soft tap upon the door drew our attention to the portal. Margrete reached for my rolled sleeve. She tugged it down to cover my leech marks and wrist, and then she opened the door. There stood a servant cub holding a wooden tray containing a few thin, dried fish and four large slices of rye bread. "Lady, here is the repast that you requested." The boy chewed these words as if they filled his tiny mouth. I went to the child, took the tray, and handed him a piece of fish. His eyes gleamed as he nibbled the middle of the leathery body. The servant cub left.

Margrete and I ate the tangy fish with thick bread. I pocketed a second piece of bread for another purpose—a sacrifice. I went to the window to view the offering place among the garden's winding paths among sparse bushes, sage, and butterbur. I saw it next to the well and below the rotating gold dials of the astronomical clock. Upon the squat stone, carved like a wave, lay an apple and a few walnuts. I wanted to go there, to gift my bread to the garden's spirits for my rejuvenation. While my personal honor was my measure of worth and was worth dying for, I knew that my life was not mine to forfeit.

Margrete wiped crumbs from her lips. "Perhaps your fate is not to return, yet, to Wittenberg. Fortinbras has not yet decided to protect us. Help me convince him, appeal to his heart or his pride."

"I have attempted it, to no avail." I looked again to the astronomical clock. Its minute dial shifted, progressing in its purpose and duty. *I must be just as persistent, just as determined.*

"Horatio…" Margrete opened her hands to me.

Although I wanted more of her, I took her chill fingers into my hands. She might have requested anything of me—I only cared that she stood before me, looking only to me, wanting something only I could give her.

She continued, "What would secure Fortinbras's love for Helsingør's people?"

"Something extolling the virtues of His Highness's youthful but wilting manhood."

Margrete's hands dropped from mine. She turned to cough, stifling a laugh. Then, she faced me, hands upon her hips, and shook her head reproachfully.

I laughed, too, but then considered more seriously: What would tease Fortinbras's pride and turn it to our favor? All of history's most powerful men are captured in books—at Leucorea I saw many such texts yet unknown in the north of Europe. If we created a document that compared his defense of Krogen to the exploits of a famous ruler from antiquity…

Then, my imagination spun gold.

"A history, written as if in the future, after the battle." I folded my hands atop my head and slowly paced. "It looks back upon Fortinbras's victory over Cristiern. By writing the history in this way, it would prove to him that we anticipate his triumph. Show our belief in his superior might. Tell how the nobles loyally fight under his command. When we win against Cristiern, it will become fact."

Margrete bloomed at me, a bright, open visage. "Include evidence about how Krogen's nobles made their allegiance to the House of Hamlet."

I grinned. "I could place Hamlet's story into this history."

"Truthfully," Margrete said.

"Of course."

Doubt skewed her mouth. "Facts must anchor your assertions."

"Indeed. As you noted, lady, I'm a scholar." I folded my arms. "But I don't know the details of the nobles' estates, of their charters with the Hamlets. I must research the royal documents." Those documents, part of the king's treasury, were locked away in the muniment room, the most secure vault in the fortress.

"Yes, the muniments. I have an idea," Margrete said. When she hooked her arm through my cocked elbow, the side of her bosom pressed against me. The scent of citrus swept over me and filled my mind.

We took a few steps toward the door. She said, "We will request Fortinbras's permission that you write this history, and he will allow you access to the muniment tower to hunt for the facts."

Such research would require many hours. I had no servitor student to help bear that labor.

"You are practiced at reading texts," I said to her.

She regarded me. Was that a trace of interest in her eyes? Was she daring me? I was enchanted.

"You are requesting the assistance of a manly witch?"

"Yes." I took from the doorjamb peg my soft, green Germanic hat, my prized gift from Papa, and set it upon my head.

Without hesitating, Margrete's arm slipped from mine and she moved past me into Wiglaf Corridor, public terrain. We were no longer joined. That was propriety. It stung.

"Let us go to Fortinbras," Margrete said. "He has chosen his chambers."

"Claudius's suite," I said with certainty, half a step behind the scrape of her slippers.

"No. Hamlet's."

That sacred place, defiled. Her news was like a punch to my belly. As we hurried, I took my bread, my intended offering, from my pocket. For comfort, I absently devoured it.

We followed the trail of lamps hanging from the ceiling like iron cobwebs cradling little suns. I prayed to them as if they were stars of hope: *Let me have another chance to save my brother. Let me not fail and perish in Satan's house.*

V.

Margrete and I entered the royal family's clamorous west corridor, lit by windows facing the late-afternoon sun. Before us stretched a steaming sea of nobles, clothed in gray and green like a Danish storm. They surged toward the housemaster, Tomas, who stood, mid-corridor, at a narrow podium. Behind him was a chamber door of ancient wood that resembled black stone.

This circus of pedigrees cried out to Fortinbras for a multitude of favors. Debt repeal. Increase in food and fabric rations. Grants of land titles and official posts. Their ambitious claims seemed to delight the wood statues of bare Danish heroes lining the east wall. Some stood in victorious conquest and others in bawdy embrace.

Margrete stood beside me and studied the crowd. Her mouth was a grim line. "Demands will not endear us to Fortinbras."

"He may be so hardened by this mob's noise that he won't receive us." For their sakes, as well as Hamlet's and mine, we had to get Fortinbras's permission to access the muniments and write the history.

We dove into the humid crowd and pressed forward. Shimmering bodices revealed full curves. Gentlemen's velvet jackets and doublets bore ribbons and medallions. Sullen faces sculpted with powders and waxes smoothed pockmarks.

A man grumbled, "Would rather eat a stone than bow to an arrogant Norwegian warrior."

Another countered, "Better than serve a ruthless Dane who sees God in his own mirror."

My breath caught as I plowed through the sour heat. At last I arrived before the secretary. I pulled off my soft hat and pressed it to my face, dabbing away sweat droplets.

Tomas did not notice me. He studied the documents he held and showed no sign of alarm. Trimly dressed in gray and black, offsetting his sculpted mass of white hair, he seemed utterly unruffled, as would a cleric standing alone in his cell, contemplating his texts, rather than an administrator besieged by a hoard.

Beside me, a young, frog-eyed woman smacked the podium. "Will Fortinbras bring a new court from Norway?"

A flushed man of middling age asked, "When will the king choose his governors?"

Tomas muttered, "Many requests of our new monarch. Few offers to assist him." He glanced up from his lists, through his shaggy brows. "Oh. It is you, Horatio. How now?"

I set my hat upon my head. "His Majesty has requested that I provide him proof of"—I leaned across the podium to continue with my voice hushed—"certain allegiances."

He regarded me now, eyes widened. Perhaps he feared that I intended to report about individuals...him, for example. "Um hmm." He looked to Margrete. "You are attending because...?"

Margrete smiled at Tomas. "Horatio may need assistance."

Tomas shook his head. "Only one will enter. Besides, my dear"—his eyes were soft with pity—"Fortinbras has no wife. No need for a principal lady."

Margrete looked down at her hands—empty. I knew that feeling. But then, she grasped her belt sash and pulled it, tightening its knot. She regarded the secretary. "Old friend, I have always assisted with facts. I have mediated between our monarch and our people in the past. Do you not recall?"

The secretary held her gaze. Without turning he reached behind and rapped a slow, insistent beat upon that door, which—I remembered with a wistful pang—had once been Hamlet's. It would no longer mean friendship to me.

The door opened. A young attendant beckoned us with a flourish. We followed his rolling haunches through a candlelit sitting room, passing seated noblemen. A few stared sullenly at us. However, one man, wearing a plumed hat and yellow sleeves trimmed in black, stood facing the hearth. He gripped a short blade and was carving into the mantle: *RoC—11 June 1513.*

As we passed him, the young attendant wagged his finger. "Stop that."

The man turned around and glared at us. I knew him—Reynaldo of Castile, a damnable cheat at cards and reputed former spy for Claudius's deceased counselor, Polonius. When Reynaldo saw that the attendant had escorted us to the royal chamber, he darted toward us. He lisped in the Castilian tongue, "I have waited the longest. They have not had to wait one minute."

The attendant ignored Reynaldo and thumped upon the door to Hamlet's sanctum sanctorum.

From within, Fortinbras's voice boomed like a cannon. "Come."

The attendant pushed open the door. Margrete and I entered, and the door closed behind us.

We stood in Hamlet's large wood-paneled bedchamber lit by an enormous diamond-paned window and mostly filled by a grand table and an immense bed. Its posts displayed immaculately carved fish heads and large-bosomed mermaids.

By our feet, near the door, lay piles of Hamlet's abandoned effects. Prints from woodblock etchings showing tavern life, bare-breasted women, and hooded Death stalking the jaunty soul of Pride. Crumpled shirts discarded like old husks. A bundle of letters addressed in Hamlet's hand to Ophelia.

I, too, felt like a remnant in that moment.

In the center of the room, at the table, stood Lanier. He bent over dozens of charts and documents fixed with red ribbons and wax medallions. Lanier glanced at me, slowly removed his hat, and nodded sharply—a signal that I attend to etiquette in Fortinbras's presence.

Because grief had distracted me, I had not noticed that, across the room, Fortinbras slouched, legs crossed, in Hamlet's well-molded study chair. Behind him, upon a wall, hung a small tapestry depicting a family crest guarded by two dogs. It stunk of dung and musty elements, probably the muck collected in Fortinbras's battle campaign tents.

I quickly pulled off my hat and bowed in deference. Margrete made a deep, nearly hip-breaking curtsy and remained crouching.

Fortinbras squinted one eye at me. "I dismissed you, Hor-a-ti-o, for failing me. You gave me no information about whether Krogen's nobles contributed to the fall of the House of Hamlet, whether they deserve my trust and protection. Are you here to serve me more blithering sentiment, like that eulogy?"

I stung from the rebuke, but I straightened and replied, "Sire, I can prove to you that Helsingør's noble tribes were loyal to the House of Hamlet and, therefore, that they will also be loyal to you. They will be worthy of Your Majesty. To do so, I must research the Hamlets' royal muniments. There, I will find the evidence I need. I will write a history that not only states these facts for your use, highness. It will be an account of your defense of Helsingør's people against Cristiern."

Fortinbras uncrossed his legs. His landing foot slammed upon the floor. "I have no time to discuss this. I need soldiers." He scowled at Lanier.

God, assist me to convince him, I prayed. I stood straighter. "A history would contain statements of your right of inheritance to Helsingør. It would assert, for all who would challenge you, that the House of Fortinbras commands Helsingør not by chance but by God's ordination through your familial line. Would you permit me to write this history?"

Fortinbras, considering, rubbed his chin. "That may take too long." His crushing stare swung from me to Margrete. "I did not call for you."

Margrete, at last, rose from her curtsy. "My lord, we would defend Krogen for you if you train us to battle our enemy."

Fortinbras scoffed. "Do you hear them beyond, in the hallways? They are not demanding military drills." He pointed at me. "This scholar supposes that I should trust these nobles who were so enamored of the Hamlets. You, woman, want me to believe that their greed will make them excellent soldiers."

Margrete opened her hands. "Your Majesty, do you not wish for your lineage to be exalted for your protection of Helsingør, its castle, and your subjects?" She slowly approached, daring to stand directly before him.

Fortinbras smirked. "I know what I want."

He lunged and grasped Margrete. Her arm clenched to her bosom and her fist guarded her *belle chose*. He pulled her to sit upon his loins. Before I could move to her, Margrete fought to free herself. She slid from his lap. Margrete stood before him and smoothed her frock.

Jealousy burned in me.

Grinning at her, Fortinbras said, "You should not refuse your king. Is not your father currently the royal fabrics assessor?"

Margrete blanched. She must have feared that her father would lose his status as administrator of the inventory and tailoring of fabrics. No one other than the housemaster so greatly influenced the court's beauty, comfort, and assurance of status.

Fortinbras stood and crossed to the table where Lanier examined scattered maps. Fortinbras jabbed angrily at them. "I would not have to rely upon these people"—he flung a gesture toward the noisome corridor—"if you had already found me the mercenaries I need."

"*Mon seigneur*," said Lanier, "I have sought them." His hand swept across the maps. "I continue to seek them. Few men between Copenhagen and Helsingør will risk battle against Cristiern. The blockade starves many. We may not be able to harvest enough men for an army."

Fortinbras struck his fist into his palm. "I need soldiers. We must appeal to the Holy Roman Emperor. Lanier, you must convince Maximillian to break his mercenaries' leases."

Lanier moved to the other side of the table. His fingers smoothed his mustache. He looked across the table at Fortinbras. "We have no time. He would decline. Already Maximillian is spread too thin in Italy and throughout Europe."

Fortinbras opened his arms wide. "*He* is spread too thin?" Fortinbras skirted the table toward Lanier, pointing his finger like a dagger. "Then go to France and get me soldiers from King Louis."

Rubbing his jaw as if struck, Lanier said, "I beg you. No, sire. I cannot go to France."

"You are failing me in Denmark, but you will succeed in France. Louis is not winning his wars. He has no need for mercenaries now. Meanwhile, Cristiern is probably already on the march to Copenhagen. I wager he will continue north and attack Helsingør. His ships have tightened the knot of his blockade. This is now a siege. We must break it."

"*Mon seigneur*, Cristiern will be upon us before I could return."

Fortinbras leaned close to Lanier. "You found Germanic mercenaries to fight for me in Poland. We won that battle. Assemble my army immediately, or I will send you to France to bargain."

Lanier's face turned as white as birch bark. "King Louis will not barter with me."

"Christ's bones." Fortinbras grasped a book from the table and hurled it. The volume flailed, spine split and pages unhinged, like a bird struck by an arrow. I looked down at the cover and saw that is was Livius's *History of Rome*. I treasured that book, which Hamlet had once lovingly pilfered for me. He had taken it from his father's collection safeguarded in a chest within the muniment room.

Lanier raised his leather-gloved palm as if in oath. "I will find soldiers. Better to send me to the Hanseatic ports. There will be men, all hungry for work and willing to fight Cristiern's subjugation of their native countries under the Kalmar Union. They despise it."

Fortinbras walked away from Lanier, toward me. He stopped and leaned back slightly, head cocked and eyes narrowed, assessing me. "I think that you intend to capture the story of your dead prince in this history you are promising me. Has it occurred to you, commoner, that Hamlet may not deserve memorial? By your own account, he killed at least three men—Polonius, Laertes, and Claudius." Fortinbras raised three fingers, counting the offenses. "Probably ordered the murder of his two escorts to England. Also, I have heard"—he lifted a sixth finger—"that Hamlet may have defiled Ophelia with no actual intent of wedding her. I see this situation more clearly than you. Hamlet was a criminal destined for the abyss, and he wanted to drag everyone into it with him."

My fists knotted to repress my rising blood. I doubled my wager upon fortune and bent truth toward my benefit. "Majesty, Hamlet was a good, intelligent man. He wisely likened your future glory as Helsingør's sovereign to Beowulf's fame."

Fortinbras's iron glare and peaked brows challenged me to astonish him further.

"Hamlet said that you'd be like the most eminent of the Caesars. He foresaw that you'd add towns to your empire and protect your adopted subjects with paternal love, not for ambition's sake, like that of Cristiern, but to express the true nature of your great soul."

Margrete cast me a heated cautioning glance.

I looked again to the maps, the feather-edged documents, the fractured book—all captured history. I went to the table, picked through the rolls and sheets and saw a leathery page with swooping script. "Highness, what is this archaic text?"

Fortinbras collapsed into his chair. "The muniments keeper brought it. He could not read it but said that if Krogen held any record of my family's heraldry tied to this land, it would be contained in that document."

I sensed an advantageous shift of the proverbial wind. I trimmed my sail to glide with it.

"You need a scholar to decipher it for you," I said. I went to the window, held the curling document high to capture the fading light, and pretended to examine it. "Highness, the muniments keeper is correct. This is evidence of your inheritance."

Fortinbras clapped his hands. "Let me hear it." He closed his eyes as if concentrating.

Lanier's raised hand drew my notice. The warning shake of his head was slight but firm. Then I glanced at Margrete for assurance but saw her silently mouth the words, "Do not lie."

A flick of my hand flattened the document. I pretended to read. "*Nach neirborg eissen...*" I blathered nonsense.

Margrete looked to heaven and Lanier folded his arms and looked down, chin to his breast. Fortinbras, however, nodded at my invented dialect as if his soul recognized his tribal elders' wisdom.

I lowered the document and said, "Highness, this is ancient lore, indeed. Its translation exhausts my faculties. I'll tell you plainly what it states. It says that Fortbraegen, the celebrated chief of the Danes and Norwegians..."

"That must be my great-great-great-grandfather."

"A very distant ancestor, most assuredly, highness," I said. "He made his home in the old lands of the Danes, where a knob of land jutted into a narrow throat of water, at Helsengia—that must be Helsingør, majesty, at the strait of Øresund between Denmark and Sweden."

Margrete covered her face with both hands.

I ignored her and feigned struggle to read the script as I crafted the fable. "He battled heathens in foreign lands and was the victor. Brought booty, metals, and new ways, such as better forging of pikes, to his people. He built a stronghold for his clan and made them a superior tribe."

Stroking his chin, Fortinbras nodded. "You said his name was...?"

"Um..." I had forgotten my invention. For assistance, I looked to Lanier. He rubbed a knuckle into the notch of his eye, as if in disbelief.

To my surprise, Margrete replied, albeit incorrectly. "'Fortengarth,' was it not?" Her fingers strained against her temples. I felt guilt that my new lie had tempted her complicity to buttress it against discovery.

Fortinbras leaned back in his chair and studied the ceiling. "A true Norse name."

I spread another layer of manure. "Very true, highness. His people's land was fertile because the goddesses admired him and—oh, highness, this is interesting." I pointed at some faint, brown script, hardly legible. "The gods blessed all chiefs of his line such that they, as righteous men, cared for all whom they ruled."

Fortinbras's outstretched hand demanded the document. I handed it to him. He puzzled over it, chewing his lower lip. Then he folded the sheet and thrust it inside his boot cuff. Fortinbras stood and, with a skeptical grunt, said, "I had never heard that story."

Although Fortinbras approached me, I avoided his gaze and chose to focus, instead, upon the chainmail overlaying his shirt. The triangular links were crusted—rust, I thought, until I realized they were blood-caked from battle.

"Hor-a-tio." As he spoke my name, each syllable dripped with scorn.

Fortinbras edged closer to me, but I did not retreat. Our toes and noses nearly touched. In my sight his face took the form of an angry Cyclops. The brown bands of Fortinbras's eyes were gold speckled, like gilded wood. He said, "I will ask about that tale. Your translation had better be the truth."

I held my breath against his mouth's sharp odor and said,

"Fortinbras likened to Caesar. *That* is what I'd write into the history of Helsingør's rulers."

"You have convinced me. Include my victory over the Poles. Say that I bested the warring Danish houses of Hamlet and Oldenburg despite my forces of untested nobles." Fortinbras raised his chin. "You, commoner, will earn your supper if you find evidence in the muniments that proves to me that these people, who once pledged themselves to the Hamlets, will be loyal to me. You will write the history quickly and truthfully for me."

I bowed and quickly straightened. I doubled my will against his scrutiny. "I will, majesty."

Out of the corner of my eye I saw Margrete look again to heaven. She moved to stand before Fortinbras. This time she did not curtsy. "My lord, the kingdoms of the Kalmar Union will honor you if you deny your enemy, Cristiern, the trophy he desires."

Fortinbras fumed. "They should not suffer because they have been ruled by Denmark's barnyard of asses."

Margrete added, "By protecting Helsingør, show Cristiern that it will never fall to him."

"Copenhagen must not control all docks and tolls," Fortinbras said. "I will defend Helsingør until Cristiern relents or this castle is blasted to rubble. If I cannot have it, no one will."

Margrete said, "If you train Krogen's nobles to fight, we will reinforce your army of mercenaries. Lead us to victory. We await your command."

Fortinbras's breast puffed. His jaw squared. What magnificent, shrewd influence Margrete worked upon his pride. I guessed that she must have honed her craft each day in service as principal lady. I believed that Margrete in her workshop, the queen's offices, had learned to expertly meld women's and men's conflict into comity, while pampering bruises and designing new frames for peers' broken perspectives. Those were the qualities I most admired in Leucorea's provosts. Here, I saw them in practice by a capable woman administrator.

Fortinbras rolled back his shoulders. "I will deny that thieving viper—and for my father's murder, I will own his killer's fortress." Fortinbras turned to Lanier. "Go once more into Helsingør Village and tell those peasants they must fight for their king, for their lives. Then go to the ports for mercenaries. They must sign a contract or will not be paid. Tell the nobles: I will teach them combat at battle stations along the ramparts and outer wall. You, also, will train them upon the killing field. Make haste."

Lanier removed his hat. With front leg extended, he bowed only slightly at the waist, denying Fortinbras his deepest respect. Then Lanier, with a sweep of his cape, departed.

Fortinbras ruffled his hair, then flicked a hand at Margrete. "You, take the commoner to the muniments keeper tomorrow morning. The hour is too late now to read in that dark tower."

I bowed. "We are most indebted to your mercy and grace."

Margrete curtsied. "We pray to God for your blessing."

Fortinbras eyed her, then pointed at me. "If the history you write fails to justify my time wasted waiting for it—or if you are not telling me the facts, you will hang." He folded his arms. "If any of those greedy, conniving nobles betray me"—he looked to Margrete—"I will kill you and your family as examples to others who were loyal to the Hamlets." His severe brow and firm mouth riveted his point.

I felt the barbed carcasses of Failure and its cousin, Death, rise at my shoulder. Their stink of flesh rot made my gorge swell. I could not swallow.

In haste, side by side, Margrete and I stepped backward to the sitting room door so as not to turn our backs on the king. I gagged and closed the door, and Margrete stormed through the sitting room and into the west corridor. I followed her into the simmering mob.

Margrete raced ahead, pressing through the crowd. I hurried to match her stride. She abruptly stopped and faced me. "Horatio, how much of the Fortinbras family legend was a lie?"

I beheld her, softer than I expected, eyes pleading. How could I risk angering her? I replied, "What legend is all truth?"

"Why do you lie, Horatio?" She clasped her hands, trembling. "Your lies have ensnared us. Should Fortinbras defend us against Cristiern and then discover that his decision was based upon your tricks, he will kill you. Because I know of your lies, I am complicit. He will execute me as well."

At that moment I realized the depth of our danger, in part because Margrete knew my secrets. I would hang by my arms, suspended and shackled, in a filth-pooled dungeon and beg for death at the muck-polished gallows leaning from overuse.

Margrete clenched her middle and said to me, "You will write the truth. Or else we will drown in your trickery."

"I may tell a strategic lie if necessary."

"Any lie can be deemed strategic. The better strategy is honesty. If we are truthful to ourselves, we will be honest with others. You would not rely upon lies in courtship, would you, Horatio?"

What a blow she could level at a man's bits. I regarded her. "No, I wouldn't."

Margrete's expression softened, but she held her ground. She accompanied me to my chambers to retrieve her bowl of leeches and her chart. We parted in silence as the dying, orange sun faded upon the astronomical clock's dials.

I lay sleepless that night. Failure of honor and deed meant death. I suddenly realized: if I succeeded in honor and deed but Cristiern found my manuscript, he would kill me for treason. *But one monster at a time*, I thought. To resolve Fortinbras's doubts in my favor I would have to write the most interesting, useful history ever conceived.

Terrified, I rose from my cot. With my *Book of Hours* open in a patch of moonlight I fervently prayed that the muniments would contain the magical elements I needed to concoct a triumph.

VI.

That morning, the twelfth day of June, Margrete and I entered the counting room and climbed the muniment tower's gently curving trail of stairs. We stood before the muniment room door. It was narrow, as dark as black moss. Through its panels' seams leaked the itchy essence of old parchment and ancient wood compartments.

Three gnarled locks in the door forbade entry; however, Margrete held three triple-notched, bony keys. Ribbons trailed from their hollow oval ends. She pushed a key into each lock and cranked them a full rotation. With each rattling turn, a bolt slid within its tumbler and clacked open. Then, she pocketed the long-legged keys and pushed upon the vault door's grainy face. When it swung inward, I saw that the room's stone walls were two hand lengths in thickness, resistant to external fire. We stepped through the deep threshold into the tall, vault-ceilinged room.

We stood upon a luxurious tricolor floor. Its small square tiles—yellow, black, and red—bragged of riches. Below the peaked ceiling, a high, single window emitted dim light from the blazing dawn. Two walls were covered by wood cabinets containing dozens of small, rustic boxes, each faintly labeled. In the center of the room was a single, massive table.

We peered upward at the matrix of boxes. Each listed several patronymics. Mikkelsen. Dvergr. Swertingsen. Which ones contained evidence of the nobles' devotion to the House of Hamlet?

I asked, "Each box contains the papers of a noble family?"

"At least one, yes. Only Erik, our muniments keeper, knows which clan is which." Margrete pointed at one box six rows above her reach. "Birgersen. Can you get that one?"

I grasped a ladder, which was propped against the box-filled wall, and climbed its swaying spine. When I pulled the desired cubby box, squeaking from its tight space, the container's dusty breath filled my nostrils. I coughed.

Margrete asked, "Did you attend services this morning?"

Her question, the first personal comment she had made that morning, relieved me. *Thank the Almighty, no more condemnation from her.*

I replied, "Early Mass. Then I went to the hall for cheese with bread, and a cup of beer."

"I took my meal with my parents in their chambers," she said. "We read scriptures. But I slept little, thinking of our predicament of lies."

I assumed too much.

I clasped the box in one arm, descended to the floor, and set it upon the table. "Please, let's discuss more about lies." I regretted my sardonic comment, however, the moment it escaped my lips.

Margrete faced me, her hands folded across her waist. "During the night a question came to me. Horatio, as a scholar you learned the discipline to study and analyze, to debate and write. Your persistence and determination as a friend and brother are amazing. Why are you not also determined to learn the discipline of truth telling?"

Never before had I considered that question. And at that moment, I was not predisposed to do so. My response was instantaneous. "As do many people, I take comfort in those things that do not bind."

"If honesty is a discomfort, how inconvenient are the vows of marriage?"

I reached into the box and removed from that shadowy cradle a handful of stiff, folded packets. Some were tied with coarse thread. I pulled at these sinews, freeing the texts.

"Study and books have been my mistresses," I said. "I have not met many women I would take as a wife. Margrete, I told you last night: I wouldn't lie in courtship. Why would I do so in marriage?"

Margrete picked up a document. She examined it but seemed to read the same line three times. Then she set it down. "I believe that a man who can learn Greek also can learn to think in the language of honesty. That would be a worthy challenge, do you not think so?"

I glanced at her and grinned. "Where would I find someone qualified to teach that curriculum?"

Margrete's lips pressed together but could not best the upturning corners of her mouth. "I cannot imagine."

She took in hand a packet and shuffled through the pages, reading. "Registers. Nobles' testimonies against one another—do not show those to Fortinbras. Pledges of loyalty to Gertrude and Old Hamlet. Useful."

We leaned close as we examined the pages. Despite the parchment's stale odor of animal oils, I sensed Margrete—sea grasses and flowers—and was transfixed by her. Tapered sleeves covered her wrists, and a blue satin hem brushed her slippers. A tall collar ascended from her low bodice and fair-skinned bosom. When I had initially seen her that morning within the vaulted stone passageway, waiting for me at the door to the muniment tower's counting room—and I beheld her trim elegance magnificently canopied by the passageway ceiling's crisscrossing sandy-yellow arcs—my breath caught.

In my perspiring hands, the pages felt slick.

"Nothing else in this box," Margrete said. I agreed. She brushed past me to bend over a chest resting on the floor against the wall. I beheld her curves. She pulled open the chest's jaws and extracted a short stack of volumes. She dropped them onto the table before me. "Perhaps these will help."

I sifted through the tomes. *Land Grants, 1473. Sound Toll Ledgers, 1502–1505.* As though unfolding frozen limbs, I lifted the brown, withered covers. The naked, gruff script was as primitive as tribal tattoos on ancient skins. My fingers and nose itched. However, I pulled more boxes from the cubby cabinet. Soon the massive table was crowded with disgorged boxes, their brittle organs extracted, examined, and discarded.

Margrete moved close to me...to flick a hair from my tunic. Her hand lingered. "At first I wondered why our prince Hamlet befriended a commoner. But I see now: you are different from the men of the court. They are lovely, but politics rules their affections, and they seem to know more of trifles and entertainments than of the world."

I regarded her. "We commoners live practically if we are to survive."

"Your intelligence...your perspective, they are not shaded by greed for title or tomorrow's favors. I believe I must take more commoners as friends."

"As friends only?"

Margrete's smiling aspect opened like a morning flower. Never had a woman looked at me in such a way. I felt a fresh surge.

"You mentioned that you do not know your destiny—"

I interrupted. "I'll decide how to align my fate with God's will. My hope of a school built with Hamlet is lost. Somehow, I'll teach Denmark's cubs the principles of *humanitas*: to delve into original sources and learn to think for themselves. To never rely upon priests and judges blathering contrived interpretations."

"If Fortinbras appointed you schoolmaster to the nobles' children, would you remain at Helsingør?"

Her question surprised me. I considered: as a teacher of privileged children and a servant of Krogen, I would never want for shelter. I could teach as I wished. Dialectics. Rhetoric. Philosophy. Theology. I would have meaningful purpose... and I would be near Margrete.

She slid a winding strand of hair behind her ear; I could fit into Margrete's life, tucked away like that. Her finger traced the lace of her bodice where it dipped at her bosom. Margrete's courtesies fed my lust. I wanted to untie her restraints. I would free the soft bend of her hips and pull her onto me.

"This month's customary labor is courtship," she said. "We should consult the astronomical clock for its calculation."

"Its gold dials for the sun, the earth, and the moon, rotating and aligning with zodiac signs, will tell us."

Margrete's flickering grin, easy and confident, was like a summer evening's final golden shaft of light that rendered the world immortal and perfect. I reached for her hand. She allowed me to take hold of her fingers and kiss them. I desired no space between us. I wanted our flesh bare, grinding and wet.

Then Margrete stepped back. Her hand slipped from mine. She smiled and said, "I want to show you something."

She was inviting me to coitus, I was certain. No one would know of it, in this secluded tower. I looked to the cluttered table. It was sturdy, would serve us well. To create space, I hurriedly removed the boxes and documents to the floor.

Into the vacancy, Margrete dropped another box. This one was larger than the others. Deflating, I stared at it.

Margrete took from the container a limp manuscript and handed it to me. "A Carmelite friar named Poul Helgesen is permitted to use the muniments. This is his manuscript: a complete factual history of all of Denmark's kings. He calls it a *Historia Compendoise*."

My heart flattened. "This monk, Poul, is writing Hamlet's story?"

"No. Hamlet does not qualify because he did not reign. Poul's text may include Claudius and Old Hamlet, however. Perhaps Poul will allow you to read his manuscript as a source you might use about the House of Hamlet. We must ask him first. He is brilliant, but he can be an angry ox." Margrete pulled from Poul's box additional documents. "It seems he was using these scouts' reports to Old Hamlet."

We spread the stack upon the table and, alternating, read them aloud. We found no historical gold. This failure soured my hope. I finished this fruitless task while Margrete, prying among the chests, found the supply of salt, and the chapel's gold and silver chalices: treasures usually protected in a royal muniment tower.

As I refolded packets for filing, Margrete said, "Horatio, behold this grand treasure."

She won't trick me again. I did not look to her or hope for seduction. "What is it?"

"Take this four-hundred-year-old lady into your arms."

Relenting, I regarded Margrete. Her outstretched hands offered a stack of square, tattered parchment. Its head and rump were covered by gritty wood plates blackened by age. A cord secured the stack. "This," she said, "is the ancient record of Danish lore and traditions."

Impossible. The Hamlets couldn't have owned Denmark's fabled masterpiece lauding Danish glory. I scoffed. "The *Gesta Danorum*?"

Margrete nodded toward the dimmest corner of the room. There sat a chest. Its open lid was a marvel of locking dials and levers.

"Is the lost grail there as well?" I asked. "And Jesus's own gospel accounting for it?"

"No one is supposed to know the *Gesta Danorum* is here. The muniments keeper, Erik, showed it to me once. Even he does not take it beyond this room. When Erik tells stories to evening audiences in Freyja Hall, he recites parts of this book from memory so that it always remains here, protected."

Curiosity overtook me. I moved near to Margrete and looked upon the corpus she held. The title, notched into the cover plate, was fashioned by tiny triangles linked to form each letter. Largest were the letters G and D.

Could this be the famous book? I scooped it from Margrete's arms. It was not heavy.

I laid the fragile creature upon the table, tugged at the cord, and let it fall away. Gingerly, I lifted the cover, releasing an acrid scent. I tasted the dust of centuries.

On the first page, stained by age, was a list of names written in tight script. The largest was Saxo Grammaticus.

"Who was that?" Margrete asked.

"A twelfth-century master scribe and grammatical teacher. Legend tells that he directed an army of monks to compile the *Gesta Danorum*. My professors at university said that its existence was mere speculation. No one had ever seen it. They said that mention of the *Gesta Danorum* in another old book, the *Chronica Jutensis*, was not enough proof of its existence."

I turned that page to find the beginning of the narrative. Runic tails looped and clasped across the pages. Gorgeous script sculled, line by line, like gliding Viking craft. An elegant hand, the strokes measured and sure, declared:

Dan igitur et Angul, a quibus Danorum coepit origo, patre Humblo procreati non solum conditores gentis nostrae, verum etiam rectores fuere.

Then I read the text aloud. "Now Dan and Angul, with whom the stock of the Danes begins, were begotten of Humble, their father, and were the governors and the founders of our race."

Margrete looked to me and grinned. "You read it almost as well as Erik."

"Why is the *Gesta Danorum* here? Is it being withheld from copying? Helsingør doesn't have a scriptorium, and not even Copenhagen has a printing machine."

"Erik says that Old Hamlet took it as booty from an unknown foe."

On many sheets I saw that scribes had marked additions and changes that squeezed and crept between larger script and spilled down the margins' channels. This was a true original, the source of our faith in our tribe, not a master copy made to guide a printer's work. It was memory itself. If lost, then forever lost. I felt as though I held the scrolls of Moses's five volumes.

"The world still harbors miracles awaiting discovery," I said. Trembling, I stroked the pages. *You ancient beauty.*

"In our churches we revere the saints," Margrete said, "but in our halls we cheer the gods." She grinned. "I love all tales—of Freyja and the small cats that pull her chariot. Stories of Beowulf, too. The seafaring bravery of the Spear-Danes and the Ring-Danes."

With her mention of Beowulf's legend, its heavy burden settled upon me.

Margrete took the *Gesta Danorum*. I stole a final touch of its smooth face as she placed it in the relic chest. She closed the lid but did not lock it. Was it usually kept unlocked?

She returned. When she looked to me, her smile faded to a sad line. "What is wrong?"

"I am thinking of loyal Wiglaf and the difficult charge that his dying friend and king, Beowulf, gave him. Wiglaf carried his friend's gold hoard back to his people and built Beowulf's memorial barrow on the site of his funeral pyre." I felt a twinge in my breast.

Margrete leaned against the table. Her bodice pressed to full capacity. "Horatio, are you not happy that I showed you the *Gesta Danorum*?"

"Of course, I am."

"I did so because I trust you, just as I trust that you will no longer lie to Fortinbras."

Behind us a man blurted, "Ahem."

We turned to see, standing within the doorframe, a man of medium stature wearing a monk's course habit. His pate and fuzzy blond ring at his temples were a natural tonsure. His scowling, angular features were sharp. How long had he stood there?

"Poul," Margrete gasped. "You tread most quietly upon the stairs."

"The pope should declare lies to be one of the deadliest of sins," Poul said. "After all, Satan was a liar." He glared at me and then glanced at the boxes upon the floor and the table.

I, too, regarded the mess. His manuscript lay within my reach. We had not yet returned it to its box and shelf.

Poul saw the vacant place, low in the cabinet matrix where his carton belonged. As quick as a deer he stormed past me, his habit bearing the grassy draft of the fields. The cross he wore on a beaded chain swung and struck the table. He grasped his unguarded manuscript and sputtered, "You are stealing my work."

"No," I replied.

"You are a thief and a liar."

"Brother Poul," I said, "let us have a proper introduction, and let us reason together. I am Horatio. You may have overheard our discussion—"

"You are taking *these* documents?" He gestured at the scattered boxes. "Erik promised my exclusive use of them."

"Poul." Margrete, palms pressed together, approached him. "Erik gave us access to the documents. Fortinbras permitted it. No one read your manuscript."

"If so, why is it removed from its box?"

Margrete said, "I hoped for your return, that you would let Horatio use it as a source. His work only concerns the House of Hamlet… specifically the noble families and Prince Hamlet, who is not included in your work, as you once told me of it. You, alone, are writing about all of Denmark's royal houses. Now, about our conversation you overheard, allow us to tell you—"

Carrying his box, Poul stomped away. On his descent to the counting room his sandals slapped the steps. He bellowed, "Unlock the door." After issuing another flash of abuse, Poul departed. Erik closed and secured the tower's portal to the vaulted passageway.

Margrete covered her face with both hands. Her breath shuddered through her fingers.

I did not want Poul, that fuming ox, to own our fate. I asked, "Will his temper cool? He'll keep his counsel?"

Her hands dropped, revealing ice-pale cheeks and red-rimmed eyes. "Poul will tell Fortinbras that you have lied to him, and that I knew of it. It is more grounds for our execution. I must follow Poul, divert him from Fortinbras."

She gave me the muniment room keys. I kissed her hand tenderly.

Margrete said, "Your advances are one more secret we must keep." She moved to leave, then glanced over her shoulder. "Unless you court me properly."

"A commoner could learn the rigors of chivalric courtship."

"While taking lessons in honesty?" Margrete's smile was a spark that lit an ember. "I dare you to prove it."

She turned away. As she moved through the room's arch to the stairs, I watched her swaying hips and expected she would cast a challenging grin at me, over her shoulder, in case her point needed punctuation. But she did not look my way. I heard the tap of her slippers upon the descending stairs to the counting room and then her lilting voice tell Erik that I possessed the keys. My heart and all else swelled.

How could I proceed? Chivalry's stiff etiquette and battery of skills were not taught to commoners. I did not care for the challenge of honesty that Margrete favored, but I would apprentice in knighthood if that meant I could pursue her.

Puzzling the matter... I returned to my task, climbed high upon the wobbly ladder to pull the age-bronzed boxes from their square catacombs. I shuffled through them. After three hours of searching, the only new political evidence I discovered concerned another prickly affront by the Hamlets against Cristiern's House of Oldenburg. Old Hamlet had bribed high clerics to separate the Ecclesiastical Court, and Gertrude then moved it to Saint Olai Church in Helsingør, from the bishop's seat at Copenhagen's cathedral. By appointing the magistrates, she secured the Hamlets' influence over nearby primary courts. These facts only proved deceit by the Hamlets.

I needed sources, good ones, to complete the account. Poul's were rich enough that he wanted to hoard them. How might I sate his anger and convince him to share those muniments?

After securing the three locks of the muniment room, I carried some documents down the tower's winding stairs. Upon the landing I passed another three-lock door and entered the counting room of the royal treasury, which was the only other room in the muniment tower.

At its center was an examination table piled with documents. Some lay open and pinned by small weights. The floor, like the muniment room's, was tiled in red, yellow, and black. At eye level were a dozen shelves bearing two dozen banded boxes. Beside a narrow slit of window stood two easels. At one sat Poul, his back to me, with a sheet propped before him that was half-filled with tight scrawl. Had he already sought Fortinbras and told of my lies?

A gravelly voice, to my right, asked, "Where are the keys?"

I looked to see Erik, the royal muniments keeper, with his thick palm open and waiting. He stood only as tall as my breast. In brown cape and cap, with leathered skin and creases at his eyes, he seemed to be made of tan parchment. Erik looked windblown, although the air in the room was still. I pressed the ribbon-tailed keys into his hand.

Erik crossed to the table and heaved himself atop his stool. He surveyed the sea of anchored texts before him. "I could not even attend services today, God forgive me, because of work to appease the king. We risk damnation either way, do we not?"

Poul grumbled. He slid from his seat and reached to the floor for a bag to pull from it a scholar's riches. Packets of ink powder and a pot. Quills. A short blade. Sheets of vellum parchment.

I walked to Poul and, gripping my hands behind my back to hide their quivering, asked, "Did Margrete find you? She remembered something that our housemaster wanted you to tell the porter at your priory." I easily lied.

Poul's jaw jutted. He looked warily at me. "No."

Worry pushed me to collapse upon the other easel's stool.

Then, Poul mounted his scribe's stool with the confidence of a crusading knight. "I will finish my book." He braced his arm against his easel's broad plane. "Every Dane will know the history of Denmark's great monarchs compared to the tyrant of Copenhagen."

To appeal to his pride I said, "You Carmelites journey far in your ministrations to the poor. Your observations of suffering where monarchs govern harshly must be profound."

"I have seen inhumane sovereigns...and I have seen kings guided by wisdom and care." Poul tore open an ink packet and dumped the powder into his tiny pot.

"Your expertise far exceeds my own."

He sniffed. "No doubt."

"Your treatise will bravely combat Cristiern's ambition."

Poul passed his hand over his tonsure. "The people need the truth, not stories justifying politic maneuvers. Cristiern will put before the people anything that casts him as the very stamp of Danish tradition, that reminds them of his anointment by God. But what if someone told the truth about him? What if"—Poul rapped upon his easel—"no. Mark *this* question: How did his father, Hans, really die? Eh? Was it truly a mysterious drowning at sea? Or did Cristiern kill him?"

"People say that Cristiern thought his father was impossibly weak in all things political."

"Someone must bring the truth to light." Poul beamed with arrogance. He gripped a quill, spat into his inkpot, and mixed the ink.

I was ready to dive into the deep water of persuasion with Poul. Thus, I took a breath and began, "Have you found, friar, that women say odd things at times?"

Poul glowered at me from a corner of his eye without ceasing his preparations. "When confessing?"

"Oh, no. I mean that sometimes women seem to imply one thing when they mean something else entirely."

"Women usually say precisely what they intend. However, they change their minds so often a man cannot track their purpose." He dabbed his quill into the ink.

"Exactly." I pounded my easel for emphasis. "Such was true earlier today when Margrete said—"

"You have lied to Fortinbras." This time, Poul did not look to me but to his quill. With a tap of his finger, a droplet of ink fell from his point into the pot.

A knot rose in my throat. With difficulty, I swallowed. "How often do women believe we're lying when we know we aren't? Margrete is mistaken. No one has lied to Fortinbras."

Poul's glare pinned me. "What, then, did she mean?"

I rubbed my temple, feigning an ache. "We were arguing a hypothetical situation because I had misspoken to her… it is a convoluted story."

Poul winced. He looked down at his hands. His long thumbnail scratched raw skin along a finger.

I continued, "She is tortured by fear that Fortinbras may abandon Helsingør. That would be a catastrophe."

"No, worse." Poul picked up his quill. "If Fortinbras battles Cristiern for Helsingør and loses, Cristiern will use his triumph to threaten all rulers of the Kalmar Union countries into capitulation."

"Indeed. Margrete's trepidation is well-founded."

Regarding me steadily, Poul pointed the quill at my heart. "Leave me and my materials alone." He turned to face his manuscript upon the easel and resumed writing.

Had Poul dismissed Margrete's statement? Had I succeeded? Would he ever share his sources?

Poul's scratching quill flew in loops, pushing thoughts across his page. Envy bit me. Poul composed without hesitation. He could write a longer line with a single dip in his ink than anyone I had ever seen. If he doubted his course of authorship, he made no sign of it.

Erik provided me some sheets of parchment and a quill. I began to scribble notes ordering the flow of the history I soon would write. Within a few hours I had created a concoction of words, lines, and arrows that appeared like the tracks of a mad bird. The page was busy, but the concepts were incomplete. I needed inspiration. Neither an imagined conversation with Papa nor meditation on Minerva, goddess of the arts, helped me. I stared at the pages, bruised by my inked fingers. My mind, empty of ideas, was as frothy as sea-foam.

Poul mumbled the sentence he was composing then added, "Do not gawk at me. Write."

"I'm stuck," I said.

Poul slapped his head. "Why? You promised to write Hamlet's story, correct? You were his friend. You know more about him and his family than any letter or report in these muniments. You are the original source, more qualified than any man to confirm the facts."

His assertion astonished me. I could only blink in reply.

Poul continued, "You are a student at Wittenberg's Leucorea University, yes? Then you should know the answer to this question: Erasmus exhorts us to do what? To go where?"

In unison we declared "*Ad fontes,*" and then spoke the translation: "Back to the source."

This unexpected reminder of *humanitas*—previously I had only enjoyed such discussion with Hamlet—dissolved my mask. I admitted, "Hamlet never heard me pledge to tell his story. His dying words were 'the rest is silence.' What did that mean?"

Leaning close to his script to examine a word, Poul said, "Perhaps, 'be quiet.'"

I continued to wonder. "My own silence, since he never heard me affirm his request? Or his story and life, forgotten, equals silence?"

Poul scowled. He set down his quill and, stretching, pulled at the straining cords of his neck. "You, not Hamlet, decide whether the story ends in silence. Now, let me be."

I am the source, I thought. I turned to face the tall sheet of parchment leaning against my easel. I began to write. My quill point gained speed and traction across the page. I raced against the sun's arc. By the end of the day, a few pages had grown to two dozen.

When the glowing celestial orb sank onto the horizon's western fields, the counting room darkened like the crypt. Because candles were not permitted, I ceased my work, eased from my perch, and, standing, bent backward for relief. I peered close at my handiwork, excited that the history I had written thus far was good. Also, I was elated that perhaps I had dissuaded Poul from harming me. But what of Margrete? Under threat, would she trade her family's safety for my blood? How could I be certain she would protect my artful claims made to Fortinbras? How could I navigate the perils of his whims and rage? I had to keep my lies a secret to avoid execution.

I bid Erik good night—he locked the exterior three-lock vault door behind me. I went to pilfer fish and beer from the cook, and then searched for the only man who could both teach me the intricacies of courtship and help me survive a mauling in this court. Lanier.

Where would a man exhausted from negotiating mercenary contracts find rest? His chambers, I surmised—sleeping or drinking and enjoying a lover. Thus, I stood among cabbage leaf remnants in the courtyard garden, looking up at the glossy windows embedded in the surrounding brick walls. I shielded my eyes against the dying reflected sun, gold and orange like little ponds, and tried to guess which window was Lanier's.

Then I heard, from the covered arcade bordering the garden, the plucked notes of a sad lute. It accompanied a low voice as somber as a French mason singing the epitaphs he carved.

So pretty was she, so lythe—brunette and fair—
Passion burning, hot and bright, ended by the knife.
Her eyes were green.

I followed the sound into the arcade and walked its stone floor past several brick arches and columns. Around a corner, I found the musician. Lanier sat upon a stool, eyes closed and tilted back against a column, playing the lute. Its round body lay in his lap. He twisted a tuning peg of its long neck. I observed Lanier's noble bearing—aquiline nose and white teeth. As usual, every thread he wore was black—doublet, pantaloons, cape—but his white shirt. His hat lay upon the floor by his boots. His usual scent of cloves was stifled by the stench of the road.

"Lanier, I've been looking for you. I need your assistance, friend."

When his eyes opened, I saw that they were pink, strained. He raised a finger to quiet me and then completed a slow strum of a minor chord. Then he raised his chin in anticipation.

I continued, "Margrete knows about…facts I told Fortinbras that were…exaggerations, to encourage his patronage."

Lanier, leaning back, suddenly dropped his stool forward. Its legs smacked upon the flagstone. "The document, the family legend that you translated? I was there, *mon ami*, and I hoped it was truth. You lied to Fortinbras?"

I nodded. "And about why Hamlet favored him. Also, that Hamlet didn't arrange certain murders. Margrete told me that her knowledge of my…fibs made her complicit." I crossed my arms and added, "I told Fortinbras what I thought was best. But now he has threatened to kill me, either for lies or late provision of the history I am writing. He also said he would execute Margrete and her family if the nobles betray him."

Lanier sucked his teeth. "Why did you just tell me? Now, I, too, am involved in your lies." He stretched his fingers upon the fingerboard, making an awkward chord. He strummed and sang:

Il faut bonne mèmoire, après qu'on a menti.

"'A liar should have a good memory.' A nice serenade, Lanier. For better effect, you should sing it like a lecturing old woman."

Lanier rubbed the bridge of his nose as if easing a pain. Then he regarded me and gave a dismissive wave. "Pah."

"What's wrong?"

Lanier's gaze turned stale. "No mercenaries in the northern provinces, not even the Swedes, will sign leases to fight against Cristiern. Fortinbras is furious with me." He plucked a few forlorn notes.

A dismaying vision of our enemy swept before me. Hundreds of horse-mounted armored soldiers. Clattering battle carts. Cannon and catapults launching against Krogen's fortress walls. For balance I leaned against the column.

Lanier, omitting each H, said, "That history you promised Fortinbras. A story of the House of Hamlet might inspire men to fight for Helsingør. When will you finish writing it?"

"It is nearly completed. I need more sources, more facts."

Lanier gave a nose-wrinkled laugh. "Invent them. That is your talent."

Looking away I saw, past the arches, dusk's lavender glow settling upon the courtyard garden. A breeze mixed the garden's scent of sage with that of seagrass from the bay. I took a breath to calm myself. "I need your help."

"I will not tell of your deceit. But Margrete?" He scratched his black mane. "She may tell him that you have lied if doing so protects her. You must control her somehow."

"That was my thought—and I want…I have never met such a woman. Captivating and intelligent. Certain of her person. She likes to dictate matters, but"—I scratched my chin—"her charms render me dumb."

"Women keep their seductions in little boxes, one for each man. They believe they can deal from those boxes how they choose. But ruined women have few options. Her stain does not repulse you?"

"No."

Lanier grinned, fox-like, at me. "You must lure her into your adoring arms."

I squatted beside his chair and confided, "Courtship would bind her honor to mine. By betraying me, she would risk herself. She invited that I court her. But as a commoner, if I reach beyond my station, I will be punished for impropriety. Higher taxes."

Lanier wagged his finger. "There is an exception. A commoner may court nobility if he remains subservient—"

"A lifetime of servitude to a woman?" Subjugation to a female was an unnatural condition. Also, I did not want more rules. I rubbed a sudden ache at the back of my neck.

Lanier regarded me with one brow raised. "*Vous êtes un imbécile.*"

"I know parts of the chivalric code, but not much of it. A man doesn't need such training for liaison with a peasant woman."

Nearby, the castle's main portal heaved outward on its hinges. From the yawning gap emerged a trio of gaggling young women onto the garden path. Next came the guards Barnardo and Marcellus carrying torches to light those resting in cradles along the arcade.

Lanier picked up his hat, and we stood. With a tilt of his head Lanier gestured at the vacant walkway ahead of us. "Let us walk." He carried the lute under one arm and swung his other arm across my shoulders. As we sauntered along the arcade, Lanier's voice dropped barely above a whisper. "Most commoners are unaware that chivalry's opportunities can apply to all men, not only to knights."

I pulled my hat from my head and examined its soft crown. "I suppose we have precedent for a common man taking a noble woman for his spouse. Old Hamlet. He was a commoner at birth. He learned propriety."

Lanier slapped my back approvingly. "*Exactement, mon ami.* Chivalry is about pure love, about placing the beloved on a golden pedestal. Your skill as a suitor should deftly magnify her bright sparkle," he said with a flourishing hand. "Any light that illuminates your existence is merely cast from her being."

"That's absolute manure."

Lanier grinned. "*C'est vrai.* Absolute manure is how we get what we want." He set his hat upon his head. "Such is life in the courtier's realm."

"You know a lot about it."

"*Oui.* Born to it in beautiful Autun, not far from Beaune. I can teach you about the pure manure art of chivalry."

I patted Lanier's shoulder in thanks. His exquisite cape crushed slightly under my fingers.

"Tomorrow I will train you in the chivalric arts of falconry and archery. You will compete in a tournament the following day. I will arrange it. The people need diversion."

Lanier turned on his heel and, leaving me in the arcade, stomped across the wasted, moonlit garden. He called over his shoulder, "We will meet at noon in the east killing field." He reached the opposite arcade walk and, whistling a soft melody, entered the castle's main door.

Hope lifted me. *I may win Margrete*, I thought. *My writing will achieve my promise to Hamlet and will satisfy Fortinbras. Margrete and I will be safe. Perhaps good fortune is mine.*

I entered the castle's main corridor and sprang up the spiraling stairway into Wiglaf Corridor. Tapestries and lit torches lined the walls. I approached my chamber.

Suddenly, I heard a familiar voice. "I cannot trust anyone but you, Horatio."

I stopped, then looked to a nearby door. The speech seemed to have emanated from that portal, which, I knew, concealed a vein of passageways that threaded between private compartments throughout the castle. Once, Hamlet and I had quietly trod those hidden lanes, which were illumined only by slivers of candlelight shining through cracks in the walls. We had listened to nobles' rancorous discussions, heaving intercourse, drunken pleas...

I went to the hidden passageway door and, opening it, peered into the dim, narrow channel. No one stood within. With sadness, I closed the door.

But then the voice crackled in my ear, "You are the most reserved, rational man I have ever known."

I spun around to discover the source. "Hamlet?"

Nothing. Was that his nisse, his guardian sprite? Or was it a daemon? My heart pounded in my breast.

I crossed to my chamber, softly singing a wisp of verse to ease my fear.

> *A pilgrim, young and fat, tilled the road abreast a donkey,*
> *Bound for Old Jerusalem to pray a dead brother's blessing.*

Beside my door hung an enormous tapestry. *That wasn't there before,* I thought. The housemaster was rotating hangings again. This one was impressive, but it crowded my door.

The tapestry's loose threads fluttered, but no breeze traveled the corridor.

I moved nearer to inspect the work. It was a faded weave that depicted a crowd cavorting upon a red field. Leading the revelers was the Hamlet royal line, resplendent in blue, yellow, and green. I saw that one figure—Hamlet—lay deceased at the feet of his towering, armored father. I was amazed, for this tapestry was musty and the design could not have been changed since Hamlet's death. I beheld this terrible vision of fate actualized, and I trembled.

My heartstrings were pulling apart. I spread my hands in appeal to the tapestry and said, "Hamlet, I may be rational, but I suffer terribly from grief. I struggle to find the Golden Mean, divine balance, in myself."

The threaded prince's eyes opened. He turned his face to me and spoke. "If you love me, endure every burden to tell my story."

My innards roiled. I almost shrieked but replied, "I began by reporting to Fortinbras—"

"He is one man, and a poor audience."

"In your eulogy, I told Krogen's people about your cause. I'm writing—"

"And dreaming of a conquest."

I poked the tapestry. "That's hardly fair. Your legacy depends upon mine now. But what is my fortune? I've no idea." I paused to gather my thoughts. "Perhaps a wife, a family."

"That woman will want only what is best for her." The woven visage of Hamlet grumped at me. His flat figure sat up. "Do not avoid your promise to me."

"*You* have never delayed action, have you, Hamlet?"

The tapestry's threads pulled taut, straining all faces therein. I stroked its surface to ease the spirits and to steady myself. When I touched Hamlet's face, it changed, seemed to rot like a sponge. Death's pinching stench made my gorge rise.

The dissolving face rasped, "Conduct yourself as a Dane, not an antique Roman."

I began to shake. Was I a shaggy Norse warrior, bent on lasting self-glory and memorial? Or a helmeted Roman, fighting the enemy for instant victory of a grand cause?

"Something greater will come," Hamlet said.

"What do you mean?"

Suddenly, the tapestry's bottom corners bucked. It flew above my head, tore from its nails, and crashed against the ceiling. I leapt back. The tapestry dropped in a heap upon the floor where I had stood.

I crept to the pile and, pulling at it, unfolded its creases until I found Hamlet's depiction. Once again, the figure rested in death's repose. I glanced about, disbelieving that his spirit had departed. "Where are you, Hamlet?"

Upon the wall beside the tapestry's vacant place, a torch flashed as if splattered with oil.

I stepped around the mound of fabric and said to the torch, "Hamlet, you deserve my faith, and I deserve yours. I also deserve affection in life."

The torch went black. *More proof of Hamlet's bad death*, I thought. Quaking, I rolled the heavy weave, lopsided. As I did so I prayed the final lines of the Hour of Terce. "May the souls of the faithful departed...rest in peace. Amen." Then I shoved it against the wall.

My quavering legs carried me into my chamber and my bed. Exhaustion crawled over me, but I lay for hours, frightened and brain-jumbled. *Hamlet doesn't rest...because of me.* What did he mean: A greater thing is coming?

I watched the moon arc and orange-rimmed crescents persistently trek across my floor's grainy planks. *Destiny's sign, prompting me to march onward*, I thought. *Tomorrow, under Lanier's tutelage, I'll begin pursuit of Margrete's hand in marriage, and I'll work harder to complete the history.* My life, honor, and soul depended upon both.

VII.

When the next morning's sunrise blinked through the horizon's cloudy gray sheet, clanging bells released us from Mass services in the chapel. My efforts to preserve us, by courtship and by authorship, had filled my prayers and dreams.

After a meager meal of dried herring, bread, and beer, I joined the nobles for an hour of battle practice. Still no word had come of Cristiern's location or his army's camp. All fretted that he could not be far from Helsingør now.

I leveled my focus upon my purpose and met Lanier on the lush, grassy expanse of the killing field, which was flanked by the fortress's towering sheer stone walls. The killing field, if filled, would have been a moat that nearly encircled the fortress, making an ideal trap for an enemy breaching the outer wall. In peace, however, Krogen's killing field was a place for festivities and games... that had become sour because of the stench of dead birds starved upon the bay's shore. The water held few fish. Many had been netted to feed hungry Helsingørians.

Upon Lanier's thick-gloved forearm sat a regal falcon. It looked arrogantly through me.

"This morning," Lanier said, "you will learn only the basics of the art of falconry and the primary skills of archery. You will compete in both during tomorrow's tournament. You will show your skills as a man of refinement worthy of a noblewoman's attentions."

A quiver of trepidation swept me. *Calm thyself.*

I held, for Lanier to see, a small rolled parchment. "I brought a poem I wrote for Margrete. Will the bird also deliver it to her?"

"For the bird, it is an easy task. But for you, as its master, requesting the delivery is an advanced skill." Lanier clucked at the falcon. He eased a loose feather from its red tail. To me he said, "Read the poem aloud."

I unrolled the sheet. "My Lady is a morning rose—most fair, starlight caught and dawn awakened."

"*C'est bon*, but try 'starlight caught and ruby-bloomed.' That would be better. For the next line, mention the stars you consulted, what they told you about your love for her."

"But I didn't—"

"Put it there. It will work magic. Also…" Lanier pulled from his cape pocket a small charcoal stick. He reached for my poem and scribbled a title across the top of the slip. *A Dedication to Lady Margrete.* "When she reads this, she will swoon."

I read the rest, and Lanier nodded his approval. With faith I rolled the sheet and tied it with ribbon.

The bird's massive wings opened, eager and insistent. I stepped back. Lanier cooed to the bronze-feathered beast, "You are lovely, Catrina. *N'est-ce pas?*" Then he asked me, "Ready?"

I nodded.

Lanier gave me a heavy leather glove and sleeve. He taught me to hold, receive, and release the bird. Then he swung a baited lure to entice its flight. The falcon soared along the walls and up the battlements. Lanier's sharp whistle brought its return. The creature's wings, arcing in flight, were glorious, but its landing—a flapping drop upon my shoulder, not my arm—was an instant of terror.

"She plays a game with you," Lanier laughed. "Be firm." He pushed my arm higher in the air. "She is to land there. Show her."

Recovering, I said, "I have a question... about chivalry. Why must courtship depend upon a lady's choice and control?"

"Chivalric love is offered by a gentleman committing his person fully to his lady. She decides when she is won, if she is won, and by whom. That is the chivalric code."

I needed no code to care for Margrete as she deserved. And what of my own honor? Could I possibly live an entire life of shame bending to a woman's will? Yet, I supposed no one dared question Old Hamlet's manhood for his similar choice. I pondered this for a moment.

Lanier leaned downward, into my vision, to hook my attention. "I have no time to teach you use of the lure: it prompts the bird's flight. At the tournament tomorrow, when you step upon the platform, I will be in hiding and I will cast the lure for you." Lanier gave the falcon to an unflinching servant boy. "Before I go to look for mercenaries in other villages, I must teach you archery."

Lanier held out a quiver of arrows and a bow borrowed from the armory. We stood a short distance before a lopsided stack of hay bales into which Lanier had plugged fabric strips to frame the target. "I will teach you some fundamental skills. If you concentrate on them you will do well, and Margrete will cheer for you."

Lanier slid the notch of an arrow's shaft onto the bowstring. He stood sideways and extended his bow arm straight, elbow rotated outward. He drew back the string, aimed, and, exhaling, released it. The arrow sailed true and landed within the boundary of fluttering strips. It appeared to be a simple task.

When releasing my bowstring I persistently held my breath, forgetting a slow exhale. However, eventually my arrows began to hit the stack, then the target markers and rings within.

"You lied again. You are accomplished in archery?"

"No." I lowered the bow. "Another question. The divine order of creation is that women want to marry and be protected by their husbands. Why is this parade of intent necessary?"

Lanier removed his hat and rolled his fist within the crown, pressing it into a rounder shape. "Does it matter? Keep Margrete close. If she reveals your lies—pah. All of us will hang."

The noon sun now beat upon the horizon and Lanier left. I hastened to the muniment tower and pounded upon the dense vault door until Erik admitted me. I stepped past him into the counting room and saw that Poul had already arrived. He wore his hood up and was seated at his easel, furiously scratching ink trails across his lightly lined sheets of parchment. I wondered if Poul was writing about the Hamlets as well.

Erik retrieved my manuscript from the locked muniment room and gave me fresh parchment. Immediately, I resumed work, and within two hours had etched into my narrative every shred of information I knew of the Hamlets. I could not finish without additional facts. Were those in the reports and missives that Poul had amassed?

Erik and Poul climbed the stairs to the muniment room to search for a document Erik believed he had already given Poul, but that Poul said he did not possess. I was alone in the counting room amid Erik's table laden with documents, the banded boxes upon the dozen shelves, and our page-laden easels.

I went to Poul's unguarded manuscript and looked behind it for documents. None were of value to me. Next, I quickly read his writings to find the fruits of his research. He had listed royal relations like biblical genealogies. His narrative proclaimed the tenures of stout Viking rulers such as Gorm the Old and his son, Harald Bluetooth. Their coarse, long hair and sinewy muscles had been woven into an everlasting ancestral brawn. My imagination reached for these Danes, as my finger traced the script's jagged tails.

"What are you doing?"

I looked up to see Poul standing beside Erik's document-strewn table. His hands were empty, but his red face was plump with anger.

"Your work is wonderful," I said. "I wanted the benefit of your wisdom so that—"

"Enough. I know a cheat, a plagiarist, when I see one. Others may choose to tolerate your deceit, but I will not."

"I did not copy your text. I'm not lying to you, Poul."

He began to sweep his manuscript and implements from the easel into his bag.

"Where are you going?" I asked, fearing that his destination would be the royal corridor.

"Where you cannot molest my work." Poul spat at me.

I ducked his missile.

Erik reached the bottom of the tower stairs. He stopped within the threshold and looked at us. His face scrunched in sharp disdain.

Poul charged across the counting room to the vault door and stood before it, his foot tapping. "Unlock the door, Erik."

I said, "Poul, you misunderstand me. Let's discuss this."

Erik moved to the door. The keys jangled in his hand. He inserted each one slowly into its tumbler. Then he turned to face Poul. "I do not care what you write or what your complaints may be. But, Poul, your conduct is intolerable, and you injure these muniments every time that you visit. You make a shambles of their arrangement. You never return the documents to their proper boxes and in the correct order. I am forever repairing your messes because, once lost, the documents are rarely found, and our indexes become useless." Erik turned each key slowly. Poul bounced like a penned goat awaiting release. Again, Erik looked up at Poul but now with the steady eye of a master archer. "I will watch you every moment that your fingers paw these muniments. I will not endure more of your liberties with the collection." When Erik pushed open the heavy door, Poul ducked under its low arch and scooted into the vaulted passageway. He was gone.

I returned to my easel and rested my forehead against it.

Erik closed and secured the door. He wearily climbed upon his stool, rubbed his fatigue-rumpled face with both hands. "That Poul is a burr to the arse. No wonder the priory father would rather let him rage here than in their cloisters." Erik regarded me. His eye twitched. "Are you ill?"

I wanted to kneel upon the hard tile and pray that Poul's heart would soften, that he would not go to Fortinbras and reveal my lies. But I lifted my head and sat hunched upon my stool. "Without more sources, I can't complete my work. I must deliver it to Fortinbras soon."

"Scholars think they know everything," Erik muttered. He went to a low cabinet and opened its narrow door. From that cubbyhole he pulled a small book. Erik flopped open its soft leather cover. His stubby finger pointed at certain cryptic document titles. Old Hamlet's campaigns. Clever battle trickery. Glorious banquets and festivals. Spells cast upon enemies. Each listed a box name. Erik held out the index to me and pointed at a list. "Did you use these?"

I peered, incredulous, at the page. "No. Why didn't you tell me of them before?"

Erik leaned close to my face. The bite of stale beer wafted from him. "You never asked me."

We retrieved from the muniment room soft parchment rolls, tightly folded packets that crackled upon touch, and smooth leather-faced volumes. These grouchy creatures marked me with acrid odors as I disturbed them. I found many useful facts, which I included in my manuscript. Erik, too, made a discovery. He confirmed that Poul had pilfered three more documents.

All afternoon I sat at my easel, reading and writing, so engrossed in my work that I missed taking supper. Eventually the worm of hunger twisted my gut. I noticed, through my window, that twilight's violet plane had settled upon the western stretch of the killing field. A fragment of the moon hovered like a shard of glass in the cloudless night sky. My work was still thick in my head, but the darkness of night halted my progress. I removed to my chambers to sleep and ready myself for my competition the next day—my first public, official attempt to woo Margrete.

The morning's sun raced in ascent and issued a hot glare promising my victory. Golden rays burned upon the forest's bushy peaks. Dew steamed from the killing field, warming the observation benches set opposite the falconry platform. A menagerie of women and men filled the grounds. Ladies fat in rustling skirts, chattered like excited badgers.

Men, smooth-skinned in leather and linen, pursued the women. Little girls wearing lace caps clung to their parents. Boys punched one another and ogled girls. Graying elders, huddled closely together, wagered for and against tournament competitors.

After several contenders flew their birds and earned mediocre applause, I stepped upon the platform with my massive bird perched on my arm. One talon clutched my scroll, as Lanier had affixed it moments beforehand.

Within the crowd I located Margrete. She was resplendent in her gown of white and black, and she sat with her ladies and an elderly couple, her parents, I assumed. Next, I looked to see Lanier, crouching behind the crowd. Suddenly, he flicked a long cord that tossed a nugget of meat high into the air. I thrust my arm upward. The falcon ascended, trailing the red ribbon that bound my missive. The people pointed and marveled. Some, I could hear, gossiped about the courting commoner. My bird dove upon Margrete as if to pulverize her. The ladies seated near Margrete screeched.

Lanier had moved to stand behind the ladies' benches. He flicked the meat-bearing lure high into the air. The bird soared over Margrete and dropped my scroll to fetch the bait.

Margrete saw that the missive tumbled toward her head. She reached, hands open to receive it. My writing was my heart, my life, entrusted to her. It dropped into her palms, softly landing. She raised it, looked to me, and grinned triumphantly.

The elderly woman turned to face Margrete. Her lips pursed, much like Margrete's sometime skeptical demeanor. I could read her crisp question. "A commoner?"

Margrete immediately unrolled and examined my poem. Her sight riveted upon the text, her lips parted, moved with her reading. Margrete, her head still inclined, looked to me. Her serious countenance melted into a soft smile.

The father, at Margrete's other side, looked past his daughter to the old woman. He reached across Margrete and patted his wife's knee, as if consoling her.

I hoped that my next performance, in archery, would secure their acceptance.

That afternoon, woolen skies blanketed Helsingør and drizzle fell upon the huddling crowds. I was the last competitor of nine, none of whom had performed perfectly. I stood before the same archery target that I had used in practice with Lanier, and I drew back the same bow that had been mine while learning. I held my breath. My trembling hands stilled. Each of my shots struck the target's rings. One hit the center.

A young man called out, "The commoner rules all."

The crowd cheered my bowmanship. I leaned upon one leg and let the bow slide through my hand to rest upon the ground. I feigned no surprise at my prowess, as if I awaited a sculptor to record in marble my magnificent deportment and talent.

Margrete beamed. Her father rubbed his chin, seeming to assess me. However, her mother's frown was like a wilted vine.

I thought perhaps I could be at peace with games rendering control to women and their rules.

My next test, however, was dance. I feared wicked failure; my feet were made in the brick house. Before the festivities began the following night, what tool could I find to chisel away my clumsiness and free my heels?

The following morning Lanier came to my chamber door.

"You look like a clubbed rabbit, *mon ami*."

"I don't know how to dance."

Lanier, in jest, staggered against my doorframe. Grinning, he sucked his teeth to irk me. I ignored him. He recovered. "Do not worry so." Lanier stood before me. His knees bent to approximate a lady's height. His arse stuck out and his toes pointed inward. He raised an open palm. "Your lesson begins. Take my hand."

I did so.

"Stand this way, one foot forward, your weight upon your back foot. Place your hand atop my—no—my hand. Now walk beside me. Good. Turn to me and guide me to your—ouch."

After my lesson concluded Lanier helped me select the most elegant attire found within my wardrobe, which Hamlet had lent to me. Lanier brushed dust from a sleek black tunic, dark gray leggings, and black boots. Finishing, he bid me good fortune.

I proceeded to the muniment tower's counting room. Erik allowed me to light a candle, which I set upon the window ledge. Facing westward, no one would see it. I received the additional benefit of reflected light.

Working into the evening, I used every scrap of evidence, scraped my memory bare for details that Hamlet had told me, and deduced everything else I needed, but sensibly. The history told of Gertrude and Old Hamlet's usurpation of Helsingør. How they gathered nobles from their lands into Krogen and moved graves into the crypt. The order of the nobility and resources they brought to the Hamlets.

Hours later, in Krogen's Freyja Hall, I joined one hundred fifty nobles at supper. All were exhausted from battle practice with long-swords, longbows, and buckets queues. Above the clatter of our empty wooden trenchers being removed by servants, the nobles grumbled about our dwindling fare now limited to dried fish and ordinary roots from the fields. To divert them, two jesters leapt upon the dais and acted out depravity and flatulence that the rich suppose are commoners' daily pleasures. Their jibes were rude but funny, and they performed until the sun set. Then, servants removed the tables, pushed the benches against the walls, and lit hearth flames that crackled and roared. The dance began.

The drum, flute, and lute filled the grand, timber-ribbed hall and encouraged our lively procession about the room, beneath the high-hanging pennons of families ever loyal to the Hamlets. Among dozens of couples turning and cycling toward new partners, Margrete and I met. She wore a long dress of blue silk and silver trim, as if she were enfolded within a brilliant piece of sky. Her hair was swept behind and collected within a tiny blue snood. My breath snagged on my heart. She looked up at me in full smiling regard, as if I were the entire world before her.

We lightly stepped toward one another and away. Again, we moved toward one another. I took her hands in mine. Then we were to turn away, but I bumped her and trod upon her foot. I apologized. Although she winced, her closed, smiling lips never flinched. "When did you learn to dance?"

"This afternoon."

"Oh." Her hands deftly slid from within my grip to, instead, hold mine. "Now the musicians will play a more complicated measure. But we need not hurry. Watch my feet. Take half a step...now—no, there." She piloted our course.

Some, prancing past us, shot smug glances at me, the uncouth peasant. A few gleefully clapped to encourage my blooming stink flower of dancing courtship. I ignored them.

Margrete said, "Only a man of great modesty can receive a lady's guidance in good spirit."

"You mean a man of great chivalry."

"Indeed. Have you read the guidance manuals on chivalric love? The man's ability to relinquish control is a sign of genuine modesty. Consider that Old Hamlet succeeded with Gertrude leading."

"It was he who fought and won campaigns. She did not plot his battles."

The pearl dangling from Margrete's ear shook. Its luster favored her cheek. "Very true, but Gertrude's heraldry justified their claim to Helsingør. Her husband's victories legitimized it. He trusted her rule over Helsingør during his absences. While her husband was away, battling enemies, she ensured order over society and in their home."

Our palms touched, and we held them high above our heads. We pivoted full circle, just as Lanier and I had practiced, this time with some ease. Margrete smiled at me, and my hand began to melt against hers.

"Is your writing nearly complete?" she asked as she took a step backward.

I advanced toward her. She turned to stand beside me and her hand rested lightly upon my forearm. I said, "I will finish tomorrow."

We began a slow promenade... but her hand slipped from its perch. "Did you—?"

"No. Everything is factual. Erik and I found more sources." Her hand returned to my arm. "Margrete." I leaned slightly to ask in a whisper, "Did you find Poul when he left the muniment room? Did he tell Fortinbras about my... exaggerations?"

"I did not find him. But I have not heard that he visited Fortinbras."

"You're certain that Fortinbras knows nothing, from anyone, about it?"

Margrete stiffened. "I do not believe so." She regarded me, her eyes hardened. "Do you think I would tell him?"

Her offense was sincere. Perhaps I was wrong to have feared her disloyalty. Thus, I decided to risk telling her the truth, in a way.

I took her hand and reclaimed the rudder of our dance. "I believe you would do anything to protect your family."

Margrete looked straight ahead. "You are correct."

"I was orphaned. I can only imagine the responsibility of sheltering one's children or parents."

"We each have a devotion of love. Yours is your pledge honoring your friend and brother, and my prince."

The orderly promenade of couples quickened, pushed by the drum and lured by the flute.

She continued, "But is it too much for a man to ask his friend to bear every burden to achieve a promise? Why did Hamlet ask that of you? Gertrude never required such of me, although she knew I would do anything she asked. My purpose would be to achieve that pledge."

I beheld her crisp elegance, every aspect in its place. "Perfection is also your purpose."

"People judge others based upon their own beliefs, not upon others' misfortune."

"No one can be perfect," I said softly. "Not even the gods. Only the Almighty."

"That is true." Margrete touched a tear in the corner of her eye. Her voice, however, did not waver. "No one will question my integrity."

Margrete suddenly chose different discourse. Her fingers clipped onto my elbow. "I am concerned for you, Horatio."

I made a mocking frown. "How have I erred now?"

Margrete gave a slight laugh, then regarded me seriously. "I hope that you no longer harbor dark thoughts. Wish for self-slaughter."

I raised a hand as if making an oath. "No. I use my razor only to cut my whiskers. Do you favor beards on your suitors?"

"I do not."

I thought, happily, that I would keep my smooth countenance in my preferred Germanic style. Then I asked, "Dare I ask: Have many noblemen pursued you in the past?"

"I do not wish to discuss that."

Her slight pressure on my elbow attempted to steer me. I turned the opposite direction and, walking backward carefully, brought her along, facing me.

"A dozen?" I asked. "And all failed their chivalric tests?"

Margrete's lips pressed. She regarded me. "I have not finished my question. If great difficulty rises again for you, Horatio, would you likely harm yourself?"

"Margrete, I usually look to the light and choose the road, not the ditch. Otherwise, I would have remained in an orphanage only to become a beggar. I would not have discharged myself from that place and found an apprenticeship, or sought Papa, chosen him as my guide, and earned a berth at the university. For one to kill himself, or think of it, is an act against God. I confess that sin at every Mass."

"My parents say that life serving a tyrant is worse than risking eternal punishment."

"Is that your belief?"

"No…" Margrete considered. "But while we have choices within God's plan, sometimes we cannot perceive the options."

The drum slowed. The flute softened. We passed the hearth. The rich scent of embers snapping sharpened my senses. Firelight gilded Margrete's hair, her nape, her bosom. A flush of confidence swept through me. I looked above, to the dusky ceiling and the scattered stars seen through the high windows. I said a silent prayer to Venus that Margrete would love me.

But a troubling itch overcame me. I asked, "Margrete, I don't doubt your regard, but I don't understand why a woman of noble status would take interest in any commoner."

"Two."

I regarded her quizzically. "Two what?"

She looked ahead, ignoring my stare. "Two noblemen courted me before I was dishonored. After my reputation was ruined: none did so."

I realized that the brute had stolen Margrete's future within the tribal nobility of Krogen. *God's eyes.* I wanted to trap and whip that spawn of a troll bitch until his genitals…

"I want to have children," Margrete continued, "and to be certain I am with the right man. That is my prayer." Her hand, at her side, brushed mine. Her fingers hooked into my palm. "Do you want a child, Horatio?"

Loneliness. Too many evenings passed in reading, or taverns and empty liaisons, or self-gratifying exertion. I had tired of those companions.

"A family would be a wonderful comfort, but fatherhood is an enigma to me."

Softly she said, "Fatherhood is love and courage, teaching and protection. Gertrude once told me, regarding Old Hamlet, that despite their native differences, she found his devotion and perseverance most alluring. As a commoner, he was bred to survive dangers she did not know. He was unlike any man she had ever met."

Margrete smiled at me. Her hand rested upon my shoulder now. Her citrus scent filled me. It takes only a grain of encouragement to grow a bushel of confidence in a man.

"Your falconry and archery yesterday were superb," she said.

"What of my poem? Did you like it?"

A wisp of hair fell from its binding and trailed down her cheek. I tucked it behind her ear. Her smile softened, lingered. "It was most pleasing."

We turned a tight circle. I noticed, by the hall's entrance, Lanier. He leaned against the doorjamb's stone molding, arms crossed, and watched us from beneath the brim of his hat.

I looked again to Margrete. Happiness was mine. I serenaded her softly, in rhythm with our steps, a few lines remembered from the popular song-tale "Habor and Signild."

> *From Signild's head to tie his limbs but two hairs did they take,*
>
> *And, such the love he felt for her, that band he could not break.*
>
> *Nay, lovely maiden, hear me now, and fear no lack of care,*
>
> *At table you shall sit with me, my bed too you shall share.*

She wrinkled her nose. "That is your choice of lyric to woo me? Obscene love among the unmarried is a criminal offense."

I feigned surprise. "Did I mention intercourse?" She laughed, and I added, "The magistrates are wrong. It's a sin, not a crime."

The music stopped. Margrete stepped back from me. I bowed to her; she curtsied. When straightened, I looked to Lanier for his reaction, but he was gone.

"Your dancing improved," Margrete said. "I will tell my father that your talents deserve advanced opportunity in courtship."

"Tomorrow night I will properly grace you with an original song upon the lute. Before I compose it, I must finish writing the history—factually," I added hastily.

Margrete nodded. She may have believed her influence had changed me.

I continued, "It will convince Fortinbras to defend us, I am certain of it."

Margrete smiled, broad and lovely. Her eyes filled but she did not dab away her feeling. "Horatio, you have saved us."

Joy overtook me. Perhaps Margrete wanted a champion after all.

Three ladies approached. Margrete allowed them to sweep her away.

I exited the hall and hummed as I walked through the torchlit corridor and up the stairs to my chamber. There, I jotted notes, planning how I would complete the history the next day, thereby avoiding the dungeon or gallows.

The next morning, dawn's razor glare lit my easel, where I sat by the window in the counting room. Elation for my conquest in love and anticipation of my completed work sped my scribbling quill. My narrative declared which families were the Hamlets' most ardent loyalists and why, especially for Old Hamlet's battle campaigns. The account also unfolded the curse of the House of Hamlet, from the drowning of youngest brother, Jons, to Old Hamlet's murder and Hamlet's madness, and his struggle to avenge his father's death. The history ends with a summary of the ambition, fear, foolishness, and treachery that decimated their line.

As bells tolled for midmorning Mass, I proudly dipped my quill into my inkpot and wrote on the last page "Finis" with a thick, swooping flourish. "All laud and glory to the Almighty," I said to Erik, "on the seventeenth day of June in the year of our Lord 1513 I have completed my work, a sixty-page manuscript." Erik merely shrugged at me. I took no offense and thought, *I must pray that Fortinbras and Hamlet's ghost are satisfied, that the history proves so useful to Fortinbras he forgets expulsion and execution.* Our lives would be spared. Thus, I went to the chapel and left my drying pages upon my easel.

After the service I returned to the muniment tower. I pounded upon the vault door. Erik opened it only slightly. He thrust his face—it was pale, unlike his usual tanned-parchment countenance—into the narrow crack.

"Why won't you admit me? What's the matter?"

I peered past Erik and saw my manuscript shuffled upon the easel. Every page was ripped down its belly and across its flanks like a gutted deer.

In God's name. I pushed past Erik to rescue my work. The damage was worse than I first believed. The slashed pages were illegible even if they could be sewn.

My best attempt. Ruined before the world could see it. Destroyed before Fortinbras could accept it. Dishonor. Death. My stomach wrenched tight. My legs buckled. I collapsed upon my stool, numb, clutching the remains.

A terse baritone spoke. "I told you, scholar, not to touch my manuscript or use my sources."

I looked over my shoulder. Poul sat at the far end of Erik's table, loosely holding a double-edged knife.

Despite his weapon, I dropped my pages and flew at him. "My work had nothing to do with yours...yet, because of jealousy and pride you sabotaged me. A learned man of God—you—a devotee to *humanitas*? I did as you advised. I wrote facts pointing to truth, not dogma."

Poul rubbed the blade's handle with his thumb. "I returned to give Erik a few items I had borrowed. And I read your dry testament. Flat drivel. You used my work for your own gain."

"Not so." I grasped his hand holding the blade. I wanted to plunge the point into his hypocritical heart.

"You have lied to me," Poul said, "about pilfering from my work, and to the king about your intent...I heard you and the lady speak of that. You are too lazy to create your own work or to tell the truth. I will personally tell Fortinbras all about your falsehood."

I tried to twist the knife from Poul's grip. I punched him in the side and, with my other hand, pried at his fist but to no avail. When I struck a blow to Poul's chin, causing a flushing bruise, Poul jammed his shoulder into me.

Erik pulled upon my arm and pushed against Poul. Huffing, he said, "We found other records, Poul. Horatio did not plagiarize your work."

At last, I wrenched away the knife. Poul scrambled to the other side of the table. Panting, he said, "You have no fire in your belly. No rebellion in your heart. Boldly proclaim the truth."

I bellowed, "I wasn't issuing judgment against the world. I wrote a simple historical account about the nobles, Prince Hamlet, and his family."

Poul wiped his forehead. "I did you a favor. You are no longer saddled by that rot."

"I was to deliver this account to Fortinbras today."

"Truth telling," Poul said, "is like standing naked in the commons square. Once you present yourself bare and unabashed, it is as easy as lying."

That arrogant, quail-necked swine. For my dishonor I might have run to my chamber, taken my razor, and either murdered him or ended my life before Fortinbras could do so. But I was too angry.

I scooped up my shredded pages. "Poul, I'll tell the truth. Mark that." Carrying them, I rushed to the door. Erik hurriedly unlocked it. But Poul and I jostled through the narrow portal. I pushed forth and lurched into the cool air of the vaulted passageway. We raced to the twisting stairway and upward toward the royal suites. Poul's sandals slapping the floor, slowed. He puffed behind me. I dashed ahead, into the perennially fuming crowd of beggar nobility. I pushed through the rancorous throng to reach the unruffled, distinguished housemaster, Tomas, at his podium. Poul arrived behind me, panting. After Tomas ushered us through the sitting room and into Fortinbras's chambers, he departed and closed the door.

We knelt abreast before Fortinbras. Poul tilted forward onto his hands and knees, wheezing. Gasping, I leaned against my one raised knee and dropped the pieces of my manuscript at Fortinbras's feet.

Fortinbras's brow crunched, a fleshy pile of purple folds. He grumbled, "This is the history you promised? I cannot read these fragments."

A MAN OF HONOR

I pressed my hands flat upon the cold floor and stared at his mud-caked boots.

"Majesty, I regret to report that this friar destroyed my manuscript. He is a wicked man. I completed my work this morning and was about to present it to you, as I promised."

Poul lay flat, prostrate before Fortinbras. "Your Majesty, I failed to report to you that Horatio and the Lady Margrete have conspired in continuous lies to you. He is but a pharisee, and the lady has known about his—"

"Highness," I said, "Margrete has no role in this matter. She deserves no punishment."

"I have suspected," said Fortinbras, "that Margrete's family ardently supported the Hamlets from the time that Old Hamlet killed my father."

"This commoner is the culprit," said Poul. "He also stole from my work."

"I did not," I bellowed.

Poul said, "I repent of not alerting you to his lies sooner."

Fortinbras grasped the back of my tunic's neck hem. He jerked me upward. His iron glare cut deep. "I permitted you to write an account proving the loyalty of Helsingør's nobles to their sovereign, even to include some mention of your friend Hamlet while telling of my command. But I just learned from my brother's letter sent from Oslo that your translation of my inheritance and family legend was a lie. What lies did you write about the House of Hamlet, I wonder? About the nobles? Does anything but deceit rule this place?" Fortinbras dropped me and dug into my back with his heel.

I huffed for breath. "I wrote the truth, sire. I would have brought the information to you intact. It showed the loyalty of Helsingør's people, of the nobles of Krogen. Why they deserve your mercy and protection. I beg your forgiveness, but Poul is to blame."

The boot heel skewering my back slid away, and Fortinbras hoisted me by my collar to stand. Then he gripped Poul by his cowl and yanked him to his feet. "I do not abide roguery. You both are expelled from the castle. Leave within the hour, or else I will use your skulls to test the readiness of Krogen's crossbows."

Poul and I staggered backward in retreat. We turned and burst through the sitting room door into the corridor. Poul rushed through the crowd bound for—I did not care.

Mercury himself could not have raced to Wiglaf Corridor faster than I. As I neared my chamber door, I looked over my shoulder. No one pursued me, but I took no comfort in that.

As I stuffed my belongings into a sack, I resolved to risk capture in order to find Margrete. I could not flee Krogen without warning her about Fortinbras's threat and properly ending our courtship. My heart splintered to bid her goodbye, but I would not forsake her—especially not by cruel, silent dismissal. Margrete's hate would hurt me more than would Fortinbras's arrow points.

VIII.

A procession of black iron chandeliers guided me as I ran, my sack of belongings slung over my shoulder, down the south corridor. I reached the end, where the high nobles resided. Carved into each door was that family's emblem that hung in Freyja Hall. I slowed to assess each door's symbol of ideal family, and I pushed down upon my rising envy for the comfort in which I imagined they lived. Where was the door of the Royal Fabrics Assessor and Tailor?

Only the last portal seemed likely. The door resembled a softly rippling sheet of cloth. My rapping brought no answer, no sound of movement within. I shifted my sack onto my other shoulder and knocked again. Time was precious. Fortinbras probably had a guard counting the expiration of my one-hour allowance to leave Krogen, until he would haul me and Margrete to the gallows.

I turned to depart. But then I heard shuffling at the door. The portal opened slightly. Margrete's walnut-faced parents peeped at me.

"Begging your pardon, I must speak with Margrete."

The man said, "Horatio, it is past time that you talked with us.

Come inside."

Stepping past them I moved into their paneled sitting room. "I have little time," I said, although I paused in surprise at the blaze in the fireplace. It could have melted bone due to the nearing summer solstice. The mantle's ornamental stone, which bore a chiseled Viking ship, and their large windows' swirled glass, denoted their wealth.

"Where is Margrete?" I asked.

The parents sat upon a plush bench near the fire. The man pointed to a chair close to the fire. The woman's lips clasped tight. "Perhaps we will call for her. First we have some questions for you."

I sat in the chair and set my bag on the wood floor. I pulled my hat from my head in impatient deference.

The man began, "I am Hendrik. My wife is Estrid."

Estrid coughed, then croaked. "Horatio, have you any children?"

"No such blessing."

"Our Margrete is our only child," she said. "Margrete should have many children."

A droplet rolled down my brow. I brushed it away. "How many?" I asked.

"You are from Tønderensis," Estrid continued. "Were you baptized there?"

"Yes. I have little time—"

Hendrik slapped his knee. "Ah, yes. That explains your accent. Good people there."

Leaning to her husband, Estrid loudly whispered, "A commoner from a market port town closer to Hamburg than to Copenhagen. Why would Margrete want him?"

"I'm not here to ask for your daughter's hand."

The parents looked to me, unblinking, like snowy owls on a perch. Estrid's smirk melted. "Only yesterday you... but now you do not want our Margrete?"

I heard, from the adjoining main room, thudding objects and heels striking the floorboards. "She is there?" I asked.

Hendrik pointed, not at the adjacent room but the wall behind him. There several drawn portraits hung. "Has Margrete told you of our tribe? We are an accomplished people."

I stood to inspect the portraits. The center picture was the largest sketch. Firm, elegant lines formed the fresh, contented face of a woman perhaps ten and six years of age. She wore a thin headband. Her hair flowed down, over a high-collared jacket to curl upon her modest bodice. She held a chess piece in one hand, a bunch of wildflowers in the other. It was Margrete in early maidenhood. That image pulled at me.

"Hendrik made that drawing," said Estrid. "He made all of them."

The encircling drawings presented men, old and young, smooth and bearded, and ladies, proud and dignified. They stared back at me. All seemed certain of their place and destiny, hardly in doubt of future atonement and entry into paradise. What was it like to feel so assured of one's heritage and place in life?

"We are proud Danes," Estrid said. "This is our home. If we must serve the Norwegian, so be it. But I will die before I serve Cristiern. He starves and hates us."

"Fortinbras will be our victor," Hendrik said.

"He will bring Norwegian nobility to *us*." Estrid raised both hands. "*They* will see our Margrete and then..." She glanced at me, and then quickly looked away. "Hendrik, it is like winter still. Add another log. Commoners probably never see such a grand fire, not even in those taverns they frequent. Horatio, you would know—I hear that the sins committed there make the saints weep."

Still standing, I asked, "I must speak with Margrete. I beg you."

Hendrik rose. He regarded me, gestured at the hat I held. "May I?"

I obliged him. Hendrik slowly rotated the hat to test its balance. The excess material in the crown, which I always wore flopped to one side, hung and rolled as the hat revolved. "Good. Could be better. Faded green dye. How old?" He returned my hat to me.

"Fifteen years, I suppose." I took and stroked my hat as if comforting an irritated cat. I set it again on my head.

Hendrik scratched his cheek. "Horatio, another question. Are you a widower?"

At last, Margrete swept into the room. She wore a shimmering, layered gown, likely her father's creation to armor her against men's penetrating eyes. When Margrete saw me, her brow arched with surprise. She draped a blanket around her mother's shoulders and then said to me, "You have come to perform your composition for me privately? Where is your lute?"

"Margrete, I apologize that I'm here to tell you—" I reached for her hand, but she pulled away. She stepped back. Her rejection stung.

"Hendrik," Estrid said, "we should discuss—we do not know his family."

"Horatio," Hendrik asked, "have you a family?" He looked to me but floated a sardonic draught toward his wife.

I could not bear more of this. "People I loved as if my family, yes."

Estrid quickly asked, "Did your people go slovenly to Mass, or were they coffer cheats or incessant borrowers?" She folded her arms as if to shield from me the emerald pendant that lay nestled in the withering sponge of her bosom.

My throat tightened. "No." Turning to Margrete, I said, "We must speak privately."

Margrete turned upon her heel and strode into the adjoining chamber. I followed her.

We stood within a sun-splashed room that contained rows of fabric bolts leaning upright against one wall, a black velvet divan, and a broad table bearing an unfolded bolt of pink silk, a ruler, shears, and a chalk stick. Margrete, arms akimbo, faced me.

I said, "Poul told Fortinbras of my lies, and he destroyed my work, which I had just finished. I can't give him the history I promised. He says he will execute me. I came to warn you. He knows I invented the translation of his document."

Margrete gasped. Her hands covered her face.

I reached for her. "Forgive me." She allowed me to embrace her. "I adore you, but... I have no choice: I must leave immediately."

Margrete pulled back. Her eyes were full. "You can remain in the village. Write Hamlet's story there."

"No. To protect us both, I'll leave Helsingør. I'll find a way to honor Hamlet. How or where, I don't know."

I could not bear to watch her cry. I turned toward the sitting room to leave.

Margrete charged past me and stepped into my path. I stopped. She wiped her eyes. "You will not stay in the province?" Her eyes flashed anger. "Were you true to me in your proclamations of love, Horatio?"

"Of course."

Her folded arms flattened her embroidered bodice. Margrete's scent of citrus blossom was stronger with her heat, but never again would it make me drunken, I believed.

The sun was running its course and pulling time in its wake, burning minutes from my allowance and risking my life. However, I could not leave undefended. "You demanded my purity of heart. I've been true to you."

"Then, determine how you will remain near Helsingør."

"I can't further endanger you, Margrete."

Margrete's face snapped at me. "Negotiate again with Fortinbras." When I stepped back from her, Margrete added, "The man who dishonored me, raped me, and broke our betrothal. He, too, proclaimed love."

I pulled off my hat and ruffled my hair in frustration. "Margrete. I haven't played with your affections. I didn't intend to hurt you."

Margrete's face blanched. "Do not leave Helsingør."

I kissed her hands, caressed her cheek. My fingers trailed down the nape of her neck and stopped at her bodice's hem. Then I cupped her chin in my palm. We kissed fully, tenderly. She pressed herself to me. Her bosom, full and soft. My arms wrapped her, and I pulled her closer.

"Margrete," Estrid called out.

Our embrace broke. Margrete patted her cheeks to calm herself. She went into the sitting room and, over her shoulder, cast me a beseeching glance.

I tugged down upon my tunic and followed her.

Estrid sat straight—cocked chin, piercing eyes, and puffed breast. Hendrik squinted at me like a troubled mole wanting the safety of its burrow. Probably they had overheard our argument.

"Pardon, but I must be—" I began.

"I should not have let you wallow." Estrid shook her finger at her daughter. "I should have made a marriage contract for you. But here we are. A tarnished line is better than none."

I beheld Margrete. She had borne dishonor and evil. I admired her for resilience and perseverance. She had saved herself. I knew that she did not need me as her hero. I also knew that the dwindling sand of the hourglass was pushing me away from her and all of Helsingør.

"Margrete, I must leave." I took her hand, her slender fingers nestled within my palm, and kissed it. "There's nothing else I can do. God be with you and be safe."

Margrete's eyes welled. Her fingers slipped from mine.

My heart rent. I bent to retrieve my bag. Then I slung it over my shoulder and crossed to the door. I turned to look at Margrete. I expected that her face would drip passion. Instead, her visage was as hard as an iron-forged mask.

"If you run from Helsingør," Margrete said, "I will know you are a coward."

"Perhaps I am. I would rather not give Fortinbras reason to kill you or expel your family from Krogen. This way, you may live. Someone will give you the children you want."

Sadness washed over me. I touched my hat to bid farewell. Estrid grinned at me. Hendrik managed only a discouraged frown. I closed the door upon them.

The castle's East Gate, my only certain available exit, seemed remote. I began my trek by charging up Wiglaf Corridor toward the stairwell's yawning mouth. As I neared the steps, to my left the hidden passageway's door suddenly popped open. The gritty scent of musty old wood met me. Into my path stepped Reynaldo of Castile, the man who I had seen carving his initials into Fortinbras's hearth mantle.

In his yellow sleeves and doublet, both trimmed in black, black pantaloons and brimmed hat with yellow plume sitting atop a mass of copper hair, Reynaldo looked every bit the illegitimate spawn of a wasp and an ass. But he was not stupid. Hamlet and I once watched him, at one of Claudius's soirees, deftly crease cards he dealt, enhancing his winnings. He seemed to enjoy pulling men into his debt, shackling them for sport. A nomadic ruffian, his vile ambitions surely ruined many. As a man, he was an artful marvel of ruin.

I passed Reynaldo. His boots flew in step with mine. His full sleeves swung in cadence, and his hat's plume bobbed from side to side—an extreme annoyance. I charged toward the stairway's low arch. "I see you still enjoy dressing like a bee. I've no interest in your gambling traps, Il Bastardo de Castile."

Grimacing, Reynaldo wagged his finger at my accurate insult of his birth. "I…" His Castilian tongue dragged a syllable—*aim*—as he considered his response. "Yellow is the color of good fortune. Of God's favor and happiness. Is it not?"

"Are you here searching for free coins?"

"I search for one thing only."

"Your patron is dead. Why are you still here?"

"Why are *you* here still? Hamlet is dead." I despised Reynaldo's Danish. When he spoke the Hs, he rendered Hamlet's name and mine with an aspirated kick as if hacking spit. He continued, "The English ambassador received gold as his 'thanks.' But I did not. I am owed, but Fortinbras refused to pay me. As for you, the Hamlets no longer need you."

I glanced at Reynaldo only to see his eyes and mouth pull wide in delight. He must have realized that his barb had hit a raw target.

"They do, more than you know," I said.

When we reached the stairwell's arch, Reynaldo grasped my arm, stopping me before I could drop onto the first step. "Where is Lanier?"

Why would I betray Lanier to this scoundrel? I shrugged. "Who?"

Reynaldo's eyes narrowed to slits. He pulled from the back of his hat's outer band a stemmed barrel, from his pocket some flint and a wad of dried leaves. Then he pressed the leaves into the barrel and struck his flint over it. A spark caught, and he puffed on the stem. A bitter smoke seeped from his nostrils—a daemon to his very core.

"What is that wretched stink?"

"I see you like it. Tobacco. Very popular. It is from the Americas."

Waving away the haze, I said, "You're wasting my time. What do you want?"

The barrel glowed in Reynaldo's hand. He drew a breath on the stem. His half-closed eye judged me. "Tell me. Where is that Frenchman hiding?"

"I don't know anyone hiding. Why do you care? Did his patron saint thrash your patron saint?"

Reynaldo's nose puckered as though he smelled a wet goat. He glanced past my shoulder and then aside, as if looking for another hiding place. "I know that you know Lanier. But...you do not know the company you keep." He drew a breath and expelled another smoke stream. "Years ago, after a card game in Madrid, I went to the dock to find Captain Pinzon, bound for America to find spices and gold. With a fraction of those riches I could have bought the Church's permission to return to my native town. The edict had forced us away, but I am not a Jew...my father was. When I joined Pinzon's crew, Lanier also was indentured to Pinzon. That is how we became friends."

Reynaldo's claim that Lanier had trusted him instantly soured his story. My doubt soared.

"But Lanier betrayed my friendship. That rat swine cost me my stipend. I almost died on that island." Reynaldo turned aside and spat at the floor. Then he straightened. "Where is he?"

Heavy boots resounded in the stairwell. Guards? I had to reach the East Gate.

I lurched ahead, but again Reynaldo grasped my arm. "Then, tell me—where is the muniment tower?"

"Why would I tell you that?"

At that moment the noontime bells clanged a summons for the hour of Sext devotions. Several doors along Wiglaf Corridor expelled women, children, and men wearing high collars, tight caps, and long wrist cuffs for modesty. Each carried a *Book of Hours*.

One passing man bumped hard against Reynaldo's shoulder and rambled onward.

Reynaldo grumbled, "A shrinking world expanding with idiots."

Past Reynaldo I saw, mid-distance in the corridor, Fortinbras stomping through the crowd. He was accompanied by the old guard, Marcellus, who held a pike and loped timidly beside him.

Fortinbras pointed menacingly at me.

I darted into the stairwell's mouth and down its winding stone gorge. I heard Reynaldo call after me, "Tell Lanier I am coming for him."

Within an instant I landed within the cool darkness of the castle's main door. I pushed upon its sullen face to slip into the arcade. I ran through courtyard garden. Its drying herbs in the warm sun made hunger twist in me.

At the opposite end of the garden I entered the fortress tunnel and exited onto the killing field. I heard the slap of running feet behind me.

I ran faster.

When I reached the East Gate and guard's tower, I grasped the bars and rattled them until its stone frame seemed to shake. Barnardo stepped from the entrance and stood beside me. "How now, Horatio." He pushed a bony key into the large iron box in the gate.

"Hurry, Barnardo. I am leaving Helsingør."

Barnardo glanced at me from the corner of his eye. He cranked upon the key, turning it. He whispered, "Where are you going?"

"I don't know."

A voice behind me grumbled, "Barnardo, if Fortinbras regains his wits and wants to break bread with any of the mendicants, he can call for me at the Carmelite Priory."

I turned to see Poul. Despite the warm sun, he wore his hood up, perhaps to shield his bald pate. He gripped a bag. He nodded at me as if we were friends. I spat at his feet, and he ignored me.

Barnardo's hand lingered on the gate. "Friar, will the gods ever blunt your tongue?"

"If I cannot be truthful to kings, or about them, who will?"

"Your bag," Barnardo gestured at his sack.

Poul puffed. "Now you are searching us?"

Barnardo took Poul's bag, opened it, and removed Poul's crumpled manuscript. He ruffled the pages and, seemingly satisfied that it did not contain stolen documents, handed the pages to Poul.

While rolling and securing the sheets with thread, Poul said to me, "Forgive my sin against you, Horatio. When the Devil has me by the throat, I rage."

I glared at him.

He sighed and slid his papers into his bag. "Somehow you will memorialize Hamlet. You do not need reports to help you tell his story, or to legitimize your account. You are the authoritative source. Like God's witnesses who recorded divine events for posterity, you are the unique observer of the profound troubles and glory of the Hamlets."

This comparison to the holy authors struck me with awe. Poul was right—I, too, bore the honor and burden of presenting evidence that was dangerous to power.

Poul cinched tight his bag's cord. "God rewards the truth tellers, Horatio." He looked to the guard. "Barnardo, open the gate."

Barnardo pushed upon the bars, and the gate swung ajar, groaning. Poul passed through it first. Again, I bid Barnardo farewell and, with sad relief, exited.

I stood outside the gate, uncertain where to go. From my elevated ground—Krogen stood upon Orekrog Point, jutting into sapphire Øresund Bay—I watched Poul. He walked down the narrow southbound path leading to his white-walled priory, beyond Helsingør Village, which lay curled in the sun like a sleeping cat.

Where should I go, and what should I do? Immediately east was the dock's bare pier. Like a parched tongue it reached to the water. The dock once had hosted noisy barterers. Danes, comfortable in their warm cloaks and boots. Fur-wrapped Swedes and Norwegians. Germanic traders laden with stoles embroidered with their princes' crests. Italians wearing wide, pointed caps and shiny doublets. Frenchmen from southern climes shivering in thin capes. The dock once thrived as it had born the casks and crates brought by Hanseatic traders from Europe's ports. All were gone now because Cristiern's blockade had choked Helsingør.

The bay's sapphire chop and its white shore were peaceful, enticing.

I looked, too, to the distant north. There I saw thick forests of gaunt birch. To the west, beyond the castle, lay a mat of fields that also stretched southward to the village. Above the village's mass of thatched cottages loomed the spire of Saint Olai Church. Its prayer benches were known as friendly to distressed travelers.

I needed God's direction to a destination away from my ordeals. I looked to see that Poul was already far along his path. He neared the village and seemed to be an ant passing other ants upon the trail. I began my downhill plod bound for the church.

The trail I walked was a razor-straight ribbon of dirt cut by peasant feet hastening to and from their place of labor, the Fortress and Castle Krogen. The road was their tether of survival. Helsingørians worked the garden and stables and filled Krogen's workbenches in the masonry, forge, and mills. In exchange, they once enjoyed hunting rights on the surrounding lands two days per month. No animals remained, however, because the nobles had eaten all.

As I trudged down the path I stepped aside for the people. Dogged women. Grimy children. Grizzled, sinewy men in rags. A few suffered from burns or twisted joints. Some on the way hesitated when they saw me—a man who yielded to them, dressed in an embroidered tunic, fine leggings, and a soft, green hat. I greeted them in a saucy tongue shared by lowborn Danes. They laughed with hands raised and cheered my audacity, for all commoners know that, despite our meager homes of mud and straw, we are the heartbeat of the world. We also know that for all the promises made by prideful, greedy sovereigns that waste the populace, we should fear the heartlessness of castles.

I hastened toward the village's cluster of shaggy roofs skirting the outward ring and passed the hulking Carmelite Priory emitting its buzzing chants. The mendicants' boundary wall of piled stones guided me to the base of the spire that towered like a heavenly pike man's spear point. At the churchyard's wooden gate, I pushed through to enter a tomb-crowded yard. Ahead stood the tall arches of Saint Olai's west entrance.

When I pulled upon the heavy door, warmed by the midday sun, it exhaled a mellow scent of burnt wax. I removed my hat and stepped into the church's cavernous nave. Sweet incense met me. I beheld the church's red and black brick walls. They were vented by tall panes of stained glass that scaled to meet gray arches and capstones. Humbled, I looked downward and saw that glowing patches of yellow and pink anointed the stone floor that had been glazed by centuries' flow of contrite, shuffling feet.

Builders' bricks and fresh planks crowded the entrance. I stepped around them to reach the center aisle. The faithful filled three dozen benches facing the priest and the altar. The only available seats were near the front, so there I sat. Upon the altar rested the small reliquary box of Saint Olai's bones. I bowed my head to pray—not to that saint, however. In life he was an ancient Norwegian tribal warrior who, much like Cristiern, had claimed that God willed his rule over all of Iceland, Sweden, Denmark, and Norway.

Instead, I prayed to my patron saint, Niels the Holy, known in life as Niels of Aarss. Pinned inside my hat was my tarnished pilgrimage badge. I rubbed my thumb over the primitive etching of a figure—me, I imagined—kneeling at Saint Niels's tomb. He understood me, I believed, because he had rejected his father's course of life and moved from his home to perform his anointed work. Niels was both a brave Dane and an antique Roman, in his own way.

I asked Niels to intercede for me to God, and for a sign instructing me how to tell Hamlet's story and where I should journey next. Should I return to Wittenberg? I begged for release from my mess of lies and promises. I confessed that my fibs, feeding upon my arrogance and ignorance, had grown large and squeezed me out of Krogen. As a result, I was alone again. I clasped my hands in fervor until they ached.

The far end of my bench crunched. I looked to my right and saw a person wearing a black robe with its hood up. He was seated before the memorial to Saint Olai. His rough hands were piously folded before his face. The robe's hood, broad shoulders, and hem were trimmed with gold braid, like the drawings I had seen of ancient Viking warriors.

Was it Fortinbras? Trembling, I shielded my face with my hat.

When the service ended, the stranger quickly departed through the south door. The congregation flowed down the aisle and out the west door. I sat alone, near the altar, in the quiet sanctuary. I was not ready to leave because I did not know what to do.

Behind me, the west door opened. The nave flooded with light. I turned to see Lanier enter, followed by a peasant woman—a curvy, deliciously sun-bronzed creature. Her black, straight hair brushed her hips. "Sir, the items you requested at the market."

Lanier stopped and turned to face her.

Smiling, she held in her outreached hand a small candle and a tiny red rose made of knotted threads.

"Oh. *Merci*," he said. His tone was as warm as brandy, but his demeanor was as halting as a bitten snake handler.

She moved closer to Lanier, offering the objects in one hand. Her other hand was open, awaiting payment. Into her palm he dropped one coin, then another as if careful not to touch her although he wore his gloves. He plucked the items from her other hand and pocketed them within his cape.

"Anything more, sir?" She waited.

Oh, Lanier. By Venus's name. Soon one of us must find his way to the comfort of a woman's bed. Fortune had not helped me successfully chart that course at Helsingør.

The woman pulled down her bodice, revealing the full plum of her areola. She moved to press herself against him. Lanier pulled back. With a swirl of her skirt, the woman left. Lanier closed his eyes and leaned into the wake of her scent.

A wicked temptress cavorting in the Almighty's house. I stood. "Lanier."

He warily strolled to me. Because of his irked blush I decided against mercy and righteous modesty. "She was ripe for your picking, but you did nothing. To think I took you as my master teacher to learn chivalric courtship."

Lanier confronted my laughter with a stony stare. He pulled his gloves from his hands and folded them into his belt. "Hope is expensive."

"Without hope and persistence, we're like kindling. Spent. Dead."

Lanier looked away, then down at his scuffed boots. "Moses had hope. Then God led him to paradise and refused him entrance. Moses had faith in God, but did God have faith in him?"

"Moses was God's indispensable link, achieving his cause for the Israelites. God wanted him."

"Pah." Lanier collapsed upon the bench. The resounding crunch echoed back to us. "What good is the free will you scholars debate? I come to God, but he will not have me."

"Lanier, why such thoughts?"

"He does not hear my prayers."

"How do you know that?"

Lanier's cutting glance silenced me, but I held him in my sight, struck by the irony that some who are most qualified to enter heaven are haunted so keenly by their sins they cannot imagine their redemption.

His eyes turned dull. "No contracts yet. I fear that Fortinbras will do as he threatened—send me to France for them. But Helsingør's guild master promised to bring some men to me this afternoon at the tavern. They once offered to fight for Claudius, but that imbecile never garrisoned an army." Lanier snorted in disgust. "Today we must have good fortune. If not…maybe one day you and I will journey together, eh?" He smiled at me.

"But never to France?"

His grin flickered but vanished like an extinguished candle. "Not France."

The church door opened, admitting more glaring light. The shriveled priest shuffled up the nave toward us. His slippers scraped the aisle. His brown habit was too large, and his white hair was as delicate as a fading dandelion.

"I arranged to meet the priest. It is time for my devotional." Lanier stood and started toward the cleric.

"I'm leaving Helsingør."

Lanier stopped. He turned toward me. His head jerked back. "Margrete cast you out?"

"Poul destroyed my finished manuscript and told about my fibs. Fortinbras ordered…he will take off my head."

"Ach." Lanier puckered as if to spit. He looked over his shoulder at the slowly advancing priest. "Fortinbras needs soldiers, most of all. Sign a contract with me. He will let you stay."

Me? A warrior like the great Roman solider Horatius Cocles? I scoffed and said, "I must go." Hurt flashed in Lanier's eyes. Regret welled high in me, for I had come to like this Frenchman. I added, "I nearly forgot—Reynaldo is looking for you."

Lanier's eyes narrowed like a hawk's. He rolled his shoulders back. His cask-like breast swelled, enlarging his moderate frame. "Where is that Spanish weasel?"

"I don't know. I last saw him near the stairwell on Wiglaf Corridor. He had come out of the hidden passageway. He said he's coming for you. What does he want?"

"Money. Revenge." Lanier's thumb and forefinger traced his mustache down both sides of his frown. "Nothing else will satisfy him. He stole from our captain. I uncovered his scheme and retrieved the gold. We dropped him at an island."

"Alone?"

"*Oui.*"

"That will make an enemy, surely."

The scraping slippers drew nearer.

I grasped Lanier's forearm in farewell. "Goodbye, Lanier. Thank you for teaching me chivalrous courtship. I hope to never attempt it again."

Lanier laughed. He grasped my arm. "You will return to Wittenberg?"

"Probably." I shrugged. "Perhaps the provost will readmit me. But my absence exceeded his permission."

"Farewell, Horatio." Lanier flashed a grin at me, then turned to face the priest. Lanier took from his cape pocket the small candle and woven rose, and he pressed them into the elderly man's clawlike hand. "My offering. Father, will you also pray for my friend's destiny? He will travel into the Germanic lands."

The priest regarded me. His continuously shaking head released a few white strands of hair that wafted above his head and twisted in a beam of light. "I will not pray for you."

That wretched old bat. His refusal stunned me. Lanier, too, seemed beset. He rubbed his jaw as if struck.

"I will bless your journey. Your prosperity, however... that is a different matter. Pray to learn that you are not the key to your locked destiny. You are only one notch in one tooth of fortune's key." The priest smiled slightly. Then he added, "Take heart, my son. There are many possibilities beyond those you perceive."

That counsel was familiar. My brain's gears spun to locate the original source. Then I recalled—Hamlet, on the killing field, had told me the same. Amazed, I bent against my knees.

The priest patted Lanier's arm, signaling their departure.

When I raised a hand in farewell to Lanier, he replied, "*Bonne chance, mon ami.*"

Together, the men moved beyond the altar toward the arch of an alcove chapel.

I hauled my bag over my shoulder and walked down the aisle. When I reached its midpoint I heard, from the alcove chapel, Lanier cry out, "Condemned and begging forgiveness, oh Lord."

Alarmed at the agonized confession, I turned and darted up the aisle. Beside the alcove entrance, in the wall, lay an engraved block. Chapel of the Dead.

For what sin did Lanier need forgiveness? What guilt pained him? Curiosity beckoned that I advance, but conscience forbade. I whispered,

"Heaven keep you, Lanier."

Turning away, I left behind the shade of the church. I expected that when I pushed past the west doors the sun would blind me. However, the afternoon sky had thickened with the threat of rain. I looked to the heavens and thought that destiny wanted my journey to begin on bleak terms. Solitude's hollow pit sank deeper within my breast.

Because prayer had not illumined my path, I guessed that reason would determine it. I considered my options. A southward road would deliver me to the nearest port but also would likely send me into the midst of Copenhagen's army. However, a northern route would take me to the dock at Gilbjerg in half a day. Somehow, I would earn passage on a ship bound for Rostock and the Germanic provinces. Thus, I looked northward to the trail leading past Krogen.

I beheld a plume of smoke billowing from the castle's towers and rolling into the clouds, dyeing them like dark fleece.

Fire? *Christ's bones.* What destruction, and what of Margrete? I could only envision charred, suffering people like the burning heretics I had witnessed as a young child in our town square.

Insensible of execution, I ran to the East Gate where I dropped my bag and joined two dozen peasants, who had run from their work in the fields. Barnardo opened the bars wide and waved us past the killing field and through the tunnel. Our mob tramped into the courtyard garden. Looking up, we saw the smoke rising from the muniment tower, beside the keep tower. The nobles had formed a queue and were handling buckets of water from the well in the courtyard garden to the vaulted passageway. Margrete was not among them.

I dashed into the castle and peered through the tangy haze at the line of people handling the water. I ran along that queue from the main corridor into the vaulted passageway. Above my head black smoke tumbled across the ceiling's beautiful arches like an upturned, hellish river. It seemed like the suffocating current of the Tiber River that challenged my boyhood hero, Horatius Cocles, or the legendary rapids of the Furious Host, its horse-drawn sleigh carrying Death and sweeping up dead souls from our villages.

Rolling obsidian clouds poured from the counting room's open maw. I ducked into the counting room. Flames leapt across the table, cabinets, easels, shelves—all were fully ablaze except the stone walls. Erik, coughing, flailed an iron spade upon scores of books and scrolls. They were strewn across the floor like gutted, burning fish.

The *Gesta Danorum*. I cried out to Erik, "The muniment room. I'll go upstairs and—"

"Everything's burned," Erik coughed.

Disbelieving that the marvelous collection could not be saved, I raced up the stairs with the rising smoke. The door was open to the muniment room. Inside I saw that the trophies and evidence of the House of Hamlet already had curled into glowing orange flakes and were flying, cinder and ash, throughout the doomed vault. An acrid cloud drifted out of the window. Piles of smoldering embers and metal lay where the towering cabinet matrix of boxes and the wide table and chests once stood. The secure trunk that had cradled the *Gesta Danorum* was only scorched debris with its locking gears half-melted.

This was the carcass of the Hamlets' legacy and memory. I saw the corpses of Hamlet and the royal family lying lifeless upon the dueling square. A searing bubble of vomit cracked in my throat. My head spun.

I wobbled down the stairs into the counting room. Erik was beating his spade against the weakening flames. I had no weapon against the fire. Thus, I tucked my hat into my belt and pulled off my tunic to whip it at piles of burning deeds—all to no avail.

With the small army handling buckets, Erik and I doused the lingering, limp fires in the counting room. The people departed sadly.

Erik wiped his eyes of tears and soot. From his charred, blistering hands the three bony vault keys dangled by their ribbons.

"Is Margrete all right?" I asked, donning my singed shirt.

"The ladies were sent into the tunnels, below the fortress, for safety, near the stables."

Fortinbras would come, would find me. "I have to go."

Exiting the counting room, we stepped into the dim, vaulted passageway. Above, the graceful, interweaving arches now were tinted as gray as a storm. Erik locked the muniment tower door, from habit, I suppose.

I took a few steps toward the corridor but sensed I walked alone. Turning, I asked Erik, "Was it a candle in the counting room that did this?"

"No. I was outside this same door, unlocking it when someone clubbed me." Erik rubbed his head. "Next, Marcellus shook me awake. Said the muniments were burning."

Reynaldo, I recalled, had asked me where he would find the muniment tower. "Did your attacker wear a yellow shirt?"

"I didn't see him. Fukkit damned..." Erik bowed his crinkled, streaked face. "Everything destroyed, and the *Gesta Danorum*, too." Sobbing, he sank to his knees in a puddle upon the wide flagstones.

Urgency to flee tore at me, but I could not abandon the poor man. I reached for Erik, but he would abide no comforting. For a moment, we grieved the cremation of centuries, and I knew: with the Hamlets' muniments ruined, now I was the only remaining source of Hamlet's story. I had to be both a Dane to achieve his memorial and an antique Roman to survive the ordeal. How could I be both?

Rising, I gripped Erik's arm to help him stand. We embraced. I bid Erik goodbye and then dashed to the East Gate before Fortinbras could sense my presence.

There, I retrieved my bag. I decided that I would write Hamlet's story at Leucorea, in Germanic environs safely distant from Helsingør. Perhaps fate would lead me to a patron who would sponsor the means for Hamlet's story to travel the globe.

But before I could embark upon a long return journey to Wittenberg, away from ghosts, women, and tyrants, first…a meal. I was desperate for fish and a tankard of beer. The few kreuzer coins in my belt pouch could buy sustenance. I pulled my hat from my belt, placed it on my head, and struck down the path, bound for Helsingør's village tavern.

IX.

Under a charred afternoon sky, I entered Helsingør village for supper before I would depart for Wittenberg. I passed an outer crust of ragged huts, garbage pits, and empty animal pens, then a section packed with guildsmen's bushy-roofed abodes. When I arrived at the village's secular heart, the commons square, I saw women splitting small logs and men bearing yokes carrying heavy water buckets. There, the tavern squatted beneath its roof of sloping thatch.

Rain began to fall from the heavens in handfuls, tossed by the Lord like an old farmer scattering feed to his chickens. The menacing sky cracked, and the rain fell faster. People dashed for shelter, and I hastened across the square to the tavern. I pulled open the door's grimy hoop latch and ducked inside.

The stench of over-boiled fish and cabbage permeated the large, windowless common room. Men filled the benches and hunched over the tables, devouring the sloppy bowls. Those not feeding sat in groups. Some slapped cards into piles, gambling for goods rather than fight for them. Others sought different sustenance. By the barkeep's cage the cook's maid, a haggard lizard with chin hair, leaned her scrawny hips into the kneading hand of a lust-drunkard reaching up her skirt. I watched them and thought of a finer interlude with Margrete.

Hunger drilled my belly. I wanted a foaming tankard. I went to a small table at the back of the room, sat upon a chair, and dropped my sack of belongings beside me. I asked a passing cook's maid for a bowl of stew and cup of beer, which she quickly brought. I paid her with my last coin and began to eat and drink.

Through the clamor of banging wooden plates and arguing men, I heard the door open, then slam shut. The storm's wind tore through the room. I looked to see Lanier stride into the room followed by Reynaldo, cradling a wrapped bundle in one arm.

"Filthy dog," Reynaldo barked at Lanier.

Lanier wheeled upon Reynaldo, barring his vulpine teeth. "Stop pursuing me."

"Rat monger. You will not rob me this time." Reynaldo spat fury despite the soft flip of his Rs.

"Steal what, you whoring swine?" Lanier felt for the silver crucifix dangling outside his collar. He tucked it inside his shirt.

"I will drag your carcass into the French court," Reynaldo said. "King Louis will kill you."

Instantly, Lanier punched Reynaldo's sneering face. The Spaniard's nose flushed a stream of blood down his shirt and doublet.

Reynaldo cried out. His plumed hat fell, releasing his flame of hair. It flared like a snake's hood. He spat blood at Lanier and then, groaning, cupped his face with one hand. His other hand clutched the bundle. "Burgundian witch."

When Reynaldo blew thick blood from his nose, men at the

nearby tables laughed at him. Reynaldo smirked at Lanier, "You are a homeless tramp working for the Norwegians. You are not a true Frenchman." Then Reynaldo's grin peeled like chaff burning from its stalk. "The House of Valois will have your severed head, and I will have the bounty for it. I will be rich, and Louis will have justice for two murders."

Lanier grasped an empty tankard from a table and cocked his arm, but before he could hurl that weapon a crash at the door sent a chill rolling over us. Everyone looked to the tavern portal.

Eight men wearing helmets stood with their backs to the shut door. They gripped clubs and swords. One soldier, leather-clad and mail-breasted, braced a hand cannon against his hip. From the weapon's underbelly hung a long, slow-burning cord, its tip glowing. Its master's square face and iron helmet seemed to have been hammered in the same forge. Beside him, arms folded across his robed breast, was the hooded devotee of Saint Olai I had seen at the church.

I ducked under the table and peered over its top. *Fortinbras came for me*, I thought. *He has found soldiers. I'll be captured and punished.* My heart pounded my breastbones.

"Men of Helsingør, behold your king," the cannon bearer called out to the grumbling throng.

The cloaked man pulled back his hood, revealing an angular, blond visage. It was not Fortinbras. I did not recognize this man.

A drunken cleric called out from his seat, "If you are the King of the Danes, Cristiern, why are you starving your subjects?"

Cristiern had arrived. I had no weapon. I nearly wet myself. I crouched deeper in hiding and barely peered above the table.

"You and your general burned my people at the Castle of Alvsborg," the cleric added.

Cristiern spoke to the man holding the hand cannon, "Willem, we became brothers that day."

Willem grinned in response. From his belt hung a sword, a vine elegantly engraved along its blade. Its hilt was fashioned in magnificent twists.

The cleric stood. "You say you care for all people of the Kalmar Union, but your sins against the Swedes are heinous. Come with me to the church and beg God's forgiveness."

"Sit down. Do not abuse my patience," Cristiern told him. He removed his robe. He wore mail and leather. Covering his breastplate was Copenhagen's royal standard—three blue lions and nine red hearts upon a yellow field.

When Willem said to the soldiers, "You men, take all the beer for yourselves," four soldiers strode into the barkeep's cage. Each hoisted a cask upon his shoulder and carried it out the door. The proprietor watched helplessly. Not one man attempted to resist them.

Cristiern solemnly addressed the crowd. "This is a good beginning. Because I love my subjects, I have come to tell you directly—to warn you—that you will serve no monarchs other than the House of Oldenburg."

From the back of the room a man called out, "We will never renounce Old Hamlet. He was a splendid warrior, a great king."

Rage simmered in Cristiern's face. "Old Hamlet was a criminal. He attacked my garrison while I was posted as Norway's governor."

The same man responded, "The House of Oldenburg is weak."

The crowd was as still as stone.

Cristiern replied, "Fool. My father gave away his power to

Copenhagen's merchants and clerics. I have rectified that." He stepped closer to the crowd. "Every man and woman of Helsingør is a traitor for supporting the Hamlets."

The people shrank from Cristiern. A few stumbled and fell.

He continued, "Helsingør is the last remaining parcel of Denmark to unify *my* kingdom. I have had enough of usurpers. First the Hamlets. Now, Fortinbras. He is deluded. He may be Norway's prince, but I rule Norway as the Kalmar Union's monarch. He will not keep Helsingør, and he will not take the Union." He flung his arms wide. "I have decimated Fortinbras's army. I will take back everything that the Hamlets stole. And I hear that today my spy Reynaldo burned the pretenders' muniments. Marvelous."

Reynaldo stood nearby, only two arm lengths away, pressing a bloodied cloth to his nose. The fire's culprit was Reynaldo—I was correct. That Spanish whore-slave.

I quit my hiding place and, glancing about, saw an unguarded meat knife lying upon a nearby tabletop. I leaned slowly to grab it and then, holding the knife low, I moved behind Reynaldo.

Cristiern regarded the crowd. His sight rested on me and seemed to calculate something.

I froze. In my palm I cupped the knife's handle, hid it within my sleeve.

The crowd began to churn.

"Reynaldo, where are you?" Cristiern called out.

"*Aqui, mi señor*," came Reynaldo's nasal reply. He dabbed his swollen, crimson face.

With chin raised, Cristiern asked, "Did you find the *Gesta Danorum*?"

The ancient book survived?

Astonished, I watched Reynaldo unfold the bundle to reveal the wood cover that shielded tales more magical than prayer, more priceless than our most holy relics. Sight of the renowned treasure made the crowd gasp. Their raised hands reached for it as Reynaldo pushed past them to deliver the *Gesta Danorum* to Cristiern.

Cristiern declared, "The most famous record of Danish history and legends. All the people will share in it."

In disbelief that Cristiern would yield the book for good will, I clenched my knife tighter.

Smiling broadly, Cristiern caressed the cover's notched title. "The *Gesta Danorum* is the soul of Danish glory. It teaches us the merit of Danish courage and might, proves that Christ and the gods favor Denmark." He lifted the book for all to admire. "Old Hamlet stole our ancient treasures. I will bring those trophies back to Copenhagen, for the glory of all Danes."

The soldiers cheered with some in the crowd. Willem and Cristiern each drank from a cup of beer.

"Reynaldo," said Cristiern, "did you fight a legion of dragons to rescue this book?"

"I bested all of Krogen's guards, Your Highness, and the muniments keeper, a stupid troll." Reynaldo cackled, grating and flat.

Lanier leaned against my shoulder. He whispered, "Lay down the knife."

"Reynaldo must be rewarded."

"True. But why now?"

The *Gesta Danorum*, that lovely tome suffering in Cristiern's greedy hands. The thought sickened me, but then my imagination began to spark. I recalled seeing in the *Gesta Danorum* the scribes' writing squeezed between lines and within its margins. What if Hamlet's story was added in that volume in such a way? Would that be like defacing Holy Scripture?

Lanier peeled his bloodied gloves from his thick hands and turned them inside out to polish his gold rings. "Stay here," he muttered. "I know how to talk to swine. It is my special talent." He took a step toward Cristiern.

Before Lanier could confront him, I called out, "What will you do with the *Gesta Danorum*?"

Cristiern clamped the book under his arm. He squinted through simmering fury. "I declare to all assembled that I will add the truth about the wickedness of Old Hamlet, my thieving cousin Gertrude, and their mad son. I reclaim Helsingør for the one, true Danish crown."

Such lies, I thought.

That was the moment I realized, with stark clarity as if I had seen a fireball streak across the night sky, that a well-crafted legend could preserve Hamlet for all time. Hamlet's story could be an epic one if I adjusted names and circumstances to fit the ancient world of the sacred *Gesta Danorum*. Who would know that it was not also the work of Saxo Grammaticus's monks three centuries ago? In this way crucial truths about Hamlet and his cause would not evidence my treason against Cristiern. When his suspicious censors inspected the book, they would not recognize the trick, and I would remain anonymous and protected. It would be my most daring lie. I would do what I must in order to achieve my promise honoring my friend.

Cristiern added, "I will send the book to even the lowest of Danish villages so that the people will know their history as it happened, not as liars would tell it."

No, I thought. I would carry the book and be Hamlet's storyteller. My idea emboldened me. I could not curb my incensed tongue. "We'll honor our loved ones and heroes as we choose."

"We will honor worthy Danes. Do we fight as our legendary Viking warriors fought?" Cristiern grimaced. "No. We have been weak but no more. We Danes must not surrender to the corruption of Europe."

Willem said of me, "My lord, that mongrel obviously was raised by a bitch dog who didn't teach him proper respect." Then he demanded, "What is your name?"

Reynaldo replied, "That is Horatio, Hamlet's friend." He distorted our names with his detestable aspirated kick.

Cristiern cocked his head with exaggerated surprise and delight. "Truly?" When he stepped toward me, cradling the *Gesta Danorum* within one arm, the crowd separated, making a clear path between us.

I hid my knife behind my back, within my cuff. I knew I mustn't kill a king, a grave sin against God. However, I would defend myself against those soldiers.

Cristiern approached slowly. "How could you have been Hamlet's friend? You allowed him to die." Cristiern stood before me. His pitying stare melted into a satisfied grin. "You were no friend to Hamlet."

Stinging, I replied, "You know nothing about it."

"I know more than you think." Cristiern smiled. "Due to my tenacious spy. But I need no agent, Horatio, to know that Hamlet would have been a terrible soldier. He could not have defended Krogen from me. He was too soft, too much a philosopher. How did you know the pretender prince?"

"We met at university."

"Schoolboys," he mocked. "Well...Hamlet could not have earned glory."

In my trembling hand, the knife's handle was slippery. I gripped it tighter behind my back. The crowd jostled.

"You knew Hamlet well." Cristiern regarded me, eyes narrowed. "Horatio, by killing you I would remove the last witness to the Hamlets that the people might believe. However, your testimony is precisely what I want. Do not gawk at me. You heard me aright. You will write of Hamlet as that limp example of a Dane. Help me correct the affections of those in Helsingør and the northern provinces."

Cristiern hefted the *Gesta Danorum*. "I command you to write a codicil to this book. Testify to Hamlet's madness, his family's ruin, and the consequences of acting against one's king, God's most anointed. I will have storytellers read the history to those who have yet learned to do so, although I provided for them to learn to read their scriptures. Once the people realize that they might have been ruled by a mad king of Helsingør they will thank Christ and the Virgin for Cristiern the Second."

"You want only to fashion your own legend. I won't be your scribe," I said.

Cristiern looked to the ceiling, eyes wide as if beholding a grand vision. "The people will be inspired. United and filled with fervor for Danish glory, they will fight for Denmark's everlasting lordship of the Kalmar Union." He looked to me. "You should thank me, Horatio. Scribes' work is the closest you will ever come to being a warrior."

A grumble at this affront rose from the men, but none dared move.

Such pride and arrogance, I thought bitterly of Cristiern as I beheld the gold trim of his robe. But then a scheme occurred to me. I could best this king and gain traction on my promise to Hamlet. My spirits brightened. I knew what I must do.

"Perhaps you are correct, sire," I said, kindlier than I felt. "I will be your scribe. May I acquaint myself with the legends, peruse the volume?" I reached to receive it.

"Sire," Willem said with a shake of his head. "Reconsider. Hamlet's friend is no more trustworthy than the pretenders themselves."

Cristiern looked to me. His jaw squared. "You advise me well, Willem." Cristiern approached me. The book lay within his forearm. "We will take you prisoner to Copenhagen. From my dungeon you will write the truth about Hamlet and his traitorous parents."

"I surrender," I lied and let my knife, held behind my back, slide down my fingers so that Lanier might relieve me of it. I felt his hand take the blade. Then I lunged at the *Gesta Danorum* and tore it from Cristiern's arms.

The crowd raged and swirled like a tide and pushed me backward, away from Cristiern, as if urging me away. Cristiern staggered, slack-jawed. His astonishment at my bold move delighted me.

I turned and ran toward the door. Midway there, a soldier stepped into my path. He waved his club menacingly. I could not determine which of his crossed eyes looked most directly at me. He swung at me and missed.

"Stand at attention." Willem's raspy bark. I looked over my shoulder and saw him swing the hand cannon in my direction as Lanier pushed men aside to reach me and the door.

The crowd roiled in panic. Like a raging current it swelled and pitched.

Cristiern, a crimson-faced tempest, bellowed, "I will not be bested by a commoner. Surrender that book, or I will kill you. You are to blame for death today." He gave Willem a signaling nod.

Willem grasped the hand cannon's dangling, slow-burning cord and pushed its glowing tip into a side hole in the weapon's barrel. With the hand cannon's loud crack, a man beside me tore open and fell. People cried out and scrambled for any shelter. Soldiers wielded their swords and leapt at the throng. Willem poured powder into the hand cannon's mouth and fired it again. Another man next to me collapsed, gutted and squirming.

Where's Lanier? I could not leave him among the crushing, anguished mob. He, however, found me and pushed me onward. "*Allez, allez.*" I forgot my bag and, lurching ahead, careened into the wide haunches of a man lumbering ahead of me. I fell onto my back. One soldier bent to pry the *Gesta Danorum* from my arms. I kicked him in the face, then clambered to my feet, still gripping the book. I saw another soldier raise a club to swing at the back of Lanier's head. When I called out to Lanier, he bent low and avoided the downward-sailing bludgeon. The hand cannon's volley shot past him, the iron ball shattering an overturned table next to me as well as a man behind it. Lanier, still crouching, slashed the knife's blade at his attacker's unguarded flesh behind the knee. The stabbed soldier howled.

Then a yellow streak—Reynaldo—passed us. I wrenched the knife from Lanier's hand and lunged at Reynaldo, swiping at him. My point caught his arm. He cried out but continued his flight, over bodies and through the puddling bile and urine, to the door.

One more soldier stood at the threshold. He permitted Reynaldo, Cristiern's spy, to bang open the door. Reynaldo scrambled out and into the rain.

Lanier and I charged, through the muck and the wounded, at that last soldier blocking our exit path. Lanier dashed ahead of me. When the soldier swung his sword in a downward arc, Lanier spun to avoid it, then gripped the sword's hilt and yanked it upward, butting the pommel into the soldier's face. I followed by jamming my knife into his neck as we passed. Again, I slipped on spilled blood and fell. Lanier gripped my tunic and, with unusual strength, pulled me backward to the door. My boots found traction on broken teeth. We burst out, into the storm.

Rain gusted across the square. Soldiers dragged corpses from the tavern into a pile. More soldiers on horseback surrounded dozens of women and children bound by jangling chains. The captives trudged in a line toward the southbound road. Souls were vanishing from Helsingør like fading shadows.

One soldier called out to us, "Buy before the pirates get them."

Horror for these innocents, shackled for slavery and carnal debauchery, cinched my gut. I slowed, but Lanier, running beside me, prodded. "Must warn Fortinbras."

Lanier and I dashed up the knob's trail toward the fortress's East Gate. Lanier's arms pumped for speed. I struggled to match his pace while hugging the *Gesta Danorum* to protect it.

Wittenberg and distance were no longer my purpose. I was determined to alert Margrete and the nobles that Cristiern's attack had begun. I accepted that Fortinbras might punish me for my return to Krogen. Or, I hoped, perhaps he would agree that a scribe's work is a worthy part, akin to that of a warrior and deserving of some mercy.

X.

Lanier and I rattled Krogen's East Gate until Barnardo lazily admitted us. We dashed through the killing field and tunnel to arrive, puffing for breath, in the courtyard garden. There we were surprised to find Krogen's men and women assembled, resting from battle practice, within the surrounding arcade. The men, slumping, held their pikes, longswords, crossbows, or longbows. The women rubbed their wrists and picked at raw blisters. They didn't know the depth of their enemy's wickedness or the nearness of his threat.

Margrete, trim in a tapered cream frock and cap, stood with the women. She saw me running with Lanier across the garden toward Fortinbras where he paced before the men. Her lips parted and her countenance rounded in surprise. She did not smile but slowly raised an open hand in greeting. I waved slightly. Did she welcome my return?

Fortinbras called out to the nobles, "The rain will stop soon, and we will resume practice."

Lanier and I, panting, bowed before him. "Majesty," I began.

Fortinbras wheeled upon me. "You dared flee my command and

now expect pardon?" Fortinbras grasped his gilt-trimmed sword and drew it from its scabbard.

Cringing, I blurted, "Cristiern has decimated the village. We saw him murder all of the men. He took the women and children as slaves."

Fortinbras hesitated. When the nobles' prattle grew to hollering racket, he said to them, "Copenhagen has arrived, in the flesh, at Helsingør, but we will prevail." Then he released his blade into his scabbard and leaned to Lanier. "Where is his army?"

"We do not know, *mon seigneur*."

"Christ's holy blood," Fortinbras sputtered. "Our only defense is a few battle drums, some old Italian guards, and an armory filled with dull weapons. I need soldiers. Lanier, by Saint Olai's soul, you are to blame."

Lanier scratched his cheek beneath his twitching eye.

Fortinbras pounded his fist. "That blasted Dane knew he could take the village. There must be a spy."

"Reynaldo of Castile," I said. "The Spanish reward whore. I saw him as I was leaving Krogen."

Fortinbras flared like a bonfire. "He had no business here." Cranking upon his sword's hilt as if turning the levers of the rack, Fortinbras added, "I know a devil's minion when I smell him. I refused his request for audience."

Margrete stepped forward. She gave me a wan smile but approached Fortinbras. She said, "The murder of your people is a profound offense against Your Majesty. By killing your subjects Cristiern has denied you tax monies. He has claimed your village as his property. You have seen us devotedly learn to battle. We will fight for you."

Fortinbras stared sullenly at Margrete. Upon her bosom rested a necklace of amber, silver, and gold. Her fingers caressed the chain. She moved nearer to him. "It is beautiful. A gift from my family. A reminder of the gods' perseverance." He regarded her hungrily.

To distract Fortinbras, I held out the bundled volume. "Your Highness, I recovered this treasure for you, stolen by—"

A sudden blast sounded from the east. A large stone ball sailed over the ramparts into the courtyard garden where it smashed into an arcade column. Above that collapsed mound of brick, a crack shot up the wall into the astrological clock. The gold dials and blue rings split and fell onto the garden.

The people screamed and scattered across the brown garden, crying out, "King Fortinbras," and, "Save us."

A second shot from the east soared a wondrous arc, higher than the first. It dropped among us and, with a sickening squash, pulverized two men.

Everyone dashed about. Four young women and men, wailing, tended to the dead. A dozen men ran up the garden's turret stairs to the ramparts to pack powder into the cannon. Others strung arrows onto their bows, no longer pretending war.

Amid the chaos, Fortinbras stood with a single arm raised. "Hold. This is not Cristiern's full attack. We must not waste our munitions. He means to intimidate us, to gain the advantage for his envoy's negotiations. Everyone, return to the arcade and wait for me." He turned to Lanier. "Come."

I followed as well, hugging the book tightly, as they bounded up the turret stairs, against the descending flow. We stepped onto the rampart's lane.

Fortinbras leaned between the merlons to observe the bay. His hand shielded his eyes against the sun's slicing edge to observe our enemy. His breastplate blazed. "Holy Mother," he said.

To the east a single ship rested upon the flashing horizon. A vertical stream of smoke spiraled above it. Fortinbras said, "Incredible range. Must be a von Steyr bombard. Cristiern must have a magnificent purse to own that weapon."

Then we saw that a distant band of gray helmets and shields stretched along the horizon but for the bay. Some long standards flew upon posts. A few mangonel catapults and battle carts bore cannons.

The sight bled strength from my legs. "Cristiern is moving swiftly against us."

"They stand beyond our cannon's reach." Fortinbras spat at our foes. "Cristiern calculated his shots for minimum damage and maximum display. He wants the castle intact. That means we have a chance to best him. We must rally the people."

We dashed down the turret stairs to the courtyard garden. Fortinbras moved among the nobles, his fist raised. "Cristiern wants to seize your home. If he attacks us, he will lose. Krogen will stand, and we will be the victors. Although Cristiern's envoy will come, nothing will justify our surrender. We will fight him. We will triumph."

"We are not yet soldiers," a man replied.

Another man, broad-shouldered and hawk-nosed, standing before me, muttered to those surrounding, "Should we be ruled by a Norwegian? Let us surrender and be subject to a Dane."

To quell treasonous debate, I called out to the nobles, "As Hamlet died, he spoke his favor of Fortinbras."

An old man behind me grumbled, "Not since ancient days has a Norwegian meant good for Helsingør."

Margrete raised her hands to the mob. "We will continue our

preparations, learn to fight, and defend our home. In Fortinbras we have a king who loves us, as the Hamlets did." She shot a simmering glance at Fortinbras, which he, surveying the crowd, seemed to ignore.

A woman, her face creased and snowcapped, stood before Fortinbras. She gripped her brocade shawl about her shoulders. "Cristiern may have killed village peasants, but he is not evil. Cristiern is a patron of the Church. He made the guilds easier to join. He educates low people to read the scriptures. Cristiern does not hate us. If we obey him, we will live in peace."

Fortinbras raised his chin and smirked. "Cristiern wants to draw us into the fields and kill us quickly so that he can preserve this castle for toll collection. He does not intend to forgive or safeguard you."

The crowd rumbled. I felt I was in the center of a steaming pot.

A tall, bearded man replied, "A Danish king will show us mercy."

"Cristiern will not spare us," I said. "Lanier and I witnessed his attack at the tavern. He declared that all of Helsingør are traitors for supporting the Hamlets, that we will be the sacrificial example to peoples throughout the Kalmar Union."

Angry curses crackled from the mob like hot oil. A young man, lean and smooth, his voice wavering, called out, "We suffer because Odin is angry. We can find an animal to sacrifice, can we not?" Many grumbled at this blaspheme, but some cheered in bold agreement.

At the crowd's outer ring, a red-faced man, cupping his hands to his mouth, replied, "We have no animals to slaughter but horses. We are eating the last of the salted rations now. Let us butcher the horses to eat them, not sacrifice."

A young woman said, "The gods never forgive without blood." She looked to the full moon rising early in the late-afternoon sky.

Fortinbras commanded, "No one will kill the horses. We may need them in battle."

Beside me, Lanier flipped his cape hem over his shoulder in apparent irritation. I saw, stitched onto the lining, the tiny sown rose he had offered at the Chapel of the Dead. He rapped on the cover of the book I held. I realized his meaning—I held a magical tool and I must use it.

I called out to the throng, "Behold"—I held high the ancient tome for all to see—"the sacred register of our greatness, of our tribes' sacrifices and glory. The *Gesta Danorum*."

The crowd gaped and shuffled. Some called for Erik to confirm my claim.

Fortinbras, brows raised in apparent surprise, regarded me. "It did not burn?"

"The spy who burned the muniments also stole the *Gesta Danorum* and presented it to Cristiern," I said. "But I took it from Cristiern." I turned to Fortinbras and added, "It's one more trophy you can deny him."

Fortinbras's eyes narrowed, and he grinned at me. That was, I felt, an encouragement, and so, turning again to the people, I continued. "This book empowers us with every reason and all the strength we need to defend Helsingør and Castle Krogen. We must not surrender to Cristiern's ambition. Our history, our legacy, our honor is at stake."

A smattering of cheers grew into a galloping applause. A few hollered, "Defend Krogen," and, "Down with Copenhagen."

Margrete went to the pile of brick, once a column, and the two bodies attended by the four shuddering nobles. She touched their shoulders in sorrow. I followed. She offered her hand so that I might help her climb upon the broken mass she would use as a dais. The mob pivoted and gathered around us. Her necklace shone, and her voice was as clear as a chime when she declared to the people, "We must have faith in our strength. Our clans are forged as one in common purpose. Today we shed the cloak of chivalry and don the armor of war. All who hear of our battle will know we are Helsingørian Danes. They will know it as our story. Our cause will be forged into memory, a golden chain across the ages. The Hamlets and the people of Krogen will not be the last link in that chain. Those coming after us will be inspired by our courage and glory, and they will build our legacy onward."

By the Virgin Mother. I had never heard a lady speak in such a way before. That she could do so was depraved, unnatural, and wickedly enticing.

The people bellowed in response. Some cried, "Praise to Almighty God," and "Praise to the Holy Mother." The crowd swelled, buoyed by hope.

Margrete looked down to me. "You have returned. Do you intend to remain with us?"

I wanted to kiss her pressed lips, ease her doubts. "I will," I said, "if Fortinbras will allow it."

Fortinbras looked away.

The hawk-nosed man called out to his peers, "We are the people of Krogen, of Old Hamlet. This is our native home. We will not fall. Even if the enemy digs into our tunnels, we will meet him and smoke him out."

Fortinbras raised his fist again. This time half of the crowd raised theirs in union. When the hawk-nosed man joined and roared to the crowd, "For Helsingør, for honor—we will be the worthy victors," more clenched hands rose.

Hendrik reached for Margrete, helped his daughter step down

from the debris. His box-shaped hat fit snuggly, framing his brow and resolute, round eyes. Margrete stood before Hendrik. He held her hands and said, "We own this ground. We will never be Cristiern's subjects."

"I understand, Father."

Estrid hooked one arm around her husband's elbow. She regarded her daughter with a slight smile of approval. Then, she straightened Margrete's necklace.

Next, Fortinbras climbed upon the debris mound to address his army. "We will not surrender. Like the Israelite against the giant, we will slay our enemy with stones if we must. We will feed rubble to him and he will choke upon it."

The crowd howled approval.

I dared to move near Fortinbras. He looked down to me and scowled. "I should hang you."

"Highness," I said, "Cristiern wants to use this manuscript, the *Gesta Danorum*, to inspire an army to defend his reign over the Kalmar Union. He ordered me to write into it lies about you, and about Hamlet. He wants to print and send it throughout Europe. Of course, I refused."

Fortinbras grumbled, "He could do the same by issuing a treatise. No way to stop it."

"No one will clamor to hear that... but legends? Those feed the people's appetite for heroes. I can ensure that we counter any such sniveling gossip. For posterity and to thwart Cristiern, I will write your story and Hamlet's into the *Gesta Danorum*."

Fortinbras's head jerked in surprise. "Write it into a hallowed text?"

"It is unfinished. The margins are filled with scribes' notes."

Fortinbras climbed down from the brick mound. "I need every defender." He rubbed his face with his hand and muttered, "God help me. I must use a scholar for a soldier's work." Then Fortinbras regarded me. "Write about me and your prince, but foremost you will defend this castle alongside our swordsmen."

I calmly nodded my understanding and knelt in thanks to my patron saint Niels.

"You are welcome. Now rise," Fortinbras told me.

Such arrogance, I thought, though I did so.

Fortinbras raised a hand to command silence. He called out, "The enemy will present an ultimatum for our surrender. Most likely, tomorrow Cristiern's envoy will arrive to negotiate those terms. I will deny them. Surely, then, we will be at war. Without Helsingør, Cristiern will not own the whole of Denmark. Without the whole of Denmark, Cristiern will not own all of the Kalmar Union." He pointed to the tunnel and the killing field beyond. "Battle practice will resume immediately. Make your weapons ready."

The people cheered and moved toward the tunnel.

Next, Fortinbras turned to Lanier and said, "When Cristiern attacks he will do so with full force and a pure conscience. He will believe he allowed us enough time to surrender or confess our sins before death." He grumbled, "We no longer have time or hope to hire mercenaries."

Lanier looked down to his boots. He wiped his nose with his gloved hand. "*Oui, mon seigneur.*"

I silently prayed, *Almighty God, send a maelstrom to wipe Cristiern's army from their camps into the sea.*

While Fortinbras and Lanier went to the killing field, I went to my chamber to deposit the *Gesta Danorum*. Then, I proceeded to the killing field to join our army of nobles.

I saw that seventy-five women and men were with Fortinbras in teams along the interior length of the outer wall. Each gathered at a ladder propped against the elevated wooden walkway lining the wall and its murder holes. At Fortinbras's command, the men climbed up to the walkway and practiced aiming crossbows and emptying buckets down the holes onto our enemies' heads. The women, on the ground, Margrete among them, threw stones into buckets and piled firewood beside caldrons of boiling water. They clamped filled buckets onto ropes they hoisted by pulleys up to the walkway. Fortinbras also barked at twenty men situated high above, on the ramparts atop the inner fortress wall. They primed cannons which, wedged between the merlons, poked out from the battlements at the enemy. Atop the ramparts, our novice archers, the strongest among us, drew and aimed their massive longbows.

Concurrently upon the killing field, to the right of the gatehouse, Lanier led fifty men in combat practice in the fortress's shadow. That was my assignment, and I joined them. We used pikes, curved messer blades, and shields to slash at foliage-filled sacks. Lanier taught us to handle the longsword. He was the only man there worth a kreuzer for his ability. Lanier spun and swung his flat, heavy blade in double-handed arcs to each side and over his head without being trapped by his cape. He demonstrated how to change grip on the handle without sinking the point in the dirt. We awkwardly imitated his actions. I understood better now why Fortinbras had wanted mercenaries.

Within two hours we were allowed respite. The men suspended activity. I went to find Margrete. She had remained at her team's rock pile, laboring while the others sat upon the grass.

Margrete bent to fill another bucket with stones. Across her bosom swayed her necklace of amber, gold, and silver, which, I realized then, was much like Goddess Freyja's fabled necklace, Brisingamen. I beheld Margrete's grime-streaked face and saw that one of her sleeves had been torn away. Battle practice had not been kind to her.

I stood at her side, picked up some stones, and dropped them into her filling bucket. She smiled meekly at me and said, "This is harder work than it seems."

"You are allowed a moment of rest, *mes amis*." I looked over my shoulder to see Lanier walking toward us, a pike resting across his broad shoulder. "I suggest you enjoy it."

Margrete straightened. Grimly she said, "Let us go to the ramparts to see what remains of my native village."

We climbed the turret stairs to the rampart and stood in its broad lane. From that elevation we saw that flames ravaged Helsingør Village. A sudden, southern breeze brought the sharp stink of corpses.

Margrete gripped her stomach as she surveyed the damage. She was as pale as the pearl earring she wore. "Why are men so cruel?"

Margrete had suffered because of a wicked man's attack. As I watched her view the landscape, my heart broke for her, and hatred for her attacker welled in me.

Lanier rubbed his face as if fatigued. "*Mademoiselle*, not all men sin with intent."

"The man who raped me intended his crime."

"But the man who killed my wife did not."

We both gasped. Margrete asked, "Who killed her, Lanier?"

"I did." Lanier's feet shuffled, perhaps seeking solid ground. "I found my wife bedded by another man, in my home. I was enraged and could not think. Collette stepped into the fight. My knife, accidentally…" Lanier wiped an eye. "I killed him. Collette died three days afterward."

To respect his privacy, I looked away, to the fading sky cradling orange-rimmed clouds.

Continuing, Lanier said, "My shamed family paid the town council and church for the burials and crosses mounted, as required, outside my door. What money they had left they dropped into the executioner's pocket to permit my disappearance. I escaped France, but the dead bastard's family knew the king's aunt. King Louis, full of hate for his ancestor's murder by my family, declared a bounty on me."

Lanier's sins relived and grieved every day were a prison I knew too well. I shuddered.

He stepped closer to Margrete, and they beheld one another. Lanier—rumpled in black, accented with ancestral crests of his sullied family. Margrete—elegant in bearing despite her torn frock and grubby face. Their unwavering stare was as straight as a mason's level. Lanier said, "I deserve punishment for my crime."

"You are honest," Margrete said.

Lanier reached inside his shirt for his silver crucifix. He patted it against his breast. He stepped back and asked, "How did you bear the pain of your dishonor?"

"Gertrude helped me and talked with me when my mother could not." Margrete looked to the curling stream of smoke. "War is coming. Our days ahead will be difficult. But personal honor sometimes justifies death." Then, she turned to me and leaned close. "I heard that you fought the flames in the muniment tower. You are not a coward." Her pursed lips betrayed a slight smile. I took in her citrus scent and longed for her.

I said, "Before war begins, I must finish writing Hamlet's story into the *Gesta Danorum*."

Margrete covered her face with her hands. "I suppose that you do not intend to write Fortinbras's story into the account, that you lied to him again."

I looked away to the bay, tinted silver under the sunset, and said nothing. The silhouettes of three ships rested upon the horizon.

We returned to combat practice and swung double-edged blades in darkness—because Fortinbras claimed that any blasted fool could fight in daylight. Servants brought some food for a brief belated supper in the moonlight. People grabbed at the stale rye bread and scrawny grilled herring. Amid this bedlam, I took a small chunk of bread and three fish, and then slipped away to my chambers.

I knelt wearily beside my table, where my *Book of Hours* lay untouched, and prayed from my heart: *Niels the Holy and Blessed Virgin, intercede for me. May Christ ease Hamlet's spirit to lasting rest. When Odin's Furious Host, his soaring sleigh drawn by thundering hooves, claws the sky, let it harvest Hamlet's soul for the Hall of the Slain. Almighty, I beg you: bless my work, may it triumph over silence that would deny Hamlet's cause. Amen.*

My day's labor was not yet finished. I lighted my lamp and set the *Gesta Danorum* upon my table. Lifting its cover, I saw that the pairs of crinkled pages lay as beautiful as the wings of a resting butterfly.

Where would I insert Hamlet's story?

The volume's edges felt ragged as I thumbed the pages, reading to learn the book's exquisite manner of narration so that I might match it. I peered eagerly into this world of tribes, gods, and codes that my forefathers believed would make them exalted and immortal. The shaggy-browed past spoke to me of battles and warriors bearing such names as Alrec, Sciold, Horwendill, and Athisl. It described practical matters. Ancient laws of marriage and inheritance, procedures of oaths and burials, voyagers' rights, and ways to collect tributes. In my imagination, legions of fur-clad, belted men carried their shields into battle and, robbed of their lives, were carried to their graves upon those same boards. Monsters hunted men, and men tracked riches and bludgeoned one another. Clans pledged blood honor so they might rise above the pyres of their dead to justify the terror of a life too punishing and glorious to be ruled by one religion. My brain filled with the cadence and language of a bygone and fantastical world.

I imagined the gnarled hands of the authoring monks scrawling their assigned passages. The insistent Saxo Grammaticus loomed over their shoulders, directing as they folded facts into legends. Those were my brothers now.

A few pages with spacious margins beckoned. That was my beginning place. I adjusted the hood of my lamp to cast more light. My quill, rolling between my fingers, felt lighter as it awakened. I stared at the runes' crafted trunks and elegant tails. What would I write, and how could my work compare to the ancient ingenuity of old Saxo's scribes? From a pocket of memory came a reminder. *The moment to act, be it now or to come, depends upon your readiness to be worthy of your part.* I did not chide myself for imaging Papa's voice—it advised me well. I so missed his teasing grin and mimicry. His spark of humor and nose-crinkled laugh. His consuming seriousness and jesting spontaneity. I still needed Papa's well-tuned, acute ear that heard more in me than I heard in myself.

"Lies destroyed the House of Hamlet." Those words—they were Papa's voice. Was his spirit there with me, or did I imagine it? What did he mean? I saw nothing of him.

I said aloud, to overpower my fear, "I will build Hamlet's barrow.

What should his name be, cast in our ancestors' mold?" Amleth, I decided.

Through the night I wrote of Hamlet as a courageous Danish hero who struggled to achieve vengeance against his uncle for his father's murder.

> Amleth beheld all this but feared lest too shrewd a behavior might make his uncle suspect him. So, he chose to feign dullness, and pretend an utter lack of wits. This cunning course not only concealed his intelligence but ensured his safety...
>
> Then his mother set up a great wailing and began to lament her son's folly to his face; but he said, "Most infamous of women! Dost thou seek with such lying lamentations to hide thy most heavy guilt? Wantoning like a harlot, thou hast entered a wicked and abominable state of wedlock, embracing with incestuous bosom thy husband's slayer..."

Hamlet's story crawled like a vine down the margins and between lines of script. My trail of ink wed Hamlet's story to the foggy past. *What a superb lie*, I thought.

My bed afforded me only two hours of terrifying sleep. I dreamed that as I composed a line of Hamlet's story into the *Gesta Danorum* my writing vanished. I labored in panic to scribble faster, to write the line backward, to do anything that would fix my words to the page. My heart thundered. Fright grew to terror as I heard Cristiern's envoy riding a screaming, frothy horse like that of the Furious Host. He burst from the killing field tunnel and soared across the courtyard garden at my window.

Argument within the courtyard garden woke me before dawn. I rose, exhaustion-fogged, in the dark and opened my window latch to push the pane outward. A splash of cool breeze woke my brain. I noticed that below my window men and women worked by torchlight, digging wide pits. Within those holes they raised sharp poles and covered finished pits with branches and leaves. Also, I saw more torches moving along the ramparts, above the courtyard, held by men hauling bags to the cannons. Probably those sacks held the only black powder that had not turned moist in the poorly attended arsenal. The faint clanging of blades in practice funneled from the killing field through the tunnel to the garden.

The tunnel. I remembered my nightmare about the envoy. Panicked that my writing had disappeared, I struck my flint to my lamp and examined the *Gesta Danorum*. My sentences lay where I had fixed them.

The hammering in my breast subsided while I dressed. Then I urgently took up my quill. By the light of my lamp and the nascent sky I wrote until a soft but purposeful knock fell upon my door.

I pushed away from my table and, rising, saw through my window the dawn's turquoise expanse. A single, ragged cloud flared bright pink. A warning?

Hesitantly, I opened my portal. There, standing alone in dark Wiglaf Corridor, was my servant cub. He wore a frown despite his jolly striped leggings of green and yellow, a red tunic, and a blue cape and hat. Undoubtedly, his mother had selected his garb to cheer him.

"You are hardly the terror I expected, for your mighty pounding upon my door," I teased him and then cowered for the child's amusement.

The boy remained the very soul of sour milk. He issued a serious request. "King Fortinbras requests your immediate presence at his offices. Our enemy's envoy has arrived."

My innards wrenched. What had I to do with negotiations about the siege?

"Thank you for your well-delivered message, child."

I hid the *Gesta Danorum* atop my wardrobe cabinet. Then, I donned my hat and hastened to Fortinbras's chambers.

XI.

I arrived, huffing for breath, at the door to Fortinbras's suite. Marcellus admitted me through the sitting room to the familiar chamber door. Lingering grief for Hamlet jabbed me.

From within I heard a baritone voice mention good beer.

Why did Fortinbras need my attention? If libations were the issue, my servant cub could have brought him that. I rapped upon the door's knuckle-polished patch.

The door opened a hand's width. Fortinbras peered out at me. His face was pinched. I smelled the acrid scent of something burning.

"It is you. Good. Where is Lanier?"

"I don't know."

"Cristiern's envoy is here. He wants to speak with you."

Fortinbras stepped aside, ushered me into the room, and closed the door.

Seated in Hamlet's beloved study chair was a man wearing wide sleeves and a long, embroidered vest blaring in yellow. A plumed hat, its brim upon the floor, tilted against his chair leg. His long thick hair, reddish brown like that of a mongrel dog, was tied to contain its flare. He held a pipe in one hand and a tankard in the other. It was Reynaldo. That wicked land pirate reclined with his foot propped low upon a box. His pipe barrel wafted smoke across a tapestry depicting the Virgin holding the Christ Child. The Madonna seemed to glower at him.

I sputtered at Fortinbras, "That vermin presented credentials? Cristiern is mocking us."

Fortinbras turned away. He went to the immense table, leaned back against it, and, facing Reynaldo, crossed his arms as he studied his foe. "Lanier also has been summoned."

Reynaldo picked from a plate of smoked fish on a table beside him. Aiming high, he spat a fish bone. It arced and landed beside Fortinbras's boots. "You brought me one rogue. I want two."

"Why," Fortinbras steamed, "do you refuse to negotiate until both Lanier and Horatio are present?"

Reynaldo grinned lazily at Fortinbras. "At times a man should take his payment before he renders service. I will own the bounty that Louis of France placed on Lanier's head." Reynaldo pronounced "Louis" with a lisping Castilian "th." He added, "Never again will I have to grovel for another patron." He set his feet upon the floor, removed his hat, and laid it on the box.

Lanier was a good man, a friend to me. I would not allow him to be sacrificed to this sack of filth. "You won't have him."

Reynaldo's face flushed. He tipped his tankard to his lips. Over the rim, smug and oily, he squinted at me. He set down his cup and wiped his mouth with the ruffled, red-stained cuff of the arm I had wounded. Then he dropped his tankard upon the floor and stood. "What do you think a man prays when left to die on an island?"

I cut toward Reynaldo. "You deserved whatever God dealt you, I'm sure of it."

"You know nothing of my life. God's bowels."

"God's bowels?" I laughed at Reynaldo. "That's an oath I've never heard before."

Reynaldo, his face darkening, veered toward me, but I stood straight and gave no ground.

"Did your people disown you?" Reynaldo asked. "You know nothing of exile." He drew a long breath upon his pipe. He instantly calmed. Smoke puffed from his mouth as he spoke. "All men are locked to their fate. You can do nothing for Lanier. You cannot keep me from my fortune."

I said nothing.

He continued, "On Cristiern's behalf, Dane, I remind you that His Majesty demands that you proclaim the truth"—his shifting eyes sought to read me—"about Hamlet's madness, that you write about the curse of the Hamlets."

"No."

Reynaldo drew another breath on his pipe and puffed. "I warn you. General Willem is an artful practitioner of the water treatment—the board, mask, and bucket. He does not need to consult the manual. If a man does not confess the required truth, Willem can drown him within seconds."

I remained silent.

Smirking, Reynaldo went to his chair, set down his pipe, and retrieved the box on the floor. He brought it and handed it to me. "You have met a friar named Poul Helgesen. An obstinate man. Yesterday Cristiern summoned him from his Carmelite Priory. Told him to write in his manuscript about Danish kings, of Cristiern's rise to reign over the Kalmar Union. Here is the result."

Poul's manuscript—the example that Cristiern expected me to follow. But the box was heavier than I anticipated. I pulled off the tight lid. A horrid stench. A bloody mass of tonsured scalp. Poul's severed head.

"Christ's blood." I cried out and dropped the box. Rising bile scorched my throat. I stumbled backward. Container and lid clattered upon the floor, landing upright. I bent against my knees, gagging but fighting the urge to vomit.

"Heed Cristiern's command," Reynaldo said. "Be his scribe and return the *Gesta Danorum* to him."

In that horrible moment I realized that Cristiern had declared war on me. My belly knotted with fear.

Fortinbras kicked the box away. It slid across the floor and bumped against the door.

The door latch pivoted downward and opened, pushing the box aside. Lanier stepped into the room. He looked down at the box's putrid contents. "That ... is a terrible gift."

Reynaldo, clenching his pipe barrel, puffed on its stem. His glare at Lanier smoldered. "The French dog smells his dinner and comes at last."

"You rancid swine," Lanier replied. "Let me be. You know it was Pinzon who chose to leave you on that island."

Turning to Fortinbras, Reynaldo said, "Give Lanier and the *Gesta Danorum* to me. Then, we will negotiate."

"You will no longer hunt me," Lanier growled.

"Whore. Devil," Reynaldo retorted. "I will take your head in a sack to King Louis. France will pay me for it."

Lanier peeled off his gloves and admired one of his many gold rings. He said to me, "*Mon ami*, did I show you the reward Pinzon gave me for finding that thief." Lanier raised a gold-banded middle finger in Reynaldo's direction.

Reynaldo flew, claws out, at Lanier who, counterattacking, charged at Reynaldo. The men toppled and scuffled upon the floor. I leapt at Reynaldo but could not knock him away from Lanier. But Fortinbras dragged Reynaldo by his shirt collar away from Lanier, then barked at Reynaldo, "I might give Lanier to you as punishment for his failure to raise my army."

Lanier pressed against the floor to stand. He defiantly shook his head, but I saw fear in his face.

Reynaldo snapped his feet beneath him and stood. He swept his mussed hair behind his head and pulled on his hat.

Fortinbras moved to stand directly before Reynaldo, whose brow only reached the height of Fortinbras's grinding jaw. He asked Reynaldo, "What are Cristiern's terms?"

Looking up at him, Reynaldo said, "You and Helsingør's nobles will surrender by dawn tomorrow. All may bring what goods they can carry to the tent in the southwest fields. Additionally, you, Prince, will cease obstruction of Cristiern's rightful rule over Norway and Denmark and forfeit all claims to thrones within the Kalmar Union."

Fortinbras slowly shook his head as if the terms hardly deserved reply.

"If you and these Danes submit, the blockade and starvation will end." Reynaldo sniffed. "If you refuse, you will die."

"Envoy," Fortinbras told Reynaldo, "advise Cristiern that Krogen's nobles will not abandon their home."

"*Señor*, if there is no surrender by dawn, Cristiern will attack."

Fortinbras turned on his heel. He walked to the door and opened it. "I will lead this band of nobles in the fight of their lives. Your audience is finished. I will escort you to the gate myself. You will not return."

Reynaldo charged toward the door. When he reached the threshold, he whipped around and, bristling, said to Lanier and me, "I will have my reward." He stormed, plume bobbing behind, into the corridor and away. Fortinbras pursued him.

Lanier followed but slowly, toward the killing field where his novice soldiers awaited him.

I dared to miss battle practice. Much of Hamlet's story I had yet to write. Throughout the afternoon, I labored at my chamber's writing table. My quill, scrawling at maximum flow, called into being a world of ancient clannish monikers, royal banquets, forests and wolves, shipwrecked beaches, and dark holes in castles and human hearts. Into the narrative I inserted slices of truth.

> *Sayeth Amleth, "The passion to avenge my father still burns in my heart, but I am watching the chances. I await the fitting hour…"*
>
> *The uncle, Feng, now suspected that his stepson was certainly full of guile… So, he thought that the King of Britain should be employed to slay him…*

Sustenance came—a platter sent by Margrete and delivered by my servant cub. I ate while I worked, pausing only once to look out my window at the black dome of the evening sky.

When I had filled all available margins and spaces in the chosen section of the *Gesta Danorum*, I went to Tomas, the housemaster, to obtain fresh parchment sheets. I inserted those loose pages into the old tome. Despite the ache of doom growing in my belly and breast, onward I wrote. I would prove the worthiness of my name and my part.

Past midnight, despite the pounding march of our nearing crucible, I needed a moment of peace. Thus, I left my chambers in darkness to make my supplications in my Gethsemane, not the chapel but where my tribulations and this pilgrimage had begun.

From the ramparts' high vantage point I looked, to my right, down the moonlight-polished fortress walls to the caldrons and rock piles cluttering the killing field, and to the ladders leaning against the outer wall's walkway. To my left, within the courtyard garden, I saw twelve men and women at the offering place beside the well. Holding hands, they stood around a candlelit table fashioned of shattered arcade brick and stone. The group chanted in both Latin and an old Danish tongue. It was a spell imploring the Disir, female guardian spirits, to reveal future events. One of the men acted as their priest. He raised high a flapping creature, either a bird or a bat. Then he pierced it with a knife and directed its spray of blood upon the offering table. I was alarmed but not surprised that our people, in their desperation and fear, had openly turned to ancient, un-Christian rites for protection.

In disgust I looked away, beyond our fortification to the south. The enemies' winking campfires seemed to be the Devil's constellation. Flags posted on their battle tents snapped in the night breeze.

The biting stink of bloated death blew from the village. I masked my nose, fearing this was perhaps our naked future God was revealing to me.

I may die here, I thought. I looked heavenward for a sign of hope. The moon's full face hovered above the trees. It glowed like an orb of the Celestial Alchemist and cast the occupied fields in crystal. This land, its ghosts and sprites, had been protected by Danish tribes for centuries. Would I die and join those supernatural forces before I could create a family? Dread tugged at my stomach. I regretted too much time spent with books and tavern dalliances.

Merciful Almighty God, I prayed, *make your servant Fortinbras victorious. Let us triumph so that I may live to have a true family.*

A sudden wind buffeted me. I heard from the distant encampments a bonfire's embers burst and the enemy roar. That cheer rattled me. *If I am killed, then my anonymous writings will be my only begotten child: all that will remain of me besides my bones.*

In haste, I returned to my work.

When I arrived at my chamber, exhausted, I leaned against my door's cool, smooth face. My foot kicked something unexpected—a package set against the doorjamb. Puzzled, I stooped to retrieve the tied bundle and entered my room.

I tore away the thread and opened the mysterious sack. It contained a black hat with a stiff brim folded upward, fore and aft. A band stretched atop the lustrous, handsome crown from ear to ear. I turned the hat over and found, pressed into its cavity, a letter, which I have long kept.

> Horatio,
>
> Sentimentality may be folly, but I will always desire to live in the land I choose, and in the keeping of a woman I adore. I wish this for you as well.
>
> My daughter is my jewel, and I consent to share her with you.

As for this hat, please accept this gift—a new emblem for a new life. It is a fashion of noble lineage, crafted by my own hands and from my own allowances. I recommend that you surrender your beloved hat, handsome though it may be. While it is expressive, it is tired and requires rest.

In faith, I am
Hendrik of Helsingør

I removed my hat, long-favored and so like Papa's. True, it was flat and thin now. However, it was a precious reminder of him, and everyone who knew me recognized it.

In my other hand I held my gift hat—a gorgeous, black creature but stiff—prickly in the way that strangers can seem, at first. It was created by someone with expectations, and it was for an imagined future Horatio bearing new responsibilities. Who might I become if I wore this new hat, as a husband, a father? Could that hat be as comfortable as my favored one?

As a father, and perhaps as a husband, I could be someone's hero.

Did Margrete know that her father had written to me, and what he meant?

Courage dared me to wear the new hat. I put it on and pulled it down to my ears. It felt a bit taut, and I tugged at it for a better fit.

To assess my appearance, I stood at the window. Within that mirror my body seemed to float among the star field diamonds of fortune's zodiac. I held my old hat to my heart. My solitary, uncertain mien wearing new garb stared back at me. Would I survive to discover this man?

I tucked my preferred green hat into my belt, and, wearing the new one, I sat at my table to continue writing by lamplight. Through my fingers and quill point flowed my love for Hamlet and my knowledge of his heart.

> *Amleth accomplished the slaughter of his stepfather... the body of Feng lying pierced by the sword, amid his bloodstained raiment...*

By the third and darkest hour of the morning, when soft, thudding bells rang for Lauds devotions, I could no longer lift my hand or eyelids. My task was nearly done. I needed only a sliver of rest, I thought. I lay my head upon the *Gesta Danorum*.

A pounding on my door and loud bells tolling for Prime's Mass roused me. "Rise for prayer," a man called out. "Fortinbras requires all to prepare our souls before we fight."

Night was blinking to admit the gray cast of dawn. I tugged my new black hat onto my head, folded my old green hat, and tucked it into my belt, and left my chambers to join the crowd's rush to the somber chapel. The kneeling benches seemed especially hard as we hunched in rows, some kneeling in the aisles, and prayed the Divine Office. We recited the Magnificat and the Te Deum. Mass ended with Psalm 130, concluding with the words:

My soul longs for the Lord, more than watchmen yearn for the morning. Amen.

When we spoke those final words, the sun's first rays struck the windows' stained glass. Suddenly, throughout the chapel several people screeched. Startled, I looked about me. I saw two dozen men, women, and children slump. Wailing, they grasped one another, shaking. I believed, at first, that they had dropped from fright of the looming attack, or perhaps from sickness. But then, some began to quake and moan.

What was happening?

A man near me convulsed. I reached for him, but he pushed back at me. I asked him, "What is the matter?" Suddenly, he lay silent, his stony eyes fixed. I felt his still heart. "This man is dead," I cried out.

Several others collapsed to the floor. Then more fell. I saw empty vials fall and roll from their squirming bodies and open hands.

Poison. Alarmed, I found Margrete crouched in the aisle. Holy Mother. Had she taken it? Margrete looked up at me, her eyes full and grieving. She was bent over her parents, struggling to soothe Hendrik and Estrid as they writhed upon the ground.

Hadn't they talked of preparing for the attack? Then, I realized: they had chosen to resist Cristiern by denying him their lives.

Estrid shuddered. Gasping, she told her daughter, "No slavery. No road."

Margrete pulled her mother closer. She brushed Estrid's hair from her eyes and stroked her strained face. "Krogen is your life, Mother."

They wept.

The old woman's body fell slack. Margrete bent to bury her face in her mother's neck.

Next to Estrid and Margrete lay Hendrik. I tried to take his trembling hand in mine, but he, quivering, pointed at my head, at his gift I wore. One side of his mouth flickered a grin while the other half of his face wilted.

"Last night," Hendrik murmured, "the death dream came. The Furious Host hunted us, just as the legend tells. A cloud flew from the west.

Rattling, skeletal horses. Phantom hounds. The man in black on his gray horse... swept us up into his throng of the dead. Into the clouds they rode. To see Odin in Valhalla."

Margrete, cradling her mother in one arm, reached for her father. She gripped his hand.

I looked into poor Hendrik's eyes to assure him as, my heart breaking, I wished I had when Hamlet died, "Go to the grand feast. Await the everlasting battle."

Silently, he mouthed something I could not discern.

A breeze came, despite no open window, and he was gone.

Hendrik's and Estrid's frozen gazes marveled, I believe, at divine secrets revealed to them.

Margrete whispered to God, "*Fiat voluntas tua.*" She released her father's hand and wiped her eyes. Then Margrete pressed her Freyja necklace, all that remained of her former life, to her heart.

At that moment, on the nineteenth day of June in the year of our Lord 1513, the first blast hit the chapel, launching Cristiern's attack on Krogen.

XII.

When the glaring sheet of dawn slung Cristiern's bombard blast at Helsingør's chapel, a wall crumbled. Stained glass shot like arrowheads at Krogen's huddling, screaming congregants and the self-slaughtered. I embraced Margrete to protect her. Rather than fall into my arms, she shielded her parents' fresh corpses.

"To your battle posts." I looked to see Fortinbras standing at the altar before the silver cross. His face was peppered with cuts, and his mail mantle sparkled with glass shards. "Go."

Dozens rushed to the door. Several of us hovered over the deceased, who had chosen to die in their home rather than suffer under Cristiern's rule.

"I must bury mother and father for their souls' deliverance." Margrete bent over Hendrik and Estrid and spilled her sorrow upon each brow as she kissed it.

I gripped her hand. "We will, after our victory."

We joined the frightened crowd jamming the chapel's narrow

vestibule. We squeezed through the portal, stumbled across the main corridor, and out the castle doors. The crowd pushed through the courtyard garden and tunnel to the killing field.

Krogen's novice army snapped to action. I found no sword awaiting me, and so I joined Margrete and the women carrying buckets of rocks and pails of boiling water to men at the ladders. Ropes and pulleys whirled, sending the materiel up to the platform walkway that stretched the inner length of the outer wall. The enemy was not yet close enough, positioned under our murder holes to receive the scalding or jagged delivery.

High above our heads our bowmen stood atop the ramparts. Their helmet tips and erect bows, peaking above the merlons, pointed to heaven. Farther down the ramparts our cannons' short barrels poked from the ramparts' ridge like blunt gargoyles. Fortinbras, pacing among the ladder stations, bellowed a command to the bowmen. A drove of our arrows soared over our heads at the enemy in the south fields. In answer, their arrows arced over our walls, whizzing too close as we scurried between our teams.

Orders became muddled. Contradictions confused demand for ammunition. Small bags of explosive powder went to those who had no hand cannon to fire from their post, while others needing that agent received none. Alarmed cries for powder rang through the teams, up and down the walk. It was a maddening mess.

Our blasting cannon hurtled great stones at the enemy. Fortinbras strode among us, calling out commands. Lanier ran from ladder to ladder and clarified instructions. Then Fortinbras, apparently anticipating more complications from those actions, barked at Lanier.

Margrete gasped from exertion as she quickly filled another bucket.

A MAN OF HONOR

"Thank the heavens you finished Hamlet's story last night."

A man beside a ladder frantically waved for materiel. I ran to deliver a pail to him. When I returned, I told Margrete, "I couldn't finish."

Margrete, arms slack, straightened. "But if you die, your soul will perish for your dishonor, for your failed pledge." Her concern for responsibility was indomitable. She said, "Your writing table must be your battle post."

I reached a bucket over a cauldron's searing lip to collect boiling water. "I risk my honor if I don't fight."

"Regardless, your honor is at risk, Horatio. You must complete the story and achieve your promise."

How could I scribble while she fought?

"Lanier," Margrete called out.

Responding, he ran, ducking arrows, to our side.

She said, "Horatio must go complete his writing. Is his chamber the best station?"

Lanier clasped my shoulder. "No. If the enemy breaches our walls, they will ransack every compartment for survivors. You must go to the muniment tower."

"I can't leave you. How can I compose among ashes?"

"Soldiers will not waste time looking for trophies there," Lanier said. "They know it was already sacked."

"Erik," Margrete cried out to the crinkle-faced muniments keeper, who was pushing logs into a blaze lapping a caldron's haunches. "Do you have the muniment tower keys?"

He trotted to us and held out the three bony implements. "Do not lose these tokens of my burned pets," he said.

Margrete knelt and kissed Erik on his cheek, grizzled from grief's neglect. Then she pressed the keys into my hand. "Lock yourself into the muniment room." She pointed at an extra ladder lying on the ground. "Take that. You can see our status from the tower's high window."

Margrete kissed me. Her lips were soft upon my unshaven face. When she stepped back, I saw in her eyes the frost and fire of rekindled grief. She said, "Your oath to Hamlet is your honor. You are his devoted friend and my knight."

I had craved to hear Margrete utter those words. I kissed her fully, lingered with her. I said, "Come with me, away from this carnage."

She shook her head. "Sequester your person in the muniment tower. Lanier and I will come for you."

Two explosions against our outer wall blew a hole high in the outer wall. Mangled bodies, splintered planks, and broken stone littered the field below. Another enemy bombard blast smashed our archers. Five of our bowmen fell from the ramparts onto the killing field. They lay, twisted and bloody, as our people, carrying buckets and weapons, ran around and over them.

The carnage lit fire to my heels. I carried the ladder, running through the tunnel and courtyard garden, into the castle. After I retrieved from my chambers my bag of writing paraphernalia and the *Gesta Danorum*, I grasped the ladder, book, and bag and hastened to the vaulted passageway.

The vault door to the muniment tower's counting room was ajar. I entered, shut that door behind me, and slid the keys into their tumblers. Each clacked when it locked. After I pulled out the keys, I crossed the ash-covered floor strewn with lumps of iron that once had been the ledgers entrusted to Erik. I tramped over the charred wood that had been his massive tables and shelves to reach the open door to the muniment tower stairs. I stepped past that door, closed it, and, using the keys, also fastened its three locks.

My throat itched. As I climbed the tower's stairs to the muniment room, I buried my nose within my collar to shield my breath from daemons. I crossed the open threshold and pushed the cold, heavy door to close it behind me. Once more, I turned the three keys in the door's locks until the tumblers clacked shut.

The square floor and tall walls were soot-coated. I felt as if I was surrounded by ashes of the decimated past, that I stood among the gray, depleted corpses of the Hamlet dead once again. My breast tightened. I had to complete my task while my friends risked their lives in battle. I brushed away ash from the floor to sit upon a patch of red, black, and yellow tiles, among the ruin of the House of Hamlet. The dust in my mouth and nose was the gritty taste of destruction, the shambles of legacy. I lay the *Gesta Danorum* before me and opened it. Using the floor as my table, I bent over the book and my sheets to write, secreted in the shadowy chamber that once had been Krogen's cloister of memory and history. I forged onward and struggled to ignore the bellowing war—catapults rattling, cannon booming, and wagons rumbling nearer to the fortress. The clash of blades and men's cries unsettled me most.

Sentences spilled from my flurrying quill point and filled my page. I paused, once, to wonder if I dared to identify Hamlet by name. I had been calling him Amleth, a clever rearrangement of the letters, to fit him into the archaic world of the *Gesta Danorum*. This license I took with the truth, I thought, was a cunning wager: it shielded him and me. If the treasonous book was discovered, Hamlet's name might not be evident and his story would escape destruction and continue to be known. Also, my authorship could not be inferred. I decided to retain it.

I finished my task. Hamlet's legend was complete—a miracle, I believed. I prayed, let this legend survive and work on mankind's minds and hearts. At that moment I was insensible that the legend I had called "a superb lie" would bring enormous consequences.

A spot of light landed upon my text, from the high window admitting the advancing sun. Hours had passed, I guessed. Had we won? To assess the situation, I leaned the ladder against the wall and climbed to a precarious upper rung at the window. I saw no activity in the courtyard garden, but in the fields, small enemy battle carts lay upturned and splintered, their tattered battle standards strewn upon the ground. That sight filled me with joy.

Craning to look eastward, I saw a portion of the dock. Its ruined piling stood in the water, reaching askew like fractured fingers. That sight quelled my excitement. Into my view of the field came horses pushing wheeled battle carts, bearing cannons closer to Krogen. The carts stopped. Soldiers loaded massive round stones into the cannons. I expected a crack from those munitions but heard from the fields, instead, an unusual sound, like the snap of a stretched rope. I saw a catapult's cup fling a body in rags that arced and fell, I presumed, over our outer wall.

Then I heard a triple blast and a tremendous crash. A triumphant cry arose. I imagined that Cristiern's bombards had broken the East Gate and Porter's Tower into a pile of stone, wood, and iron.

A man, perhaps atop our ramparts, cried out, "They come."

I heard tramping boots. Cristiern's forces in roaring fury swept over the ruins of the East Gate. From my window perch I saw a stream of soldiers' glinting helmets flow from the tunnel into the courtyard garden. A few screams came from what I hoped were soldiers and not our nobles. Had they fallen into the pits, lying impaled upon the pikes within? The thought made me squirm.

Then I looked to the ramparts. Soldiers pushed our archers along that narrow stone lane to the turret stairwell. They emerged at the bottom of the stairs, in a corner of the courtyard garden. More soldiers brought our people, captured on the killing field, through the tunnel and into the garden. By the well and offering place stood Cristiern, his helmet clasped under his arm. Across his breastplate stretched the royal standard of hearts and lions. General Willem, mail and leather-clad, strode among the cowering nobles. His elegant sword, hanging from his belt, was blood-smeared. Willem commanded, "Throw them into the pits."

Cristiern began to pace among the six holes as he watched his soldiers push screaming families to their tortured deaths. Cristiern stood at the lip of a pit and declared, "Like our great, ancient King Valdemar the Dane, I will vanquish encroaching princes, nobility, and clergy. Sweden and Norway will pay tribute to me. But *you*, traitors, will suffer."

Where were Margrete and Lanier? I began to shake for fear that Cristiern had already killed them. I gripped my ladder harder.

Cristiern glanced into each pit. He called to Willem, "Not all traitors are accounted for. Where is Horatio?" Cristiern looked up and about, and then to the towers, straight at me.

I ducked. Frightened, I clambered down the rungs.

The *Gesta Danorum* lay unguarded upon the colorful floor. Cristiern must not take it again. He would strip Hamlet's legend away. Where could I hide the book?

I looked for a secret place, a hole once covered by cabinets or chests. But the four soot-caked walls were entirely solid. Next, I fell to my knees and tore at the small, square tiles to make a hole. The only result was bloody fingers. I could not pry away even one tile.

Somewhere near, Cristiern called out. "Horatio, give me the *Gesta Danorum*. Be my scribe as last witness to the Hamlets' treachery."

There could be no failure now. Not at the cost of my honor. The hours of knuckle-straining, scribbling labor. If this second manuscript was lost? My God. The heavy burden of my impossible promise. Hamlet's phantom would never rest.

I scooped up the book with pages inserted. I wanted to howl for Margrete and Lanier.

Cristiern added, "Do not follow Poul's demise. Do not come to an end in a box."

Clutching the *Gesta Danorum*, I stood with my back pressed into the corner farthest from the door. My heart crashed against my breastbones.

A deafening explosion shook the floor and reverberated throughout the muniment tower.

I crouched and waited for the floor to drop, but it did not happen. Then I heard Cristiern.

"They would have surrendered immediately after praying the Office of the Dead. They would have gone to purgatory with clean souls." His muffled voice came from below, within the tower. He had blown off the vault door and was in the counting room, I guessed.

Willem, with gravely tone, replied, "We lost men. The traitors are not clean, and they are weak warriors."

Then, a second detonation struck, closer and louder than the first. The noise hurt my ears and rattled the muniment room door. Cristiern and Willem had blasted the second door at the portal to the stairs. Only the muniment room door remained between us.

My only weapons? Jangling keys ready in the door for my escape, and a ladder. If I survived the next blast, a broken ladder could make a good spear.

I heard boots, plodding and steady, begin to ascend the twisting muniment tower stairs.

In one hand I clumsily gripped the ladder. My other arm clamped the *Gesta Danorum* to my breast. If the next explosion blew the door away, it might also hit me.

Within the stairwell Willem asked, "Who did you direct to print your *Gesta Danorum*?"

Cristiern answered, "My cleric legate, the canon of Lund. Assigned to the archbishop of Sens in Paris."

"Wasn't he supposed to find the book for you?"

"Yes, but I never should have expected competence or loyalty from a Helsingør native."

"Can you trust him to print it?"

"His scriptorium at the Hôtel de Sens will see to it. Their work is good."

Printing of the *Gesta Danorum*. I suddenly realized that writing Hamlet's legend satisfied only half of my promise. Without a way to afford its distribution I would never see the *Gesta Danorum* grow gnarled wanderer's feet or trek the globe. Even if I survived and smuggled the *Gesta Danorum* to safety, Hamlet's tale would be stillbirthed if I could not bring it forth to the world. With grudging thanks to Cristiern, I now knew who might render help... if I survived.

"Horatio," Cristiern called from the stairway, now nearer to my locked door. "Submit now or die."

With an explosion, the door would fly at me. I clenched my eyes against death's strike.

At the moment that I expected the deafening blast, I heard, instead, someone yowl within the stairwell. Next came grunting and a clatter, as though the cook had dropped an armory of bowls and kettles down the stairs. A shuffling, clashing fight raged outside the door.

I waited, hardly able to breathe, and held my book against my pounding breast.

The door exploded. It soared at me. I fell to one side and was almost crushed by the torn metal slab.

I expected Cristiern, but into the smoky room ran Margrete.

"Almighty God be praised," I cried out.

"Help me," she cried and turned against her assailant: Willem. He charged into the room, panting like a tired ox. He wielded his bloody blade at us.

"Where is Cristiern?" I asked.

"Thrown down the tower stairs," Margrete said.

Could she have done that? I thought, and then saw who had delivered that blow.

Lanier stormed in after Willem. One eye was purple and swollen half-closed. He rotated, hand over hand, a long staff missing its pike head. He bellowed, "Murderer! King Fortinbras will be avenged." He pivoted, twisting, to whip the rod against Willem.

"What? Is this true?" I scrambled to my feet and looked to Margrete.

"Yes, and our people are dead," she cried out. Margrete stood, and Willem veered toward her, advancing, sword raised to strike. She fell back as the blade swung at her.

I grabbed an end of my ladder and heaved it at Willem. The uptilted rungs caught his swooping blade and twisted the weapon from his grip. The sword crashed to the floor. When Lanier and Willem scrambled to retrieve it, both fell upon the ladder and broke it.

A splintered piece of the ladder lay near me; I grasped it. As Willem and Lanier wrestled, I tried to jab the stake into Willem's back. But his mail shirt foiled my attack.

Willem got up and turned to strike me, yet it was Margrete, not I, who attacked him first. She kicked at his unshielded loins like a lowland pit brawler.

Lanier now possessed Willem's sword. The men grappled for control of it. Lanier, cocooned in his cape, raised the blade high. Willem reached up. His tainted armor shimmered black and silver. Lanier, one arm holding the sword away from Willem, with his other hand grasped the lip of Willem's breastplate. He yanked it down to expose his neck. Willem tried to twist away, but I kicked him behind his knees. When Willem fell to kneeling, Lanier pivoted the blade point down, aiming for Willem's raw patch of flesh. Then with a double-handed grip upon the hilt, Lanier squatted. His full weight pulled the sword into Willem's neck and down through his torso.

Willem, gawking upward, beheld his own weapon that skewered him.

Panting, Lanier stood up and released the sword. The body tilted back against its heels but, supported by the blade, remained upright. Lanier stepped away and held a cuff to his eye.

I looked to Margrete, never more grateful to see her lovely, dirt-streaked face. The beauty of her Freyja necklace, paired with her ragged frock now missing both sleeves, seemed like royal gems worn by an orphaned peasant. She sat heavily upon the floor and wiped her face with one hand.

Lanier squinted at me through his engorged eye. He grinned.

Relieved, I turned my back to the door. But instantly someone stomped behind me, seized me, and threw me to the floor. I heard the painful crunch of my body. I dropped the *Gesta Danorum* and lay stunned. The back of my head pulsed. I touched my head for blood and realized that my hat, gifted by Hendrik, had fallen off. I saw it upon the floor, trampled and ruined. I was disheartened, but then felt at my belt and found my papa's hat tucked there.

Looming over me, Cristiern laughed. A side of his face was puffy and scraped. His blood-caked gloves held the *Gesta Danorum*.

Lanier called to Cristiern. "Your Majesty."

Cristiern turned to him and saw Lanier standing beside the impaled general, his hand resting on the sword's pommel.

"Christ," Cristiern bellowed. He dropped my book and, in an unholy rage, ran at Lanier. To ward off Cristiern's jabs, Lanier grasped the blade's hilt and pivoted Willem's body between them like a shield.

"Get the book," I said to Margrete. She scooped up the tome and the scattered pages.

My head and side pained me, but I crept behind Cristiern and leapt on his back, clawed blindly at his eyes and nose. Cristiern turned and grasped my neck. "Traitor. Dung-eater."

Lanier sneered, "I killed Willem."

Cristiern released me. He tackled Lanier and Willem's corpse. Cristiern sat atop Lanier and pummeled him as Lanier, arms bent, tried to buffer the blows.

From Margrete's arms I took the *Gesta Danorum* and leapt back at Cristiern. I raised the volume and, summoning every drop of strength in me, smashed that book across the back of Cristiern's head.

Cristiern tumbled face-forward and lay still. I stood over the tyrant. "Consider that my delivery of your trophy."

Lanier reached up to me. I pulled his hand to help him stand. Then he drew the sword from Willem's upright body. It crumpled. Lanier strode to Cristiern lying facedown. Standing over him, Lanier raised the blade high, double-handed.

"Stop," Margrete cried.

"Don't," I told him.

Lanier hesitated. He looked sharply at me, then at her. "We must be certain he is dead."

Margrete implored, "We must not kill a king. God forbids it."

The blade point hovered above Cristiern's head, rotated with Lanier's tightening grip. He said, "Perhaps God intends this man's death, *mademoiselle*. Cristiern is not my king." Lanier's fists rose higher for better leverage.

"Only God may determine a king's fate. He may be dead. Do not desecrate the body." Margrete reached for Lanier's arm. "Our souls will perish."

I said, "This act would be neither defense nor accident. We'd never be absolved."

"Too late for me. God condemned me long ago."

Margrete said, "Already we have committed the sin of treason against this king."

"*Exactement*. And he killed Fortinbras."

Margrete cried, "We must not kill a king."

Lanier replied, "Hamlet did."

Margrete's pointed finger shook at Lanier. "And see what befell him. Cristiern, too, will receive his own punishment from God."

I gripped Lanier's shoulder. "If you won't protect your soul, at least don't surrender your honor."

Lanier's raised arms, holding the sword, slackened. He lowered the blade, stepped back from the body, and wiped his brow. He pointed at the *Gesta Danorum* in my arms. "That book had better be worth our jeopardy."

"It is."

Lanier tugged loose his cape's ties. He tossed it to me. "Swaddle your child."

"Thank you." I wrapped the *Gesta Danorum* and held the bundle tightly.

"Please tell me," Margrete said as she walked a circle around Cristiern's still body, lying face downward, and watched him for movement. "Did you finish writing?"

"I did," I said and allowed a little relief to wash over me. My belly rumbled with hunger, but we had no time to scavenge for food.

Cristiern stirred. Alarmed, we jumped back.

Margrete whispered, "The stables. Follow me."

She soared down the muniment tower stairs, pausing only to clamber over the small bombard cannon discarded there. Lanier, grasping Willem's sword, and I, carrying our treasure, flew after her. We passed through the counting room, then hesitated at its yawning threshold. We listened for soldiers. Detecting none, we ran into the vaulted passageway and nearly tripped over several dead nobles and a few soldiers beside the fallen door.

At the sight Margrete moaned, "Too much death." She bent and vomited. Her rancid gut stink nearly made me wretch. Lanier turned away and belched.

Margrete wiped her mouth. "You have never seen a lady spew?"

"No." We gagged.

"Precious men. Hold fast your skirts and follow me."

She led our loping gait out the vaulted passageway onto the west-end patch of the killing field. We followed the curving fortress's wall. Buoyed by the absence of soldiers, our pace grew to a sprint. However, when the wall straightened into a long stretch of masonry, we saw at its distant end a mass of armored men.

We stumbled to a halt.

Like nailheads struck by a single mallet, in unison the helmets pivoted in our direction. Then the devils ran toward us. Their shaking chain mail made lightning from sunlight.

We turned about and dashed, retracing our path along the curving wall. Beside me Lanier, carrying the sword, swung his other arm to pump breath into his barrel breast. He gasped, "Where now?"

"The passages to the underground tunnels," said Margrete. She ran in bare feet, slinging her slippers in both hands to race ahead.

We ran into the vaulted passageway. I expected that we would pass the corpses strewn below the doorless arch to the counting room, enter the main corridor, and then reach the passages and tunnels leading to the stables.

However, before us, in the throat of the vaulted passageway, stood a figure, his feet planted wide. He pointed a sleek hand cannon at us. It was Reynaldo.

XIII.

Lanier, Margrete, and I stood terrified in the corpse-littered vaulted passageway. Grinning, Reynaldo leveled the black mouth of his hand cannon at us. It seemed like a dark snake hole harboring the deadliest monster. He grasped the slow-burning match cord hanging beneath the weapon, held its glowing orange tip near the barrel's explosive touch hole, and said, "*Hola, mis enemigos.* Now, you will give to me Lanier and the book."

"*Mon Dieu.*" Lanier scowled.

Reynaldo tipped the hand cannon's lip at Lanier. "France will pay me well for your skull."

I won't surrender Lanier—my brother in commiseration and combat, or the Gesta Danorum—*my promise to Hamlet fulfilled.* I summoned every shrewd instinct. "You think that Cristiern will reward you for the *Gesta Danorum*?"

"Yah," said Reynaldo, mocking my accent. "That *Gesta Danorum* is ugly. But it will bring a good price."

"That's unlikely," I replied. "Cristiern is dead."

Reynaldo snorted in refutation but then chewed his lower lip. "Not... possible."

I asked, "Would Willem's sword be ours if Cristiern was alive?"

Lanier, perceiving my cue, held out the crimson-streaked blade for inspection.

"That blood is Cristiern's," I added.

"You killed Cristiern, the Dane of Copenhagen." Reynaldo's words dripped skepticism.

"We did," I said.

Margrete nodded.

Lanier said, "*La vérité n'a qu'une couleur; un mensonge en a plusieurs.*"

"The truth has but one color; a lie has many, you say?" Reynaldo scoffed. "Truth or lies always present best in gold. Come and bring the book." Reynaldo tilted the barrel upward, bidding Lanier.

We remained still.

"Come."

Dread seized me. "Wait. You risk enraging the entire House of Oldenburg." Counting, I raised one finger. "They will be angry that you stole their property." I bent back a second finger. "They have the primary right to prosecute us for murder and for thievery. If you interfere, they'll come for you."

Reynaldo, rubbing his chin, seemed to puzzle my point. Then he grinned like a drooling dog. "They would not pursue me where I am bound. Lanier, I will drag your maggot-eaten corpse to Louis. Come."

Lanier went to Reynaldo. Our enemy cradled his hand cannon upon one arm and with his other hand snatched the sword's leather-wound grip from Lanier. He slid the blade within his belt and yanked out a loop of rope. He tossed it at me. "Now, bind Lanier." To ensure I understood his threat, Reynaldo pointed his hand cannon at Margrete.

Ire burned in my breast, but I said nothing so as not to further endanger my friends. I set down the wrapped book. I tied Lanier's wrists. Trembling, I awaited Reynaldo's next order.

"Give me the *Gesta Danorum*." Reynaldo aimed his hand cannon at me and held the smoking match cord closer to the weapon's touch hole. "You cannot chase me if your legs are blown off, *señor*."

I hesitated, wondering what else I could do.

Reynaldo barked, "Give it to Lanier."

The approaching trot of soldiers echoed within the vaulted passageway. They had seen us from their distant position at the southwestern end of the killing field and pursued us. I had no weapon to fight that force and no lie to save my cause. My gut twisted.

I handed the cape-wrapped *Gesta Danorum* to Lanier. His bound hands clamped it to his breast. "I am sorry," he said.

"The shame is mine," I replied. I watched Reynaldo press the hand cannon to Lanier's back, prodding him to the entranceway. Lanier turned to give me a last, grim look before Reynaldo pushed him into the dim main corridor.

I heard a groan behind us. I turned to see Cristiern stagger into the vaulted passageway. He clutched his head.

Margrete screeched at him, "Murderer."

Soldiers stamped into the vaulted passageway. At the sight of their swaying king they stopped.

Cristiern regarded them incredulously. "Why do you wait?" he rasped. "A bounty on all their heads. Kill the traitors."

Margrete and I ran from the vaulted passageway into the corridor.

With every stride my heart cracked for Lanier and for the loss of the *Gesta Danorum*. I wanted to rescue them both.

Behind us clambered a dozen soldiers. From the vaulted passageway Cristiern roared, "I will launch God's judgment at them."

We dashed down the corridor. Through windows upon the courtyard garden arcade I glimpsed the pits and many angular bodies scattered everywhere, seeping and writhing.

In our path along the corridor lay more bodies, gashed and moaning. At the sight of the tubular lumps of entrails, Margrete cried out. She ran past.

I stood and saw the person to whom those guts belonged. The bloody, parchment-like face was that of Erik. I could not help him.

Behind us, soldiers pounded in our direction. At their rear Cristiern limped, urging them onward.

We reached the stairwell and climbed the spiral to the landing of Wiglaf Corridor. At the top step we heard trampling, raucous soldiers passing. We stopped. They laughed about their victory as we hid inside the curve of the stairwell and huffed for breath.

After they turned toward the royal west corridor, we went to the hidden passageway. Margrete grasped its latch and flung open the door. I followed but feared that the army was inside, crawling throughout the castle like ants through a mound.

The passageway snaked between the walls of nobles' residential apartments. We scurried down that musty lane between thin plank walls separating chambers. I heard men talking in the flanking compartments, and I slowed to quiet my steps.

Margrete hissed, "At the bottom of the south stairwell there is a door to the underground tunnels. We can get to the stables."

"Someone is in the walls," came a shout.

Behind us came a crash. I looked over my shoulder to see a hole ripping into the passageway. Soldiers climbed through the gap into the lane. They began to chase us like a thunderous sea storm raging toward land.

We raced southward the length of the passageway. Then we rammed against a simple, hewn door and barged into the south corridor. Margrete took a lit torch from the wall and hastened down a narrow, winding staircase. I followed her, fleeing the pounding boots overhead.

At the bottom of the stairwell Margrete led me behind the stairs and pulled upon an iron ring in the wall. Stone blocks swung inward, revealing a dank space. The stench of wet rot filled my nostrils. Margrete held the torch in the opening to show me the earth-hewn steps that descended into the shallow mass of tunnels that Old Hamlet had made for escape.

Above us, soldiers were tramping the stairs in descent. They were nearly upon us.

I pushed the door shut behind us. We plunged into the darkness, lit only by the torch, and down the dirt and sand steps. Along the path ahead we ran, batting away dangling, stringy roots. From our bobbing torch, shadows fell and swirled around us. Alternative paths opened upon our approach and shut in darkness as we hurried past. Vermin screeched at our intrusion. We swerved to avoid them.

Margrete said, "This way," and led me into a joining tunnel.

The soldiers, shouting a distance behind us, had found and entered the tunnel and were stumbling through the dark. They called out threats to us and to the underworld spirits.

Suddenly we came upon more dirt steps. We climbed to reach a door cut in the ceiling. When I pushed upon it, urine-soaked hay and old manure dumped upon our heads. We sputtered and climbed out into the glaring light, onto the stable floor. I was partially blinded by the aging sun. Margrete dropped the torch into a water pail, shut the door, and covered it with hay. I searched the stable to find Lanier and Reynaldo.

The drum and grunt of a galloping horse alerted us. We rushed to the stable entrance and saw, racing away along the curving south wall, one black horse. It bore Reynaldo, flailing for speed. Lanier, seated before him, was visible only by his black-clad arm and leg.

Margrete said, "Probably they are headed toward the East Gate, but it is a ruin now."

I secured a lady's saddle upon a gray mare and quickly harnessed the horse. Using a stone block, I helped Margrete onto that horse, both legs to one side, and handed the reins to her. Although Margrete appeared pale and wan, she urgently slapped her heel against her mount's flanks and lunged after the men.

The tunnel door in the stable floor began to rumble. I jammed a bit into the jaws of a startled white steed, saddled and climbed upon it, and tore after Margrete. I kicked my horse for more speed and looked over my shoulder at our pursuers. Soldiers filled the stable. Some were mounting horses. Others were loading crossbows. I did not see Cristiern.

An arrow whizzed past my ear, barely missing me. I huddled close to my horse's flying mane and rallied it onward. The wall I skirted appeared like a long smear of stone. I drew close behind the pounding haunches of Margrete's mare.

The clatter of enemy hooves behind us, conducted along the wall, sounded like a legion one thousand strong. When I looked again, however, I counted ten soldiers whipping their horses to overtake us.

I kicked my bellowing horse and shot forward alongside Margrete. The vision of her—trailing waves of auburn hair, determination sculpted in alabaster, and a chain of gold and amber rising with her bosom... I forgot my fear for a moment. She was the most beautiful creature I had ever seen. But she did not look to me. When I saw that tears streamed down her face, my own sight blurred.

Lying in our path was the body I had seen flung by the catapults. It was a child. The little body was a contorted stump. I prayed, *God keep you.*

Ahead lay a large pile of rubble, the columns and iron ruins of the East Gate. Margrete's horse sprinted directly at the pile of twisted bars, wood planks, and jagged stone. Should we hurdle that mound? My heart beat in my throat, but I flailed my horse. We shot faster than I imagined we could fly toward the heap. It seemingly grew taller. I foresaw our animals smashing against those rocks like sea-wasted vessels, our bodies bent and broken upon the strand. I was amazed I did not soil myself.

Ahead, our prey neared the hulking ruins.

"Bounty is mine," Reynaldo cried out.

An arrow grazed my ear. It stung mightily. I tried to ignore the blood trickling down my neck. I leaned forward, nearly flat against my horse's drenched neck smelling of hot leather.

Reynaldo's horse soared over the jumbled tower of debris. Then one moment Margrete and I were at its base and the next moment, like herring caught in the lap of a curling wave, we ascended, riding on horseback a swelling current of air.

At our arc's crest, I glimpsed below, set outside the ruined East Gate, the dripping head of Fortinbras. Skewered upon a pike, eyes and mouth agape, it appeared to melt in the sun. I shuddered. Cristiern had made a horrific example of his challenger.

We landed heavily, all eight hooves, outside the fortress.

Two soldiers on horseback managed to also jump the wreckage. They chased us.

Reynaldo and Lanier galloped a distance too far ahead for us to immediately catch them. I saw, once, Lanier turn to look back at us. I could see his grin. He raised his bound hands, probably encouraging us, perhaps celebrating that he had not fallen. This bravado earned Lanier a hard slap on the back of his head from Reynaldo.

We skimmed the fortress wall past the fortification boundary and the Pond of Hearts. Then we bolted into Helsingør's northwestern fields. All around, feathery green caps topped a rustling sea of stalks. Ahead lay a horizon of leafy jade where the fields met the birch forest. Behind us, the huddled village of Helsingør and Krogen's reaching spires shrank in the distance.

Margrete turned to take a final look at her only home. It was her seat of influence from youth into adulthood. Where she had learned to wisely garner and spend political currency. To anticipate and serve her queen's needs. To sense the needs of others for protection. Where Margrete had first learned resilience.

Krogen was the place where our legacies died.

I, too, looked back to bid farewell to the cursed abode of the Hamlets. Once glory-seeking, it was now a wasteland of generations. A furnace of spirits. My beloved brother's death place. Where perverse ambitions begat cruel destiny. Where my future self perished.

However, that desecrated fortress also was a sacred site. It was where Hamlet had professed to me his brotherly love. Where I had met Lanier. Where I had met Margrete.

At that moment, as we raced through the open fields, I felt vulnerable and frightened, as if I myself had been shot from a catapult, like that unfortunate child, and in flight had no way to steer my path to safety. I was in pursuit to rescue and was also being pursued. I had no security of a scholar's cell and no destiny as the proud chancellor of Hamlet's and my university. I had no physical home. No hold upon my place in the world. Neither did Margrete, I believed.

We crossed fields, pulling along our lengthening shadows. They seemed knit to our horses' hooves. Behind, the two soldiers neither turned back nor gained upon us. Ahead, Reynaldo and Lanier dove into the forest of bushy treetops. We kicked our panting mounts and followed, plunging into the shade, upon the trail that wove among the chalky trunks. The trees' looming canopy gripped my imagination. I believed I saw ancient spirits skitter from branch to branch, their wings straining and lungs bursting to lift them, screeching, to a primitive moon.

Behind us, from the fields, a horse screamed. I guessed that the soldiers' exhausted animals had refused to confront the tree-dwelling sprites.

However, I was certain of Reynaldo's porcine-stinking presence ahead. I asked, "Can't we go faster? We'll lose their path."

Margrete said, "They are going to Hundested, probably."

"What's Hundested?"

"A northwestern port and fishing village. Very prosperous."

We followed the downward-arcing sun. Under a fire-streaked sky, we broke through the forest's western boundary. Ahead, a sandy clearing met a wind-whipped sea and a small village. The horse bearing

Reynaldo and Lanier thundered toward the shore where several small craft wobbled in the current. Beyond the surf a few large ships were moored. He'd escape with my book only if he killed me first, I thought. I spurred my horse.

Margrete called after me, "Wait."

I raced, bearing directly at the men riding ahead. My horse wheezed as it pounded across the sand littered with fish heads. It skidded in fright at the pebbly eyes.

We were nearly upon Reynaldo and Lanier when they slid off their horse. Lanier, still bound, tried to run away, carrying the *Gesta Danorum* clamped to his breast. The volume was partially unwrapped. The folds of his cape trailed, shedding pages upon the dry, white sand. Reynaldo dropped his hand cannon and, swiping at Lanier with Willem's sword, chased him to the mirror plate of soaked sand where it met the water. Lanier stumbled, fell into the water, but he managed to hold the book above the foamy current.

I leapt from my mount, landed clumsily on the dry sand, and ran after Reynaldo. I grasped him around the middle. We tumbled. I punched his face.

Reynaldo twisted away from me and scrambled to his feet. He chased Lanier, who was racing back to one of the wandering horses. But Reynaldo tripped him and ripped the *Gesta Danorum* from his arms. Reynaldo, at the tide's edge, waved the sword menacingly at us. He waded backward through the water in the direction of a shallow-moored landing boat. "Come, get your book," he called to us.

I ran into the water after Reynaldo. He turned toward the boat and lunged after it in breast-high water, holding my beautiful book above the surface. I swam after him. Reynaldo reached the small boat and heaved the *Gesta Danorum* at two boatmen sitting within it. They caught it. When I was within an arm's length of Reynaldo, he faced me and, smirking, wagged his sword point at my face.

"Return it, now," Margrete screamed from the shore.

Reynaldo, grinning like a wicked dog, held up a small, soaked purse to one of the boatmen. That crusty devil gave a shrill whistle to a large ship anchored farther out at sea.

"You bastard fiends," I cursed them. Reynaldo held the sword point at my head even as he was grasped under his arms and lifted into the landing boat. The oars dipped into the water. They pulled away toward the ship. Reynaldo, seated backward, leered broadly at me.

I treaded. Hopelessly, I watched the men row, then reach their ship. They climbed its rope ladder to board it. Within moments, I expected, the vessel's sails would fill and draw toward the twilight horizon. I could not bear to watch my book, the last hope for my promise and honor, disappear.

Feeling defeated in body and heart, I paddled back to the shore. I was glad for Lanier's rescue but was bitter for my loss. My arms and legs ached from fighting and the weight of my saturated clothing. I limped from the water.

Lanier, now freed from his bonds with Margrete's help, stood arms crossed, glaring at Reynaldo's ship. However, I did not see Margrete. "Where is she?" I asked Lanier.

He watched the ship. "Sails dropped. He waits, dares our pursuit."

"What can we do?" I asked. Burning from my loss, I scooped up the few scattered pages of my writing that had fallen from the volume. I stuffed them into my damp tunic pocket, then pulled my wet hat from my belt, wrung it, and put it on my head. Although I flopped it to one side in Papa's fashion, I did not feel better for doing so.

"Where is Margrete?"

Lanier pointed. I turned to see her, a short distance away upon the shoreline, near the fishing village. Margrete talked with four craggy men and gestured at the ships nodding beyond the tidal flux. Three men shook their heads and walked away, toward the village. However, one man, burly and bundled in silver fur, spoke longer with her. Within moments they ran to us, Margrete as graceful as a doe and the man huffing like a walrus. Frosty curls peeked from his brimmed seaman's cap. He seemed familiar, but I could not recall why.

Margrete told us, "The others will not risk trouble with Cristiern, but this man"—she smiled warmly at him—"has agreed to be our captain."

The captain did not look to her but regarded Lanier and me suspiciously. "Running from Cristiern?" he gruffly asked us.

We nodded in reply.

The captain's jowls worked on something tucked into the recesses of his cheeks. A rising breeze stirred the elegant fur on his shoulders. We, however, grimy and bloody, appeared as though we had crawled from a raw waste pit.

Reynaldo was likely far away now. To confirm my guess, I looked over my shoulder at that ship and discovered, to my surprise, that Lanier was correct. The ship remained, seemed to hover on the horizon, as if waiting for us. I turned to Margrete. "We've nothing to buy our passage. Only these horses to trade, but that's not enough."

"He will take them and also this as payment." She held out her necklace to the captain.

My heart plummeted. She would surrender that beloved keepsake? I could never ask her to do so.

"Eh, now." The captain fingered the lovely nuggets of amber, gold, and silver hanging from Margrete's hand. His flakey, swollen face pulled taut with his grin. "I always enjoy breaking Cristiern's blockade."

I grasped Margrete's outstretched hand holding the necklace. "No."

She twisted from my grip. Her fist dug into her hip. "In honor of the hundreds who died. For the House of Hamlet. And for you…" Her voice broke.

Margrete's care rendered me speechless. No one had ever sacrificed for me, had been my champion. For another to share my burden—that was a foreign and uncomfortable aspect. I recalled the counsel that the priest at Saint Olai Church had given me. A turning key is made of many notches, and I was only one of those, dependent upon the others.

"I'm forever your servant." I took Margrete's other hand and kissed it.

A sad smile was Margrete's only reply. She pressed the necklace, the remnant of her broken past, to her lips. Then she dropped the necklace into the captain's salt-cracked hands. His eyes lit at his new wealth. He pocketed the necklace.

"We must go." Margrete clapped her hands. "We cannot lose sight of that ship."

The captain whistled to his crew. From the village three bushy men approached and collected our horses.

The wet shore shimmered in twilight's descent. We hastened across it, into the tumbling surf, and waded to a small craft. It bore us across the crystalline, watery sheet to an angular three-masted ship. Its name, *Master Yorick*, scrawled along its bow, sparked my memory. This captain, loyal to the Hamlets, months beforehand had brought me from Rostock through Cristiern's blockade to Krogen, so that I might help Hamlet in his grief. Although he did not seem to recognize me, I suddenly felt I was in better care.

We scrambled up the rope ladder, over the rail, and onto the deck.

The captain's booming commands sent his men scrambling above our heads, across the yardarm. The sails unfurled and, at first, flapped like lazy wings. With a sudden burst of wind, however, the triangular sails bulged and spanned the length of the craft. We lurched toward the sea and the ship harboring Reynaldo. It, too, instantly opened its sails and took flight.

"Where's that Spanish hornet leading us?" I asked Lanier.

"We will see, *mon ami*," Lanier said grimly.

Our vessel surged west toward the last sliver of God's fiery aura. After His banner melted into the watery, indigo blanket, the sky thickened to the ink of misty night.

Throughout the night we rode the sea as if drawn by an enormous water serpent, rising and falling with the monster's undulating back. Although the crew wrestled the lines governing our sails, Reynaldo's ship leapt far ahead. I watched until it vanished into the horizon's shadow.

"Never fear," the captain barked into the wind that whipped his silver fur. "We'll draw close and sidle with him like a daemon calf."

As our ship lurched into oncoming waves, Margrete, Lanier, and I gripped the rail for balance, buoyed by our faith such as we proceed in life, we prisoners of the current.

XIV.

On the first day of our seafaring journey in pursuit of Reynaldo's vessel, our ship, tumbling across the ocean's silvery swells, drew nearer to the enemy's rocking stern. Through our captain's scope I could see Reynaldo scurrying across the deck, the *Gesta Danorum* in hand. I wanted to wrest it from that vermin, to catch and squash him. A prejudicial wind, however, carried his craft farther ahead.

That evening I stood at the rail, watched the sun drop and seep across the watery table like a broken egg. A few sailors above, scaling three lateen masts, called to one another. Some below the deck sang jaunty tunes with flute and drum. Others played raucous games of cards. I, however, could not make merry or retreat. A cutting wind assailed me, within and without. Would I ever hold my book again? How would I afford its printing? If I could not, how would I keep my promise and save my honor? Punishment by fire and pinchers surely awaited. Heavy dread of unending death filled me.

My rumination benefited nothing. I could not see my future path any better than I could glimpse a landmass beyond the frosty halo of the horizon. My mind was caged, and our ship was like a prison. I was surrounded by a vast, monstrous moat and by my tormented friends.

I turned my back against twilight's last rays to behold Margrete and Lanier, bedraggled and sitting upon the deck. We gnawed pieces of hard bread that the captain gave us. Their faces were pallid and shallow—I probably appeared much the same—fitting for anyone shackled to his life's debris. We suffered heart fever. When we were not smoldering beneath an ashen crust of fury, we were chilled from despair. This variance caused no little share of confusion.

For example, one moment Margrete seemed to want her privacy, keeping to her cot among our beds in the ship's berth deck, in the aftercastle. The next moment, she appeared to want my company, when she leaned against me while we watched sailors angrily lose their card games. I wanted to comfort her but always seemed to choose the wrong approach. That always earned from her either a dejected glare or a huff of disgust. I contained my impatience because her pain and difficulties exceeded my own. I confess, however, that I struggled with the debt and dishonor levied by Margrete's forfeit of her precious necklace. She had rescued me whereas I should have been her champion.

During our second afternoon at sea, Margrete came to me where I stood on deck, upwind of rancid sailors and watching their contest as they flipped knives at the mast pole. I cupped her chin and saw her red-rimmed eyes. She had been crying. Margrete leaned into my arms. I stroked her hair, kissed and embraced her. She pulled my hat from my head and wore it upon her flowing locks. I liked that she remained shielded within my arms, covered by my hat and nestled into my shirt folds. Her breath upon my skin brought a sweet itch. At last I was her protector, her knight.

Margrete asked me, "What are we to do now?"

"Go to my cot," I would have replied. However, when I flopped the hat's crown aside so that I might see her expression, her hollow-eyed sadness curbed me. Instead, I said, "Get our *Gesta Danorum*. Somehow print it."

"I mean that none of us has a home. Where will we live?"

"Fortune is our guardian and will provide for us somehow."

Margrete shuddered. She looked up at me. Her mouth was a dour line.

I stroked her shoulders. "We will find our destiny, even if we must hunt and shackle it."

"I want to have children," she said. "I told you of my rape but not of the consequences. My attacker impregnated me, but my child was stillborn. I carried it to term because my womb would not give up the dead baby. That was my punishment for his sin, but he was protected."

My bliss shattered, and anger at that filth-eater welled in my breast. "What was that witch bastard's rank?"

"He was a son of Krogen's highest noble line."

"Old Hamlet or Gertrude could have expelled him. They should have given him to Helsingør's council for trial."

"He served his penance and more," she sniffed. "A fever overtook him last winter."

I held Margrete tighter, believing my arms could give her anchor, replace her lost status and security. I shared with her some dried meat and a cup of water that a gaunt sailor brought us.

But a moment later Margrete pulled away. She handed me my hat. Confused, I looked to her.

She said, "Why would a man abide my stain of dishonor? His happiness as a husband would be impossible."

"Was this a concern while I courted you at Krogen?"

She wiped her eyes. Then she stood straight and, smoothing her frock, looked away.

Her assessment against men was unfair to me, for I was not heartless. I wanted to rave, *What did she want?* Instead, I made a bridge of my fingers and began, "I understand—"

"Only a woman can know—"

"That our lives are upended. That now, as always, our role is to act honorably." I replaced my hat on my head, gave its crown a firm downward tug.

Margrete stepped back. That sudden, little space between us felt to me like a great gulf.

I felt helpless but tried harder. I opened my arms, saying, "Only moments ago we were enjoying…allowing ourselves a few moments of—"

"Horatio, tell the truth. You courted me for the purpose of your own protection because you feared that your lies to Fortinbras would be your ruin."

"I courted you because I love you."

Margrete folded her arms against me. "Another of your lies."

"No." Stinging from her abuses, I regarded her. I did not know what to do with the woman…other than surrender to her will, to her preference that she always control the moment.

The next morning, I saw Margrete upon the deck, squinting into the glare pinching the horizon, as if reading our fortune in the tides. I did not approach her even once that day.

Therefore, I was much amazed when that night Margrete came to me at my cot in the aftercastle, undeterred by the dozen snoring men surrounding us. She loosened her corset's front laces and joined me under my blanket. Beneath that cloak we explored and tasted one another. I was wary of her, but desire overcame me. I allowed her command of every motion until I could refrain no longer. Then, I steered us, straining and swallowing, to become one, our moans obscured by the creaking bow. After culmination I spied a sailor's greedy stare, but I cared not. I held Margrete until dawn's light pierced the deck's planks above us and shone into our eyes.

She sat up, wrapped herself in her restraints, and climbed up the ladder onto the deck. But that day she only greeted me cordially, a cutting reversal. "Hello, Horatio," was all she said as she passed me. I wanted to embrace and fondle her. In agony I pondered what I'd done wrong. That night we enjoyed a little reprieve, as we stood in the moonlight upon the deck. She kissed me lightly on my cheek. However, no more favors opened to me.

Grumpy and uncertain of Margrete, I turned to Lanier for company. I found his demeanor only a little less perplexing than the lady's.

At times he was sanguine and evidenced buoyant disposition, and was so during an instance, after four days at sea, when we turned from the English Channel into the mouth of the Seine at Le Havre. At the dock, Lanier helped us hurry, with the captain and crew, to disembark from our ship and board a boat suitable to travel the river. Reynaldo had already changed conveyances.

Through the milky haze of sunrise, we chased Reynaldo's vessel.

That thief's stink spoiled the otherwise sweet convergence of salt air and the river's green breeze. I gripped the rail and jubilantly cried out, "We're nearly upon him now," although we were no closer to Reynaldo. But then I remembered the danger to Lanier—Louis's warrant forbade his return to his country—and I cringed.

I abandoned my celebration and crossed the deck to stand with Lanier. "You shouldn't enter France. We're risking your life. We don't expect you to—"

Lanier jerked backward as if I had struck him. "You do not value my friendship?"

"Yes, but already you have done much—"

"Pah. You insult me." Lanier, with a chop of his gloved hand, dismissed my objection. "There is no debt between friends."

"Not debt, but perhaps other obligation. Did I ever tell you of my dream about the skull?"

"No. I would remember that."

"I dreamt, once, that Hamlet handed me a skull..."

Lanier's brow arched. "A man's severed head? Was it mounted on a board? A pike?"

"No. A bare skull. Hamlet disappeared, and then the skull I held became Hamlet's. Then you appeared beside me, and I handed the skull to you."

"Ach. I hope I did not accept it."

"You did accept it, and a little girl stood beside you and you gave the skull to her."

"*Mon ami*, that is depravity."

I considered Lanier's point. "She didn't take offense. She seemed interested in it. I believe it is about our journey together, my promise, and honor. But why and how would a girl champion my promise?"

Lanier shrugged. He bent at the waist and leaned upon the smooth rail, examined his thick hands.

I propped myself beside him. "Do you have a daughter, Lanier?"

"None reputed to be mine," he said wistfully.

"Nor do I," I said, sharing his melancholy.

Together we watched the vista. Emerald fields and sloping embankment lumbered past our creaking deck. A road paralleled the river. Upon that path trundled an ox-pulled cart. At its head stood a frail old man. He held the reins. Two small girls beside him clung to the cart's dilapidated, shaking sides. The man took both straps in one hand to pat one girl's round cheek. The other girl stroked his shabby sleeve. The children settled against him, like ducklings seeking protection. Lanier seemed transfixed by the scene. "Look how they care for one another."

"That cart and ox might be their only earthly possessions," I said.

"Regardless, they are rich." He leaned near my ear—his scent of cloves was as warm as a hearth—to say in confidence, "I envy that man, *mon ami*."

"Why so?"

"Their company is his home. A man cannot doubt he is loved." Lanier examined his hands. "I have no home, no family, and no hope for one. Probably, I will die a vagrant."

"Even wanderers must rest, find people who know and love them. Every man has significance and a place in the world."

"Does he?" Lanier picked at the skin rimming his fingernails. "Before I became a Hanseatic agent, before I joined Pinzon's ship crew…before the deaths—as a young man I only knew how to work horses. My father's line trained them for the courtiers and royalty. My mother's line were musicians. I tried to play, but most instruments rejected me."

"Not the lute."

Lanier shrugged, flicked away a sliver of fingernail. "The horses: they liked me."

"You can return to that life, can't you?"

"It was long ago." Lanier stared ahead. "New opportunities come. I take them."

"Perhaps fortune will carve a fresh slate for you. A home you don't expect. Or a gullible woman who smells like a horse."

Lanier laughed. Then, he grinned sadly at me and clasped my shoulder. "*Mon ami*, I like you. You give me hope."

"Good."

Lanier briskly rubbed his chin. He leaned, forearms upon the rail, and looked again to the riverside, the old man, and the children. "I would take Nicolas in a cart like that. Show him the world."

Surprised, I regarded Lanier. He continued to study the scene. "Who's Nicolas?"

"A son, perhaps one day. Or a nephew. It is a family name. Do you wish for a son?"

His question awakened an ache in me. I nodded.

We continued to observe the little family. Distance shrank them to mere wavering forms upon a long, muddy trail. They seemed to meld with the elements under the cobalt, cream-streaked sky.

Lanier's demeanor was enigmatic to me. Despite his wistful moments open to hope, at times he was despondent. One night, during the final two days of our voyage, Lanier, Margrete, and I stood silently upon the boat's deck. Lanier suddenly scoffed. His eyes and teeth caught the glow of the hazy pearl moon in the starless expanse.

I cast a question to lure conversation. "What does the moon portend?"

Rather than look heavenward, Lanier looked down the hull's bowed side. He watched the sea fold upon itself. "That my fate is set. I can only do what I must."

I said, "We've some choice in our part and how we act it. A wise man, my papa, taught me that."

Lanier removed his hat, turned the broad brim round in his thick hands. "Who decides one's part?"

"You decide for yourself, my friend."

"Not God?"

Margrete said, "He cares for us and marks our life's boundaries. Our end, ultimately, is determined by our Heavenly Father."

Lanier considered. His clenching jaw seemed to pump worry through his temples. He turned to her. "You bought your destiny with sacrifice of your necklace."

"And prayer."

He looked away but then glanced at me again. With a dull flicker of mirth, he asked me, "If we are captured by Cristiern's bounty men, how will we be executed?"

I made an exaggerated frown. "After imprisonment, probably hanged. Possibly dismembered."

Lanier's finger traced each wing of his mustache. He countered, "Burned."

"No," I said, jesting. "Too conventionally English. The sword and block are coming into fashion against nobles."

"A quick death for me." Lanier nodded. "For you, I really think"—

he grimaced mockingly but his eye glinted—"you were right the first time. You would be hanged."

"Stop." Margrete's straining fingers jabbed at us as if casting a spell. She closed her eyes and took a deep breath. Her voice struck a lower register when she said, "You laugh at death, but we have serious matters to consider. Lanier"—she turned to him—"fear not. We will deliver you from France."

Lanier, stoic and steady, regarded her. He did not reply.

She added, "The family offense is remote, now. How can Reynaldo take you to Louis and expect a substantial reward?"

"Louis would grant it to him. Reynaldo is a fool, mademoiselle, but he is convincing, and his reputation as a rogue is well-earned."

Margrete shook her head. "Louis should have no concern with you."

"Many Burgundians have fled France for fear of Louis's judgment and abuses. Hatred between the Orleans and Burgundian family lines is a common dish at the Valois table."

"Your entire family has fled France?" she asked.

"Not yet."

"What has this to do with you?" I asked.

Lanier looked up at our bulging sails. He seemed to read them like huge pages writ upon by the wind. "My great-great-grandfather was Jean the Fearless, a powerful Burgundian of the House of Valois. He arranged the savage murder of Louis's grandfather, the Duke of Orleans. That death caused the duke's wife, Louis's grandmother, to lose her wits. She wrote of her despair upon the walls where she lived. That was Blois Palace, where Louis lives now."

"Your ancestor's trial must have been an unruly mess," I said.

"He had no trial. He fled and was pardoned. Within a few years the family lines publicly reconciled. But Louis...he never accepted his father's forgiveness of my ancestor."

I began to weave an understanding of the trouble. "The families of the dead appealed to Louis?"

Lanier nodded.

"Louis thinks that because you—"

"Killed two people," Lanier quickly stated.

"You are like your ancestor."

"An unpunished Burgundian murderer. Consequently, a nomad." Lanier grimaced.

I looked down at the water, seeking hope's mark of encouragement. The ribbonlike flow along our hull seemed to be a sign of continuity. "Margrete is right. We won't allow Reynaldo to take you. He probably wants the easiest reward, which is why he took the book. He might try to sell it to rich merchants in Paris. If we can follow him, we can take the book and run with it to the Hôtel de Sens. Cristiern said that's where the canon of Lund is stationed, that he awaits the *Gesta Danorum* to print it for Denmark."

Margrete added, "If we cannot salvage the whole manuscript, we will rip Hamlet's story from it before Reynaldo can get his recompense."

Lanier seemed to chew his words. "I will be a prisoner of my ancestors' sins forever." He pounded the rail. "*Mon Dieu*, I have had enough." Lanier glared at Reynaldo's boat. He fumed like a hunted boar.

"The hour is late," I said, steering Margrete by the elbow toward the aftercastle. "I will guard her at her bed, for her ease."

Soon after Margrete fell asleep I returned to the deck. Lanier, still at the rail, studied the water. He muttered, "*Je suis perdu.*"

"You are not lost."

A MAN OF HONOR

The moon's thready trails seemed to reach for Lanier. He braced against the rail and remained silent. I left him alone.

I had scarce ability to help my troubled friends. And God was testing me. My puzzling situation with Margrete, my fight waged at Krogen, and loss of my work and treasured volume—altogether these were, I believed, a trial to prove my heroic merit. I bore a greater burden than even the Horatii brothers and Horatius Cocles. They had never confronted their friend's ghost.

On our final morning during seven days upon the water I stood again at the boat's rail to breathe in the sweet scent of the Loire's riverbank. The lovely environs would, I hope, unlock my mind and inspire revelation. How would I distribute Hamlet's story?

While awaiting the muse, I watched activity on the embankment. People, bending, pulled at vegetables. One man in particular caught my notice—something familiar about his bearing. He wore a wide-brimmed hat and a ragged straw-colored vest over his shirt. When he straightened and raised his hat to look at me, I recognized his face. It was as beloved and dirty as on the day that he had returned to Helsingør, fought Laertes, and died.

I cried, "Hamlet." He cupped his hands to his mouth and called to me, but I could not hear him.

What's he telling me? I slung my leg over the rail to dive and swim to him. "Hamlet."

Hamlet waved both arms, as if panicked. Why couldn't I hear him? With every previous visitation I could hear Hamlet speak clearly to me. I closed my eyed and rubbed them. Was I mad?

I opened my eyes. Hamlet was gone. The farmers dug onward.

Shaken, I climbed back over the rail and stood on deck.

A nudge at my elbow made me jump.

"You ogle my mother country?" Lanier scowled at me in jest. He waved a proud hand across the lush panorama.

"Lanier, on the riverbank—I saw…"

"Hamlet?"

"Yes. You saw him?"

"No, *mon ami*. I guessed." He gave me a wry glance. "Are you well?"

Lanier's easy recognition of my longing stung like a skinning. I closed my eyes, recalled Hamlet's urgency. Was something wrong?

I wished for illumination but, to me, there was only blackness. My hands itched to rescue the *Gesta Danorum* and stage it before the eyes and ears of the world. Further, I felt liable for my friends' safekeeping although they had elected to join my crusade. I had to succeed, to justify the risk they bore.

XV.

At dawn the next morning, the Seine, cascading like a ribbon into an inviting bosom, delivered us to Île de la Cité. This was ancient Paris, the lovely heart of Lanier's perilous motherland. A crusty point of land loomed ahead, splitting the river.

Reynaldo's boat sped onward, right of the point. We chased and shortened the distance.

Our captain clasped me on the shoulder. The silver fur of his coat fluttered in the uncommonly cool summer morning breeze. He handed me my last ration of hard bread and beer, then squinted against the morning sun and said, "Your thief'll be in chains soon enough." He called out to his crew, "Full sail. At approach ease starboard."

Lanier, Margrete, and I moved to the bow and saw, a short distance before us, Reynaldo watching us from his stern. His plumed hat bobbed. He doffed it at us. Our boat drew closer. He called out, "Make yourself ready, Lanier. In God's name, I will deliver judgment."

Margrete screamed at Reynaldo, "You are a troll and a blasphemer."

I anticipated Lanier's retort to his enemy and so looked to him.

Lanier said nothing. His eyes were bloodshot but sharp.

"How now, Lanier?" I asked him.

"*Mon ami*, you are absolutely certain that this book is worth our trouble?"

"Yes. It will teach of courage, our need for good kings and good friends."

Lanier looked out over the river. Beneath the darkening sky, its gloss was like an iron sheet. He nodded. "I hope so."

Our bow followed a half-length directly behind Reynaldo's stern. I began to climb over the bow toward the bowsprit, intending to somehow swing from that pole onto the enemy's bouncing stern. However, Lanier grasped my arm to restrain me. He pulled me back onto the deck. "Only a few moments, *mon ami*, and you will have your *Gesta Danorum*."

Ahead, the busy dock lined both flanks of the point. A gray stone fortification wall, like armor, channeled voyagers along the dock to the towering stone gatehouse to pay the toll. There began the main road that became the town's spider web of lanes harboring markets, workshops, homes, and churches.

Reynaldo's vessel slowed, veered to the right side of the point. Following close in his wake, we glided nearer to the dock. It was filled with stacked barrels, boisterous sailors, and wandering passengers. Our crew groomed our sails and turned the boom away from the wind. Reynaldo's boat drifted portside toward the dock. As his crew flung ropes down to men to secure the boat, Reynaldo gripped a rope ladder and dropped it over the rail. As the boat's hull bumped against the dock, he climbed downward.

Our sailors called out to one another, cast ropes to men on the dock. A millennium seemed to pass as our vessel settled alongside the sturdy planks. There, Reynaldo stood, *Gesta Danorum* raised in one hand and sword gripped in the other. He leered at us.

Lanier flung our rope ladder's end over the side of our hull. "*Allez.*"

I grasped the prickly cords, clambered down the wooden rungs, and jumped down upon the dock. Immediately, I reached up and assisted Margrete's descent. When I turned to face Reynaldo, he thrust Willem's sword point at my face.

To guard Margrete I pulled her behind me. "Give me the book," I told Reynaldo.

Lanier landed beside me, a heavy thud upon the dock.

Reynaldo laughed. He wagged the sword point and shuffled to the edge of the dock. Then he held the *Gesta Danorum* over the water. "Give me Lanier." A corner of the bundled cape dangled: some pages peeked out. "I have no use for it, now that Cristiern is dead. It was the cheese that brought my rat to me. Lanier, we have a king to visit in Blois. Come with me or no one will have this book."

I said, "If you destroy it, Cristiern will hunt you as well."

"Probably not, *señor*. Dead men pay no reward."

"Cristiern lives." I grinned. "My lie bested you. I smashed that book against his head. It felled him but he revived. His soldiers saw you take the *Gesta Danorum* from us."

"They did not see that," Reynaldo sneered.

"They did," I insisted, "and now, you're the thief he's cursing. Cristiern is enraged, and he'll come for you, Reynaldo. You can wager Christ's bones on that. What will he do to you if you destroy his book?"

Reynaldo bristled.

Lanier said, "If only you had remained at Krogen, Cristiern would have rewarded you for delivering the book, and us, to him. The bounty would have been immense. As usual, you lost. *Quel dommage.*"

"Lying witch," Reynaldo accused me. He jabbed the sword at my head. I swerved but my beloved hat suffered a cut in its floppy crown.

"Swine. If you give Horatio the *Gesta Danorum*, then I will surrender to you."

"Lanier?" Margrete said, standing behind me.

Alarmed, I grasped Lanier's sleeve and demanded, "What're you doing?"

Ignoring us, Lanier continued to feed Reynaldo's boiling greed. "Forget the book. Louis will pay you much more for a live Burgundian that he can torture, especially me."

Reynaldo's shoulders dropped, as if the thought of Lanier's misery lightened his burden. At that moment, I lunged at the book—but the blade point aligned with my heart. I halted.

Lanier stepped closer to Reynaldo, and the sword targeted him again. Lanier told him, "Release the book to Horatio and Margrete. Permit them to go. I will come with you to Blois."

Margrete's fingers clamped my hand like iron bands. "Horatio, we cannot allow this."

I could not bear this madness. "Lanier, cease this blasted negotiation."

Reynaldo pointed to a scar on the dock and said to Lanier, "When you cross that mark to stand with me, there I will drop the book."

I pulled Lanier close. "Why sacrifice yourself?"

He looked dubiously at Reynaldo's sword point. "What are we to do? Your cause, Horatio, is why we stand here, upon the point of Île de la Cité."

I shook my fist at him. "Don't force me to choose between my promise and... between the dead and the living."

Lanier's hand capped my fist. He pushed it down. "*Mon ami*, we each contribute to destiny. Some men do this by living. Others? If God wills the fall of a sparrow, believe there is singular fortune in it."

"This can't be your destiny," I said.

"Take the book. Do your duty, your part, as you say. Continue your chivalric courtship but improve your dancing. Don't disappoint me." Lanier smirked, but I could not laugh.

Lanier looked straight ahead at Reynaldo and took a fortifying breath. He walked forward as if sauntering to the barkeep for a tankard of beer. When he passed the scar, Reynaldo tossed the wrapped *Gesta Danorum* at the mark, short of my stance. The tome's heavy landing cracked its bottom wood cover.

I picked up the partly shrouded, broken *Gesta Danorum*. My heart, too, was splintered. I had failed to protect my brothers, first Hamlet and now Lanier.

Reynaldo tied Lanier's hands behind his back and tightly cinched the knots. Lanier winced. Reynaldo's lips curled in a blasted, triumphant smile. He told Lanier, "I will remain at Blois for the festivities of your hanging, to watch you suffer. Or, perhaps soon after we arrive there, your head will go on a pike, like Fortinbras at Krogen."

At blade point, Reynaldo pushed Lanier through the toll gate to a horse trader stabled at the base of the road. Reynaldo glanced over his shoulder and shook the sword at us, warning us away. Within moments they mounted a burly, wooly horse.

Despite the gate separating us, Lanier called out, "Horatio, do this for me: find my brother, Jean. Search the marketplaces and taverns here. He is a flute player. Wears a black cape, like mine. Tell Jean the situation."

"I'll look for him."

Margrete and I watched the men ride onto the town road. Among the milling throng they trotted past the cottages and shops. Where the road bent toward majestic cathedral towers, they disappeared from my sight.

In that moment I beheld Lanier akin to Horatius Cocles. Each risked himself to save others, not knowing if he would survive the act. With this realization a weight dropped from my heart into a purse of regrets from which nothing could be spent or given away.

I hugged my book, feeling bereft and wanting comfort. I reached for Margrete's hand, but she pulled away.

"Why?" I asked her.

"Stop pretending love."

I, whom Hamlet had once praised as the most reasoned man he had ever known, was nearly overcome with frustration. I wanted to scream at her but quelled that heat. "I'm not pretending."

Despite Margrete's apparent revulsion at my touch, I took her arm and, carrying the *Gesta Danorum*, guided us along the dock. We walked among the herds and carts laden with cabbages and furs ready for transport toward the gatehouse tower. At the gate we joined a large group as they paid their toll and, en masse, squeezed through the opening. We pushed past mail-layered guards, standing aloof as they observed the creeping throng.

Once free of the crowd, we stood in a broader lane. Swarming merchants, eyeing their competitors, filled the road ahead. Men and women pulled their carts, adjusting their signage and wares to attract the gullible and curious. Peasants dashed to complete errands. Yoked horses and mad derelicts relieved themselves in the road.

Panic roiled in me. We had to find shelter. And we needed to locate

Jean.

Across the road stood a long timbered tavern. It was not an acceptable refuge for a lady, for no women but a cook's maid or a whore would inhabit a tavern. However, Lanier's brother might be there. I led Margrete to stand beside the tavern portal.

"One moment," I said and reached for the latch. "Perhaps Jean is inside."

"Or bounty hunters." Margrete's hand slapped upon the door to hold it shut. "Soon many will know about the prize for our heads."

I looked to the passing crowd to identify ruffians. Ragged peasants, guildsmen, and workers in their thick smocks and leather pantaloons, finely cloaked merchants—all trudged up the road lined with cottages and shops, distracted by their purpose. No one noticed us. Thus, I grasped the tavern latch and flung open the door. "I'll take care. Stay here."

Margrete nodded. She hugged herself tightly, stood with her back to the wall, and watched the procession of humanity.

I stepped into the tavern. The room was hazy with lingering smoke. In the fireplace a heap of coals still glowed, perhaps from the previous night's grand roast. Throughout the room a few plainly dressed people reclined in stout chairs. Some slept. None wore a black cape embroidered with a family crest like the one wrapped around the book I held. None held a musical instrument.

I went to a muscular man, the barkeep, tending casks beside stacks of tankards.

"Is Jean the flute player commissioned to play here?"

"Who?" he grunted as he wiped a cup on his sleeve.

Because Paris would be packed with taverns, a recited list of them would be useless to me. But Lanier also had mentioned markets as possible sites. Therefore, I asked in simple French, "Please, tell me if the marketplace is near here."

The barkeep, gaps showing between his teeth, muttered. "One big market near the churches. The other, farther north."

I also wanted to know where I would find the Hôtel de Sens, which was—as I had overheard Cristiern telling Willem—the archbishop's home where the canon of Lund, the official Cristiern had ordered to print the *Gesta Danorum*, was posted.

"Thank you. Please, where is the Hôtel de Sens?" The barkeep winced quizzically at me, and so I added, "Where the archbishop resides?"

"Up the road north, then west at the churches. Cross a footbridge. Up a hill. Down a hill. Mansion's there. Go to the end of that road."

He held out his open palm. I had no coins to render for his service. "Bless you," I said and touched my hat to salute his courtesy. He frowned at me and grunted again.

I exited the tavern. Margrete turned to me, arms still crossed against her bosom. "Horatio—"

"The Hôtel de Sens is a slight distance. The canon of Lund may offer us shelter when he sees our book. I will ask him to print it with Hamlet's story intact. But he may not agree."

"We should find a patron not connected to Cristiern." Margrete still shielded herself and scrutinized the passing masses for a sign of the enemy. "Why has Cristiern not followed us or sent a minion to fetch the *Gesta Danorum*? He would not have abandoned pursuit of it."

She was right. I looked down the road to the gatehouse and dock. "No soldiers yet. As Lanier asked, we must find his brother," I said.

"We will not forsake Lanier. Let us go now to the Hôtel de Sens."

"Not yet. Let's find Jean and rescue Lanier. Then, we can go to Wittenberg. In that town somehow I'll find a way to print the *Gesta Danorum*."

Margrete swept a tress of hair, sticking to her perspiring face, behind her ear. "We have no means to journey there. Do you know a printer in that town?"

I looked down at the book I held and tugged a corner of the cape to reveal the hard, smooth face. "No, but several printers thrive there."

How could I find in Wittenberg a patron to pay for creation of the manuscript and a patron to afford its printing? If a single patron, he must have access to a scriptorium. To an army of scribes. To crates and allies who would carry the book to points afar. He must also be willing to test Cristiern and all of Copenhagen.

The canon of Lund as patron seemed to be my only option. He might, as Cristiern mentioned, be a son of Helsingør. But would he dare betray a king he served, print a forbidden story within a book he was ordered to produce? I swallowed my doubt and set firm my resolve. Somehow, I needed convince the canon of Lund that my cause deserved his charity. He had to help me create the perfected manuscript needed by his printer to birth a multitude of *Gesta Danorum*s.

Fat, icy raindrops began to pelt us. I bunched Lanier's splendid black cape around my book and pages and tucked the bundle under my arm.

Margrete sighed. "We cannot find Jean. We must find safe harbor."

I looked across the road to the leaning cottages abutting one another under a black wool sky. Each seemed to bear too many occupants already.

Margrete pointed up the road. "The Hôtel de Sens is this way?"

We hastened from the tavern up the foul-smelling, noisome road lined with an odd variety of abodes—thatch-topped shops, dwellings made of humble straw and mud, and others constructed of brick. We darted past merchants' doors, beneath their hanging tokens depicting cobblers' shoe molds, tanners' strips of animal hide, and bakers' loaves. Where the road turned, the crowd thickened. The people pressed toward a structure rising in our path. Like ribs unearthed from a windswept grave, the buttresses of the Sainte-Chappelle arced. From its west gable a celestial eye of stained glass watched all whom the bells summoned to Mass.

Then, a steady rain broke upon us. Because our appearance was suitable only for the hogpens, we could not seek refuge at the church during devotions. However, ahead, we saw tents stretched across a commons. It was the marketplace. We ran there and ducked beneath a canopy.

While Margrete lingered at a dry table and examined weasel skins, I dashed about in search of a flute player clad in a black cape. I heard the hollow thud of drums and bright strum of a lute. However, I detected no one resembling Lanier's description of Jean. I began to realize that he would not be so easily found.

I fetched Margrete and, together, we ran from the marketplace to a narrow bridge, which we crossed. Along the uphill road we passed mansions whose broad faces of stone and brick gawked at us. Their sloping roofs, adorned with fanciful Italian carvings in the parapets and dormers, were like elaborate hats invented by clever children.

The road turned slightly downward and ended at a massive garden gate. This, I guessed, was the boundary of the Hôtel de Sens.

We pushed through the unlocked gate and stepped into a garden. At its far end loomed a palatial home bearing a smooth edifice of stone. Its tall windows blinked, betraying flashes of life within. Coned turrets and peak-roofed dormers towered above. These adornments were not like a child's cap but more like a rich man's hat and cape worn to a High Feast Day celebration.

Cold seeped into my bones. The sight of the residence ahead, likely warm and perhaps generous with food, urged me onward. I clamped the volume to my breast and ran through rows of bushes to the tall, arched door. I saw no knocker and so pounded upon its dense planks, jarring my fists...until I noticed the double-knotted bell rope hanging beside me.

I pulled upon that cord, which was massive enough to clash the bells of Notre Dame. But it made only a delicate, faerie-like ring behind the door. We bore the soaking rainfall and waited. No reply came. My second attempt issued the same bright, tentative request.

Margrete, then, flailed at the door. Her stringy, wet hair and wild demeanor belied any former hint of nobility. I joined her tempest by kicking at the door. "Are they deaf?" she asked.

The door drifted finally inward, cackling upon its hinges. The attendant, a short, older man, glared at us. He was round and pink, like the wedge of pulpy fruit he gnawed. Nectar dribbled down his chin. He examined the door, where we had kicked it, and spied a blot. "Wretched filth-mongers. What do you want?" He cursed at us in his native tongue—words we did not understand, but his rumbling tone was malicious.

I stood at nose point with the attendant and made a clenching grin so broad and tight my teeth might have cracked. "Pray you, escort us to the canon of Lund."

"Not without an appointment." He pressed the door nearly closed upon my face.

A sheet of rain swept my back, and I heaved myself against the door, making a gap. The attendant pushed against it, but I held it fast. He growled, "No more audiences today. None available until the thirteenth day of July."

"What day is today?" I pressed back against the door.

"The twenty-sixth day of June." He snorted.

Margrete blurted, "Stand aside. Is this how the Paris bishopric welcomes Danish nobility?"

The attendant's rasping laugh was an affront. With one hand I reached through the gap and grasped his collar. I twisted it and pulled his face close, squeezing his cheeks between the edge of the door and its portal. "We will see the canon."

"You...will...not," he panted.

Margrete might have clawed at him, but she cooed, "Horatio, we are mistaken." She looked to the attendant. "Oh, my dear man, we are sorry. It is the archbishop we seek." She slid his hand into her sleeveless frock and onto her wrapped bosom.

The attendant's eyes bulged at her. "The archbishop is not here today."

"Oh. Then, are you certain we cannot speak briefly with the canon of Lund?"

The gap widened. His fingers wiggled for access.

She purred, "Just a few words with the honorable canon?"

He seemed not to hear. He licked his lips and reached to feel her again.

I grasped his arm, twisted against his elbow. He yelped. I fumed. "The canon...or I will report you for defilement."

The attendant sputtered, "She offered."

Margrete smiled bewitchingly at the attendant. He opened the door a bit more, then grasped Margrete's other breast.

I banged open the door. We barged into the large whitewashed foyer graced by candlelight, tapestry, and sculpture. Margrete slapped the attendant's face. He stumbled backward. She said, "Take us to the canon."

He blinked at her as if confused about the terms of purchase. Then he rubbed his cheek and scowled. "Follow me."

The attendant, waddling, led us past twin marble figures of the pope and the archbishop of Sens, square in comportment, each clasping the Holy Scriptures to their breasts. The mosaic floor we walked shimmered like the gloss of pearl. We passed through an arched portal into a bright passage lit by windows on the left side that looked onto the garden. Along the right side, a vivid mural depicted the Stations of the Cross.

At the hallway's end was a wide, white door secured by a gold latch. The attendant ushered us into that cavernous, unoccupied office.

The broad floor was a sea of interlocking planks. The lower walls were lined with shuttered cabinets. Through their latticed windows peeked the gold-tooled bindings of many books. Above the cabinets, tapestries scaled the white walls and reached the ceiling adorned with painted flowers. At the room's far end, a grand table was moored by its gilded feet. Upon it two tall candles burned. Stacks of books and piles of manuscripts and scrolls covered the table from end to end. Set upon a smaller table in the corner were stacks of vellum accompanied by two inkpots and a scale. In another corner stood a rack upon which a few manuscript sheets hung to dry. The pages bore sweeping script bordered by delicate, vine-like illustrations of gold, green, and blue. The riches contained within this single office filled me with awe and envy.

Behind the table was a great chair, the seat in which the archbishop studied his treasures, I guessed. Opposite it, facing the table, were three small cushioned chairs, side by side. The attendant waved at them. "Sit."

Margrete and I timidly sat in the lesser chairs.

After several minutes passed, the latch pressed downward, and the door opened. A man, tall and gaunt, entered the room. Gray hair curled below his tonsor. He wore a white habit trimmed with gold. His bushy brows arched—perhaps the attendant had not mentioned our presence. He approached and his open hand levitated within its sweeping white sleeve. "Alms are not distributed from these offices. Who are you?" The canon's question floated upon a lyrical arc. His dignified Danish cadence was softened by the lilt of his acquired Swedish accent.

Gripping the *Gesta Danorum*, I knelt beside my chair. "Master, I am Horatio of Tønderensis, Denmark. The lady is Margrete, daughter of Hendrik of Helsingør, Denmark."

"Hendrik? Truly? I knew his family once."

Margrete curtsied. When he glanced, narrow-eyed, at Margrete, she gripped her hands before her middle.

He continued, "I am Christiern Pedersen, canon of Lund."

It seemed to me a dark omen that the canon shared the name of a murderous tyrant. With some trepidation I looked up at him.

The canon tugged his brocade rope belt, cinching it tighter. He appeared more like a long, bound sheaf of wheat than an influential church official beholden to a Danish king. "Rise, and tell me: What do you want?"

I said, "Master, the people of Helsingør are dead, killed by Cristiern of Copenhagen and his general, Willem. Cristiern decimated Helsingør—"

"It cannot be." The canon's mouth drooped. "Not my village."

"He declared us traitors," I continued. "Cristiern wanted revenge against the House of Hamlet and to make an example of Helsingør and our defender, Fortinbras of Norway, to all resisting his ambition." I touched Margrete's arm. "We escaped from the carnage at Castle Krogen."

The canon's chin raised in assessment of us. He frowned.

"A friend also was captured, sacrificed himself for our case." My belly suddenly pained me. I braced against my knees to gain air and balance. "Master, we've risked much." I took my bundle from my chair. "I've written into this book…"

The canon scowled. To convince him, I unpeeled Lanier's cape and showed him the book's dark face and notched title.

"The *Gesta Danorum*," he said. The canon's jaw dropped as if unhinged. His long fingers touched the carved letters, examined the tattered edges of the parchment stack. When the canon raised the cover, his eyes sharpened at the text.

I shuffled the manuscript into his arms as if passing a baby to him. "Master, I made a promise to the late prince of Denmark, my dear friend, that he would not be forgotten. I wrote a tale about Hamlet into the manuscript—"

"You defaced an ancient book?"

My face grew hot in embarrassment. "I did, but I had few options. Already there were edits in the margins, made by the original scribes. I also wrote on some separate sheets." I held my loose pages of writing in the candlelight, turned them to show my thrift and judgment in using both sides. "Master, Cristiern must not erase the Hamlets from memory."

The canon supported the manuscript upon one arm. He slid the leaves over one another and swam through the text. He whispered snatches of Latin script. He held one page in mid-turn and regarded me with a skeptical frown. "By what right do a beggar woman and her consort possess this trophy?"

Margrete said, "Indeed, Hendrik was my father. I am a daughter of the noble house of—"

"Enough." The canon turned his back to us and went to a lattice-faced cabinet. He pulled a key from his pocket, unlocked and opened the cabinet door. Then he pushed the *Gesta Danorum* and its wrap into the cabinet.

"Master?" I cried out.

The canon shut and locked the door. He pocketed the key.

Must I lose my book again? Risk my honor and suffer lasting death? I burst at the canon, wanted to grasp him by his neck, but he stood, tall and unflinching, staring at me. I restrained my attack and cried out, "The *Gesta Danorum* was in the royal treasury at Krogen."

Margrete stepped toward the canon. "You have no right to it."

He regarded her calmly. "Yet, *you* claim it? Under Cristiern's orders I searched every abbey and hut in Denmark for that book. I have it now, thank the Almighty."

I flew at the cabinet. I gripped the lattice and shook it, rattling the hinges. The doors hardly budged: it was like a fortress. "I brought this to you in good faith. Give it back to me." Again, I shook the cabinet.

"Cease your tantrum. Sit down," the canon said.

I peered through the lattice. Among tan scrolls and thin books with red-dyed bindings lay my *Gesta Danorum*. Its pages reached to me from between its pocked covers. Lanier's cape lay beside it like a shrunken rind.

The canon walked to his table and stood behind it while Margrete regarded him with the hot glare of the inquisitor. He told her, "Woman, this is not your court."

Margrete did not recoil at this rebuke. She said, "Thou shalt not steal."

The canon said, "I assure you, I will do Cristiern no favors. I will not allow him to use the *Gesta Danorum* to embolden Danes to wage war."

I opened my hands to beg. "It is a treasure to be shared. It is all that's left of Helsingør."

"I will stop Cristiern from luring Danes to die for their imagined glory," the canon said.

"The *Gesta Danorum* must be printed," I replied. "It will teach the people about good monarchs and princes. Hamlet must be remembered."

The canon grasped a lever on a cabinet. When he pulled down upon it, the lattice across the entire bank of cabinets slid closed. He said, as solemn as an Old Testament magistrate, "No one will ever see the *Gesta Danorum* again."

XVI.

The *Gesta Danorum*'s imprisonment within the locked cabinets of the archbishop's immense, candlelit office made me captive to the canon of Lund. Once again, malicious fortune impeded my advance and threatened to rob me of my honor, of my promise achieved. The canon's intent—to thwart Cristiern's ambition by never releasing the book—he believed was virtuous, but I deemed it wicked. That treasure belonged to all people. Its legends honored worthy men such as Hamlet, not Cristiern. The *Gesta Danorum* would not lead the people to mistake bad seed for good, to wage war on behalf of Cristiern's ambition.

I banged upon the cabinet's black lattice concealing the *Gesta Danorum*. "Give me that book."

The canon's face was a palette of flickering light and shadow. He pointed at the three chairs placed in subjugation before his table.

Although I stepped back from the cabinets, I did not sit. Neither did Margrete. She knelt before the canon. "Your Excellency, you may hide the *Gesta Danorum*, but soon Cristiern will demand it from you."

The canon looked down his narrow nose at us. "Why would he?"

"He knows I possessed it," I said. "When he hears I came here, he'll assume you have it."

Rubbing his face, the canon stormed to his table. He paced behind it. "Then, let him require its return. I never intended to follow his order for its printing. He will not use it against his people as a clarion to their deaths on his battlefield. Someone must resist this man."

I countered, "This book will show the people good kings and warriors. Its legends will inspire them to fight against a fiend such as Cristiern, not for him. You must print this book."

Margrete's hand lingered upon her bare neck where her sacrificed Freyja necklace once rested. She glanced at me and motioned, with a nod of her head, at the small chairs. I sat, although burning inside. Margrete, however, perched upon her chair's edge and beamed at the canon. "The *Gesta Danorum* will inspire defense against tyrants. Your Excellency, if you see to its publication, you might be sainted."

"I do not believe that Cristiern would destroy Helsingør. That would be impractical, even for a dogmatist." The canon's stride halted. "My village is not…cannot be…gone."

Margrete rose to stand behind her chair. Her hand rested lightly upon its back. "The Castle Krogen was my birthplace. Like you, I am a Helsingør native. Were it God's will, I would have lived to old age and died there. I would not be here, in audience before you, if my home thrived. Cristiern intends to punish our allegiance to the Hamlets."

She paused. The canon paled. His long fingers scratched his jaw.

"Sir," she continued, "I assure you, Helsingør and Krogen are dead. Everyone, including my parents, was murdered. Horatio and I are the only people who escaped—"

"There is one more." I stood with Margrete as if we pled before the assembled court. "Our friend, Lanier, traded himself to our enemy in exchange for that book"—I pointed at the cabinet—"that we might bring it to you for printing."

"I respect your persistence. However—"

"And this lady sacrificed a family necklace most precious to her. She used it to purchase our ship's passage here."

"A pity." The canon passed his hand over his tonsor, a perfect oval, below which his peppery hair curled. "You are more stubborn than I had given you credit withal." He regarded us with stale patience. We silently stood—dirt-streaked, wind-mussed, and spattered with dried blood. We must have appeared like Hell orphans. He asked, "When did you last eat something?"

The canon's question caused my belly to waken and twist. I said, "This morning. Our last ration was hard bread and some beer aboard our ship."

He reached behind his table and shook a bell. The attendant immediately appeared at the door, and the canon ordered that he bring meat, cheese, bread, and beer.

I wanted food, yet I would not yield to the power this man held over my ability to accomplish my purpose. It was a weighty torment. I sensed my fate shriveling like a slug on a sizzling rock, but I persisted. "Master, there's a better way to oppose Cristiern than to refuse his order."

The canon's hawkish, blue-eyed glare darted at me. "What do you mean?"

"Build a lasting memorial to those who thwarted Cristiern and the House of Oldenburg. Remembrance of the House of Hamlet through legend written into the *Gesta Danorum*—that would be your triumph."

He gave a dismissive wave. "All of my money is obligated this year. My scriptorium is brimming with work orders. My printer is working even on some Sundays—he has a dispensation from the archbishop. I can spare nothing for your cause."

I looked to the piles of manuscripts upon the canon's table. He deemed them worthier than my own. My heart fell through my soles. I was empty of ideas, of trust in the possible. I had failed.

Margrete's head bowed. She raised her pressed hands to her murmuring lips.

The canon's tongue worked against something lodged in his teeth. He looked expectantly to the door. "What of that food platter?" he grumbled.

Apparently, the attendant had some talent of value: he divined the canon's displeasure and immediately carried into the room a plate laden with white cheese, yeasty bread, and crispy, smoky meats with beer tankards. He set them on the table, atop some thin manuscripts, and quickly exited.

The canon pointed again to the three chairs. I sat and wiped my mouth to mop my hunger.

Chewing upon a piece of cheese, the canon said, "A memorial to mad Prince Hamlet whose family defied the House of Oldenburg. Hmmm."

I looked again to the locked cabinet, that tiny fortress that held my book. "Master, I beg you, don't imprison Hamlet by either condemnation or false impression. Rather, free his story and give it flight. To all he will be the very mold of a desirable prince, his honor devoted to opposing a wicked monarch such as Cristiern."

The canon, chewing, replied, "Hamlet is dead. People wish their heroes to live."

"In his legend as I have written it, Hamlet survives," I said. I took a piece of shredded quail and bit into its dark flesh. "But, in life, Hamlet chose the wage of honor. It was the part worthy of him."

Then I turned to Margrete and offered to her a small chunk of meat. Her lips twisted in sour refusal. "It's good," I encouraged her, but she shook her head. "You're ill?" I bit into some tangy cheese.

She nodded, "A sudden ache." She sat back in her chair.

"We don't know when we'll eat again," I said. "Don't reject our host's kindness."

She took a bite of cheese.

I gobbled the food. My stomach ground like an alchemist's pestle.

The canon dabbed his mouth with the back of his hand. He reclined in his broad chair. "You wrote a legend. Through it you tell lies softened by truths, and truths cloaked by lies. Is that not a grave sin?"

The arrow point of that question glanced off my armor of ignorance. I could not consider the poison of my lie because I did not recognize it then. Thus, I was silent.

"Why should the Church publish Hamlet's story?" the canon asked.

I looked to an empty chair beside me, where Lanier might have sat. "Because without the legacy of courage and sacrifice, the Church is nothing."

The canon squirmed, then leaned forward upon his knees and asked me, "You speak of legacy. What is Hamlet's legacy?"

"He was a prince who did his best for the sake of honor. He failed often, but he persisted in trying. He was beloved. He would have been a good king to his people."

The canon's hand braced his head against his temple. His fingers pulled one eye to a slit. His other unwavering eye studied me.

"Decisiveness. Hamlet was not known for it. Yet, that trait is most important in a monarch. Otherwise, a king is merely a water bearer for those unanointed." He shook his head. "I do not see the legacy."

That man's judgment of my cause was like a torch cast upon the stake. Its heat lapped at my hope. I attempted again. "Master, Hamlet's story shows his determination to act honorably."

The canon's stare only sharpened. "You have said that you are a Dane. You do not speak like one. Are you Danish?"

"I am," I said but did not attempt to convince the canon of my native birth. I could not be certain whether in my heart I was Danish. Was I a Dane, persevering, as did our ancestral Viking tribes, to forge lasting memorials despite the adversity that snuffs life? Or was I like an antique Roman? Could I ever emulate the heroism of Horatius Cocles and the Horatii brothers?

I sensed a presence in the empty chair beside me. Seated there, a strengthening outline of a man took shape in the sepia candlelight. Lanier's ghost? I jolted. Is he dead?

Then, I recognized the specter's head—glinting red locks silvered with age, flowing in short waves. I beheld Papa's countenance. He examined an open book upon his lap. The *Gesta Danorum*.

My book, however, remained locked in a cabinet. The copy that Papa scrutinized was its mystical twin. He touched the tawny pages. The script's trunks and tails wriggled. Like struggling newborn calves, they seemed either to be coming to life or squirming in death.

The sight of his spirit—I had never seen it before—was an amazement. To the others, however, the phantom was unseen. Margrete stared at the canon, and the canon picked at his fingernail.

Papa patted a page, pinning the characters to their mat. He looked to me. His scowl lidded his frowning jowls. *Lies have never protected you, Horatio.*

At that moment I did not understand the true meaning of Papa's statement. His criticism, rather than his usual encouragement, shook me. I answered Papa aloud. "Hamlet's tale sits well among the legends collected by Saxo. The story will burrow into our tradition. It'll rise in familiarity and, at the same time, remain cloaked from enemies who would extinguish it."

Papa, still frowning, looked down upon the book resting upon his lap. He closed it. The vision dissolved.

Aching, I touched the seat cushion he had occupied. It was cold.

The canon, from his comfort in the archbishop's chair, conversed as if I had spoken to him. "If Hamlet is hidden in an imagined past he will not be easily recognized. That will defeat memorial of him." The canon tore a piece of bread from the loaf and examined it. "I think that you stole the *Gesta Danorum* from Krogen. I am not convinced that the village is decimated. Therefore, I will not release the manuscript."

Margrete said, "Your Excellency, we will swear an oath upon the Holy Scriptures that we escaped the decimation wrought by Cristiern."

The canon raised his chin. "No one could have escaped murder of that scale."

"Master," I said, "not only did we flee, but our friend, Lanier, killed General Willem."

The canon scoffed.

I continued, "Cristiern has set a bounty on each of our heads, especially Lanier's."

"No doubt. With Willem dead, Cristiern's force would suffer."

The canon nibbled from the piece of bread. "Prove you killed Willem. Perhaps I will believe you."

Charged by this possibility, my mind raced. What evidence existed? I realized that only one dangerous notion lay before me.

"Master, if we bring you the general's sword, will that suffice?"

The full weight of Margrete's incredulous glare swung to rest on me. I did not turn to meet its force. I looked instead to the canon. His brows arced like a broken bird's nest. "Willem's engraved battle sword?"

"Yes."

The canon leaned forward. "I saw Willem carry it at Alvsborg, at his victory ceremony over the Swedes. He and Cristiern committed abominations there." The canon pressed the remaining bread he held into a ball. "I would take that as proof that you killed Denmark's most treacherous general and somehow escaped Cristiern."

I dared to add, "Will you also be my patron? Print and distribute the *Gesta Danorum*, including the Hamlet legend?"

The canon dropped the bread nugget upon the table. He glared at me. "Perhaps."

At last, a turnabout of fortune and a pledge from the canon. I had to find Reynaldo, take the sword, and secure Lanier's release. The notion that the *Gesta Danorum* would no longer be captive lifted my spirits from a bog to a bright sky.

I slapped my knee and stood, ready to depart and pursue Willem's sword like a crusader seeking the Holy Grail. "Master, thank you. We'll return with that trophy, worthy of your love and patronage. I pray you, may I have my friend's cape?" I pointed at the cabinet that imprisoned it and the book.

The canon frowned. "That will remain locked. Earn the book, then you will have both."

I leaned over Margrete and whispered, "Come." I strode from my chair toward the door.

However, I sensed that I walked alone. I stopped and, looking over my shoulder, saw that Margrete remained in her seat, facing the canon.

"Margrete, gentle lady, let us go now," I called to her.

She sat still. The canon watched us, his hand bracing a temple.

I returned to Margrete's side and, bending to her, whispered, "What's the matter?"

Looking to the canon, she said, "Horatio made his request of you. I have one, as well."

"Speak it," he said.

"In return for your assistance I will pray incessantly for your salvation."

His fingertips touched, making a bridge. "I pray that God will hear you."

Margrete hesitated. Her hands clasped in her lap. "I wish to be removed to a convent some distance from here. I can no longer bear the dangers of the road."

Stunned and smarting, I sat beside Margrete and turned in my chair to face her. Margrete glanced at me, pulled at her fingers. This was the woman who had swung at Willem. Who had fought as valiantly as any knighted nobleman. Yet she would abandon me now?

"Why?" I asked her.

"Distance can be a healing remedy."

The canon's finger arch dropped. "You are not married to one another?"

Margrete shook her head. She truly meant to leave. Did she not love me?

I reached for her hand and looked to her. "We could be married."

Margrete's hands remained clasped. Her eye twitched. "Horatio, I need a home."

"As do we all."

She looked away. "I cannot stay at the Hôtel de Sens or the abbey, or any other place that is full of men."

"That is true," said the canon.

Her hands began to shake. "I must learn from women how to be a commoner."

I gripped the sides of my chair to anchor myself. "You can learn this in the convents of Paris, near this place."

"Horatio, I must remove my person."

The canon shrugged at her. "You hold no regard for this man? He would make a poor husband?"

"I hold him in great regard." Her words were slight, like individual raindrops squeezed from a reluctant cloud.

The canon silently assessed her. At last he asked, "You trust no one?"

Margrete's lips pressed together. She closed her eyes and answered, "I do not trust the future." She bowed her head. "If it please you, where may I make my devotions for my dead parents?"

The canon replied, "I know where to send you." He reached again for his service bell. "I will provide you a letter and an escort."

At that moment I realized that I must choose between my causes. I must decide my part. Either I would serve a brother's ghost, or I would serve a wife.

I knelt before Margrete to mimic illustrations of courtship I had seen in chivalry manuals. Margrete beheld me. Her eyes were like twin moons. I said, "Margrete, I adore you. Do you love me a little?" Her grim mouth softened. She squeezed my hand. Heartened, I continued, "Will you be my bride?"

"You cannot choose husbandry above your sworn pledge to Hamlet." She released my hand. "Achieve your purpose. That is your calling."

I could no longer lose people I needed and loved. I reached for her hands in her lap and cupped them. "Margrete, if we are one and do as we should, God will bless us. We'll have hope. We'll have a home somewhere, and much will be better."

Margrete's shoulders drooped, eyes glossed. "The convent is best."

"I beg you. Reconsider."

She was silent.

"When will I see you again?"

"I do not know. Pray that the Virgin Mother will guide us."

The door opened. The attendant entered and the canon instructed him, "Take the lady to Mother Anne for escort to the convent at Poissy."

"God keep you, Horatio." Margrete softly kissed my cheek. Then she rose from her chair. I, too, stood, although my shattered heart remained at my feet.

She walked away from me, through the open doorway and into the hallway's bright light. I watched her follow the waddling attendant toward the main door. Then, my vision blurred. Her curves and angles became a small silhouette.

Margrete's image lingered in my thoughts and dreams, especially that night as I lay in the abbey, as permitted for one night by the canon. I tossed upon lumpy bedding in a small cell shared with a fat, gurgle-snoring monk. On a single date, the twenty-sixth day of June in the year of our Lord 1513, I had been shut away from my purpose and my honor, lost the only woman I desired, and lost a brother. I do not believe my heart beat that night.

When the bells for Terce devotions clanged, the monk snorted and woke. He rolled from his cot onto the floor and knelt upon a plot of moonlight cast from a single window. He mumbled the hour's office, well memorized. I, however, would not join him. For the first time in my life I felt that God would not hear my prayer. I lay upon my back, closed my eyes, and admitted, "Lanier, now I understand you."

As I was instructed by the canon the next morning, I followed the smirking attendant who ushered me to the main door. He closed the portal behind me. Whereas I had been allowed entry due to Margrete's shrewd favors, my only hope for return—to reclaim the *Gesta Danorum*—was to bring Willem's sword or other evidence proving Helsingør's destruction.

I carried nothing. No purse upon my belt. No dowsing rod to divine Reynaldo's location with the precious trophy sword. No map to direct me to the Palace at Blois. My best prospect was to seek Lanier's brother, Jean the flute-playing Burgundian, and request his assistance. I determined to search for him at the great central market, where, I reasoned, I would most likely find him practicing his art, soothing both merchants and buyers.

The flagstone path led me through the dewy garden to the gate. I pushed upon that thick door and stepped onto the muddy road. Immediately, a dozen carts trundling past might have flattened me, but I pressed myself against the garden wall and survived that first challenge.

Whether it was hope or desperation that inspired me, I know not: I leapt through puddles, asking the cart drivers if they would convey me to the market. For a time, none obliged me…until, at last, I reached out to a passing man—he was flicking a light whip at a yoked ox—and poked him on the shoulder. I said in French, "Please take me to the central market. In gratitude, I will beg the saints for your speedy passage through purgatory."

The man scratched a thinning patch of his brown beard. He looked over his shoulder at me and winced. "This crowded road is hell enough. I fear I'll never escape it. But I welcome some company." He nodded at his cart—a hay-burdened platform on wheels. "Come along."

Even when we falter in our prayers, sometimes the Almighty delivers a bit of good fortune.

I gratefully doffed my hat and scrambled onto the rickety cart. While swaying upon a bundle of straw, bound for the central market, I scratched at my memory to recall the regal shield of Lanier's family crest. That mark, Lanier had mentioned, would be worn by Jean on a black cape much like Lanier's. I worried for Lanier and chafed that his beautiful mantle rested, not in my hands where I might compare it to others, but captive with my book and my honor—remote, just as Margrete also was now beyond my reach.

XVII.

Paris's boisterous central market was a colorful jumble of the goods and garb of a voracious people. I had just arrived on the cart that had borne me from the Hôtel de Sens. I strode among a multitude of bulging tents and laden tables in search of Lanier's brother, Jean. Would he help me rescue Lanier and Willem's sword? Would my *Gesta Danorum* be freed?

My hunt took me through earthy scents of muddy pottery, and of ripe tomatoes and yellow squash still warm from sunny fields. I passed servants, in firm-stitched vests or bodices, haggling with life-worn peasants. I brushed by fluffy bunches of dyed wool and hastened away from the nose-biting odor of bloody pig and lamb carcasses.

I turned a tent corner and heard the wispy notes of a soft flute. I stopped. The sound emanated from a closed tent. Before it stood a brawny man whose bald head was too small for his body. His eyes, like hard, black pebbles, regarded me coldly. He lifted the tent flap's ragged corner. I peered inside.

At the center of the musty, sloping tent a dozen young women and girls stood in various stages of disrobe. They were surrounded by twenty men wearing plush capes and pointed hats. The men bartered as they cupped the concubines' rounded flesh and stroked budding breasts and flat hips. In one corner, clothed women sat on stools and conversed in furtive, hushed tones. They warily watched the tent's entrance.

A wealthy couple asked a grim-jawed trader, "How many piss buckets can she carry?"

Another corner harbored a few eunuchs wearing skirts open at the groin. They stood for inspection by a merchant and two monks who asked, "By when will he have worked off his father's debt?" I crossed myself, grateful that as a youth I had escaped servitude's fate and found Papa's protection.

In the farthest corner stood a man playing a long, wooden flute. He wore a black cape, tied at his neck and draped over his shoulders. It bore, at the breast, an embroidered red crest.

I passed the ogling hoard and went to the flute player. As I approached, he watched me and continued to blow upon the slender pipe. His frame was thicker than Lanier's. So, too, were his fingers, which tapped and slipped over the flute's holes to play a tripping melody. I stood before the man and asked, "Are you Jean?"

The man stopped playing and lowered his flute. His visage brightened. "If you have a commission for me, I am."

"Your brother sent me to find you."

The light in Jean's eyes extinguished. His mouth drooped. "Tell him he should not have bothered."

"He wanted me to tell you he is captive, taken to King Louis at Château de Blois."

"Someone will enjoy a grand reward for his capture." Jean looked down at his flute, carefully placing his fingers to block a few holes. "If so, then he is lost, and now the rest of our suffering family is found. Why are you concerned with Étienne?"

"I'm a friend."

Jean's smirk plumped his face. "Étienne has a friend?"

"I know him only as Lanier."

"Our surname. How did you meet him?"

"He was an aide to Fortinbras of Norway. We met at Castle Krogen, Helsingør."

Jean's head jerked back. "He fled a far distance, even for him."

I glanced aside at the bound, part-naked women. "He sacrificed himself for me. Traded his freedom for my treasured book of legends."

Jean snorted. "Not surprising that a man of failed dignity gave himself for a book of lies."

Anger flared up my spine, but I ignored that heat. "He was protecting my honor, as would a good friend."

"*Your* honor? The Lanier family should be his cause. When Louis condemns Étienne to death, our curse finally will be lifted. It is time my brother acted righteously."

"You won't go to Blois?"

"I did not say that."

"You will rescue your brother."

"I did not say that, either." Jean tucked his flute under his arm. He sniffed. "His crime reignited Louis's hatred of us Burgundians. Because of it I lost my post as a court musician at Blois. I would have become wealthy, and then Rouen would have been my home. Generous patrons. Banquets." Jean looked about the tent. His jaw ground in disdain. "But I will forever be here, in the shadows. So much for our family's honor."

Jean strode to the tent flap and exited. I followed. We stood in the morning's fresh breeze.

"Help me find Blois and release your brother. Perhaps your dream of life in Rouen will be restored."

"That will not happen unless Burgundian blood is forgiven," Jean said. He fished in his cape pockets, withdrew a handful of glinting coins, and counted them. "I can remain here among filth. Or I can go to Blois and do what I must to reclaim my position. Request an audience with the king."

His selfishness sparked my suspicion. Through gritted teeth I asked, "What is your decision then?"

"I will go to Blois."

"Please bring me with you. You're a French noble. I'm not. I need your help to enter the palace gates. I must recover a sword stolen from me by the same man who captured your brother. Because I brought you news of your revived opportunity, I deserve your consideration."

Jean's brow crunched. His fist, clutching his coins, rubbed his chin. "It is a long day's ride from Paris to Blois. I will get us one horse. No need for two."

"Thank you," I said but wondered why Lanier had wanted me to find this obnoxious man, no matter their sibling relation.

Less than one hour later, as the sun reached its apex, Jean and I rode a sable horse away from Paris's encircling stone arms. From the town's gates we traveled the road southwest. We passed villages packed with bowing roofs clustered around church spires. Between settlements lay fields of cabbages, small leafy crops, and purple flowers. Scores of hulking cows tore at thick grasses. Under the setting sun's pulpy orange and pink clouds, sloping green velvet valleys brought us to the gentle plateaus of the Loire.

By the time we arrived at Blois, under a speck of moon hanging high in the black gloss of night, we were exhausted. We followed a tall, bending wall that encircled the royal chateau. At last, our mount's clopping hooves stopped before the palace's gatehouse. I looked past the gate's medallion, an arc encircling Louis's regnal number XII, to the grand courtyard and residence. Fanciful crisscrossed brickwork. Clusters of chimneys. Protruding balconies rested like magical nests upon curved braces. It seemed a place of charm, not misery and grudge.

I slid down from the horse and bent backward to rest my arse. Jean dropped to the ground and shook his legs.

From a peak-roofed porter's lodge, which sat well behind the gate, a guard leaned out the doorway. He wore a mail hood and a gold-trimmed, blue robe, and he hailed us with a most courteous welcome: "No. Return tomorrow. The porter cannot come for you now."

I rested my hand upon the cool bars of the gate. In fractured French I said, "Your porter will want to quit his bed when you tell him of our arrival."

The guard raised his chin. "Why?"

To create some beneficial confusion, I wanted to claim that I brought the infamous murderer, Lanier the Burgundian, to Louis for the promised bounty. However, before I could speak, Jean handed me the horse's reins and stepped up to the gate. He asked the guard, "Was a man called Étienne Lanier brought captive here?"

The guard nodded. "By a Spaniard. They await an audience with the king tomorrow."

"I am Jean Lanier, brother of the accused. I demand an audience as well."

"Upon what grounds?"

"I once was a court musician here." Jean's face was as round as that of a well-slopped hog. He pulled from his cape pocket his wooden flute, waved it at the guard. "I wish to reclaim my post."

"You came at midnight to beg work? You think I am like an instrument, easily played?"

"No, by the saints," I said. "You are a good man. But the Spaniard is a thief. Did he carry a sword? Its hilt sweeps outward, and the blade bears an engraved vine along its length."

The guard scratched his chin. "Yes. Quite beautiful."

"Those witch bastards stole my sword." I pounded the gate. "Will the king hear my claim and see to return of my property?"

"Can you prove ownership?"

I gripped the bars and motioned to the guard to lean close. He did so. I whispered menacingly. "Admit us or"—I looked up to the moon—"I will cast upon you a spell so wretched it will grow maggots in your gut. You'll wish to die."

The guard shrugged. "Had that last year. Cast by an Italian shepherd woman in the market. You should have seen the slop that came out my—"

"Enough." Jean dug his fist into his pocket and drew forth a shiny goldgulden—a healthy sum. He held it out in his open hand.

The guard's jagged grin spread wide. He took the coin from Jean and winked at me. Then he unlocked the gate and pulled it open. "Tie your horse at this post. Come along."

Jean led the horse through the gate and secured the reins there. He scoffed at me. "A spell, indeed." In the moonlight, his wide eyes were milky orbs.

We followed the guard down a pathway across the dirt square to a squat, round tower opposite the palace.

"What accommodations are these?" I asked.

"Walk."

We entered the tower through a low archway to stand in a dark, dank space before a small door. The guard unlocked it, then pushed Jean and me into the black cell. He secured the door.

"Release us," Jean cried out.

"*Si*. This is improper treatment of a gentleman."

I recognized that voice and looked over my shoulder. Beyond a patch of moonlight cast from a barred window, two men sat upon the dirt floor. One was the vermin Reynaldo. The other was Lanier.

The guard replied, "Sort out your differences. Kill one another if you wish. Then, I will not have to bother with you." His departing footsteps crunched upon the exterior walk.

Reynaldo went to the window and gripped the bars. "Thief."

Even in the darkness I could see Lanier's haggard but beaming face. He leapt to his feet and we embraced. "*Mon ami*, you found Jean. *Merci*."

Lanier turned to his scowling brother and grasped him by his shoulders. "*Mon frère*, Louis will have my head. And you will have your old post once more."

Jean stepped back from Lanier. "Your rage, *mon frère*, cost me my livelihood, my destiny. You brought dire shame upon our family."

"I am a sinner beyond salvation. But your talents will save you," Lanier said. "Somehow you will marry and raise your family in Rouen, as you have always wished."

Jean spat at Lanier. He moved to a corner, leaned against the wall, and glared at us.

"Why does he deserve your love?" I asked Lanier.

Lanier wiped his cuff across his face. "Jean has been wronged. He needs his honor reinstated. And I need mine. Perhaps I will earn it through death."

I did not accept Lanier's logic, and I wanted to pummel both Jean and Reynaldo. However, I turned my attention to monstrous trouble. How would I rescue Lanier and the sword?

The cold, lumpy ground made for fitful sleep. When dawn's bright spear shot through the prison window and struck me in the eyes, I sat up. The other three men sat apart from one another, their backs against the walls.

By midmorning the guard dropped a sack inside the door—the previous night's remains of roasted goose. We tore into the greasy, mauled carcass. The guard told us that we would be brought to the king for a noon audience.

At the twelfth toll of the royal chapel's bells we four stood, side by side, before Louis in his sunlit, glossy stone hall. To my left, Jean. To my right, Reynaldo and Lanier. We were flanked by silky, chattering courtiers resting on black-pillowed divans.

Louis, an aging narrow-framed man, sat upon his carved throne, packed into his seat with red pillows. His long simple tunic, festively embroidered vest, and leather leggings were the long-past fashion of a huntsman. His straight, gray hair flowed from his gold crown of large gems and curled upward at the tips. The style might have been handsome in his youth. From his wide leather belt hung Willem's sword. It had been shined. The engraved vine was a black trail upon a silver plane. I wanted that trophy.

I looked toward heaven, hoping for the sword's deliverance to me. Painted upon the ceiling planks was a scene of the royal hunt. A crowned man on horseback chased boars, stags, and pheasants. I understood the panic in the animals' large eyes and snarled mouths.

Louis wheezed. Then he made a long, hacking cough. His speckled hand beat his breast. When he stopped, he peered at us through slightly swollen eyelids.

A door opened in the wall behind the throne. A man emerged, wearing a red cardinal's cap and a gold chain medallion over his red robe. He carried a gold staff. The counselor handed Louis a kerchief and leaned close to whisper. Louis regarded us. His frown was a like a pile of rock from his brow to his chin.

He said, "Two of you are Burgundians named Lanier. Which of you is the murderer?"

Reynaldo pulled off his hat and bowed low. He pointed at Lanier and replied with a thick French tongue no better than my own. "This is the man who killed the woman known as Collette and her lover. He is the Burgundian descended from the man who killed your ancestor. I have come to your beautiful chateau, sire, hauling this vagabond to your judgment. The reward belongs to me."

"Not so," I replied.

Louis's eyes, heavy with disgust, shifted from Reynaldo to me. "Who are you?"

"Horatio of Tønderensis. Scholar and witness to the thievery this Spaniard has committed upon me and my friend." I rested my hand upon Lanier's shoulder.

Jean stepped forward, extended his right front foot. His bow folded his rotund middle. "Highness, I am not the murderer. I am, however, of the Lanier family. Musicians and artists. I was one of your court flute players, sire. Your Excellency, do you not wish to resolve, for all time, the offense against the House of Orleans?"

Louis, visage sagging, nodded wearily.

"I attest that my brother"—Jean pointed at Lanier—"is the murderer you seek." My furious glare at Jean did not dissuade him from adding, "Because I can ensure that you not condemn an innocent, I am the man who deserves compensation."

Reynaldo twisted his hat. Tufts of yellow feathers dropped from its plume. He knelt, groveling, before Louis. "I brought you the devilish killer you wish to punish for your family's suffering. In addition to his murderous crimes, he has stolen the fortune of many others."

The counselor tapped his staff upon the floor. He said to Reynaldo, "You speak as if you, not the king, is most aggrieved."

Reynaldo began to weep. He chewed upon his lips as if he would wail like a child. "*De sol, a sol.* I have long sought vengeance. My ship's captain abandoned me on an island. That man"—he pointed again at Lanier—"was the cause of it. I nearly died." Reynaldo crept to the base of Louis's throne and raised his hands in supplication.

Louis and the counselor, looking down upon Reynaldo, regarded him as if he were a leper.

Reynaldo continued, "I lost my gold stipend promised to Pinzon's crew. Your Majesty, that man I brought you is your declared enemy. The bounty should be mine."

Lanier said, "Sire, this pig writhes in fantasy—muddy lies. He stole from the captain."

"Is that true?" Louis asked.

Reynaldo lifted his face to beg. "I swear on my soul."

"What is that worth?" the counselor jeered. "Swear an oath upon the Divine Soul."

First Reynaldo hesitated. Then he rolled back from Louis to squat upon the floor. He stood and, again, twisted his hat.

Lanier added, "This malefactor was sentenced to death upon an island for a reason, sire. He is blessed to be alive."

Louis crossed his legs and arms as tight as a barrel. "Spaniard, your injuries are no concern to me. As for you Burgundians, I might as well hang you both. At last my grandfather and grandmother would be avenged."

"No, highness," I said. "I beg you."

Louis's raised brows both questioned and condemned my outburst. Jean whimpered and knelt low. His cape seemed to melt around him. A few courtiers chortled.

The counselor grumbled, "No more trouble from Burgundians."

I dared to continue, "Majesty—as an honored king concerned with righteous revenge and justice—would you condemn to the gallows a man who, albeit a sinner, does not deserve death?"

Louis looked to Jean. He lay prostrate upon the floor with arms out and legs straight, positioned like a cross. Louis also regarded Lanier, who stood beside Reynaldo. Louis said, with a sweep of his arm, "True justice is my concern."

Reynaldo began to grin and shake with seeming anticipation of victory.

"I can read a man's lies as if they are writ upon his face," said Louis.

Me—he spoke of me, I thought. A bolt of panic shot through my breast.

Louis stared at Reynaldo. "You are a damned liar."

Reynaldo bowed low and shuffled. "Most gracious highness, I beg—"

"Revenge does not righteously serve greed. I know greed. I see it in you, Spaniard. You are an unjust thief not deserving my bounty." Louis turned to his counselor. "François, go to my treasury and bring the reward. Give it to that man." When Louis pointed at Jean, Reynaldo shrieked and crumpled upon the floor.

The startled courtiers flapped and cackled.

The counselor waved to beckon the guards who stood barricading the tall doors. Two guards grasped Reynaldo's arms and raised him to his feet. Reynaldo's wobbling head tilted up. He barked at Lanier and me, "I curse you. Blast your souls to Hell."

Lanier calmly shook his head at Reynaldo, but Louis regarded him sharply. "You know more of explorers' treasure than you admit. You will tell us of it." Louis looked to his soldiers. "Return the Spaniard to the dungeon. *Allez.*"

Two guards carried Reynaldo, howling objections, from the hall. One guard remained at the door.

"Bring the reward," Louis said to the counselor.

The counselor said, "The man screams as if we will torture him, but he will eat better there than a peasant." He moved behind the throne, pulled upon the door, and departed.

Louis instantly paled like chalk. He pressed his kerchief to his mouth and coughed.

Jean pushed himself up from the floor to stand. He mumbled to Lanier, "You have remarkable talent for inspiring men to want to kill you." Next, he said to Louis, "Your Highness, the compensation I requested was not money. Please, the post of musician."

Lanier knelt before Louis. "But for my sins, my brother now would have a life among Rouen's renowned artists. A commission at Blois would return that hope to him. He deserves it—"

"He doesn't, majesty," I interjected. "Sire, what good man sacrifices his brother for his own gain? What virtue or honor is that? Jean wishes for his brother's demise. That's why he leased only one horse for our transport. *N'est-ce pas*, Jean?" I regarded him with disdain. "You never expected your brother to return with us to Paris."

Jean ignored me. He looked only to Louis.

The door behind the throne popped open. The counselor, taking small steps, bore a heavy iron box secured with straps. He carefully stepped down the polished steps of the stone platform and set the box at Jean's feet.

Jean bent and pushed the coin box to the base of the steps. He straightened. Jean's mouth was a grim line. "I do not want money as reward. I want to gain my way in life upon my merit, to be reinstated to my post within the court."

"Your greed is like Reynaldo's," I said. "Your concern isn't for your king, and it isn't for your blood."

Louis looked down at his spotty hands, rubbed and stretched them. He looked up at his counselor. "François, I am old and tired."

"Indeed, sire," said the counselor. "The physician insists that you unburden your person."

"Too easily said," Louis grumbled.

"We have talked of this heavy curse of family sin and anger, of your desire for your soul's light penance," said the counselor.

Louis sighed. He wiped his face with one hand. His other hand rested upon the sloping hilt of Willem's sword. I needed that blade, to exchange for my imprisoned *Gesta Danorum*. My heart hammered in my breast.

"Why would I want a bitter, scheming flute player in my court?" Louis looked to Jean and shook his head.

The counselor tapped his staff upon the floor. "The king has decided."

Jean's head hung low.

Next came my turn to make and justify my requests. A torrent of fear beset me. If I failed, my purpose and promise would turn to ash. I would be the one deserving death.

"Most Excellent Majesty," I began, "I've heard your people speak of their love for you and your love for them." The counselor rolled his eyes, but a spark of interest lit Louis's face. I continued, "Not once did I hear your subjects speak of serving or favoring either the line of Orleans or the Burgundians. I heard only of service to the House of Valois."

Suddenly, Louis made another rattling cough. After he settled, rasping and teary, I continued. "Whether kings or commoners, we each consider how we'll be remembered, what acts will secure our honor. Will your people's love for you be sustained if you put a man to death because of an ancient offense the House of Valois resolved long ago but which you never forgave?"

Louis's shoulders drooped.

I opened my arms, inviting reason. "Is it just to punish a man who willingly offered his life to make amends with his brother, despite being betrayed by him?"

Louis leaned forward and rested his forearms upon his knees. The baggy flesh beneath his eyes cinched. "Perhaps. However, not as you state it."

I dared ask, "What honorable act would prove worthy of your people's regard? Would most benefit your soul?"

The counselor glared at me.

Louis made a sputtering cough. He leaned back in his chair. The corners of Louis's mouth turned downward, but he nodded. "It is good counsel." Louis looked up, quizzically, to his counselor. "Why have you not said such to me? Your uncle, D'Amboise, always advised me well." The counselor's jaw clenched in apparent frustration.

Louis glanced at Lanier. "I rescind the bounty." He gave a sharp, dismissive wave. "Do not return to Blois."

"The king has decided." The counselor tapped his staff.

Lanier bowed low and thanked the king. Jean slightly bowed. They began their retreat down the lengthy hall, walking backward to the door.

I bobbed, elated by this victory. I had done the impossible—influenced a monarch's change of reason. Encouraged, I bowed again and dared ask for more. "Begging Your Majesty's patience, I've a simple claim of an item stolen from me by the Spaniard."

Irritation snagged Louis's mouth. "What is it?"

"The common sword you wear."

Louis looked down at the weapon hanging from his belt. "You think it common? François, you said it was handsome." He turned in his chair to scowl suspiciously at his counselor.

The counselor smirked at me. "How is it yours?"

"Oh, it's not mine. I was carrying it from the smith, returning it to my master's porter, when the Spaniard accosted me and took it."

From his perch the counselor studied me. I, however, regarded him with a light and steady gaze, the very essence of innocence.

Louis asked me, "Why would your master want an ordinary sword?"

"Personal value, sire. That sword was given to him in his youth by his grandfather."

"Oh." Louis looked down at the sword again and frowned at it.

The counselor sniffed. "The king will not relinquish property because of a foreign peasant's beggary. Let your master come to the king and make his request."

I would not relent. I bowed my head and said, "Today His Highness rendered gracious judgment resolving his family's predicament."

"Do not address the king regarding his private matters."

Louis glanced at his counselor. An amused smile tinged Louis's tired face, perhaps at the volley between his counselor and a commoner. "Proceed," he bade me.

The counselor stiffened, and I continued, "All tribes, whether peasant or royal, suffer private battles. Often it is one person who resolves the strife. Is that not true? Today, the king, in his wisdom, did so because he is a good king. Unafraid as he was to step forward and issue a righteous decision."

Louis considered, nodded.

I raised my head to address Louis directly. "Highness, your care about right action honors the Almighty. I pray that your goodness will please God, that he will invite your eventual passage into heaven."

The counselor descended a step. He bent toward me and hissed, "Who are you to advise the king concerning God's satisfaction with his soul?"

Louis leaned forward. "Cardinal François Guillaume. Even a peasant acts wisely twice a day: when he rises from his bed and when he returns to it. Let him speak."

I waited for the counselor to ascend the platform and stand beside the king. He did so and glared at me like a furious goat.

"Highness," I continued, "the scriptures inform our understanding that a man's goodness is his honor, his honor is his life, and his life's virtue is his appeal to God for salvation."

Louis, jaw squared, regarded me. Suddenly, coughing racked him again. He covered his mouth with his kerchief. His face, contorted and purple, was an agony to behold. I looked down to my shoes. Indeed, he was ill.

When his convulsion ceased, Louis dabbed his eyes. "I have made my penances."

I looked up. Louis was watching me. "For your blessing I would testify about your goodness to everyone I meet, sire, should you enable me to return my master's sword to him. Your generosity would ensure my safe trek homeward should I need to defend myself."

Louis examined the sword. "I am old." He sighed, then said, "I need no weapon taken from a low noble." He drew the sword from its loop on his belt and handed it to the counselor.

When the counselor gave it to me, pointed downward, he hissed, "You do not fool me, scholar."

Gratefully, I bowed again and might have run from the hall that moment... but I had one more perilous request. I bore my fear and stood before Louis.

The counselor bent to hoist the heavy coin box. He noticed that I lingered and said, incredulously, "Come now. You cannot want more."

I said to Louis, "Majesty, God favored me to own a book. As a poor scholar it is my treasure. But it is being held without cause by a stubborn church official in Paris. He inspected it for impurity—of course, it contained none—yet, despite my pleas he has not returned it to me."

Louis's face scrunched. "Why do valuable objects so often quit your possession?"

"Sire, I wonder that as well."

Louis shifted upon his throne. He shook his head. "I have given you enough."

"If it pleases Your Majesty, may I have some parchment, ink powder, and a quill?"

Louis grunted. "François, give this beggar those meager supplies."

I pledged my gratitude to Louis. With sword in hand and my tunic pockets filled, I departed the hall.

My mind was flush with amazement. I realized that I could reason with a king, even to wrest kindness from him. It was a power I had believed belonged only to magicians.

I exited the hall's foyer and stepped into the bright sunlight of the dirt square. Lanier and Jean stood, talking. Lanier was leaning against the brick edifice of the palace, warming himself. He embraced me.

"You are marvelous." He leaned back and, grinning, patted my face. He noticed the sword I held at my side. "A knight's suit of armor would complement it well."

"I will never have my musician's post," Jean said.

Lanier faced his brother. "Jean, let us go to Rouen, eh? Why not? You will be appreciated there. It will be difficult at first, but we will not be poor always."

Jean spat, this time at the ground.

"We can be a family," Lanier added. "You can have the wife and children you wish. Perhaps, I can begin again by marrying a widow. You can teach your children their instruments. They will learn magnificent art. In time they may regain our family's honor if we cannot."

Jean looked away. "Perhaps."

From the tower came Reynaldo's voice, arguing with a guard. I said, "Let's get the two horses and return to Paris. We shall go to the canon of Lund and exchange this blade for my captive book."

Lanier scoffed. "I went with Reynaldo so you could have the *Gesta Danorum*. And then you lost it to a cleric? Imbecile."

"*Très stupide*," Jean agreed.

"Wonderful," I said. "At last, the Lanier brothers agree."

We crossed the dirt square to the young guard at the gatehouse. We requested, by description, the horse that Reynaldo had brought and the one that Jean had leased. Lanier and I mounted Reynaldo's horse, and Jean, the other. We quit Blois. By the time we trod the Loire's northernmost boundary, the descending orange sun was melting and spilling across the fields. When we approached the gates of Île de la Cité, velvet night had long settled upon us.

At the market's dark flotilla of tents, abandoned for the night, Lanier and Jean agreed upon one thing more: they would meet at a tavern the following day to discuss the possibilities of Rouen. Thus, we took our leave of Jean.

Despite the silence of the aged, moonlit heavens and slumbering town, I galloped our horse along the downhill-uphill road to the Hôtel de Sens. We entered the garden and closed the gate behind us. I allowed the horse to eat freely of the shrubs while Lanier slept under a pear tree. I pulled from my pockets the writing implements and, by dim moonlight, crafted a letter as if written from Louis XII to the canon of Lund. Then I sat with William's sword in hand, watching for the imminent dawn and the mansion's first sign of life, ready to pounce upon the attendant and demand another audience with the canon of Lund.

XVIII.

Despite the usual dim prospects of negotiation in the archbishop's candlelit office, I stood with Lanier, determined to reclaim the *Gesta Danorum*. We faced the canon of Lund across his table as he, seated, ignored us and wrecked the Sabbath by signing papers. My heart was in a state of storm. I gripped Willem's sword, point downward, for the canon's inspection. He had agreed it would be proof that we had killed Willem and escaped Krogen. It was a trophy worthy of trade for my imprisoned book. I wanted to swing that blade like an antique Roman warrior to slash open the cabinets lining the walls and take the *Gesta Danorum* by force. However, such an act would destroy any possibility that the canon would agree to be my patron.

"Master—" I knelt before the table, as did Lanier beside me. I offered the canon the sword lying flat across my outstretched arms at the table's height. "Your Excellency—"

"Oh, now I am Your Excellency?" The canon peered at me across the thin rim of his round lens. With one hand, he balanced the spectacles upon the bridge of his nose. His other hand held a quill over a document. It dripped a blot of ink where his signature would have landed, beside his white robe's sleeve. "You want something of me. I suppose that promotes me in your esteem."

Had he forgotten our agreement? Tumult roiled my gut. Surely, because I had been able to influence Louis's forgiveness of Lanier, I could also convince the canon to release my beautiful volume.

Still bowing, I raised my arms higher than the tabletop, for the canon's easier viewing of the blade. "I have brought, as promised, the sword that belonged to Willem, Cristiern's general. You said that our possession of it would prove both his death and our escape from the slaughter at Helsingør."

The canon stood. The table creaked when he leaned against it to inspect the sword. "Graceful crafting. Long blade. I recognize the stone set atop the pommel. This is the sword I saw Willem carry in ceremony after the slaughter at Alvsborg, Sweden, that Cristiern ordered."

My arms began to quake from their prolonged extension. "I beg you, receive it." I stole an upward glimpse at the canon, hoping for a serene nod of acknowledgement.

The canon rounded the table and took the sword. With his knobby finger he traced the decorative etching along the blade. "All of Helsingør, dead?"

"Yes, master," I said. Lanier and I rose to stand.

Assessing Lanier from head to heel, the canon asked, "Who is this?"

"My friend, more like a brother. He killed Willem."

The canon stepped closer to Lanier. "Do you swear upon God's blood that you killed General Willem of Copenhagen?"

Lanier stroked his jaw with the back of his hand, seemed to consider the oath. He sighed, perhaps wanting no more talk of murders committed. "I vouch that when Willem and I fought at Krogen, his sword was in my hand when it dispatched him."

The canon squinted at Lanier, then nodded. "You killed him."

"Master," I said, "we have proven that Margrete and I truthfully attested to our situation. Now, will you help us avenge the dead of Helsingør? Will you release the *Gesta Danorum* and print the Hamlet story in it?"

Carrying the sword, the canon moved behind the table to a black chest girded with leather straps. It seemed as old and traveled as the holy ark. He laid the weapon upon the chest.

"As a native son, I despise the havoc that Cristiern has wrecked upon Helsingør." The canon sat heavily in the archbishop's immense chair.

"Then, let's make haste, advance Hamlet's story through distribution of the *Gesta Danorum*. Every day that passes is another day wasted."

The canon looked aside to the bank of cabinets, the nearest of which held my manuscript behind its closed lattice. "No."

I might have burst with fury. But I possessed one more weapon, concealed in my tunic pocket, which could leech conviction from that man's stubborn vein of aspiration. I drew forth the writ I had forged in Louis's name, much like Hamlet's trick. "Are you certain, master?"

His brow bunched. He took the missive from my outstretched hand. "Where is its seal?"

"It must have fallen away during my journey."

The canon regarded me suspiciously. He pulled open the packet and, holding his spectacles before his eyes, read it, mumbling aloud. "Heretofore, you must release to Horatio of Tønderensis the manuscript you have garnered—" The canon leapt to his feet. He waved the letter in my face and stammered with rage. "You dared complain to the king? Threaten my livelihood?"

What did I care of his state? My own teetered on a ledge. A broken promise to Hamlet would shatter my honor and deserve eternal death. I took a breath to contain my fear.

The canon's nostrils swelled like bellows. "Yesterday I received a letter from Cristiern. He warns me that if a Dane named Horatio brings the *Gesta Danorum* to me, I am to take the book and capture him and anyone in his company. Further, I am to make Horatio add to the manuscript Cristiern's achievements and the truth about mad Prince Hamlet's demise. He wants the volume printed and sent to him in Copenhagen."

"Cristiern's writ insults you, master. He assumes that your loyalties are not to your native land first."

Rising to pace behind his table, the canon said, "I will not tell him that you came here. But I will not print Hamlet's story. Should Cristiern discover it inserted in that ancient book, he might send his assassins for me. Do you understand that?"

Woefully, I glanced at Lanier. He looked down at his boots and shook his head.

"Master, if you print the *Gesta Danorum*, wouldn't Cristiern accept your word that you followed his order?"

The canon's stride halted. He laughed at me.

I persisted. "There is a political advantage to updating the *Gesta Danorum*. It is a four-hundred-year-old book. The facts of Hamlet's life are buried in the legend. We won't include Cristiern's story." I looked again to the locked cabinet. "Master, let me show you that text."

The canon flung his arms wide. "I do not want this book to inspire Danes to fight for Cristiern's ambitions."

"No such thing will happen. I beg your pardon, master, but you are wrong, as is Cristiern." I stood before his lanky frame and rolled back my shoulders for illusion of height. "People are subject to kings, but they needn't surrender their hearts to them. Stories of Hamlet and Old Hamlet pitted against Claudius and other enemies will encourage Danes to pledge their loyalty to good rulers, will inspire them to fight for noble kings and virtuous causes. Why isn't *that* your greatest concern?"

The canon puffed a breath. He seemed to mull the question.

I looked to Lanier. He stood, head cocked, curiously regarding the canon.

For effect I swept my hand at the cabinet banks filled with books. "Writings are a substantial legacy. So much greater would your legacy be if, through the *Gesta Danorum* you, a son of devastated Helsingør, dealt a blow against Cristiern, ensured remembrance of Helsingør and the House of Hamlet. All will know that Helsingør was wonderful beyond measure. You would be the patron of all Danes…"

"*Your* patron, you mean."

"Revered like a saint for saving the history of your native martyred village and its lords."

Folding my false writ, the canon shook his head.

Boiling frustration overtook me. "Master, you're abetting Cristiern's erasure of history. He could decimate any town within the Kalmar Union. Do you want the havoc that befell Helsingør to afflict more people?"

The canon crumpled the missive. "I will give you the book, but I will not print it." He threw the packet to the floor, stepped forward, and ground it beneath his slippered heel.

I knelt before the canon's table and folded my hands as if praying.

"Gracious Almighty Lord, do not condemn this cleric—"

A slight rattle at the cabinets alerted me. I glanced behind me and saw Lanier standing at a cabinet. He tugged on the lattice, testing it. I motioned slightly, guiding him to the one that held the *Gesta Danorum*. Lanier moved there. The canon, arms crossed and glaring at me, did not seem to notice Lanier.

I continued, "Oh God, do not damn Christiern Pederson, the canon of Lund, to the Hell of obscurity for abandoning his native village, which the House of Oldenburg obliterated."

Opening my eyes, I saw the canon's visage set like stone. "I will not print it," he said.

That witch bastard's heart was frozen. What else could I say that would soften him or pivot his reason? My innards wrung from this turmoil.

For any inspiration, I looked to the bank of cabinets. Atop one section lay a single volume upon its side. *Nicomachean Ethics, Book II* by Aristotle. An idea struck me.

I rose from my knees and, planting my fists upon the table, braced myself and leaned toward my opponent. It was my most effective posture used during debates at university. I said, "Excellency, God's design requires balance, symmetry, does it not? Even the pagan ancients recognized this in the principle of the Golden Mean. In this tradition you can still the chaos of Cristiern's ambition by countering it with the good of Hamlet's story."

Seemingly bored by my commanding pose, the canon sat in the archbishop's chair and, without even a twitch aside, barked at Lanier, "Stop molesting those cabinets."

Lanier pulled again on the lattice. "You said you would release the book." Lanier came to my side and sat in a chair facing the canon. I, however, would not be seated.

The canon wiped his face with one hand and then looked up at me, across his table. "Horatio, I must do that which is right, despite the gales driving at me from all compass points. You are not going to direct, cajole, or trick me otherwise. I will not print the book."

His pronouncement rattled me. I had failed in my promise. Every agony, every risk had been for nothing. I didn't deserve brotherhood. I wasn't a Dane, establishing eternal glory. I wasn't an antique Roman, achieving victory in this life. I collapsed upon the chair beside Lanier.

Then, a clash erupted in my ears, followed by silence and searing pain. I clutched my head.

Lanier's hand upon my arm steadied me. He leaned close. I felt his puff of speech but heard nothing.

"Speak louder," I told him. His mouth made motion. Lanier studied me. His face was blanched with fright. He jostled my shoulder.

The ache in my head intensified. I prayed that the pain would cease.

"Horatio."

That voice, I heard it. It came from above. I looked up to behold a face hovering before me, red-orange like a glassmaker's molten bulb.

"Do you see it?" I asked Lanier. I pointed to the face.

Lanier leaned away, regarded me with hard eyes. "No." He fell to his knees beside my chair and, hands clasped, began to pray.

The canon squinted at me in judgment. He opened a book upon the table. He glanced at it, then at me. He quickly turned the pages, searching for information.

The spirit cried out, "Remember me."

I asked, "Which Hamlet are you? Cursed king or betrayed prince?"

The face transfigured, became Hamlet's pale visage with blood-speckled eyes, as he had appeared the instant that he died.

The next moment the ghost's eyes rolled upward under half-closed lids. The face became like boiling flesh beneath shimmering skin. The sharp stench of roasting tissue filled my nostrils.

Again, the form changed. The roiling face wore a sable beard and helmet, like that of Hamlet's father with visor lifted. The phantom said—in Hamlet's voice but tuned to a tortured key, "Your life and honor depend on your promise, Horatio. Prove your worthiness as both an antique Roman and a Dane."

I beat my shuddering breast. "I've not said enough Masses for you."

Lanier grasped my shoulders and shook me. Although he said something, mustache bristling and eyes questioning, I could not hear him.

The canon grasped an aspergillum from a cradle behind him. He rounded the table to stand over me. When he shook the rod at my face, water sprinkled from its silver ball. The canon held a book in his other hand and read from it. I could not hear the rite he was performing on me, but I knew what it was, and I was horrified.

"You think I'm possessed?" I could not hear my own words.

The only sound I perceived was Hamlet's voice, strained like a string about to break. "Immediately, you must make this man commit to my cause, or all is lost."

The canon shook the aspergillum high in the air. Like a bonfire doused by a sudden storm, the ghost vanished.

When the canon shook more holy water at me, I heard him chant, "*Vade retro Santana.*"

I pushed away the canon's waving arm and stood before him, our noses almost touching. His rancid breath smelled of sour milk. I grasped his collar and rasped in his face. "Master, the souls of Prince Hamlet and Old Hamlet are imprisoned by the Devil. They command that you print Hamlet's story. If you fail, your life and soul will join theirs in perpetual torment."

The canon shook water faster in every direction and repeated his incantation.

I said, "Persist at your folly. The eternal blaze awaits."

The canon's face was as gray as a bloodless corpse. I yanked the book and rod from his shaking hands and dumped them into Lanier's trembling arms. I declared to the canon, "Your sin is black though you are an officer of Christ. You claim to protect people from assisting Cristiern's destructive ambition. But by denying them choice and risk, you obstruct men's capacity to learn evil from good."

The canon stumbled backward, waving his arms as if warding away a swarm. I pursued him, and Lanier followed me. The canon collapsed to his knees, quaking. "Your daemon forbore the cleansing and now persecutes me."

"You rob them of wisdom," I added.

Kneeling, the canon pressed his forehead to the floor. "Have mercy on me, Christ Jesus."

Satisfied that I had at last hooked this evasive fish, I looked down upon the canon. "God's angel commands you, Christiern Pedersen, to swear an oath that you'll print the *Gesta Danorum* containing Hamlet's legend."

The canon cried out, "Why must I swear an oath? Why must I be more imperiled?"

"Fear the capture and torture of your soul."

"I fear it, and—"

"If you won't swear to print the *Gesta Danorum* and Hamlet legend, then make your confession before you are damned. Say it thus: I, Christiern Pedersen, canon of Lund, confess to God, and to the Blessed Virgin Mary, and to all His saints because I have sinned exceedingly in life. I forfeit my wretched soul. I am ready to endure perpetual fire in my body, the pinchers and worms that will eat my—"

"Propose the oath," the canon cried out. He raised his hands, palms pressed together. He closed his eyes, face lifted to heaven. Lanier knelt beside him, hands clasped.

I stood before the canon and rested my hands upon his shoulders. "Say thus, canon of Lund: I swear to the Almighty God, and upon my ephemeral life and eternal soul, that I shall release the *Gesta Danorum* from my possession, and..."

The canon, trembling, wiped his brow and repeated the phrase.

I continued, "I shall ensure creation of the new master version for the printer's use. It will include Hamlet's legend, found in the original manuscript's marginal notes and inserted pages."

During the canon's repetition he paused. His forehead furrowed, and then his mouth twitched. But he completed the phrases.

I added, "I swear I shall see to the block-setting, printing, illustration, assembly, stitching and binding, and to the allotment of copies sent near and far—"

Lanier, the negotiator and master of contracts, looked up to me and whispered, "And pay for it."

The canon opened one eye and scowled at Lanier.

I hastily added, "I, the canon of Lund, swear to pay for all obligations incurred by these tasks."

The canon haltingly repeated the phrase.

Concluding the oath, I said, "Finally, I swear that the copy work be administered by Horatio of Tønderensis. Amen."

The canon grumbled that final line of the oath. He stood, trudged to the archbishop's chair, and sat heavily in it. From that seat of authority, he slowly asked, "What shall I report to Cristiern about how I obtained the book?"

I replied, "Tell him that a Spaniard sold it to you. He'll believe it."

"I just swore an oath to God, and now you want me to tell a calculated lie?"

"Yes. You have high purpose and there's no other way."

The canon regarded me sharply beneath his thick canopy of brows. "How long to complete the copy work?"

"It depends on how many scribes assist me." I turned a circle, arms outstretched at the cabinets containing the vast wealth of books. "For each volume made in your scriptorium, master, on the average, how many scribes were assigned to produce it? A dozen, perhaps?"

The canon wagged an index finger. "I have too many orders for manuscripts. I can give you the supplies you will need, but no scribes."

"You intend that I, alone, write the new master version of the *Gesta Danorum*?" I dropped my arms in helpless objection. "It's said that Saxo Grammaticus had an army of scribes to create his original *Gesta Danorum*."

"If that is the case, when you forced me to take that oath you should have made me swear to give you a legion of scribes. I will not forfeit them. Saxo did not have Paris's archbishop piling orders upon his scriptorium."

"Surely you'll provide me a corrector, a rubricator, and an illustrator."

"Only an illustrator. I cannot give you more."

"I must identify my own errors? Draw my own chapter headings and paragraph capitals? A millennium will pass before I might finish the task—at least five months." The canon's miserly offer wracked me with disbelief, but I had no recourse. "Very well," I said.

Lanier strode to the cabinet containing the *Gesta Danorum*. "Monsieur, you owe my friend a book."

The canon leaned back in his wide chair and folded his arms. "Not before *I* exact a promise from *you*, Horatio. I will not have you sitting among my holy men, laboring at their easels, without a tonsor. You will wear a habit and get yourself to the barber-surgeon."

I had hoped to escape that itchy tradition. My full head of hair, enjoyed since leaving Leucorea, had been a comfort.

"You must endure that humility," the canon added. "Do as they do and be as they are."

"Must I rise in the dark of night for Terce Hour devotions?"

The canon sucked his teeth. "No, you may sleep," he muttered.

My *Gesta Danorum* awaited. The canon rose and went to the nearby cabinet. He pushed an angular key into the cabinet lock, twisted it, then swung open the lattice-face door. My precious treasure lay upon Lanier's cape like a sleeping cat upon a bunched blanket. Lanier reached for them, but the canon shut the door upon his fingers. Lanier whisked away and nursed his hand. The canon told me, "You see that the manuscript is well. First, your tonsor. Then, I will give you the book and rags."

"My cape." Lanier, frowning, looked to his bruising hand and said to me, "It is torn but you may keep it for bundling the manuscript. I needed a new one in any case." He turned away.

That night Lanier took our horse and departed for Jean's home, and I submitted myself to the barber-surgeon's razor. Then, I hastened through the evening breeze, patting my bare scalp to ease the stinging, to the Hôtel de Sens' abbey and to the small cell I had shared with the snoring, fat monk. He groaned in slumber nearby. I lay upon a cot, using Lanier's cape as a pillow. Some comfort came from hugging the *Gesta Danorum* to my breast. My possession of that volume was momentous. However, because the square, wood plates covering the parchment were broken and cold in my arms, so unlike Margrete's soft curves, it gave me less joy than I wished.

Lying awake, I looked to the cell's small window. The moon, a tiny, white disc, traced a course across the pane. It seemed to me that all the world was made of distant, icy stuff.

What was Margrete's life now? Could she thaw and give me warmth? Did she watch this moon and think of me with regret or hope?

I slid from my bed and knelt in the moonlight, suffering the floor's bite into my knees. I whispered an oath. "Gracious, Almighty God. Hear me, blessed Niels the Holy. I swear that when I've earned one day's rest from my copy work, I'll find the convent harboring Margrete. I beg you, soften her heart toward me."

XIX.

For a fortnight I labored upon my copy work as if beset by a fever. I wanted, as I had pledged, to earn a day of rest and seek Margrete at the convent at Poissy.

Every day at the abbey, which stood adjacent to the Hôtel de Sens, I sat in the large, white stone scriptorium. It was well lit by windows and filled with dozens of sour-smelling, somewhat inebriated monks. On their stools they sat perched before their easels, scratching and scribbling. We gestured conversations to one another to keep the required silence.

Amid this crowd I worked at two easels. Against one lay the ragged *Gesta Danorum*, containing in its margins my writings about Hamlet that spilled onto additional, rough parchment sheets. Upon the other easel rested smooth vellum pages, laced at the center into leaves and faintly lined. On those pages I neatly wrote a new version of the *Gesta Danorum* that integrated the original writing and Hamlet's story, a grand lie.

Each morning after Prime Hour devotions and a cup of breakfast wine, I piled upon a small table, beside my easels, the items I would need for the day—ink packets and pot, quills, rulers and charcoal sticks, stacks of polished, chalky parchment, and a small knife. A bowl of walnuts sustained me between meals. Each day I carefully stroked long script onto the pages, using the blade to scrape away mistakes. I wore my itchy habit's sleeves pushed over my elbows to avoid ink stains.

From sunrise past sunset, day after day, the hours flowed with the continuous turning of pages in the scriptorium, with sparse meals of roasted meat and cheeses and beer, and with devotional readings and prayer. Onward I worked, although the season beckoned. Hot afternoon breezes carried the grassy scent of the wheat harvest, July's customary labor. The days' waning, honey sunlight stretched shadows across the gardens. The warm scent of spices wafted from stew pots and evening hearths.

On Monday, the eighteenth day of July, I sat at my easels, dipping my quill in my inkpot for the one thousandth time that morning when, suddenly, my concentration faltered. I thought of Lanier. It seemed a month, not a fortnight, had passed since he had bid me farewell, departed Paris to go with his brother, Jean, to settle in Rouen. They, unlike me, were making their family and future. My life, in comparison, was unsettled. I had no sense of my destiny. For me, Lanier, like Hamlet, was another brother adopted and lost.

Sadness sat heavily upon me. I set down my quill.

Then I could think only of Margrete. I imagined her at the convent, in a tiny, dim chapel kneeling in prayer upon the stone floor. A single pillow beneath her knees for comfort. Her pink curves and russet strands hidden by a gray, stiff nun's habit.

Why, I wondered, would she prefer that existence to wifely

obligations? Why didn't she want me? My heart ached, for I wanted to be that man I had seen, mirrored in my nighttime window at Krogen, wearing her father's gifted hat. I would love her and lay with her. We would plow until a brood filled our home, making me a proud patriarch.

I had to go to Margrete, to ask once more for her love. Although her rejection could poison like an asp's bite, I would not waste another moment. My day of absence from my labors had been earned and I had satisfied my oath, I decided. I would seek Margrete immediately, convince her to quit her seclusion and return to me.

I went to my cell, dropped my monk's habit as if it were a leper's drapes, and donned my cleaned, mended clothing. It was a joy to wear my beloved green hat once again. I flopped its crown to one side, fully covering my tonsor.

Half a day's trek, at times along the Seine River, which was as glossy as onyx, brought me to Poissy. I quickly found the women's fortress. It was a white, low-roofed, high-walled abode. I pulled upon the bell rope and was greeted by a girl as wispy as a reed. When I asked for Margrete she brought me to a stone bench within the arcade of the nuns' cloister. She pleasantly but firmly instructed me to sit there and wait.

I complied but fidgeted while I beheld the environs. The arcade walk, the ceiling, all plain white, were graced with delicately carved detail—vines, flowers, and fish. I wondered how this refined haven, long situated and endowed by nearby ancient estates, could teach a noblewoman to understand a commoner's life.

At last, Margrete appeared. She was well-collected within her cap, tall collar, and loose frock befitting a nun. I was disappointed that her appearance was as stark and rigid as I had feared. Nothing remained of her trim, shimmering elegance from Krogen.

I stood and reached for Margrete's hand. She allowed me to kiss it. Then I moved to embrace her. She pointed above in warning, to a large window immediately above us. From that perch a glowering old crone, the mother superior, watched us.

We sat stiffly upon the shaded bench.

"Why did you go away?" I asked.

Margrete's hands, in her lap, interlaced. "You need no distraction from your promise, and you need shelter. I could find a bed and meals at a convent. Where else could you have gone?"

"But why so far? There are convents in Paris. Come back with me."

She asked, "Did the canon agree to be your patron?"

"I convinced the canon to print it."

Margrete brightened. "Indeed? The legacy of Krogen."

"I'm the scribe, editing and copying." I removed my hat to show her my tonsor. "I'm a counterfeit monk."

She touched her habit and smirked.

I wished to free Margrete of every confining strap and layer. Yet, I remained on her path of discourse. "My progress is good. Two dozen pages written and one hundred yet to produce."

Margrete nodded slightly. I expected that next she would remark upon a sanguine topic. However, she did not. She asked, "Why do you want to marry me? I have no dowry. No birthright. I am stained by molestation. I cannot make a home as even common women know to do."

I wanted to tell her: *Because I love you.* However, the pinch of skepticism in her eye cautioned me. I clutched the edge of our bench, hooking my fingers beneath its stony lip, and replied, "Doesn't love inspire vision? Tint disgrace? Soften scars? It is our daily medicine."

She regarded me with the woeful pity of a nurse informing a child that Odin does not always bring winter solstice treats, even to good little Danes.

Reconsidering, I changed my tactic. "Dowry, birthright, and domestic perfection are not the qualifications for heaven. As for your... shame, I admire you. Your courage. Your perseverance." Margrete blinked. I saw her bearing ease, as her shoulders dropped and she sat taller, and so I continued, "You're not a nun. I beg you. Return with me to Paris."

I beheld the unfathomable ocean of her—until a beacon, a flicker of a smile, played upon her lips. She told me, "Return when you have completed the book."

Disappointed but determined, I trudged back to Paris.

Throughout August, September, and October I worked. Dozens of candles burned down to pasty stumps upon my scriptorium table. My toils, confined within walls, were unlike those of most men. Their monthly customary labors, harvest among grapevines and fields, allowed them to share their company and work. I, however, was surrounded by monks but alone in my effort.

After months had passed, my heart could no longer bear solitude. I feared that Margrete had devoted herself to a nun's oath. Uncertainty of her intentions consumed me.

On Wednesday, the ninth day of November, I borrowed a cloak from my cell brother. Buffeted by a chill wind, I walked the mucky bankside road and crossed the fields to the convent. I hoped that when I arrived Margrete would be waiting for me, seated in a private white alcove box surrounded by windows, wishing for rescue from tedious, constant chores. When she beheld me, she would smile happily, or tearful regret would drop from her full, brown eyes for time wasted in that dry crone's prison.

I pulled upon the gate bell's cord. A frosted, smiling spinster led me through one side of the cloister's arcade into the garden's center. She pointed to the opposite side of the arcade, to a carving post within the shaded walkway. A woman stood there. "There is Margrete," she softly said and departed.

Never would I have recognized Krogen's former principal lady. Margrete was tanned from months of harvest work. She wore a common hemp frock, rather than a habit, and a thick cape fastened at the neck. A tall block, used as a cutting table, was her work podium. Upon it she wielded a blade, loudly chopping turnips.

To gain her attention, I coughed. Margrete glanced up, across the garden. I could not read her wan smile, but when I saw her push a strand of hair beneath her cap, I knew her. She called out, "Horatio, already you have finished the copy work?" She made no move to invite me closer.

I hesitated. Then I approached her and removed my hat to show my tonsor, now grown fuzzy. "I'm nearly finished—fifty pages yet to complete. I hope to conclude it soon or else I must shave again. My script is elegant, if I dare immodesty. An excellent master version."

"Oh." She took up her knife and continued chopping. "You agreed not to visit until your work was done. Do you remember?"

"Margrete, conclusion of the *Gesta Danorum* is at hand. You needn't remain here. I ask you again to quit this place and come with me to Paris."

She looked down at the piles of roots chunked upon her board. "What do you think of my work? I used to spend half an afternoon splitting them. Now, after only an hour I am done. The women say I season and cook better than they did as novices."

I said, "Your mother wouldn't have known such craft."

"She never could have lived a commoner's life. I, however, have no choice in the matter. Without land or title, I am a peasant now. My birthright brings me no security. Horatio, I have remained in this convent because I have much to learn if we are to survive."

"We'll fare very well," I said, assuming that she meant herself and me.

Margrete set down her knife and wiped her hands upon a cloth scrap. She moved, sweeping her full skirt with her, from behind the block table. Her cape hem parted where her hands rested upon her protruding, round belly.

"By the saints' blood. You didn't have the decency to tell me?"

Margrete flushed. "I could not know my condition until the first months had passed." She stood straight, swollen with indignation and child. "All day I ruminate on fears and horrors, past and future."

Her finger traced the nape of her neck, as if seeking a dangling strand. Her motion bewitched me, as it always had.

She continued, "Now at least my physical dishonor has purpose. I am no longer a noble lady defiled. I am the disgraced mother of a commoner's child." Margrete blanched. "I am taking upon myself the burden to survive, to make a new life for myself after I lost everything dear to me."

Fear crept upon my back. "You would proceed alone? Without me? Why?"

Then, I saw that several women had gathered across the cloister and were watching us. I knew I could not escape them. Thus, I took Margrete's hand and led her to a bench at the center of the garden, within view of the mother superior's watch post. I looked above to the overseeing window and saw the old spying woman glaring down at us like a wizened cat. I said to Margrete, "If you please, sit and rest yourself."

I assisted Margrete as she settled herself upon the bench. I sat beside her. She wiped her eyes.

I softly declared, "I'm a father."

She regarded me, eyes full, and nodded.

Amazement and pride swept over me. However, I also perceived that I might never have known of the birth. That awareness kindled my hurt.

I turned on the bench to fully face Margrete. She took a breath and pivoted toward me. Her hard countenance was a ready shield.

"My security and happiness matter as well," I said. "Your silence, your abandonment, Margrete, threatens my felicity. Did you consider that? You elected to leave, to control everything within your grasp, as usual."

"All I have ever known and done was to preserve myself and others," she said. "I have no fortress. No family. No purpose. My child and I surely will be hunted in this profoundly adversarial world. What lies in wait for us? What will the future exact from me?"

"These questions vex me, also. I don't know where we'll go, how I'll provide for us and the child."

She opened her palms. "Once, a child only reminded me of desolation and ruin. Now, a child could be my hope."

"Why didn't you let us marry at Krogen? You knew that I wished to propose to you. I could be your knight, protect you and the baby, if you would allow it."

After a silent moment she said, "I do not desire a hero as my husband."

Her words seared me because I knew they were true. Facts are harsh masters.

She needs no Horatius Cocles, I thought. Then, I asked her, "What else can I be?"

"A man I adore."

"Whom you neither respect nor want."

She shook her head, seemingly flustered. "You are more sincere, more intelligent, than any courtier who ever walked at Krogen."

"If so, then why don't you want my hand in marriage?"

Her pressed lips. Her unwavering stare. I suddenly realized that perhaps I did not desire the answer to my question, but I could not reverse the moment. She said, "Once my life was a clear path. Now I do not know what I may trust."

"As principal lady, you lived in the confines of a castle and singly protected the queen, conducting favors and the court's access to her. However, you must know that in the wider, dangerous world belonging to us commoners, two persons together are better guardians, especially of a child."

"Perhaps."

"Your father—he blessed us, entrusted you to me. He wrote me a letter telling me this."

Margrete wiped her brimming eyes. She nodded. "He did."

A beetle of irritation crawled beneath my skin. "Then why don't you trust me to care for you and the baby?"

I reached for her hand. Her lithe fingers had been roughened by work.

"Horatio, into what society will I fit?"

"Margrete, the Almighty's will and our determination will forge our destiny."

"You do not understand me. I cannot trust a destiny I cannot imagine."

In frustration I whipped off my hat. "This, Margrete, is the thing I don't understand. You tell me you want our child with you on the river's flow through life"—I pointed west, toward the Seine—"but you also say that you fear the river's course, that you and the child might drown. Why don't you want me to provide the boat to convey you? Here am I, begging to provide you succor. Yet you refuse."

Her sorrowful eyes regarded me. "I do not need to be saved."

I needed no more of her wounding rejection. One moment I learned that I would be a father. The next moment I was denied the right to be that child's protector, and its mother's as well.

I stood to depart and said, "You've cleaved my heart."

She stood and said, "Perhaps I will remain in the convent."

I glanced above at the still-hovering witch. The thought of Margrete surrendered to this place released a wave of suffocating misery that swept over me. However, I fought that tide. *I must make her whole before the Almighty*, I thought, *through marriage*.

"We must make amends to God," I said, wiping my eyes and trying once again. "We would be good helpmates to one another. We could go into exile." I beheld the perfect arc of her belly. "There's safety in a brood."

She clutched her hands and regarded me sharply. "A family is a tremendous commitment, scholar. A bigger promise than you have ever made. You once told me, while we danced, that fatherhood is an enigma to you. Horatio, you should consider whether you can choose fatherhood above all other things. I do not want your instant decision based on pride or anger or joy."

I did not want the everlasting sadness of a man such as Lanier, a vagabond, pining for family and home. He, at least, had departed to build again that which he had lost.

Margrete said, "I will endure here for the present." She took both of my hands in hers. "Are you all right, Horatio?"

I felt I was drowning, rather than swimming this current. Did she want me, or did she not?

"I'm well," I lied. "Come to a convent in Paris where I may visit every day and help care for you."

Margrete faced me and, apparently willing to risk the mother superior's wrath, kissed me lightly upon my lips. A warm surge flooded my parts. She leaned back. "When you are done with the *Gesta Danorum*, return and tell me why fatherhood is the pledge you most desire."

Again, I looked up, not to the window but to the clear, dark blue sky of dying twilight. It inspired simplicity, and so I stepped away from Margrete and spoke plainly to her. "I pray you believe that my promises of love have always been sincere. I wish you could see that."

Margrete blinked. Her lips parted as if to reply, and her fingers interlocked across her belly. "I see that I have put you to trial. I never meant for you to pay the wages for my past injury by another man."

"Margrete, I'll care for you. I'll honor you always."

A breeze stirred wisps of hair, which had escaped her cap, across her forehead. Her hands dropped to her sides, and she softly said, "I know the desire to protect one's person, and I know that you do, as well, Horatio. For a father to guide his child, he must choose to step from his cell into the fray. Go back to Paris, finish your work, and consider why you desire fatherhood. Then you may return and tell me your answer. I will await it."

Margrete gave me a parting nod. Then she turned and, stroking her belly, wandered back to her cutting block. Standing behind it, she took her blade and chopped off a turnip's stringy arse.

The hood of night was closing. I waved farewell to the mother superior and departed the convent, taking a lit torch offered to me.

During my return to Île de la Cité my torch died, abandoning me to the dark fields and perilous riverbank. Worse, fear assailed me—could I bring into being the image of the husband and father I had seen reflected to me that single night at Krogen, when I received and wore Hendrik's gifted hat? I could not bear my loneliness any longer.

I arrived at the abbey's weathered wall and gate. The scent of baking bread for the morning meal did not lure me. I was in despair and did not want food.

Nor did I want my bed, despite exhaustion. I pulled myself atop the wall and, sitting there, watched passing pilgrims and townspeople. They spoke of navigation—about life's pathways and time's passage, of redrawing maps and planning new routes. I imagined the chatter of candles winking within homes surrounding me, calling to the stars above. I hoped to overhear their gossip of Margrete's love for Horatio, or of Lanier's welfare. However, they only chanted my soul's desire to finish the *Gesta Danorum* and recapture the heart of Margrete.

XX.

Through November and December, as frost crept across the scriptorium windows and the slicing, bright winter sun mocked my desire for heat, I labored to complete the *Gesta Danorum* master copy. I huddled at my easels, too far from the corner fireplace. With one hand I clamped my habit's cowl to my chin for warmth while, with the other shivering hand, I wrote. Because I was determined to finish before springtime's buds cracked, I paused only on Christ's Mass and Feast Day, Sunday, the twenty-fifth day of December. I prayed that when I finished my task and returned to Margrete, she would favor my explanation for pledging myself to fatherhood.

I not only consulted God, I sought a physician's prognostication as well. His globes and charts calculated that it would please God to give us the baby in good health during early spring. I privately resolved that before then I would wed Margrete.

On Thursday, the twelfth day of January, in the new year of our Lord 1514—thank the Almighty, the saints, the gods, and each of Freyja's sleigh-pulling cats—I penned the final words of the last tall, creamy page of the master copy. Then, I sat back upon my stool to appreciate its rows of jagged black script. The serifs and capitals hooked as if in dance, and the cadence flowed with the oratorical confidence of an ancient storyteller. Because time was precious and the canon had consented to insert some pictures within the text, I had already directed the illustrator to create drawings while I completed the manuscript. When I saw his magical art—gold leaf flaming beside red pigments and cooling in the company of blue and green hues—my work seemed to breathe. Relief for my achievement nearly caused me to collapse.

That same day, the canon and I carried the finished manuscript from the scriptorium to the Prelum Ascensianum, the Paris workshop of his friend, the learned printer Jodocus Badius. Master Badius placed the *Gesta Danorum* in the queue for creation of woodblock carvings duplicating the illustrations. Because I had never before witnessed a printer's astonishing hive of tempo and assembly, he allowed me a glimpse of the typesetting room. The speed of the compositors, marking manuscripts to guide accurate selection and placement of type pieces into trays, and the biting stench of dye and sweat made my head nearly float. Men ministered to hungry machines by placing the finished trays within frames, pounding them with bulbs of ink, and laying blank pages. They clamped and slid the presses' arms to make the impressions. Printed sheets of fine paper hung in a separate room to dry. Entranced, I hastened from the workshop. My feet skimmed the snow-laden ground for excitement that soon my *Gesta Danorum* would be printed, sewn, and bound—dressed to perform Hamlet's story for the eyes and ears of the world's populace.

My own story now awaited my attention. I knew that my heart's destiny would soar or sink depending upon my response to Margrete's question. How would she answer me when, once more, I asked her to be my wife?

The following morning, the thirteenth day of January—the Feast Day of Saint Hilary of Poiters, a gentle holy man known as The Hammer—I ignored the festivities. As determined as Thor, I went again to Poissy to woo Margrete.

I trod ice-crusted fields and trailed the frosty Seine. Winter's cold swiped at me like sharp talons. However, not even a maelstrom could have hindered me. I had left Paris the sire of a book, and I expected to return with the family I desired.

When I arrived at the convent, I was in no state of wits to ask a nun's permission to visit the mother of my child. Thus, rather than use the bell, I found discarded casks, piled them at the convent wall, and climbed over its peaked crown like a mad pillager.

I dropped from the wall into the nunnery's garden, specifically into a thistle patch—no doubt planted there precisely to ensnare ruffians. My yelp alerted the mother superior, who I saw appear at her oversight window. Probably she observed me while I, hobbling, pulled thorns from my limbs. I could not reach those jammed into my back.

The hollow-cheeked woman descended from her nest and, tugging my arm with surprising might for an old crone, hauled me to an open, hewn-beamed threshold. I ducked to pass through and found myself in a room lit only by a raging fireplace. Two women stirred boiling kettles and tended to dusky bottles on shelves. Margrete stood at a broad carving table. She skinned a rabbit, using a blade to strip the flesh as she pulled away the fatty pelt. Wet, silver beads rolled down her tanned neck.

The mother superior hovered behind me at the door. "Margrete, your trouble visits us again. Resolve it and replant my briars by the wall."

Margrete looked up as she tore away a hindquarter. When she saw me, she set down her knife. The mother superior shuffled away as Margrete waddled toward me. Her belly sphere led her steps.

I tried to bow in deference, but the barbs along my spine stabbed me. In pain, I managed to reach for her hand to kiss it. "Margrete."

She swatted away my offered hand, wiped hers on her apron, and touched a sore on my face from whence I had pulled a needle. She scowled. "Why did you climb over the wall?"

"It seemed a chivalric undertaking. More spikes are in my back."

Margrete grimly said, "Disrobe to your waist."

I gingerly pulled my tunic over my head and slung it over a bench. The ladies, remaining as her chaperones, stirred the kettles and glanced at us disapprovingly.

Margrete used small tongs to extract the thorns from my back. Bending to minister to me, she groaned softly.

I said, "Kneeling for prayer must be difficult now. Can you make your devotions for your parents?"

"It depends on the baby's position, but I always manage."

Margrete uncorked a small vial, poured an ointment into her hand, and spread it on my back, soothing my wounds. She gave me the bottle and pointed to a pantry cabinet. I hid myself there and applied the salve to my limbs, buttocks, and chest. I gingerly dressed and returned to the kitchen. Carefully, I sat on a bench.

She rested beside me and asked, in an even tone, "Have you completed your work?"

"It's in the queue for illustration block carving and printing. Soon I'll be called to read a proof copy with the pressman. I can hardly bear the wait."

Margrete nodded, smiling slightly. "Good. Congratulations." Then her lips pressed. She looked down to her hands, clenching and unclenching, in her lap. "Have you considered my question?" The fire's orange hue illuminated russet wisps in her hair. I took a breath to still my pounding breast.

My soft scribe's paws took her calloused hands. Her brows arched. A speech rolled from my tongue. I had practiced it while tramping through snow to the convent gate.

"My father didn't care for my well-being. That's why I adopted Papa. He gave me guidance and some protection. Margrete, I want to be my child's Papa and hero. I'm worthy of that part. I'll act it well for our honor."

She leaned back, seeming to take a wider view of me. "Why are you ready now?"

"I've lived a solitary life. I desire a family."

Margrete took my hand and laid it upon the round apex of her belly. "I have learned to conduct myself in the kitchen and the marketplace."

I touched her soft cheek brushed by firelight, the glow of gold leaf. Margrete beheld me, full-eyed. I cupped her face. Our kiss was full and tender. Her hand trailed down my back, rested upon my hip, slid near my groin.

When Margrete paused for breath, she whispered, "I can cook. I know the hearth I want to keep. The suppers I can roast and brew. I could be a good wife."

A hot surge overtook me. "I need more assurances, lady." I kissed her again.

Sudden clanging made me look to the hearth corner. A beacon of judgment shot at us from one of the chaperones. She held an iron fire poker and beat it once more against the kettle. I launched an answering glare at her.

Margrete asked me, "You promise that the baby and I will be your greatest care?" She regarded me with trepidation as if she stood alone upon a high, crumbling ledge. My heart quickened and I closed my eyes. My soul scrambled up the imagined rocky wall to its summit, to stand beside her. Below us flowed a dark, choppy, antique Roman river of unknown consequences. I feared its tumult but, as did Horatius Cocles, we leapt from that ledge.

I knelt before Margrete. "Two beings rely upon your love. Our baby, for even the purest baptism can't redeem a child born a bastard, and me, a lonely man leaning as near to his grave as to his cradle. Your love will be our salvation. To you I pledge my adoration, my devotion, myself, now and always. I ask you, in the presence and merciful benevolence of the Almighty, his angelic hosts, all the saints—"

I read in Margrete's eyes a soft plea. *Finish your proposal before the baby is born.*

"Will you, Margrete, make this poor scholar the happiest of men? Will you be my wife?"

She smiled. "I will."

My heart might have burst. In her answer I heard a promise of simpatico understanding. To me its essence was as sweet as a field of sun-warmed lilacs.

I desired to whisk Margrete immediately to Paris, but her transport required arrangements and payment from the canon. Therefore, one week later, on a sunny, crisp Saturday, the twentieth day of January, I held the reins of a gentle, gray-speckled mare, loaned to me by the canon. Upon that gentle animal I brought Margrete from Poissy to Île de la

Cité. I walked and Margrete, seated above on the mount, rocked with the gait. She was veiled in blue, swollen and stoic, and seemed every bit like Mary, albeit not virginal. I fed her chunks of dried mutton, eating plenty myself, peas, and fresh hawthorn berries. During that single day's journey, we became attuned in that when she, twice each hour it seemed, pointed to the roadside I helped her slide from the animal's back to the ground. Then I held a thin blanket that shielded her from onlookers as she pissed. We achieved masterful coordination in that art by the time we arrived at the Hôtel de Sens where our beds awaited. The canon had agreed to permit our temporary residence there providing that he immediately performed our most sacred sacrament.

We arrived, and, three days later, on Monday, the twenty-third day of January, in the year of our Lord 1514, Margrete and I were wed. We stood within the Sainte-Chappelle's blue and crimson upper chapel, before the altar and an audience of scribes and nuns. The canon conducted our Mass adorned in his gold-trimmed, white robes. We made our vows, bathed in jeweled light emanating from towering stained-glass columns. I was clad in a borrowed white, flower-embroidered tunic with white leggings and boots. From my shoulder draped a single article of black—Lanier's washed, repaired cape. It was a poor substitute for my friend's presence. Most lovely was my bride. Margrete's hair hung in woven loops. She wore a loaned, modest cream frock embellished with small embroidered petals similar to the design I wore but adjusted to suit her advanced posture.

Facing Margrete, I took her hands. How radiantly she beheld me, as though no other man existed under heaven! I was overcome. I could not merely repeat the canon's prompts of my vow. I raised my wrist, still holding Margrete's hand, to dab my eye. Then, I drew her closer, respecting her girth. Our fingers gripped between our hearts, and I spoke from mine. "My wedded wife. My only beloved. My life's beacon. You are the home I've long sought, the family I've forever craved. Every breath I have taken has been my life's hungering wait for you…for this very moment."

The canon raised a finger as if to beckon me from my free-willed path. But a glistening wash in Margrete's happy eyes and a quiver in her smile encouraged me to proceed. I utterly abandoned the canon's lead and completed my oath. "I pledge to you, Margrete of Helsingør, daughter of Hendrik, that I will give myself to you completely. I will adore you, and I will honor and defend the dignity of your mind and soul, may it please the Almighty."

Margrete's full eyes released a tear. Its downward glide slowed upon the plump apex of her pink, joyful cheek. She squeezed my hands, which still held hers.

The canon began, "Margrete, do you…"

"Horatio of Tønderensis," she said. The canon, dismissed again, sighed. He shrugged and stepped back. Margrete continued, "The certainty of my life's direction, that I had thought was lost, I have found again in your love. My husband, though you are a commoner, there is nothing ordinary about you. Your desire to honor those you love, the strength of your mind and heart, your persistence…no man in Krogen's court possessed such true nobility. Despite my testing of myself and of you, while I resided and worked in the convent, when you visited, my heart filled. At night, especially, I thought only of you, heard your voice, and wished for your touch. I longed to be yours. I vow to trust you, to keep your hearth, and"—Margrete's belly pulsed. Her hand slipped from mine to rest upon her abdomen and still our kicking baby—"to bear little ones blessed with your stamina and imagination."

How my breast was able to contain my bounding heart, I could not divine. "And with your beauty and grace-giving love." My reply, staggering through my emotion barely restrained, was almost a whisper.

Our sealing kiss and full embrace was greater to me than a usual carnal act. I was filled with hope. For the first time in my life I could say that we, not I, pulled the lever of destiny with God and forever changed our lives' path.

Less than two months later our first born, my book, emerged. On that blessed day, which was during the second week of Lent, on Wednesday, the fifteenth day of March, I went to the Prelum Ascensianum. In the vast room of groaning printing machines, I witnessed several wet pages lifted by waiting hands that cared for them. The pressman allowed me to hold a few folio sheets—fresh, long, and pungent. When I beheld the beautiful, stately print of the *Gesta Danorum* and Hamlet's story disguised and neatly enfolded within, I trembled with elation. I believed, with all my heart in those days of ignorance, that this lie was the best I could do to fulfill my promise.

Within a month, the canon delivered to me my own leather-bound copy of the work. It was surprisingly light, compared to the original thick, wood-shielded manuscript. I bent back the supple cover and, thumbing the paper pages, marveled at their delicate form. Then I turned back to the first page and beheld the sweeping red lettering that proclaimed its title and ancestry:

> *The histories of Danish kings and heroes in an elegant style, by Saxo Grammaticus, a native of Zealand and dean of the cathedral church of Roskilde, compiled over*

three hundred years ago and now concisely printed for the first time in a series of illustrated volumes.

    Exquisite, I thought. Badius the printer had bound the many volumes into a single book.

    The introductory page also featured another surprise: a marvelous woodblock illustration celebrating the majesty of Denmark. This drawing was not one I had imagined and requested. The canon had generously added it. Classical columns bordered the page, containing berry-inked cherubs and dragon fish at play and more infant angels riding prancing horses. At the center of the page stood a king, glorious in his armor, leading his army. Who was that? Cristiern, shrewdly portrayed and flattered by the canon? I preferred to believe that the royal depicted there was Hamlet. The notion that my falsehoods had made him a long-lived king did not, then, burden me.

    Upon closer inspection I saw, drawn within the illustration's top border, a small pendant containing a miniature portrait. A man seated at his scriptorium easel and writing into a book. Saxo Grammaticus, I initially presumed. He wore something upon his head—like my green Papa hat, flopped to one side. I was amazed and proud that the canon had honored me as if I was a lauded scholar at Leucorea.

    During the following weeks, the pressman made dozens of copies of the *Gesta Danorum* for transport to Copenhagen. Each copy bore a fresh leather cover the primitive color of russet mud. The title, like the original work, was comprised of notched triangles linked to form each letter. I helped the packers in the Prelum Ascensianum stack and place the books into crates, but first I said a prayer over each volume. "May you speed Hamlet's story to all Danes, perhaps to all the world. May all remember Hamlet and learn to be worthy of their honorable duties."

My only regret at that time was that I perceived no sign from Papa's spirit. He had always lauded my achievements while he lived. I tried to forget my disappointment; however, when I slept, sadness slithered into my dreams.

By this time, Margrete's belly had grown as large as the same ship's hull in which we had conceived the child. We dared not attract devils by speaking our fears that the baby might be stillborn, as Margrete's first conception by her attacker had been. We prayed daily. We were excited for, and terrified of, the coming day.

Wednesday, the twenty-second night of March, was blustery. White clouds tumbled across the dusky sky. All night, a midwife tended to Margrete in the most distant chamber of the Hôtel de Sens. I sat in the corridor, outside our room, on a hard bench. I begged God for an end to Margrete's screeching agony and for His blessing of a live baby. A century seemed to pass.

By dawn the next day, no one had fetched me, and I had not heard an infant's cry. I gripped my hands to still my rattling heart and stood at a window in the same hallway. I watched the sun rise, first as a blue bunt, then burn orange. Its aura stretched across a rack of clouds. Beneath that godly banner I suddenly heard a child squalling. It was, to me, as splendid as a royal fanfare. The midwife brought me a precious bundle. I peeled the hood to behold my son whom Margrete permitted me to name for the wisest of Romans.

Marcus was a gurgling, flaxen-headed, squinch-eyed little creature. In a roaring second he claimed my heart. I shook for pride, joy, and fear—the chaotic sensation known to any new father craving a true family.

The midwife allowed me to briefly visit Margrete. God's bones. She was pale and weak, having lost much of her humors. But she was alive, thank the Almighty and the gods. Recovery was slow. Within a week she could walk, with my assistance. Gradually, she gained more ease and strength.

Five months passed while we watched our little gurgling boy thrive. Our dread that he might perish at any moment gradually was replaced by trepidation that we would be captured. While in the marketplace I overheard talk of the bounty Cristiern had pledged on our heads for theft and escape.

During the sunny afternoon of Tuesday, the twelfth day of September, in our tiny chamber at the Hôtel de Sens, Margrete and I discussed our situation. Margrete, standing, looked out the window, which afforded only a view of the stark-white abbey wall and the branches of a neighbor's flat-leafed lemon tree. I, sitting upon the bed, nibbled pieces of an apple.

"We cannot hide here forever from our enemies," said Margrete. She reached into the crib where Marcus, swaddled from toe to chin, lay squirming against his confines. She stroked the baby's wrapped belly. The child retched, then chortled. Margrete bent over Marcus. She wiped his face and laughed with him.

I said, "For our safety we must remain in exile but go where none of Cristiern's bounty hunters will find us."

Alarmed, Margrete glanced at me. She tugged our only chair closer to the crib and sat. "How can we raise our son anywhere but Denmark?"

Marcus screeched. Margrete lifted him and cinched his wrap tighter. "This cloth is hard to keep evenly bound," she said as she unpinned and rewrapped the swaddling around the baby's bottom while the child, momentarily freed, kicked. I offered Margrete a piece of apple. She waved it away. She shifted Marcus onto her right shoulder, then rubbed and patted his back. "Be calm, Marcus."

At last, my wife must bear a creature that will not heed her commands. I enjoyed that notion.

"What is so funny?" Margrete's glance jabbed me.

"Nothing, dearest mermaid. I was only thinking of the childhood tricks I played in my native town, Tønderensis. That is where we could make our home. From there we could escape easily, westward by ship or southward by roads into the Germanic principalities, if we must."

Marcus screamed as if he was on fire. Margrete, her face pinched, said, "I cannot quiet him." She held out the baby to me. "You try."

I stroked, bounced, and rubbed Marcus. I hung him upside down. Cooed. Sang. Giggled. Whispered. Stared at him. Margrete watched, wan-faced, her wrist braced against her forehead. Marcus continued to wail as if horn-helmeted Odin, haggard and bloody, gripped him.

Margrete took the baby from me. She cradled him in one arm, and with her other hand yanked at the front of her gown to open the nursing flap. She pushed her plump nipple into the baby's mouth.

I said, surrendering, "That's one trick I can't manage."

The child greedily suckled, eying me with arrogant triumph.

A soft knock upon our door prompted Margrete to turn her back to it. She said, "I asked the attendant for fresh cloths."

I went to the door and opened it.

In the corridor stood Lanier. He was well groomed. Below his hat, his mane was clean and flowing. Mustache trimmed. He wore a new cape and fresh clothing. All was his customary black. However, his aspect bore familiar sad creases. He held in both hands a small stack of folded cloths. "The abbot's assistant gave me these to bring you."

I embraced my brother and kissed his cheek but knocked his burden to the floor. Releasing him, I stooped to collect the fallen articles.

Lanier also bent to retrieve the cloths. "I had hoped, in vain, to swaddle my son or nephew one day."

We straightened and I held out a cloth to Margrete. She draped it over her bosom and the baby and then turned to Lanier. Margrete smiled with curiosity. "You are returned to us, Lanier. Why aren't you in Rouen?"

"Jean and I boarded in a fine tavern. But we argued. I believed the crowded, noisy location was to blame for our trouble, and so we went to another tavern. But there we had the same fights." Lanier walked to the window and stared at the abbey wall. He sighed. "Jean thinks I am a swine. I *know* that he is one. Many artists are temperamental, are they not? In Rouen, he and other pigs will make art for snide patrons. That will be his life. And he is welcome to it."

Margrete turned away to secure herself. Then she faced Lanier and showed him our tightly bound child. Lanier grinned, removed his hat, and set it upon our chair. He reached for Marcus. Margrete let him take the baby into his arms.

Lanier unpinned the wrap.

Margrete said, "Do not."

Ignoring her, Lanier loosened the binding across the baby's middle. Then, with his finger, Lanier touched the baby's round, pink nose and spoke to him, as sweet as honey. "You are very tiny, yet so mighty." Marcus cooed at Lanier and wriggled. When Lanier tugged at Marcus's swaddling folds to separate them, Marcus beheld Lanier in wide-eyed awe. Lanier untucked one of the child's arms and waggled his freed little hand in salutation to his mother. Margrete's stiff expression softened to a grin.

She said, "For a man who is not a father, you have quite a rapport with infants."

Lanier returned the baby's limb within the swaddling and pinned it with more slack than it had been originally fixed. "My mother was a secondary midwife. I learned a few things. Best to set the binding like this." He cradled the baby so that Margrete slid her finger under the wrap and tested its tension. A putrid stench reached me. I covered my nose but Margrete merely bit her lip, puzzling over the art Lanier taught her.

She felt within the folds, then shook her head. "He is dry." She asked Lanier, "Why did you say that your hope to care for a son or nephew was in vain?"

"I have no such fortune. Jean's progeny will carry our name. Already he met a woman. She writes plays. Quite a talent. And he has impregnated her. Jean's dream of status as a court musician, his family, will fare better if I am not there. I left."

"Why?" I asked.

"One night at the tavern, a man confronted us. He had heard of Louis's bounty on me. He refused to believe it had been rescinded. He tried to capture us. Jean blamed me for our trouble."

Lanier began to shift Marcus from cradling in his arms to upright against his breast, but Margrete snatched the baby from him.

"I have no family but you." Lanier's arms dropped to his sides. I clasped his shoulder.

Margrete lay Marcus in his crib and hastily rewrapped him, binding him tightly. Marcus yowled. I went to her and, leaning close, whispered,

"Lanier needs a home just as we do. He can help us."

"To you, he is like a brother. I know that you want him with us, but—"

The chair behind us crunched. I looked over my shoulder and saw that Lanier reclined in it, holding his hat. He regarded me. Tender sentiment rounded his face.

I replied, "He is, indeed, my brother."

Margrete moved to stand before Lanier. He rose to be addressed. Margrete said to him, "Your bravery at Krogen, your courage to draw away Reynaldo so that we might achieve Horatio's promise—all was more than we deserved. You are our friend. I do not wish you harm, Lanier. But I cannot risk my child because of bounty men seeking…"

Lanier's head dropped upon his breast. His stare rested on his boots, and his finger wiped his nose. My heart cracked for him, and for me.

"Surely, you understand, Lanier," Margrete stammered. "If you and Jean drew the attention of bounty men, it is more likely that we three, together, will be recognized and caught, then killed by Cristiern. Marcus is Krogen's blood. His existence denies Cristiern his intended obliteration of my people. For Marcus to be protected, we must be safe."

Lanier looked to the baby in his crib. Marcus wailed, nostrils flaring. "Apologies, madame. I should not have intruded." Lanier turned his back to us and began to shuffle toward the door.

I reached for Lanier's sleeve and held it tight. He paused. I looked over my shoulder at Margrete. "Lanier could fight for us. Guard us."

Lanier leaned toward the portal and pulled away from my grasp. I leapt between him and the door. I would not allow his dismissal. I could not lose him again.

Marcus's bellowing sobs gave voice to my anguish.

Margrete sighed and then said to Lanier, "You need not leave us immediately." She wearily bent over the crib, lifted Marcus, and carried him to me. "You crying boys can keep one another company for a while." Still leaning against the door, I held Marcus and bounced with him. His screaming persisted. Lanier opened his arms. Into them I placed Marcus's crimson, squalling body.

Lanier cradled him close and, looking steadily into Marcus's blaring face, softly sang in French:

> *By full moon's light each summer night, I suckle the beer casks's teats—*

"Stop," Margrete and I begged. She added, "No tavern songs for lullabies."

Lanier turned his back to us, gently rocking the baby, and continued:

> *'Til sleep, that buxom whore, straddles me.*
> *Dreams never came so sweet.*

What else should I expect of him? After all, he gave a skull to a little girl in my dream.

Lanier carried Marcus to the window and stood with his back to us. He repeated the offensive verse and made an action we could not see. The baby's crying ceased. Lanier turned to face us. He showed us Marcus asleep, within his slightly loosened wrap.

Margrete did not curse Lanier for the liberty he took. "Thank you," she said. She received the child from him and laid him in his crib.

Then Lanier walked to me, where I leaned against the door. His eyes were large with wonder. He scratched the back of his head. "That drinking song is a magical spell. It also calms horses."

I looked past him to Margrete. Her long stare and grim smile signaled to me her awareness of lost ground. She approached, her hands clasped at her middle. She told Lanier, "Do children of your clan grow to be barkeeps or brothel proprietors?"

A grin flickered across Lanier's lips, then flattened. "Not yet, *ma chère*."

Encircling Margrete with my arm, I whispered to her, "I've told you, and I mean this still: I admire your perseverance and courage. Those traits are a tremendous inheritance for Marcus. Do you want him to learn fear from us? We must be examples of virtue."

Margrete, considering, bit her fingernail. She went to a high corner shelf and, reaching, pulled from it Lanier's old, dusky cape. It tumbled into her hands. She turned to Lanier and said, "Some time has passed since you last saw this."

"I wore it, draped over one shoulder, at our wedding," I said.

Lanier touched the neck clasp of the thick cape he wore. He gave a sad smile. "In that way, I attended your nuptials."

Margrete held his old, faded cape so that Lanier could appreciate her careful darning that had mended its many tears and scars. She said, "It bundled the *Gesta Danorum*. It has journeyed far."

"*C'est vrai*. It saw many battles."

"Likely, it will survive many more," Margrete said. She bent over the crib. "Oh. He is awake again. That was a short respite." Margrete tied the cape around the baby's swaddled shoulders and held him up for our view. The cape hung from his small body. Margrete said to Marcus, "Uncle Lanier will come with us to Tønderensis. He will suffer much if he teaches you filthy habits."

My heart leapt. Marcus happily squealed. Lanier's vulpine teeth flashed a grateful smile.

That night, Margrete and I packed our few possessions. Some clothing given by generous persons. Cloths and a coverlet for the baby. Our *Gesta Danorum*.

The next morning, I went to the canon, who I found sitting in the archbishop's office. I stood opposite his table, as usual, and thanked him for his assistance and advised him of our departure. After the canon looked to the ceiling and uttered brief thanks to God, he asked me, "Where are you bound?"

"A town some distance from here that will hide us well."

The canon's fist rapped decisively upon the table before him. "A most excellent response, Horatio." He opened a small chest beside the table, retrieved a few goldgulden coins, and pressed them into my hand. "That should speed your trek."

I was much amazed. Those coins would afford our journey by boat from Île de la Cité to the port of Tønderensis. "Thank you, master."

"Leave your visit at the Hôtel de Sens in the past. Good day." The canon sat at the table and took his quill in hand. Then he noticed that I remained. "What do you want now?"

I wished to give Lanier his deserved trophy. I replied, "The sword would serve us well for protection. We would never return for your help. May I have—"

"Buy one if you have need." The canon dismissed me with a wave.

I nodded my understanding. We departed the Hôtel de Sens.

Immediately, our family of four souls hastened to the crowded, malodorous dock of Île de la Cité and boarded a shallow-hulled boat. It bore us to Le Havre, the river's confluence with the sea. We disembarked to join the cargo and crew of a sleek, three-masted craft that carried us through the North Sea to a port above Rodenas. There, we boarded a ship and I surrendered more money for our final passage. On Saturday, the twenty-third day of September, ten days after we departed Paris, we approached the rattling market-port town of Tønderensis, Denmark.

As our ship neared the town, I stood on deck beside Lanier and Margrete. She held Marcus. The crew scrambled across the yardarms above us and tended the sails. We slowed and glided along the dock piled head-high with hay bales, wine casks, and stacks of furry hides. Beyond the dock, I beheld the craggy, ancient wall ringing the thatch-roofed town. I gripped the rail in fearful anticipation of our new life. Our happiness and survival, I knew, would depend upon masterful deception as we lived among the assiduous Danes of Tønderensis. I believed then that my lying habit, which I thought to be a talent, would serve us well.

I did not yet perceive how my sin had already subverted my worthiness of honor and my promise to Hamlet.

XXI.

Immediately, before September shed its warmth, we found an abandoned, tiny cottage. It was nestled against a stinky, decrepit section of Tønderensis's town wall, within a quarter that sheltered the population of ragged undesirables—an order of people native to me, and I to them.

The dwelling was a shell of a home, composed only of four walls and half of a roof. Within it our family huddled in one corner and made our hearth. There, Margrete hung broken but functioning pots and shears that she had scavenged. As Lanier and I learned thatching skills, mostly through error, our roof gradually grew to cover the entire abode. We suffered deep splinters, twisted joints, and some mockery from our neighbors, but we piled upon our home a roof that kept our family dry and comforted. Although our home was ugly, it pleased me because our industry made it our own.

Our professed family surname was an invention, and to our neighbors we asserted that Lanier was our distant, beloved cousin. No one seemed to doubt us or object to our arrival. However, some commotion revolved around Lanier and courtship. Often, he would woo a woman and then weary of some aspect or doubt himself. After he abandoned his hopes for her, or she gave up her efforts with him, he would sulk and reassert his status as a devout bachelor. Then we bore some angry questions from insulted fathers and brothers. But inevitably another woman would drift close and Lanier's imagination would embark with her.

Margrete continued to cook, improving upon her apprenticing begun at the convent. She quickly became respected among the women in our part of the town, if not for her skills then because of her willingness to work. She joined them every Saints' Day to help prepare meals for the poorest among us. Margrete seemed to take comfort in belonging to the whole.

I, too, earned some esteem. I befriended our priest who appointed me the town's schoolmaster. In one of our church's chapel alcoves, by the light of stained glass, I taught boys and girls Latin, mathematics and rhetoric, Rome's history from Livy's works, which Hamlet and I had once enjoyed, and the writings of Marcus Aurelius, beloved by Papa and me. I found those books within the church's library, a collection that generous merchants had fattened over time.

Also, I included stories among my lessons. I sat upon my stool, surrounded by children sitting upon the chapel floor, and told from memory Hamlet's story and other tales recorded in the *Gesta Danorum*. Soon, adults joined to listen. Practice before audiences improved my talent in the art of epic storytelling. Within months I was telling Hamlet's legend to audiences weekly gathered in the town hall after supper or at sundown, much as Erik had once recited from the original *Gesta Danorum* to Krogen's people.

Years passed. Sometimes they dragged fear's heavy shackles, but otherwise they raced with the speed of Mercury provoked.

Our daughter was born on Monday, the ninth day of June, in the year of our Lord 1516. While Margrete recovered from the difficult labor, I rushed the baby for christening, lest devils hold fast. My wife permitted me to give our second child, like our first, a classical Roman name.

Julia was a flaxen-crowned baby, as was her brother. However, while his temperament would flash from calm to storm, her manner was pensive and patient from the day she emerged from the womb.

As summer became autumn in the year of our Lord 1518, often at night I lay awake in bed, aware of several presences. Margrete and the children, now aged two and four, slumbered beside me issuing wispy breaths. Lanier, upon his cot across the room, slept fast, his nose whistling. And Hamlet's spirit returned. For terror I could not sleep while I watched, from my cot, Hamlet's ghost traverse my floor. Only I saw the bony phantom shimmer in a stream of moonlight, then pass into shadow and flicker like a candle flame about to collapse. It bobbed as if floundering without a guiding beacon. Why did the ghost linger despite my continual remembrance of Hamlet in my readings to audiences? What more was left for me to do?

After a fortnight of these persistent visitations and wondering about their meaning, I concluded that more people, beyond Tønderensis, must hear Hamlet's story. I would have to become a performing storyteller, more than a scholarly reader of stories, and visit surrounding villages. Venturing out, I feared, would risk our discovery by bounty men. Yet, I took comfort in knowing that, like Papa, I would achieve honor in life through teaching many people.

When I shared my idea with Margrete and told her of the ghost's return, initially it did not rest lightly with her. I persisted over weeks, plying her with my best debates. I won her begrudging consent on the condition that I alter my appearance to trick men hunting us, then she would permit me to recite to assemblies gathered in the villages one night each month.

To prepare for this new calling, I found cloth remnants discarded by the merchants, which Margrete sewed to make a scholarly robe befitting a truth teller. I grew whiskers frosty with age, and I practiced oratory in my home. My adoring children had no opinion of the text I committed to memory. Instead, when they pulled on my bushy beard they squealed with delight.

During the following two years, my audience in Tønderensis exceeded several hundred souls. At times I did not need to trek to other towns. Those who were hungry for diversion came from nearby villages to hear me tell Hamlet's story in the village common square by firelight. I was pleased to sate their interest. However, Hamlet's ghost continued to walk my floor. Before each performance and during each bedtime prayer, I privately begged, "Hamlet, *es tranquilla*: be calm."

Threat of discovery and failure persisted for another reason. I learned the dreadful facts with slicing clarity on the evening of the twenty-fourth day of June in the year of our Lord 1520.

On that day, Margrete, Marcus now six years of age, Julia, four years of age, Lanier, and I had exhausted ourselves by indulging in the festivities of the Feast Day of Saint John the Baptist. We joined the throng at the clerics' platform erected in the common square and marveled at the priest's droning translation of the saint's relic bones. After Mass, the mob devoured the summer's bounty of fish and stewed roots, roasted venison, breads, cheeses, and beer. We gluttons next danced to pounding drums and urgent flutes around the night's bonfires, which blazed throughout the town to evoke cures and cleansing. Our waving arms and stomping feet evaded the jagged claws of daemons and witches said to roam the earth that night.

When the merriment ended, we straggled under a dusky, starlit plane, carrying our sleep-struck children to our home. Midway, Lanier offered relief to Margrete and bore Julia homeward. I held Marcus, draped partly over my shoulder, the entire distance.

We were grateful to arrive at our abode. After we laid the children in the bed, Lanier went to his corner cot, collapsed upon it, and soon fell to snoring. Margrete lit three candles and, sitting by them at the table, took up darning one of Marcus's ripped tunics.

I hoped that our customary evening reading from our *Book of Hours* would be forgotten and forgiven. I wanted no more biblical recitation that day. For confirmation of my wish, I looked to the children in bed. Julia lay flat, head turned toward me, deeply asleep. Marcus, however, was propped upon one elbow, sharply watching me. "Papa, let's read a psalm."

"Indeed, Cardinal Marcus." I took one candle and the little book from our table and sat upon the bed beside him. In the dim expanse of our single room, my candle's wick was like a sun to the cosmos where only my babies and I dwelled.

I opened the *Book of Hours* to a random page. I read Psalm 7 to Marcus, continuing uninterrupted until I said the verse, "The lying mouth kills the soul."

"That isn't true," Marcus said.

"Of course, it's so," I replied. "This is the Almighty's scripture. It is precious and writ for our instruction and salvation. Entrusted to us. Why do you say it isn't true?"

Marcus rubbed his nose. "Your soul is alive, not dead."

"May it please God, yes."

Marcus shook his head. "You lie often, Papa. God doesn't punish you. Everything's fine." Exhibiting the proof, he waved his arm at the peaceful environs of our home.

I stared at my son and momentarily was struck dumb by his innocent accusation.

Margrete coughed. I looked to her. Through the candles' glow, I read her knotted countenance and brewing concern.

My inclination toward falsehoods was a trifling matter, and those instances were for wise purposes, I thought. I brushed Marcus's mussed hair, tidying it across his forehead. My tongue revived, and I asked, "What lies?"

"You tell stories to people about a prince who lied to everyone about everything, and you say that the prince lived long ago. But he was Hamlet, and you tell me how you knew him, that he was like your brother."

"That..." I took a breath and paused to think "...is a way of giving people something they need—the example of a friend and a man devoted to his promise. At the same time, we are safe from those who do not want Hamlet remembered. We keep our honor, because I pledged to tell Hamlet's story. This way, we get what we need. It's a special matter. God would forgive it. Aside from that, we tell the truth."

Marcus, clear-eyed, considered. He nodded. "God commands us not to lie. But if we have good reason, it's all right to lie. Then God's command is false." Marcus, brows raised, looked to Margrete. "Momma? Papa and God lie. Do you lie, too?"

Margrete set down her darning. Her head sank into her hands. When her fingers parted, she raised her chin, and looked to me. I read sorrow in her eyes.

Denial's heat rose in my breast. *I don't deserve blame. Marcus is confused by my conduct, not corrupted. I'll test him.* "Suppose that at Mass today a man stole a coin from the alms box beside the holy water basin. But the man ran away and dropped the coin, and you picked it up. If the constable saw you do that and asked you, 'Is that coin yours?' how would you answer?"

Marcus regarded me with squinch-faced cynicism too seasoned for a boy of six years. "Did I see the man take the coin?"

"You did."

Marcus shrugged. "It's mine," he firmly said.

"Why? You saw the thief take it from the poor."

His eyes gleamed. "No one's hurt, and I need it. It's only one coin."

My son seemed proud of his sinful logic, which he had learned from my hypocrisy, and worse—his lie justified theft. Because of me, my son thought both were virtues. I had failed Marcus. Hot guilt swept over me. Overtaken, I leaned back upon the bed, braced against my arms. I could not defend myself against a battalion of realizations.

I knew that lies had destroyed the House of Hamlet. In memory I saw Hamlet rail against Polonius, Claudius, Ophelia, Gertrude—everyone who he believed had trapped him with lies. Did lies drive Hamlet to madness? Had my lies vexed his spirit, caused his soul's unrest? Is that what his ghost on the riverbank had called out to me? *Horatio, tell the truth.*

Then, I saw that I had been blind and dumb. I had elected to rely upon a grand lie incorporated into a printed book to achieve my promise and create the foundation of Hamlet's legacy. Although I was the source of the Hamlet story, I had chosen to hide myself behind a legend, my biggest lie. I was neither a brave Dane nor an antique Roman. I had failed Hamlet.

My plan to insert my grand lie into the *Gesta Danorum* had caused Lanier and Margrete to risk all for it. I had failed my wife and my friend.

I had long deceived myself by believing that I could both manipulate truth and maintain my honor. I had failed the Almighty.

Papa's spirit, at the Hôtel de Sens, had asked me, *Horatio, why do you lie?* At the time I could not, or would not, understand his meaning. I had proceeded, negligently. I had failed Papa. Yet, Papa's disappointment in me would be nothing compared to God's judgment and my loss of friendship with Him.

I was unworthy of my part. Dishonored. Deserving of eternal death. My gut wrenched. Sickened, I bent forward. I flogged myself with accusations. *Why didn't I see? I'm upon the cusp of age, yet my wicked ignorance endangered my soul, and the souls of my loved ones.*

Marcus touched my hair. "Are you ill, Papa?"

Margrete came to sit with us upon the bed. Her hand soothed my shoulder as she said to Marcus, "Your Papa is all right. Lay back now and sleep."

The candlelight softened Margrete. I touched her hair to calm my agony. She looked to me, eyes narrowed as when, at the Hôtel de Sens, I had chastised her for teaching fear to our son. I looked away and stroked Marcus's cheek. "Look at what I've done to us." Shame clipped my tongue.

Marcus's round face flushed with alarm. Margrete bent and touched her forehead to his. She whispered to him, "All will be well."

I turned away and reached to a shelf for the *Gesta Danorum*. I carried the heavy book to the table and, sitting, opened it. I beheld my accomplishment. That printed work had been my pride. I had thought that the moniker I had given to Hamlet—Amleth—was clever: close enough to truth and opaque enough to protect me had I been discovered as its author. Now, the text appeared to me like broken twigs, chains, and charred shavings.

I had violated the Almighty's commandments and neglected my duty to train my children to live in virtue. By failing to act well my part, I had corrupted my honor. As the apostle Paul wrote, a man who does not provide for his own house denies the faith and is worse than an infidel. My selfish sins and wicked example pitched my family upon the crackling, unholy spit and fueled its eternal flames. I deserved confinement alone in a raging, molten pit but forever in darkness.

"This book is my wicked dishonor. Marcus clearly saw—but I didn't—that Hamlet's story is not honorable. It is my colossal lie, a mortal sin because of its effect upon our children."

Margrete, from behind me, wrapped her arms around my shoulders. "Not a mortal sin. You did not intend harm."

"It is the source of our damnation. I have endangered us, and I haven't fulfilled my promise to Hamlet."

Margrete released me and knelt beside my chair. She clasped my arm. "Horatio, the *Gesta Danorum* is a wonderful book, a miracle. It might have been destroyed in so many ways, but it has survived, and in it you created a marvelous story."

My knotted mind pulled tighter in digesting my predicament. "I wrote a fabrication of lies and truths."

"Truths and imagination that tell a story honoring Hamlet. People adore the tale. They walk great distances to hear you." Margrete stood and touched my cheek. "Some people understand history best in this way."

"Hamlet wanted me to tell the truth. How could I have been so blind to the consequences?" I closed the book. I raised my hands to mask my tearful face to God. "Oh, the stench of my transgression is an affront to heaven. How will I redeem myself and save my family?"

Margrete returned to the table. She sat and, through the glow cast from razor-like flames, regarded me with firm resolve. "We will think of a way. We must go to the priest."

I looked over my shoulder at my children, both now slumbering within the folds of their blankets. I had thrived in the bosom of the family I had long craved—but I had been blind to my sin.

Then, I realized that I had only admitted to myself, and prayed to God's abused ears for forgiveness, my part in Hamlet's demise. I had never confessed my pile of failures at Helsingør that had built an immense sin—a part in my brother's murder. For love of Hamlet and fear of losing his love, I had supported his initial lie of madness and acts of treason. I could not have protected him from every instance of malicious trickery or from his own decisions. Hamlet's failures were his own. Yet, I could have protected evidence of conspiracy and acted better to ease his grief for his father and Ophelia. At the beginning of the whole cursed affair had I never delivered Hamlet into the clutches of the daemonic supernatural, his fire for vengeance may never have burned. Mad or not, my friend would be alive.

My sins had multiplied as I continually lied to Fortinbras because I believed that deception helped me to protect my friend's memory. I had been insensible to the momentum my deceit had gained to perpetrate my egregious sins of falsehood. I had ignorantly believed that some lies were strategic and bore no consequences.

How could I make amends now for my pride and selfishness? How could I be a courageous father to my children?

Watching my little ones sleep, I said, "Their lives and destiny must not suffer because of lies. How will I show Marcus to conduct himself honorably?"

Thinking, I stroked the smooth, leather cover of the *Gesta Danorum*. Margrete took up her darning and pulled a threaded needle through the torn collar of Marcus's tunic. How could she be silent?

There was no escape for me—only one way to earn release. The path was not self-slaughter, however, for I had learned that lesson some time ago.

I closed my eyes and pressed my fingers to my lips. I prayed to my patron saint, Niels the Holy, "Tell me what I must do."

Then, I heard counsel spoken with such clarity I thought the deceased speaker stood before me. *Let your heart pour from your quill point. It is like standing naked in the commons square, but once you do it unabashed, you will never fret about covering yourself again.*

I was amazed. It was not, as I would have believed, Niels, or Hamlet's ghost, or Papa's spirit who had advised me.

"What is the matter?"

Opening my eyes, I replied to Margrete. "I just heard Poul, something he once said to me in the muniment room."

The dead friar's jolting words forged an idea—how I would forthrightly secure my fulfilled promise to Hamlet. Would make my humble penance to God for our souls' deliverance. Would render to my children the honesty they deserved.

"What are you planning?" Margrete's needle rested in her hand. She watched me, her brow creased.

"I must make my confession."

Margrete's head dipped in agreement. She pushed her needle through a flap and tugged it through. "I wondered when this day would come, when you would want absolution for the lies." She sighed. "We cannot afford indulgences. The priest will tell us your penance."

"Dearest," I said, "I mean, I must write my confessions. Regardless of any priest's dictates, I know *this* is my task."

Her face, shiny in the candlelight, blanched. "That is too much risk, Horatio. You would guarantee our deaths through writing the truth? That proof will destroy us."

A child's moan and squirming in the bed cautioned us. From the corner, Lanier discharged a snort.

Margrete whispered, "A priest can assign better absolution than written confessions."

With a wave I dismissed her assertion. "Our children will be lost if they've no way, once grown, to understand our situation. I'll begin my confessions by telling of Hamlet's death and my struggles. I'll carry our story to our life today, lay bare our trials and decisions so that they aren't mysteries to our children. This courage will demonstrate our honor."

Margrete set down her darning. She crossed her arms tightly across her bosom. "Horatio, we need not risk ourselves in order to teach them not to lie."

More rustling from the children caused us to pause. I looked down to the supple cover of the *Gesta Danorum*. In woe, I touched its face. "Why did I not see it?" I repeated.

When I realized that my confessions might achieve Cristiern's demand that I write a truthful account of Hamlet, I suffered a twinge of revulsion. However, I reasoned, Cristiern wanted only his version of the truth. Thus, a simple determination eased my conscience. My confessions would not contain his tiny sliver of facts but the whole plank of truth.

I said, "There's more reason I must disclose myself through my confessions. Our children will read it and will learn the value of *ad fontes*, that they may seek truth through questioning the source. Their inquiry may lead them to know me as the fallible man I am. But, in this way, they will learn *humanitas*. Perhaps they will follow my elemental belief in man and God's joint creation of wisdom."

Margrete's arms released, dropping her shield. She regarded me, lips pressed.

I continued, "If our children will be strong, be survivors as we are, Margrete, they must learn how to consider the variety of assertions, fallacies, and truths that the world will haul in buckets to their door."

Seeming to ponder, Margrete bit her fingernail. "They must learn to decide, like choosing mushrooms, which claims are poisonous."

An irritated murmur from Julia and a grumble issued from Lanier's corner silenced us. Margrete stood, went to the children, and leaned over the bed to assess them. Satisfied that they slept, she turned toward me, gripped my arm, and led me to our door. We slipped out our doorway and stood in our moonlit, craggy lane, away from a reeking puddle of excrement fed by a downhill trickle from the merchants' houses.

Margrete's face was sunken with fear. "Redemption may be had in writing your confessions, but it is a monumental chore." Then, her finger jabbed for punctuation. "Any penance you leave undone will convert to your punishment in purgatory."

I reached for Margrete's hands, rubbed her fingers to ease them. I kissed her knuckles on one hand. "I must write my confessions."

Her mien was like smooth rock, forbidding traction. "Already, we have borne enough, and I have allowed too much."

"My account will memorialize Krogen. The truth will be the people's legacy. Isn't that what you have wanted?"

I kissed her other hand. Margrete pulled away from me. She turned a circle as if seeking an enemy to club. "This is madness. Here in exile, I have been freer than I ever believed was possible. I do not want to lose the peace we have found, that we have worked hard to keep. And now, you want to charge into the open"—she flung her arms wide and took a striding step, mocking me—"'Here am I: Horatio the Dane,' and drag us with you into danger. Why do you believe that the danger and sacrifices we bore to print the *Gesta Danorum* were not worth the effort?"

I looked down at my feet. My scuffed boot toes were thin, worn from vast journeys. "I did not say that the *Gesta Danorum* was for nothing. You heard me in there." I nodded in the direction of our humble cottage. "I cursed my cowardice and ignorance." I scratched the back of my head. "I believe that the *Gesta Danorum* brought me, us, here, that it was God's will that I realize my transgressions so I may make myself a man of honor."

"Then why was our effort not enough to honor Hamlet?"

"I sought to protect myself first, not tell the truth foremost. For example, who would recognize the name Amleth as Hamlet?" I slapped my head in frustration. "I chose to proceed as I wished, to shield myself rather than bear the consequences if I told his story truthfully and was captured."

"Does he continue to manipulate you?"

A blast of rage overtook me. Through clenched teeth I demanded, "What do you mean, 'manipulate' me?"

Margrete, allowing no space for doubt, moved close. Quivering, she stood within a hair's breadth of my nose. "You and I both know that Hamlet seldom concerned his person with others' well-being."

I looked away to the milky-gray, vacant road that curved before us, hoping that a late-arriving cart would deliver a fresh supply of reason to my wife.

She continued, "The ghost's purpose has never been for good. Hamlet's demand of you has only been to serve his pride. What friend requires a man to bear every burden, to sacrifice everything, for his own glory?"

Seeking strength and wanting to quell my anger, I looked above to the cloud-streaked moon and its pale gems, the all-knowing constellations. Two stars flashed. I believed it a sign denoting pairs. Horatius Cocles and the Horatii brothers. Antique Romans and Danes. Hamlet and me. Me and Margrete.

I knew that by our feet lay precious notations written into the moon-bathed slate of ground. I looked down at those remnants of lessons I had taught Marcus and Julia. Using our favorite twigs, we had etched beloved words into the mud. Helsingør. Hendrik. Hamlet. Horatio. Horatius Cocles. Horatii. *Humanitas*. This was evidence of a story more sublime and significant than a dead man's demands.

I said to Margrete, "Hamlet saw that by requiring my promise to bear every burden to tell his story I shouldn't have cause for self-slaughter, a sin deserving eternal torment. He saved me. That doesn't factor as care? I loved Hamlet. I will do anything for him still."

She regarded me tearfully. "You still believe you must be someone's hero."

Despite standing in the cold draft of her judgment, I managed to jest, "You might have pretended surprise. Lied to me."

Margrete's head dropped. She heaved a sigh and, with fists dug into her hips, grudgingly laughed. I moved to hold her, but she stepped away and brushed a drop from her eye. Then, she clasped her hands to her forehead and called out, despite the late hour and surrounding cottages, "Hear me, Mother of God." Then, she dared to add, "Hear me, Freyja."

A neighboring woman's head poked beyond her threshold into the night air. She gave us a sharp, quizzical look.

Margrete's arms dropped to her sides. She leaned into my embrace. Her bosom was soft against my breast. Then her chin lifted, and I saw that her tired face was open, gentler now. She said, "I beg you, do not write your confessions. I agreed that you should recite the *Gesta Danorum* to your audiences. But every time you tell of Hamlet, I hold my breath in fear. If your testament is found, we will be ensnared. We will not be able to control..."

I leaned back and swiped my finger across her nose. "Always, you want to control."

"What will happen to us or the children if your confessions are discovered?"

"We'd flee again. We're well apprenticed in that skill."

Margrete sighed. She glanced warily at the muck puddle. "I love our home we have made. I thought we would protect it always. I promised Marcus that all will be well. How will we achieve *that* pledge?"

I embraced her and said, "I must record the truth, immediately." Then I offered a concession. "We'll make my confessions a secret for now, not to be released to our children until their own are born."

"The Church may hold it in trust for us." Margrete leaned back and, grimly smiling, regarded me. "Perhaps one day it will inform history that Cristiern never deserved Krogen. It will thwart his validation as a righteous monarch." I recognized in her eyes that familiar, assured spark of authority, the vigor of the queen's principal lady.

I hugged Margrete again. Her breath was light upon my neck when she asked, "We agree, then, that we will seal and entrust your confessions to a church rector who will safekeep it for our children and away from our enemies?"

"Indeed. Its lessons will last longer than our mud slate. Our children's children will learn from it and know us."

I looked again to the catalogue of "H" words we had etched into the ground. Then I realized the absence of a crucial term. My negligence at the omission, its confirmation of my sin and blindness, made me cringe. To make the correction, I released Margrete and, bending to write with Marcus's stick, scraped one more word into the earthen list. *Honor*.

After Margrete and I embraced once more we entered our home. We observed Marcus and Julia sleeping like rabbits in a cozy burrow.

I went to my seat and placed before me a few ragged sheets of parchment. I bowed my head. *Almighty God, forgive me. I am used to begging your understanding but not my family's. How does a man lay open his life, raw and squirming, before the eyes of his wife and children? I do not know how to do it. Was Poul correct—nakedness becomes bearable when the mirror becomes familiar?*

Trembling, I gripped my quill and leaned into the bite of my splintery table as shadows dodged my candles' twitching flames. Their light was meager compared to my bright love for my children, whose fire was a daily genesis in our primitive cottage, and in my ancient heart.

I had seen a written testimony baring a man's raw soul only once before. *The Confessions of Saint Augustine.* Desperate humility was his muse and would be mine as well.

My inked quill nib shook as I held it hovering above the cream-faced parchment that I had smoothed with my other hand. *The Confessions of Horatio the Dane*, I thought.

Margrete, seated near me at the table, darned a tunic. In mid-stitch she glanced, worried, at me as I launched myself upon a most terrifying and humbling journey.

Confiteor Deo, et Beate Marie Virgini, et omnibus sanctis eius.

I paused. An invocation written in Latin was proper, of course, but my story should not be veiled by that ancient language, like a code to be unlocked. My children, or their children, might never be scholars. They should not struggle to read their ancestor's tome. I had to write in a language they would understand. I had to risk discovery in this way. What else would suffice but Danish for a Dane's confessions.

> *In this testament, written in utmost contrition by my own hand on the Feast Day of Saint John the Baptist, the twenty-fourth day of June in the year of our Lord 1520, I, Horatio of Tønderensis, confess to God, to the Blessed Virgin Mary, and to all His saints my mortal sins. Truth is my offering. If God wills that I die for telling it, so be it. May my penitent will illumine my children's paths that they live for right purpose and deserve a good death.*

Over the past several months, my children, I have huddled at our table, my ink-stained fingers etching my confessions onto the rough parchment. Over time, dozens of candles melted into puddles of stinking lard, sacrificed to my labor. While I wrote I bore many interruptions, such as grousing by frustrated card players: Lanier teaching gamblers' strategies to Margrete.

At times when, in the pit of scribblers' despair, I craved inspiration, it came to me. Sometimes, Julia and Marcus, you were the source. When we crouched at our mud slate and, writing sticks in our hands, their questions loosened the knots in my mind. Other times, Hamlet's dust-thick ghost was a muse of sorts. Some nights I saw him traversing my floor. Persistent. I had become used to his visitations. Whenever I considered his madness and hesitated to tell of it, he reminded me, *Tell the full truth. If you love me, endure every burden to tell my story.*

I assured Hamlet, "Peace, brother. I'll tell the truth."

Yet, I wondered if my efforts, since the time we were students, to encourage calm in Hamlet had instead lured him toward madness.

In only one instance did I forego writing my confessions. That was two days ago: the Feast Day of All Souls. I set down my quill and left the children to riot in Lanier's company while Margrete and I went to the day-long Mass. In the church, among the kneeling congregation, we prayed the Office of the Dead for Margrete's parents, for the dead of Krogen and Helsingør Village, and for Hamlet. We asked that they be remembered, be sustained at Valhalla's banquet table, not be locked in purgatory for unatoned transgressions.

Today, on the fourth day of November, in the year of our Lord 1520, a great Mass of thanksgiving would be most deserved. With this final page, I complete my confessions.

Upon closing this opus, will Hamlet's spirit at last be retrieved by the Furious Host? Will he be received by Freyja and the Valkyries for escort to Valhalla, or will he be guided to heaven by the Virgin and the saints? The answers may escape me until my eventual death. For now, I will listen for Hamlet's lasting silence.

I am grateful for my difficult penance of confession. When I began writing, my certainty of failure caused me heart-gripping trepidation. My fear, however, gradually thawed into wary curiosity. Most valuable was my discovery, through confessional reflection, of the many ways since childhood I had clung to loneliness and how that had not served me well. I am all the more grateful, therefore, for the brotherly love I received from Hamlet and Lanier, and for my joy in fatherhood.

May you take from my example the lessons that a man's honor relies upon his truthfulness, and that lies waste time in one way or another. Time is too dear to be squandered.

Bear in patience with me a little longer. I wish to impart a few more bits of advice. It is a father's right, whether he be a lowly village teacher or a king's counselor. Thus, I bid you:

- *Act the part which is worthy of you.*
- *Be thou honest, for truth is both vinegar and ointment, dissolving the rust of turpitude and binding faith and courage.*
- *Value truth as if it is gold, for truth does not decay in a mud-scrabble world astonished by virtue.*
- *Know that if the seed of legacy is worth the love and sacrifice to grow it, its branches will become like iron, withstanding pruning and control.*
- *Teach all to go on life's pilgrimage. Let not fear leash yourself or your children, for the world apprentices*

its stout-hearted explorers in the talents of discovery and defense.

~ Should you ever fall prey to the desire for self-slaughter, I implore you to remember that you are loved. To earn eternal life you must, at least, live.

~ Lying is death's gate and an evil that ushers a legion of associated sins filling the Devil's index. You have marked the consequences in this testament.

~ In humility I ask you to accept my story, to learn from it, and to guard it as long as our enemies roam. In the wrong hands, it will prove treason.

Before I inscribe my closing benediction to my confessions, I must—

XXII.

A monstrous fortnight has passed. Today, on this tepid mid-November morning, I take up my quill and hasten to append to my confessions. I do this for the good of my soul and my family's well-being. May God have mercy on us.

※

In Tønderensis, during the fourth evening of November, I sat at the table in our home, finishing my confessions by writing advice to my children, when rude pounding upon our door frightened us. Little Julia, sitting upon the floor by my feet, wailed. Margrete hushed her. Marcus, sitting beside his sister, asked me, "Can we trade her for something useful, Papa?"

Louder beating rattled the secured latch.

Across the table from me sat Lanier and Margrete, playing at cards. I asked him, "One of your friends, come to collect a wager?"

Lanier wiped a baggy eye, pulling its creases taunt. "*Au contraire, mon ami.* Lately, I have won my games." He turned to regard the door suspiciously.

Something rammed against the portal. Alarmed, I looked to

Margrete. She had already swept up the children and sat them upon the bed. She was pulling on their booties.

I rose from this confessional document and went to our portal. Lanier joined me. I said, hopefully, "It's only a drunken neighbor, mistaken. I'll send him home."

I opened the door.

In the moon's milky beacon stood Reynaldo wearing his plumed hat. Two burly ruffians lumbered behind him. Upon recognizing me, Reynaldo's grin, now missing some teeth, cracked his grizzled, olive-tinted face. "Oh, *si*! It *is* you, *Horatio*. And my lost trophy, *Lanier*."

When Reynaldo and the men tried to pass us, Lanier swung to hit them. But he missed and received a punch in the belly. A thug pushed me against a wall. Reynaldo stood in the center of my home, infesting our peace.

Margrete's outstretched arms barricaded the children on the bed behind her.

Reynaldo wiped his drooling lips with his thumb. "The trio has become a litter. A discovery of riches." He grinned at me, greedily. "Cristiern heard of a storyteller in Tønderensis reputed to excel in the stories of the *Gesta Danorum*. He wants that man to entertain his guests at his banquet, a few days from now, in Stockholm. I wondered if that man was you, Horatio. I wanted to see. And so, I begged Cristiern to send me as escort."

Reynaldo moved closer to me. I withstood the reek of his sour breath. He continued, "Cristiern's forces defeated the Swedish army and killed their leading rebel family. Tonight, Cristiern is being coronated as King of Sweden. He now wears the crowns of Denmark, Norway, and Sweden: all three of the northeast kingdoms within the Kalmar Union.

His ambition is complete, and he has much to celebrate. Cristiern will be glad to see you, Horatio. His hunger for traitors has grown with time. Did you know, his bounty remains on your heads?"

I saw, from the corner of my eye, my children, not wailing but pale and cowering. Margrete, reaching behind, held them fast in her skirt. She glared at our intruders. The sight of my threatened family made my heart pound with fury.

"You never win, Reynaldo," I said.

Lanier added, "You will see nothing of that reward."

Reynaldo's grin lapsed to a scowl. He spat at Lanier. "For a mere kreuzer in payment I would trade you into slavery. But soon you will stand before Cristiern, at the Hall at Stortorget Square, and I will take away a fortune for delivering Krogen's escapees and their cubs."

When Reynaldo nodded at his men, one brute grasped me. The other leapt at Lanier. We fought but were pummeled.

Margrete hefted Julia onto her hip and gripped Marcus by his wrist. They fled to a neighboring cottage.

Lanier, his face swelling and bruised, and I, aching through my sides, were bound at the wrists. The ruffians pushed us atop their horses, which they mounted. My anguished heart thundered in my breast. I saw Margrete, the children, and the neighbor woman huddled within their open door.

Reynaldo slid down from his horse and stomped toward them. They slammed shut the door. He jarred and kicked the portal, but it held fast. "You will not escape me again, whore."

Margrete loudly replied through the door, "Restore my husband to me, or a band of cleaver-wielding ladies will dispatch your tiny member and feed it to the hogs."

I thought Margrete's response marvelous, exceeding all debate tactics I had ever used in university. I called out to Reynaldo, "She'll do it herself. Don't miscalculate."

Cursing, Reynaldo returned to his horse and climbed upon it. He led us onto the road. I called over my shoulder to Margrete in hiding, "I'll return to you." Yet, my breast cinched for I feared I would never see my family again.

After traveling the night on horseback, in the morning we arrived at the Danish port of Sønderborg and boarded a ship. Nearly three days later, on November seventh, we docked at Stockholm as the sun dropped behind the town's peak-roofed, spire-pierced horizon.

Reynaldo and his men prodded us, bound at the wrists and tethered to one another, from the dock to a lane, past a church and into Stortorget Square, a vast cobbled expanse. On each side, merchant trade houses towered above the square, which was filled by a throng. The people wore every kind of attire, from frocks as bright as flowers to dingy flax as primitive as dirt. I guessed that the mass of peddlers and prostitutes, officials and clerics, guildsmen and merchants were there to battle for scraps of favor discarded from the king's banquet table.

Before us loomed the rectangular, brick tower of Stortorget Hall. Gray smoke looped from its chimneys into the dusky sky. The scent of roasted meat pulled at my belly until, nearing the door, we passed a bonfire and the stink of corpses. I saw two dirt-caked, shriveled bodies packed among the pyre's logs. One was once a man. The other, a youth. Light-armored soldiers fed more wood to the flames. I tried to run, but Reynaldo's brutes gripped me and pushed us harder to the immense, bronze doors. Three soldiers guarded the hall. When Reynaldo muttered at them, they pulled upon one door, admitting us into the hall's glare and baritone clamor.

Lanier and I stumbled but regained our footing. The door closed at our backs.

Before us a vast audience of nobles and bishops—two hundred, it seemed—sat at banquet. The tables stretched the length of the hall, brightly lit by lamps and candles upon racks. The men, hunched in conversation, nibbled charred meat, salt-cured fish, and crusty bread—it must have been delicious. Servants at side tables carved roasted beasts and scurried to deliver foaming tankards. However, the eating was not enthusiastic. Few men dared to glance up, or over their shoulder, at their host.

Upon a platform sat Cristiern, alone. His table, centered against the hall's long, tapestry-covered wall, was piled with enough food to feed twenty men. Cristiern was bearded, wide in the belly now, and wore a double-banded crown. Above his head, carved into his chair's high crest, was Sweden's royal heraldry—gold crowns and prancing horses. Cristiern took a dagger from his table and cut away a chunk of meat. He slowly bit into it and chewed, glowering at his audience.

A red-robed, square-faced man trudged up the platform steps to Cristiern. The man bent, one hand balancing the miter he wore on his head, and whispered into Cristiern's ear. Cristiern smirked at him and nodded. Then Cristiern sucked the grease from his fingers and pushed back his chair. Its legs screeched across the dais.

The buzzing conversations at the banquet tables ceased. Men set down their mauled meat and fish bones. Wizened faces peered at Cristiern and his cleric.

Cristiern said, "As you know, three days ago I stood at Stockholm's most divine altar. Archbishop Trolle"—Cristiern swept his hand at the man beside him—"anointed me as your king. Your rebellion is destroyed. The family that led it is dead. After my army killed them, you clerics decided poorly—you gave them burial due only to proper Christians. My first order was to exhume their bodies."

The field of nobles and clergy, filling the hall, wilted.

"At this very moment the corpses are burning on a pyre in the square. You will have no marker for their ashes. You will not make idols to their memory."

Some men masked their faces with their hands. Others, numb, gazed inward. A few dared to level a marble-hard glare at Cristiern.

Reynaldo shoved me away from the door, toward the room's center. "Walk," he hissed. He told his men, "Leave. I will pay you later."

I shuffled forward, followed by Lanier and Reynaldo. We threaded between two long benches to the middle of the hall. A tug on the leash binding my hands halted me at an aisle before the platform.

Extending his right foot, Reynaldo bowed and swept his plumed hat with a flourish across his pointing boot. "Sire," he said, "You charged me to bring you the storyteller famed for reading the *Gesta Danorum*. Here he is, the Thief of Helsingør. I also captured General Willem's killer."

Cristiern, red and puffy, beheld Lanier and me. He grinned with serpentine delight. "Reynaldo, you have brought me two wicked villains. Well done."

Reynaldo straightened and gleamed with pride.

Standing at the edge of the dais, Cristiern loomed over his audience. He told Reynaldo, "Now, you may claim a seat among your betters."

Reynaldo's sunny face clouded. Scowling, he collapsed into a small space among three priests. Their arses shuffled along the bench to accommodate him.

Cristiern pointed at Lanier and me. "You, come here."

We climbed the platform's three steps and stood upon the dais before the gawking banqueters.

Flushed, Cristiern strode directly at us. He stood so close that his rasping condemnation sprayed spittle. "I swear to Christ Jesus, upon my honor, I will avenge Willem and make examples of you."

Arms akimbo, Cristiern declared to his audience, "The Kalmar Union is united. No longer will we be prey to the greed and trickery of Hanseatic trade agents. We will resist Europe's wars." At this mention, the audience murmured, nodded. He continued, "My glory, my deeds, my love—all are for you. However, every man and every woman must be loyal to me."

A few men sitting nearest the dais squirmed.

Next, Cristiern stepped back and leaned toward me. I bristled. He said, "I commanded you years ago to tell the truth about Hamlet. You refused. No more betrayal, scholar. You will talk now."

Returning to the edge of the dais, Cristiern pointed at me. "This man, a witness to many crimes, will tell you how a pretender prince and his debauched family—illegitimate rulers—stole land from my father, took our rightful sound tolls, and defiled Denmark's crown. They are dead because of the evil they waged against my person and my family, the House of Oldenburg. You may have heard glorifying fables about the Hamlets. All lies. Now this man"—Cristiern flicked his hand at me—"will tell you the truth." Then he turned to me. "You will save these people by teaching them."

Arrow points from two hundred pairs of eyes struck me. My tongue turned fat and dry in my mouth. I could not speak.

Cristiern watched me. His prickling force of being constricted my soul's chords to a high pitch. He prodded, "Renounce the legend of Hamlet in the *Gesta Danorum*. I do not know how you burrowed garbage about the Hamlets into my beautiful book. This is your last opportunity. Tell the truth about Hamlet's madness and the curse that the Hamlets brought upon themselves. If you do not, you will die."

My heart strained. I hated Cristiern too much to even reply.

Lanier, however, suffered no such impediment. "Go to Hell."

Cristiern, wagging his head, planted himself before Lanier. "I will slice off your head. You haven't long to wait. Make your prayers."

Archbishop Trolle untied the leash tethering me and Lanier. Then, he moved Lanier back upon the platform to stand near the wall, away from me.

Words dislodged from my brain and tumbled from my mouth. I said to the assembly, only loud enough for the first seated row of men to hear, "God will not have you, Cristiern, because you are unworthy. Should you trick your way into heaven, it will spit you out. You have no place of honor with the warrior dead of Krogen, not even with Willem."

Cristiern winced. He regarded me, as if calculating his response, and moved close. I forbore his acrid breath. "You once accused me of controlling the peoples' memories and beliefs. You, though, are as ruthless—worse than me. You lie. I tell the truth." He cocked his head and asked, "You think your lies will honor Hamlet? God hates liars. You are dishonorable. Pathetic. Not a Dane. Not a man."

I regarded Cristiern. He strode to his table, carved a piece of meat, and suckled a bone. He dared to judge my integrity as a Dane? Cristiern feared his own vulnerability. And his devotion to Willem wasn't brotherly love. He wasn't like Wiglaf, that honorable Dane who secured his friend's immortality through memorial. *I* was like Wiglaf.

My audience stared at me. I knew that the rope of lies I had woven, which had begun with one falsehood I had spoken to a king, years prior, in a different great hall, had led me to my predicament. I further realized that, in that moment, in a Swedish hall before a tyrant king, I could elect to tell more lies or I could choose to speak the truth aloud, not in writing and no longer in hiding.

Possibilities whirled through my brain. *My example might inspire this audience*, I reasoned to myself. *Emboldened by the truth, they will rise up against Cristiern and break his hold upon them. Through that act I will be like a brother of the Horatii, perhaps inducted into their family of perpetual honor.*

Consequences also gripped me. I might not survive combat. Not even brave Horatius Cocles's fate was known. After his victory on the bridge into Rome, he had plunged into the tumultuous Tiber River. Some said that he had died in the water. Others professed that he had lived. If I fought, what would be my fate?

My gut twisted, but I realized that the welfare of peoples throughout the Kalmar Union depended upon my decision.

I looked up to the hall's high-beamed ceiling to summon heaven's courage. *Almighty God, help me do what I must*, I prayed. Then I moved to the edge of the platform and made my declaration in a voice that even the dead in Zealand's barrows and Rome's crypts could hear.

"Hamlet died because of others' ambitions gone awry, because of lies and manipulations, because of pain that twists men's hearts, because of burning vengeance. In our times these plagues will kill us. They rage now because of Cristiern."

Cristiern, coming toward me, tossed a mauled meat bone onto the floor.

I spoke faster. "Cristiern murdered the innocents of Helsingør. Burned the muniments to obliterate Hamlet's history. Committed evil for his own glory and sinful pride."

Cristiern reached for me and, gripping the back of my neck, stood behind me. I was defenseless, for my hands were still bound. I tried not to squirm. He hissed into my ear, "Bastard devil. Tell the story as I require."

"Hamlet's cause," I called out to the people, "was his struggle for courage to act, for justice against the ambitions of powerful, malevolent men. We must not let fear bind us. By daring to perform such worthy acts, we prove our honor."

Throughout the room, men cried to Cristiern, "Protect us. Do us no harm."

Cristiern jerked me backward by my collar. I fell against him, but then I found my footing and stood to face him. His brick-like countenance reminded me of Louis at Blois. I had convinced Louis to decide benevolently. Perhaps I could also influence Cristiern.

I settled myself before his steaming glare. "Majesty, your authority needn't rely upon cruelty. You needn't do unto Stockholm as you did to Helsingør."

"That is not the story."

"You've spoken of your desired legacy. A king's bequest is his care for his people and their loyalty to him in return."

"You dare to lecture me, scholar?"

My bound hands quivered. I clenched them for comportment. "Would a distinguished king be ruled by a stubborn grudge? Would he imperil his soul and risk that the world would want to forget him? Make his glory dissolve to dust?"

Cristiern stepped back. He rubbed his face as if stunned. But he began to nod slightly. His expression warmed, almost to smiling as if at last he understood me. "Your favor for my soul's welfare is well considered."

Encouraged, I added, "Your forgiveness of your people would demonstrate your strength and honor, would uplift you on earth and later in Valhalla. Your subjects' lives depend upon your love."

Stroking his chin, Cristiern asked, "What would you advise me?"

I stood straight, held his stare. "What would you choose, great king?"

Cristiern regarded me with steady, stoic reserve. I could not divine his state of mind. The hall, thick with bodies and silence, allowed no room for even shallow breath.

Cristiern looked over his shoulder at Archbishop Trolle. The archbishop nodded to him. Then Cristiern slowly moved away from me, toward his table. He rubbed the back of his neck, seemingly deep in thought.

"Horatio," Lanier hoarsely whispered. He had remained, hands bound before him, near the wall. His grim glance at me was not what I expected. Didn't Lanier approve of my tack? Didn't he see the archbishop urge Cristiern's forgiveness of us?

Lanier silently mouthed the word, "*Allez.*" He looked to the steps, directing me.

I shrugged at Lanier. "Why?"

Cristiern, turning from his table, approached me. "Horatio, your wise words move me." He opened an arm, inviting embrace.

I thought, happily, that he had come to reason and I had succeeded, just as I had triumphed at Blois when I had convinced Louis to release Lanier and the sword.

I leaned into Cristiern's wide breast. "To peace throughout the Kalmar Union," I said, offering a blessing.

His embrace tightened. "To thy own peace," he murmured into my ear.

Cristiern's other arm made a quick motion. A sharp, deep pain erupted in my right side. I crumpled. Then Cristiern jerked back, gripping his crimson meat knife. My wound turned hot and wet. I saw the archbishop's distant grin. Then, I fell. In agony I lay upon the platform and pressed my side to contain my blood and bile.

"Horatio," I heard Lanier call to me, but I could not discern where he was.

Standing over me, Cristiern said, "Forgiveness makes a king weak."

"Not so," I groaned.

Lanier jumped onto the platform. His wrists were freed but scraped. He gripped a short-bladed carving knife.

Cristiern pointed at him. "You are next, French witch." Cristiern lunged, blade point leading, at Lanier. But Lanier leapt aside. He clamped his knife between his teeth, grasped my arms, and pulled me down the few platform stairs to the floor.

Reynaldo leapt from a bench onto Lanier's back. They brawled, daggers and fists.

Cristiern clambered down the steps after me. I scooted across the floor toward a table. The people scrambled away. I rolled beneath the table, beyond Cristiern's reach. Gulping breath from searing pain, I pulled myself across the floor to the farthest table. Cristiern did not follow.

Death's rude jeer spurred my determination to return to my family. I tore away my gray cuff and stuffed it into the bubbling wound in my side. The tail of fabric turned red and hung from the puncture.

Lanier's scratched face suddenly appeared beside me. He crouched below the bench and pulled me into an aisle. Then he helped me to stand among the crowd. They cried out for Cristiern's mercy. All paths were blocked to the closed doors at the distant end of the hall.

I saw Reynaldo, on the platform steps, braced against one knee as he rubbed his head. Above him, upon the dais, stood Cristiern. His bloody knife was fixed within his belt. He declared to all, "Loyal subjects need no escape. Loyal hearts need no cure. You who loved the rebels are the diseased. The best remedy for Stockholm's traitors and heretics will be a thorough shaking. Guards, secure the doors."

A resounding thud made me look right, to the faraway portal now blocked by a long bar across it. Six soldiers stood with their backs to the door, pikes upward. The people panicked and pressed toward the doors. The soldiers lowered their pikes against the surging crowd.

Lanier clamped one arm about my shoulders and pushed me toward the portal, past old clerics and young merchants, through the howling mob and its urine stench of fear. As the crowd lurched in waves toward the door, some beside us lost balance, fell, and were trampled.

I heard Reynaldo, from the platform far behind us, cry above the din, "Sire, my reward for the criminals."

"Upon Saint John's head, you will get nothing if they escape again," Cristiern bellowed in reply.

We neared the line of soldiers defending the doors. One soldier skewered an old man before us and then bent over his elderly, writhing victim to extract his pike. Lanier thrust his knife into the soldier's throat. The soldier fell. We moved into that vacancy before the door. When we and a few others lifted the door's bar, deep pain tore through my side. I felt I might collapse, but Lanier bore me up. The soldiers jabbed at blood-smeared clerics and merchants. We pressed past that ruin of plush robes and silver threads to push open the towering doors. All tumbled out, onto the moonlit, cobbled square. There, orange flames from the rebels' pyre leapt at a coal-black sky.

Cristiern's command boomed from the hall behind, "Bring me the criminals of Helsingør. Take the bishops to the gallows."

Immediately, Lanier pulled me behind a cart by the hall's entrance. There, we huddled and watched soldiers drag the condemned, scrambling and begging, to a platform with a noose standing at the far edge of the square. Soldiers drew their swords and slashed into the crowd. Peasants and merchants fell, gutted, their life draining from them.

My middle burned from the inside. Nauseated, I tried to vomit but was dry. I knelt, arms wrapped about me, to contain myself. I began to shiver. "I can't run."

"You must, *mon ami*. See the lane beside the church?"

I peered around the cart and saw, a short distance away, the nearest corner and the road we had walked from the dock to the square. Lanier grasped my arm. I took a breath to gird against the pain.

We crept from our shelter and skirted the crowd's outermost ring. In the church's shadow we turned sharply into the lane. That straight downward slope, lined by brick storehouses, ended at the dock. A few three-masted ships anchored there bore glowing lanterns enticing passengers too impatient to await departure at dawn.

I loped beside Lanier, straining against the devils that were tearing my insides. Halfway to the port I heard, behind us, the slap of running feet. I managed to look over my shoulder. Reynaldo pursued us. His huffing breath and swinging arms were in cadence with his labored stride and hat's bobbing plume.

Lanier and I reached the dock and stomped across its planks. "Ho, captain." Lanier called out to a shaggy, middling-aged man who, leaning upon the rail of his ship, looked down. A wad protruded from his cheek. Chewing, he grinned at us. "You owe him for beer?"

Before I could grasp the ship's rope ladder, Reynaldo leapt at me. He and I fell upon the dock. Reynaldo straddled atop me and raised his blade. I squirmed at meeting death's face.

Lanier dove at Reynaldo and knocked him away. They scrambled across the dock, knives swiping. I wanted to help Lanier fight that bastard Spaniard. But I had no strength. I could only crawl toward them.

A blade glinted like lightning. Someone groaned. I prayed: *Let it be Reynaldo.*

Lanier staggered to rise. I reached for him, to comfort my brother if we were to die together. Then I saw that Reynaldo lay upon his back on the splintery dock. Blood glistened on his lips. "I will kill you both," he rasped.

"Perhaps," Lanier said. He bent and stabbed Reynaldo in the breast. Reynaldo made a guttural groan. Next, Lanier yanked a purse of coins from Reynaldo's belt and then rolled him off the dock into the water. That splash was glorious.

I rose, with Lanier's help, and saw Reynaldo flailing. After a moment he stopped. I thought Reynaldo was dead. I wanted to hoot in triumph. But he thrashed again.

From above, the captain, leaning over the ship's rail, called down to Lanier and me. "Still need passage?"

That night the ship swept Lanier and me southward along the Swedish coast toward Denmark. I prayed I would survive the three-day journey to Sønderborg where, if it pleased God, we would beg use of an old horse that would bear us home.

The sea journey was hellish. My waking thoughts of Margrete, Marcus, and Julia, of resting in their care, did not ward off nightmares in which Reynaldo managed to crawl, like a damned, resurrected sea creature, from the tides onto land. Also, Lanier told me that while I slept in the ship's hull and he replaced my blood-soaked wadding with strips torn from his own shirt, he heard me repeatedly mumble, "Tiber River." I recall dreaming that, like my boyhood hero Horatius Cocles after battle, I dove into the current and uncertain fate. I remember also the grip of Lanier's hand upon mine as he prayed over me.

By the time our ship reached Sønderborg I had ceased to bleed. At that port, Lanier bought a pony, paying a low price to a female horse trader who favored him. During that day's journey I sat behind him, draped against his back. I believe that faith, the kindness of saints, and my promise to return to my family kept my soul stitched to my body.

On Sunday, the eleventh day of November, the Feast Day of Saint Martin of Tours, patron of the poor, we arrived at Tønderensis. At the crowded gatehouse the porter saw me slumped against Lanier. He waved us past the knotted, worn gate and forgave us the toll.

Along our path, to our decrepit section of the town, was the church. Upon our approach I heard the pitchy timber of a sung psalm and judged that many faithful congregants were making devotional prayers before festivities began. "Margrete must be there," I said. "Let me dismount."

Lanier stopped the horse. He alighted and helped me slide down the animal's musky flank to the ground. I braced against Lanier to hobble toward the closed door and its hovering saint-lined tympanum. Beneath the arc of figures sat a haggard woman upon a stool. A boy sat at her feet. She urged him into the church. Within moments the doors parted and

Margrete burst into the sunlight, carrying Julia suckling her thumb. A young neighbor woman followed, holding my son by the hand. Marcus wore, tied at his neck and dragging on the ground, Lanier's musty cape. Its breast hem still bore the thread-crafted rose.

Margrete's sun-burnished skin and her common frock were a most beautiful sight. She released Julia into her friend's waiting arms then ran to me, tears streaming, one hand covering her mouth. Perhaps my countenance and bearing already told her everything. "I curse Reynaldo and Cristiern. May those witches suffer greatly for their deeds," she said, and then lightly touched my face and kissed me.

"I stood before the assembly of nobles and clerics. I told them the truth about Cristiern."

Margrete sighed. "It is no wonder they…"

"Papa."

Beside me stood Marcus, looking up at me. I could nearly hear, beyond his firm stare, his mind's levers working. He feared my condition, perhaps already believed me dead, I thought. I wished to embrace him, but for the pain I could not even kneel. I touched his peaking crown of hair, let his precious, silky brown strands fall between my fingers. "I missed you, my son."

Margrete, again holding Julia, leaned her toward me so that I could kiss her round, water-soft cheek. At the age of four, my daughter's skin still smelled of early spring flowers.

"Papa," Marcus insisted, "People hurt you because you told them the truth?"

"One powerful man tried to force me to lie, but I would not. If I hadn't told the truth, he would have hurt many people in lands throughout the Kalmar Union."

Marcus grasped the long right hem of the cape he wore. He looked down at it and fingered the stiches as if counting them. "The man who took you and Uncle Lanier away…you could have lied to him, and we could have escaped. You had reason to lie."

Margrete reached for Marcus's hand. "That horrid creature knew us already. Let us help Papa rest now."

He gripped both long hems of his cape and ignored his mother's outstretched arm. Marcus's brows raised, and his lips pressed, like his mother's. He awaited my answer.

"Son," I said, "I made a sacred oath to tell the truth. My honor and our salvation, in God's sight of all things, bad and good, depended upon it. Why do you think that is?"

"I don't know, Papa," Marcus mumbled.

Had he forgotten our psalm reading, that crucial night of my awakening and debate? I hoped, with every cup of strength left in me, that my boy's six-year-old brain was puzzling the ingredients of truth telling: courage and selflessness.

In our home that night I lay in our bed, angry at my fragility and hopeful that God was only taking his time in mending me. Lanier and Margrete sometimes stood aside, by the door, whispering and gesturing. I believed they debated whether I would live. I weakly called to them, "You may consult privately, but together we will bargain about our fate."

Margrete sat upon my bed and set the children beside me. They had been playing in a nearby field. Their grassy, muddy scent filled the bed. I bent to my left and kissed Julia's head. Because I could not turn to my right, the wounded side where Marcus lay, he reached out to me, patted my face, and kissed my cheek.

"Papa, I know the answer." His face bounced close to mine, our noses almost touching. He beamed at me.

"To what question?"

"The lying mouth kills the soul."

"Ah. You are right. Wonderful boy. But what does that mean for *you*?"

Marcus leaned back upon braced arms. In thought, he stared at his knees.

"Apologies, *mon ami*. We only meant to spare you more burden." Lanier stood near my feet.

"You are certain that Reynaldo is dead?" Margrete asked us.

"I killed him." Lanier glowered, grinding his heel upon the floorboard.

"We didn't see him dead," I cautioned.

Lanier wiped his face with one hand. "*C'est vrai*," he grumbled. "I thought I killed him."

Margrete sighed. "We must assume he lives." Her brow knotted. "Cristiern knows this is our home—Reynaldo told us as much." Her hand rested upon my thigh. "We cannot remain."

I said, "Our exile must be elsewhere."

Margrete squeezed my leg. She whispered, because our lid-droopy children had begun to doze, "I fear you will not survive another journey."

I touched her cheek. "Where will we go? We can't afford even a ditch in Wittenberg."

Margrete's hands masked her face. I pulled her close to me, embraced her as best I could to calm her. Would devils never cease pursuing my family?

Lanier crossed his arms. "There is a land where Burgundians have escaped to make their home. It is a soggy place. But I hear that they make their livelihoods. I do not know anyone there." His arms dropped to his side. He looked away. "Perhaps not a good idea."

"Where is that place?" Margrete asked.

"Saint Olave Parish, Southwark. Across the river from London's town walls."

"We made a home here. We could do the same there," I said and noticed that Marcus, now laying upon his back to my right, and Julia to my left, were asleep.

Lanier grimaced, rubbed the back of his head. "No migrants are allowed inside the town. People have built camps along the riverbank, near the merchants' bridge. Those who prosper move upland from the marsh."

"Will there be bounty hunters?" Margrete asked, looking up at Lanier.

"There will be criminals, *ma chère*."

"Worse than us?" I jested.

But Lanier did not laugh. His frown twisted. He folded his arms again and looked down at the floor. "Do not leave us, *mon ami*." He turned away.

Margrete, blinking away a tear, grasped my hand. "We will leave for England tomorrow at dawn…" She nodded at our slumbering, open-mouthed children. "Or earlier, if we can rouse these little fish."

The next morning, Monday, the twelfth day of November, well after sunrise and our intended departure, we hastily bundled our household. Margrete collected our clothing and the children. Lanier gathered into a sack our tools and pots. Margrete wrote a farewell missive of friendship to our neighbors, divulging nothing of our destination, and tacked it to our table. I insisted upon a task because I refused to lay waste in my sickbed while my household toiled in preparation. I gathered our money, these confessions, and then went to the shelf to retrieve the *Gesta Danorum*, which I still loved. It was not there. I searched under our bed and through sacks already packed, to no avail. Frustrated and gasping, I wobbled out our threshold onto the dawn-bronzed road to seek Margrete's assistance. She and Lanier were hoisting a small crate onto our ramshackle oxcart. Drawing close, I said, "I cannot find the book."

Margrete's wrist wiped her forehead. She puffed. "There." She pointed at our cottage, beside the open door, through which I had passed. I had not noticed Julia sitting against the side of our abode on a tiny stool. Before her, on a small stump, rested the open *Gesta Danorum*. Her small finger traced the page's block print, and her lips moved in seeming fascinated comprehension of the Latin text.

My tiny daughter. Because she, by nature, sought to understand our world, I had come to believe that of my two children Julia would be the most voracious reader of my confessions—would become our family's legacy-bearer.

I whispered to Margrete, "Julia is pretending to read."

"No. She has learned, at the late age of four, and I was about to beg you that she join our women scribes at Tønderensis' convent."

I was about to reply to Margrete's sardonic quip, but the sight of Julia...the memory of my dream of the skull that Hamlet gave me and which I handed to Lanier who gave it to a little girl...An idea struck. Perhaps my daughter was the little girl who, in my dream, was so enthralled with holding the skull...which, we know, encases the soul. And the soul depends upon truth for eternal life.

"I told you, Horatio," Margrete said, nodding at Julia, "some need history as legend."

All converged into a ringing realization: *The skull is a symbol for my confessions and the* Gesta Danorum, *together. United, they are the bones of truth of Hamlet's story. But did my dream mean that Julia would inherit the promise I made? Would she become a teller of Hamlet's story?*

That conclusion sat uneasily with me. My daughter could grow a wise heart and a stout mind, but I had never seen the spirit of storytelling in her. Perplexed, I thought, *The child in my dream could not be Julia.* Who was the girl who took the skull from Lanier?

I mulled this question and shared it with Margrete during our voyage. The mystery bewildered her, as well. We confronted our chilling uncertainty by praying for Fortune's kindness to us all.

We arrived four days later, upon the sixteenth day of November, at Southwark, Saint Olave Parish, our new place of exile.

※

This English hut is a sturdy home. No dung stream flows by it as we had in Tønderensis, but Margrete complains that its crackling hearth can hang only one pot, that our cottage there was larger.

Now, my time wanes, but I have more to impart.

XXIII.

I lay in a cot in Southwark. Not even a bonfire can warm me, but Margrete tends the tiny hearth to coax its warmth. The meager flames struggle against the morning's damp chill on a day brilliant with sunshine. Autumn's spirit floats—in hues of red and orange in the drifting leaves, in the flames' scent of burning wood, and in Margrete's auburn tresses. She is in life's flush.

"You are especially beautiful today," I told her this morning, which is proper because time with one's spouse is a treasure to be wisely spent.

Margrete's lips turned downward in a tolerant, closed-lipped smile. "Horatio, your habit now is to speak truth about all things." She caressed my whiskered cheek with the back of her work-worn fingers, then dabbed a cloth across my forehead.

I coughed to clear my raspy voice. "A man should speak his love to his wife, especially when he hears the roaring sleigh of the Furious Host drawing near."

Only Margrete sits with me, yet the world calls to me. Blessings announce themselves through our window. I see afternoon's aging rays gild the thatch of our neighbor's hut, and, beyond, the blue sky begins to frost—haze is slowly rolling up the Thames River. I hear, among the chatter and squeals of Southwark's playing children, that of my own progeny—cavorting with Lanier, our former vagabond. He drives them, Margrete tells me, in a rattling, borrowed oxcart trundling past our door. Marcus and Julia cling to him. He shakes the reins and pats them. It is my brother's loving gift to me that in my final hours I hear my babies' happiness, rather than their mournful witness to my passing.

Has my lunar cycle run its course? Stars shining in a moonless sky serve as beacons for spirits, but they must allow me a little more time to conclude my testament.

We were a motley, small tribe that fled Tønderensis' walls. At its port we purchased single passage to sail the River Vida to deep water. Our ship descended along the bottom hem of the North Sea. Two days ago, on Friday, the sixteenth day of November, we arrived at Southwark's muddy banks and wasted no time in joining its people.

Saint Olave Parish is a gray place, Margrete tells me. The murky terrain abuts a river as dull as slate even when dawn crests. From our hut, among many poor, leaning dwellings, we can see across the water London's stalwart walls braced like crossed arms against us. We are the only Danes among this parish's inhabitants—many Burgundian, Flemish, and Germanic folk. We can hardly understand their languages but know that they call themselves the leathermen of Southwark.

Lanier told me he, cuffs rolled and hair tied behind, will learn from the leathermen how to tend their stinky, fuming caldrons, boil fat from animal hides, and tan the skins by stretching and drying them in the indifferent, moist air. He is not afraid of the burns he has seen on the workers, and he knows that the leathermen's skills are no gate to prosperity. Those men are shut out of the guilds and are refused entry to the town. Officials allow them and their women the shallow privilege of peddling skins, pouches, and bridles at the Borough Market, scraping a living in the cold shadow of the bridge.

Margrete insists that our efforts will gain us a home in the safer environs of nearby Parys Gardens. She wants a life far from ominous elements too close to us now. Prisons. Whore enclaves. Brewers. Bearbaiters. Actors. To this purpose, Margrete makes her oath, which I register here at her request:

> *Upon the Holy Mother's bones, I swear, I will protect my children and teach them to survive the pains that fortune portends—the thorns of a rose, the bite of a swan, loss of hope, or any plague visited upon the globe.*

I want Margrete to know that my greatest wish for Marcus and Julia is purity of will, strength of mind, and wisdom that they may explore and be happy. "The wonder of pilgrimage is not a controlled journey but rather the joy of receiving unexpected revelations," I told her. "They must choose how to define our legacy, for no man can decide the impact of his own life. That fact was a revelation to me. Had I never ventured upon this crucible, I would have led a cloistered life."

She told me to write those words. Thus, I did so past noontime, until our cottage door opened. In the blond shaft of light stood Marcus with Julia, holding her hand. Behind them was Lanier wearing his workman's sleeves rolled over his thick forearms and gripping his hat. "Forgive me. I tried to occupy your children, but they seem to know God's intent and will not be excluded from it."

"Let them come, if they are willing," I said. "Fortune has always thwarted my desire to have one more embrace with those whom I love. It will not best me now."

Margrete turned to regard our son and daughter. "Marcus, would you like to tell Papa the story you told me this morning?"

Marcus nodded, and Margrete beckoned them with a gentle wave. She pulled Julia onto her lap and swept her hand over our girl's wind-blown curls. Lanier closed the door and leaned, arms folded, against it, watching us.

My little son timidly walked to my bed. His hands, by his side, were nearly hidden by his cape. As Margrete watched him approach, her eyes betrayed a proud gleam.

"Do not fear, Marcus," I said haltingly. "What would you tell me?"

"This morning, I was walking by the leathermen's tents to find Uncle Lanier. In the dirt, between a post and a barrel, I found a piece of a coin. A tent was there. I took it into the tent, to a man at the table. He told me it was a farthing…"

"What is that?" I asked.

"A quarter penny, English," Lanier said. He held up a pinched thumb and finger to show me that the worth was very small.

"What happened then, Marcus?" I asked.

Marcus's eyes and mouth widened with the details he described. "He told me no one had ever come to him and delivered a lost coin before. He said I could keep it and, Papa, that when I am bigger I should come back to him for work. 'I'll always need honest men,' he said."

My truthful son. Hope filled me.

"And then what did you do?" Margrete prompted Marcus.

"Papa, as I walked home, I saw a man, a beggar, on the ground. His legs were bent in wrong ways, twisted at the knees. He was very dirty. He wouldn't look up at anyone. But I put the coin on the ground before him. And I ran home."

My boy of honor. His generous hand and honest tongue will purify his soul after all.

"I am proud of you, Marcus," I said. "Not even a saint could have acted with more virtue than you did today."

Marcus reached to embrace me. I kissed him and Julia a final time. *Until we meet in heaven, my sweet angels.* I whisked away my tears before my babies could see them.

Margrete asked Lanier to take the children outside again. Lanier, however, slowly approached my bed, lay his hat upon it, and bent over me. He kissed me on both cheeks. His dark eyes were red-rimmed. "*Mon ami, mon frère*...you took me to your heart when God would not have me. You and your wife lent to me a cot and a hearth when I had no true family or home. I will never forget you and your kindnesses."

His hand clasped atop mine. I had only a little strength to respond with tearless dignity. "You are forever welcome in this home," I told him.

Margrete wiped her eye. "You will never be an orphan again."

Lanier kissed me again on both cheeks. He took his hat, tipped it in deference to us. Then he took the children in hand and told them, "We have left your ox for too long. I hear her calling to you. She is lonely. Come." He led them through our threshold and away.

I watched them go. Sorrow welled in me. I said to Margrete, "I suffer that I will not be by your side to protect you. I beg your forgiveness."

Margrete smoothed the cover across my breast. Her lips quivered, then pressed. She closed her eyes for a moment. But then she regarded me steadily. "I have no regrets that my husband is a brave man who dared to speak truth to a tyrant and suffering people. Our child has learned from your example."

I could no longer withhold a tear. "I am no longer a hypocrite in Marcus's or, I pray, in God's eyes. I dropped my shield of lies. I am no longer the lonely man who wished to die with my brother."

I attest last to this for you, my children, who must not grieve me: my death was worth the cost to save my soul, honor, and family's virtue. I am grateful that my ravaging coals of sin produced in me, a prideful scholar, a refined ingot of revelation. I see now that my written confession also gave me practice in garnering the courage I needed to, then, stand before a fearful audience and my enemies and, as the only source of truth about Hamlet, openly profess it and potent facts that our people may forcefully wield against Cristiern. The story of Hamlet survives, truthfully told. *Ad fontes.*

I am an antique Roman; I fought my enemy and braved the consequences. But, I am more so a Dane, proven by daring to build a lasting memorial that would thwart dangerous powers. I earned worthiness of my part by acting it well. I achieved my cause and, surely, bore every burden to tell Hamlet's story. His spirit must agree, for I have seen nothing more of his ghost.

However, I have seen one spirit... Papa. This morning he stood at the foot of my cot. His serious, approving frown assured me that he is proud of me, my honor, and my achievement. Perhaps he was an advance scout for Saint Peter, or for Freyja and the Valkyries, or for both the Christian and pagan. I have always quietly believed that they all are one in God.

༺༻

The sun has arced in descent. I have spoken my final confession to the Almighty. With the priest and my wife attending, I have prayed the

Office of the Dead and received the sprinkling of holy water and last rites. Because I achieved my promise to my brother and I endeavored to salvage my children's souls and my own, unlike Hamlet I shall die a good death.

My counsel to my children now completed, I turned to Margrete. "Do you remember the first poem I wrote for you; you caught my scroll dropped by the falcon?"

She nodded and wept.

"It was my heart, commended to you. Now, you must safeguard my confessions."

Margrete grasped my hands. "That is no longer a record of guilt. It is our triumph—our legacy. I will ensure, as we agreed: the Church will hold your confessions in trust for our children when grown. They and their children will determine its destiny."

I held her in my gaze and heard her murmur, "My beloved husband, sacrificed by Hamlet. What will I tell my children of that?"

"Say that one of them, a girl or woman, will carry a great legend… beyond my frail capacity and cursed epoch. A story of honor and a promise. Tell them… my vision foretold she would bear it fully into the light."

I wanted to reach for Margrete. "Farewell, dearest mermaid. Once more, I'll make my swift return to you."

Margrete, my beloved, kissed me once more. "Horatio, you never did say goodbye to anyone. When you hear the hooves of the Furious Host claw the sky, you must let your spirit rest."

Pounding grows in my ears. Margrete's helping touch props my faltering hand.

A MAN OF HONOR

I, Horatio of Tønderensis, perhaps more Dane than antique Roman, with my mark attest to the veracity of my confessions on this eighteenth day of November in the year of our Lord 1520. Ideo supplico vos, omnis sancti angeli Dei, et omnis sancti, I beg you, all the holy angels of God, all you saints, receive and secure my soul. Amen.

EPILOGUE

The eighteenth day of April in the year of our Lord 1598

Dear Sir,

 I, Emilia Bassano Lanier, your faithful and humble servant, entreat your good grace to recall our recent chance meeting at the home of the poet and playwright Marlowe. I had visited him, our mutual friend, to deliver into his hands my latest published poems, which are now read throughout England. When my lord Marlowe mentioned to you that I have penned a play about a tragic Danish prince, you requested that I send you the text and some details. I dare mention this knowing that you are reputedly discerning in those whom you admit to your business confidences and trust to serve within your literary stable, to create with you the most successful plays put on among all of Southwark's theaters.

 The two sources for this work are my possessions in my estate, which I inherited through my family. One source is a lovely, published illustrated work of ancient Danish legends. It includes a tale about the prince. The other source is a private manuscript containing confessions written by the prince's friend. Each chronicles the prince's life differently. Of their provenance, I know only the following: family lore tells that the books descended to me from the confessor's family through my husband's granduncle, who was a Burgundian and leatherman in Southwark. As written on the hind page of the confessions, they were *"sealed and held in trust by the Parish of Saint Mildred, lessor of the residence known as the Little Rose in St. Olave, Bankside, Southwark."* If, sir, that land parcel is familiar to you, likely that is because your competitor, the Rose theater, was built where that dwelling once stood.

I offer the play, enclosed herewith, for your enterprise and considerate adoption. It must bear some cuts, tucks, and polish, but I believe it will prove worthy of the Globe's illumined stage and direction by you, our renowned William Shakespeare.

AUTHOR'S NOTE

Historical facts frame and illumine Horatio's world, as I came to imagine it through many years of research, writing, and travel. This novel, however, is "fictious history." It blends fact and fiction. Some geographical details, characters, and situations are my creation. However, several actual locations, events, and people anchor the setting (both in time and place).

The novel is set between 1513 and 1520 in Europe for a few reasons. First, Leucorea, the humanist-founded school that became Wittenberg University (where Shakespeare's Horatio and Hamlet studied), matriculated its first class in 1508. Second, during 1514 in Paris, Christiern Pedersen (the canon of Lund) and Jodocus Badius printed Saxo Grammaticus's twelfth-century *Gesta Danorum*, which chronicled Danish history and legends including the original tale of Danish Prince Hamlet. Christian II of Denmark ("Cristiern," as is written on his tomb) required that Pedersen find and publish that ancient manuscript. Third, in 1520, Cristiern concluded his coronation in Sweden by ordering the Bloodbath of Stockholm, the massacre of many dozen noblemen, clerics, and commoners.

Other salient facts include Carmelite friar Poul Helgesen's writings and opposition to Cristiern, the rift between the noble familial lines within France's House of Valois, the names of most Lanier family relations, the palace and health of Louis XII, the convent at Poissy, the Hôtel de Sens as residence of the archbishop of Paris and the post of the canon of Lund, the Prelum Ascensianum printshop of Jodocus Badius, Danish rule of the Kalmar Union and resistance to that control especially in Sweden, the migrant peoples that inhabited Saint Olave Parish in Bankside, Southwark, and the Parish of Saint Mildred as lessor of the Little Rose in St. Olave Parish. Literary history takes the form of excerpts from the original Hamlet legend, which are authentic to the *Gesta Danorum*, of references to various historic manuscripts, and in the genuine person who is the "Epilogue's" author. About places: the monikers, locations, and status of all towns, villages, and named buildings, are true... except one.

Krogen Castle and Helsingør, during the early sixteenth century, stood more like a frontier fort than a stone and brick fortress served by a buzzing village. As it appears in the novel, Krogen more closely, but not exactly, resembles its current majestic structure, Kronborg Slot. While the presence of the mendicant orders and Saint Olai Church within the village are factual, all events at Krogen and Helsingør that appear within this book are fiction.

I derived Horatio, Reynaldo, Fortinbras, Hamlet, Claudius, Gertrude, Ophelia, Polonius, Old Hamlet, the guards, and the British ambassador from Shakespeare's play, and I chose the accurate spelling of surnames "Rosenkrantz" and "Gyldenstierne" because those Danish noble families existed. Characters based on real people include Cristiern and his father, Hans; Friar Poul Helgesen; Louis XII and Cardinal François Guillaume; the canon of Lund, Christiern Pedersen;

the musician brother, Jean Lanier; Archbishop Trolle; the swedish rebel family Sten Sture and son; and Emilia Bassano Lanier (sometimes spelled Aemilia Lanyer in a few historical sources). I invented Margrete and her family, (Étienne) Lanier, Willem, Erik, Tomas, the priest at Saint Olai Church, and all other "supporting cast." Horatio's "Papa" is a different case entirely: Papa's depiction is a personal memorial, as noted in my acknowledgements. His name in the story is not intended to represent any other person, living or dead.

Here is one final literary fact: throughout the play *Hamlet*, Horatio appears steadfastly loyal and reserved, to all appearances a man of impeccable honor. However, at the end (Act V. Scene II) we see that Horatio was a liar. It is an easy point to miss at the end of an intense tragic tale. The evidence is in this part of the scene: immediately after Hamlet's death, after Horatio promises to tell Hamlet's story, the visiting English ambassador demands, "Where should we have our thanks?" (meaning: payment for the execution of Rosencrantz and Guildenstern at the request of the Danish king). In response, Horatio lies: "Not from [Hamlet's] mouth, had it th' ability of life to thank you. He never gave commandment for their death." But Hamlet had everything to do with those murders. Horatio dares to state this lie in the presence of his new king, Fortinbras.

Ironically, a fact of literature—Hamlet's reliance upon his imperfect friend to keep a difficult deathbed promise—launched this "fictious history," *A Man of Honor, or Horatio's Confessions*.

SOURCES OF EXCERPTS

Frontispiece of *Gesta Danorum* (1514). Image posted by The Internet Archive. Retrieved December 16, 2018, from www.archive.org/details/den-kbd-pil-130017585852-001/page/n12. The original language contained in this image was the source used to create translation of the frontispiece.

Gesta Danorum, Saxo Grammaticus; Christiern Pedersen, ed., Jodocus Badius Ascenshls, publisher, Paris, 1514; Urbana, Illinois: Project Gutenberg, reproduced under the Project Gutenberg license. Retrieved December 16, 2018, from www.gutenberg.org//files/1150/1150-h/1150-h.htm.

The Tragedy of Hamlet, Prince of Denmark, by William Shakespeare. Fairfax, Virginia: George Mason University, reproduced under OpenSource Shakespeare public domain provision 2003-2019. Retrieved December 16, 2018, from www.opensourceshakespeare.org/views/plays/playmenu.php?WorkID=hamlet.

"Habor and Signild." *Ancient Danish Ballads, Volume I*, Richard Chandler Alexander Prior. London, England: Williams and Norgate, 1860.

The Meditations of the Emperor Marcus Aurelius Antoninus, A new rendering based on the Foulis translation of 1742. Translated by George Chrystal. Urbana, Illinois: Project Gutenberg; reproduced under the Project Gutenberg license. Retrieved December 16, 2018, from www.gutenberg.org/files/55317/55317-h/55317-h.htm and www.gutenberg.org/files/2680/old/medma10.txt.

"Psalm 130" reproduced from the *World English Bible*, translation by the EBible.org Project (Wycliffe, Inc.) based on the American Standard Bible (1901). Retrieved on December 16, 2018, from www.ebible.org/study. The author edited the excerpt.

All other lyrics, poems, and rhymes that appear in this book are the invention of the author. Any semblance to an existing lyric, poem, or rhyme is unintended and accidental.

ACKNOWLEDGEMENTS

Numerous people, too many to thank by name, contributed in one way or another to my writing and the evolution of this story. However, I owe special gratitude to certain individuals.

Without my husband's patience and understanding, I could not have devoted the time and attention necessary for me to begin, and continue to learn, to write. Thank you, Ed Hruneni. My second, but not secondary, thanks go to my mother, Nancy Nelson, who endlessly listened and encouraged.

I may not have found the deepwater anchor of Horatio's "fatal flaw" had not my beloved friend and teacher, Pete Loomer, hinted at it. After Pete passed away and I had begun to revise this novel, I found this among my handwritten letters from him. "Did Horatio *lie* when he told the British Ambassador that Hamlet 'never gave commandment for their [Rosencrantz and Guildenstern's] death'? Act V, scene II." I also thank Pete for posthumously loaning his persona as Horatio's "Papa."

Leslie Lehr and Leslie Schwartz provided wonderful guidance and support. Beta readers of my complete manuscript gave thoughtful and detailed feedback. Thank you, Val Campbell, Susan Collins, Natalya

Kovalyova, Laura Pasternak, and (hired through Quiethouse Editing) Heidi Dorr, Max Keyes, and Fiona Tobin.

My editor Faith Black Ross, book cover designer Patrick Knowles, book interior designer Mark Thomas, and proofreader Ryan Quinn were my superb partners in helping me scrub and clothe my manuscript. Map designer Nat Case expertly crafted the maps found at the front of this book.

Input from Julian Reid, archivist at Oxford University, who was my gracious consultant about Merton College's muniment tower and its rooms, inspired my imagined muniment tower (muniment room and counting room) of Krogen Castle. Also, librarians of the Royal Danish Library ("The Black Diamond") in Copenhagen, particularly of the Department of Maps, helped me identify and then retrieved original maps of Tønderensis (Tønder), Denmark. Additionally, Latin translation specialists of Absolute Translations wrestled with the language of the *Gesta Danorum* frontispiece and provided wonderful text.

The Writer's Center, Bethesda, Maryland, and the James River Writers, Richmond, Virginia, provided resources and camaraderie.

A last "thanks" is also a note about beginnings. Reading *Hamlet* never prompted me to wonder "What is Horatio thinking?" However, once I saw Kenneth Branagh's marvelous film version of the full-length play, that question never left my mind. My thanks to Mr. Branagh for his art that inspired my initial curiosity.

WHAT DID YOU THINK OF A MAN OF HONOR, OR HORATIO'S CONFESSIONS?

Thank you for purchasing this book. You could have chosen any book to read, and you picked this novel. For that, I am extremely grateful.

If you have a moment to spare and would like to help other readers decide whether to read *A Man of Honor, or Horatio's Confessions*, please share your honest review on your preferred social media site or, if you purchased this book online, at that location of sale.

Again, thank you for your time and for your love of books!

ABOUT THE AUTHOR

J. A. Nelson's passion for exploring connections between history, literature, and evidence in written texts has shaped her life thus far—from a BA (Occidental College) and MA (the George Washington University) in cultural studies to a two-decade career at the National Archives of the United States, working with historical documentary treasures and helping people access unique stories in those records. A native of Los Angles, Ms. Nelson lives with her husband in Northern Virginia. *A Man of Honor, or Horatio's Confessions* is her debut novel.

Reach out to J. A. Nelson via the following social media:
Instagram @JANelsonWriter
Facebook @JANelsonAuthor
Twitter @JANelsonAuthor
or at via her website:
www.janelsonauthor.com.

CPSIA information can be obtained
at www.ICGtesting.com
Printed in the USA
FSHW020422160120
65959FS